I0536795

Firebird

Catherine Mesick

This book is a work of fiction. Names, characters, places, and incidents either are products of the author's imagination or are used fictitiously. Any resemblance to actual events or locales or persons, living or dead, is coincidental.

Copyright © 2012 by Catherine Mesick.
Cover Design by Mirella Santana: mirellasantana.com.br.
Credits: © Yana Bobrykova and Марина Хоменко.

All rights reserved. Published by Scofflaw Publishing.

ISBN: 978-0-9986631-1-1

Pure Series: Book 2

Firebird

Catherine Mesick

Chapter One

It was Sunday morning, and I was going to meet William.

And I was nervous.

A feeling of uneasiness had been growing on me steadily within the last month, and just as steadily I had pushed it aside. But the feeling was stronger than ever this morning, and this time I couldn't block it out.

And so I hesitated before the door.

Things are normal now, I said to myself sternly. *You no longer have visions. All of that is over.*

I *wasn't* having a vision, but there was a feeling—a barrier—something solid but invisible standing in my way. The way this strange feeling overwhelmed me reminded me of how I had felt when I *had* had visions—it overpowered my senses and threatened to blot out the reality in front of me.

This particular feeling warned me not to leave the house.

But I was determined to go—I wasn't going to let fear run my life—no matter what had happened in the recent past.

All the same, I couldn't help stepping quietly back to my grandmother's office at the front of the house and peering in through the open door. GM was sitting with her back to me, her head bent as she perused a letter, her long silver braid flowing like liquid silk down her back. I had already said goodbye to her, but I had a strong urge to say it again—as if it would be the last time I would ever see her.

Don't be ridiculous, I said to myself. *What could happen in a sleepy small town like Elspeth's Grove?*

But my own memories of a little more than a month ago rose up like an uneasy spirit to answer me.

I saw a livid face, burning eyes—I heard inhuman cries—

I shut my mind against the memory and hurried out the front door before I lost my nerve.

The morning was clear and cold—it was just past Thanksgiving—and a brisk wind kicked up, whipping my pale hair across my eyes. I pulled the strands of hair away from my face carefully.

As I pulled my unruly hair back and secured it, I wondered what advice my mother would have given me on a day like today—a day on which, if I admitted it to myself, I could feel danger in the air.

I tried to close my mind to it, but the strange feeling remained.

I hurried on toward Hywel's Plaza, which was surrounded on all sides by trees, and as I entered the wooded area, I was struck by the eerie calm of the place. There were no sounds of birds or other animals—it was as if the woods were watching, waiting for something. There were no people or houses nearby, and I broke into a sudden, panicked run.

What do you think is in these woods? I asked myself, and I found I couldn't answer my own question. I just knew that I wanted to get away from the silence and the trees as fast as I possibly could.

I ran for what felt like an eternity before breaking out suddenly on a clearing.

Stretched before me was a vast sheet of ice surrounded by a low wall. A roof made of pipes and angles, supported by thick metal poles, extended protectively over the ice, and black matting had been laid down between the ice rink and the skate house. The rink was brand-new and had only been open for about a week.

Loud, cheerful music suddenly filled the plaza, and I could see that skaters were already out on the ice. All of the sound and motion was a pleasant contrast to the watchful silence of the trees. As I stood looking out over the big white sheet of ice, the sun dipped behind a thick bank of solid gray clouds, and its harsh glare was blunted, suffusing the area with a muted, gentle glow.

The area around the rink was fairly crowded, and the atmosphere was cheerful, happy, relaxed. And in the midst of the crowd, I spotted a familiar, well-loved figure.

I hurried forward.

William turned and smiled his crooked half smile.

A casual observer would describe William as tall, lean, dark-haired—maybe eighteen or nineteen years old. The only thing that might be said to be unusual about him were his eyes—blue was not an unusual color, but the intensity of the color in his eyes wasn't quite human. There were other words, too, that had been used to describe him—*cursed, damned, outcast*—words that had real, if melodramatic meaning. There were still other words that described him—fantastical words but real nonetheless. On this particular morning my mind shied away from that last group of words—as if thinking them could somehow bring about disaster.

"You had me worried, Katie," William said as I reached him. His voice was colored as always by an accent that I could never quite place. "I was beginning to think you weren't coming."

His tone was light, but there was an undercurrent of tension in it.

I glanced at him sharply, and I could see faint lines of strain around his eyes. I was late, and that was unusual for me—but it seemed to me that William was anxious over more than just my lateness. Or was it my imagination? I shrugged the feeling off—I figured I was just projecting my own recent paranoia onto him.

"Sorry," I said. "I just got started a little later than I meant to."

William held out his hand, and I took it, marveling anew at the tingle that ran through me whenever he touched me. His skin was warm, and his hand was pleasantly calloused. I didn't want to think about anything but how wonderful it was to be with him. As I had done for the past month, I decided not to tell him about the strange feeling of dread that had stolen over me.

We started toward the skate house.

"Were you worried about trying to skate today?" William asked.

"No," I said, making an effort to be relaxed. "I wasn't worried about skating."

A strong gust of wind swirled around us then, causing me to stop and turn toward William. He slipped his arms around me, and I leaned against him.

There was laughter out on the ice, as skaters found themselves pushed around involuntarily by the wind.

We stood together until the wind died down, and then I went closer to the ice to watch the skaters for a few minutes—I had never actually been ice-skating before.

A little girl with braids and red mittens went flying by on miniature skates, her cheeks flushed with happiness. An even smaller girl with equally pink cheeks gave a tiny shriek and chased after the bigger girl. I wondered if the two of them were sisters.

The atmosphere at the rink seemed so happy and normal that it was hard for me to credit my fears of only a few minutes ago. Surely there was nothing dangerous in the woods that surrounded us.

"Do you think you can do that, too?" William had come up to stand beside me, and he was smiling at me now.

I glanced over at the two little girls who were now on the other side of the rink.

"I think so," I said, smiling back at him.

We turned once more toward the skate house.

As we reached the door, William stopped and looked around suddenly, as if he'd heard something. His eyes narrowed warily.

"What is it?" I asked. "What's wrong?"

"It's nothing," he said. He gave me a reassuring smile.

"Are you sure?" I asked.

"Yes," he said. "I'm positive—it's nothing."

I knew William could hear things I couldn't, and I felt a flash of panic that I quickly pushed aside. I told myself to relax—just because William had heard something that had distracted him, didn't mean it was something dangerous. I would have to make an effort to get my imagination under control.

We continued on into the skate house and emerged a short time later with skates on our feet.

A gate stood open in the rink, and I walked over to it and paused with one hand resting on either side of the gate. The ice stretched out in front of me, white and unforgiving.

Now that I was about to step onto it, the rink suddenly seemed much bigger than I had realized, and the ice itself seemed to glow faintly, as if it were pulling all available light into its depths. It almost didn't seem real.

I was seized powerfully by nerves.

At the same time, I felt something like relief. The fear I was currently feeling was born of the moment—it had nothing to do with the fear that had very nearly prevented me from leaving the house that morning. It was a perfectly normal fear.

As I stared at the ice, however, I suddenly saw a dark figure appear in the white surface—right by my feet. The figure was black and shifting and vaguely human in form. It looked like a human shadow, but it wasn't mine—and it was definitely something that shouldn't have been there. At first there was only one—and then there was another and another. The figures seemed to swim under the surface of the ice itself—dark phantom shapes that twisted and turned, as if they were trying to escape.

I backed away from the ice.

William was standing right behind me, and I bumped into him.

"Are you all right?" he asked. He took my arm, and we stepped away from the gate.

"There's something out there—under the ice," I said. "I can see—things."

"Those are just shadows," William said reassuringly. "It's nothing to worry about. The ice can play tricks on your eyes if you're not used to it. You'll adjust."

I looked back out over the ice again, and the strange shapes I'd seen had disappeared. Maybe William was right—maybe I'd just seen shadows.

"Go on out, Katie," William said. "Don't worry. I'll be right here to catch you if you fall."

There was more laughter from the ice rink, and I looked around. Out on the ice there were parents helping their young children, older children racing each other, smiling couples holding hands. Everyone and everything seemed so normal and down-to-earth that I wanted to join them.

For just a moment, I wished that I could be normal, too.

I stepped back to the gate. Two skaters suddenly zipped past me at what seemed like alarming speed, and I felt a little tingle of nerves again. I told myself I would be fine as long as I didn't see any more dark shapes in the ice.

"Like I said, I'll be right here to catch you," William murmured.

I waited till the way was clear, and then I stepped out onto the ice. Almost immediately I began to slip, and I grabbed frantically for the wall, catching it just in time to prevent myself from falling.

I clung to the wall, my heart pounding.

William glided around to my side and leaned against the wall, his lips twitching suspiciously.

"You're laughing at me," I said.

"No, no, I'm not," William said, but his smile grew broader. "I'm not laughing at you, really."

I continued to cling to the wall.

"So, what do I do?" I asked after a moment. "I don't actually know how to move away from here."

William reached over and helped me to prize my hands away from the wall. Then he pulled me to a standing position. As he did so, I noticed with some irritation that his shoulders were shaking with silent laughter.

Over the next hour—with William's help and with much stumbling on my part—I managed to make it all the way around the rink several times—and I even managed to move away from the safety of the wall. We kept going, and eventually, I raised my head and looked around. I realized I was moving along with everyone else on the ice and having a good time.

William gave me his crooked smile. "You're glad you did this now, aren't you?"

I could feel the cold air nipping at my cheeks, but the rest of me was comfortably warm. And William was beside me.

"Yes," I said quietly. "I'm happy I did this. And I don't just mean the ice-skating."

William bowed his head, so I wouldn't see his expression, but I could tell he knew what I meant.

William and I were together now, but it hadn't been easy to get to this point—and we hadn't been together for very long. But even though we were officially a couple, he kept limits on our time together. I still didn't know very much about him, and that included the things he could tell me—I didn't even know where he lived.

But he was here now—and that was all that mattered at the moment.

When William and I were done out on the ice, we went into the skate house and sat down on the benches to unlace our skates.

I could feel William's eyes on me, and I looked up at him. There was something forlorn in his expression.

"You don't want me to go, do you?" I said.

"No." His voice was quiet.

"We *can* spend more time together, you know."

"No, we can't." William was suddenly stern. "We have to limit our time together. No matter how much I wish things were different."

"Because you think you're cursed," I said.

"Because I *am* cursed," he replied. "All I can do is savor the time I have with you before you find someone of your own kind."

"My own kind," I said, shaking my head. What was my kind exactly? William insisted on seeing me as a normal girl—but I was far from normal.

The two of us put our shoes on and walked out into the cold. I was warm from my recent exertions, but a gust of wind kicked up, and I shivered. William put his arm around me.

We left the rink and entered the woods nearby. Another shudder ran through me as I thought once again of the fact that I didn't know where William lived. What if he had no home? What if he slept outside in the frozen night? Of course, I didn't know if William ever actually *had* to sleep. And I didn't know if he felt the cold—though somehow I doubted that he did. But I still didn't like the idea of William's not having a proper home.

"William, why won't you tell me where you live?" I asked.

"Because you don't need to know."

I felt frustration welling up within me—William gave me that same answer whenever I asked him anything about himself. I knew today would be no different, but I suddenly felt very stubborn.

I persisted. "Do you have a job? Where do you go while I'm at school?"

"Katie, it's not important for you to know these things. You know we need distance. You're too young to get deeply involved. I'm much, much older than you are, and I can barely remember my past. Like I said, someday you'll leave me for one of your own kind. Leave the heartache to me."

"William, answer my questions," I said. "Answer just one. Tell me what neighborhood you live in."

He sighed. "We've been over this territory before. Why are you bringing all of this up again?"

"I worry about you," I said. "I want you to live somewhere safe and comfortable. I want to know you're okay."

William gave me a searching look. "It's your grandmother, isn't it? She's uncertain about me. You must have told her by now that I don't go to school, and she wonders what I do with my life. She must wonder if I'm good for you."

I felt a brief stab of guilt when he mentioned my grandmother.

"It's not GM," I said.

"She doesn't ask about me?"

"No."

William looked puzzled. "Are you telling me that your grandmother has never had any questions about me?"

"I wouldn't say she's *never* had any questions about you," I replied.

"But?"

"But she hasn't had any questions about you since we returned from Russia."

"Why not?" William demanded.

"Because GM doesn't know you're in Elspeth's Grove. She thinks you stayed in Russia."

"What?" William stopped walking and stared at me, incredulous.

He continued to stare at me.

"Your grandmother doesn't know I'm in Elspeth's Grove," he said slowly. "So she doesn't know that we've been meeting?"

"No—I was afraid she would forbid me to see you."

"Katie, I insist on seeing your grandmother," William said sternly. "I want her to know I'm here. I need to—"

He stopped suddenly. He turned to look behind us.

I turned too, trying to see what had attracted his attention, but we appeared to be completely alone. William held up a hand.

As I stood looking around me, I noticed that the surrounding woods were quiet and somehow watchful—just as they'd been when I'd walked through them earlier.

I thought once again of the fact that there were no houses nearby.

William continued to stare at a fixed point somewhere off in the trees.

"William, what's—"

"Katie, get out of here," he whispered. He didn't turn to look at me.

"William?"

"Katie, go! Run!"

I turned to do as he asked, panicked by the tone in his voice.

I had not gone very far when someone stepped out of the trees and blocked my way.

I looked up and found myself staring into the calm, pale eyes of a vampire.

His name was Innokenti, and I had last seen him in the Pure Woods in Krov, Russia.

He was friendly. Sort of.

"Hello, little one." His voice, as I remembered only too well, was silky and just a little superior. His brown hair fell in a straight line to his chin, and his clothes were as picturesquely antique as they had been the last time I'd seen him—he appeared to have stepped out of the Middle Ages.

Innokenti's presence here in these woods was deeply disturbing. I had believed that I would never see him again after I left Russia—and I certainly hadn't expected him to show up today. Seeing him again was like being revisited by a nightmare.

"Innokenti," I said, taking a step back. "What are you doing here?"

He bared his teeth in a smile that was far from reassuring—especially since it allowed me to see the unusually sharp outline of his teeth.

"My friend and I," he said, "have traveled thousands of miles to pay you and William a visit. How fortunate we are to find the two of you together."

Innokenti sent a significant nod over my shoulder, and I turned.

Standing next to William now was a man I didn't recognize—young, tall, dark of hair and eye, dressed all in black. William was staring at the young man with dislike, his body tense, his expression set into harsh lines. For his part, the newcomer was smiling malevolently at William.

Innokenti gestured to the young man. "Shall we go over so I may make introductions?"

As Innokenti and I walked over to them, I had to remind myself that Innokenti had never actually done me any harm—but no matter how hard I tried to calm myself, I remained uneasy.

As we reached William and the stranger, I could see a muscle working in William's jaw, and the stranger's smile deepened as he looked me over with unpleasant scrutiny. His eyes met mine, and I was startled by just how dark they were—they were eyes with the depth of night in them.

"Innokenti, get out of here," William said angrily. "And take *him* with you."

"Now, now, William," Innokenti replied mildly. "This is a friendly visit." He gestured to the stranger. "The two of you know each other, of course. But introductions are in order for the young lady."

Innokenti gave me another one of his unnerving smiles. "Katie Wickliff, may I present my associate, Anton. You'll have to forgive us—we don't go in for surnames much in our community. Many of us don't like to dwell on the past."

I looked to Innokenti. "Is Anton a—"

"Vampire?" Innokenti said. "Yes."

"Pleased to make your acquaintance, Katie," Anton said. His voice was dark and smoky, and I had the feeling that he was laughing at me.

He lifted my hand with his ice-cold fingers and kissed it, and then he stared at me steadily as he let my hand drop. He seemed to be waiting for a reply.

I found myself momentarily at a loss for words.

Anton's amusement deepened. "Too stunned to speak? I have that effect on a lot of women."

William grabbed Anton's coat and shook him. "Leave her alone."

Malice lit up Anton's dark eyes. "I'm simply saying hello."

"Gentlemen, please," Innokenti said. "I believe you're upsetting young Katie. Our mission here is a benevolent one. We should all be pleasant to one another."

William rounded on Innokenti. "Why did you bring him? If you wanted things to be pleasant, you should have left *him* at home."

"William, your attitude isn't very charming," Innokenti admonished gently. "You should put your antagonism aside as Anton has done. This mission we are on is one of the gravest importance. Anton knows that, and that's why he very graciously volunteered to come with me."

"Why did he have to come at all?" William said angrily. "*If* you truly need to speak to me, you should have come alone."

"William, you weren't listening," Innokenti replied patiently. "We have come here to see you *and* the little one, and this is no routine visit we are on. I am a messenger here. Anton has accompanied me in order to look out for my welfare."

"He's your bodyguard?" William said derisively. "What do you need protection from? Me?"

"Vampires are strong, but we are not completely invulnerable, William—you know that. And the situation is a dangerous one—for both of you."

William's face grew grim.

"Say what you need to say. But leave Katie out of this."

Innokenti spread out his hands apologetically.

"I'm afraid I can't leave Katie out of anything," he said. "She is involved no matter how much we all might wish otherwise."

William folded his arms. "Make this quick. Then get out of here."

"Very well." Innokenti's pale eyes grew hard. "You both have your duties, and you're both avoiding them. This is unacceptable."

"Unacceptable to whom?" William asked. "To you?"

"William, you know I do not speak for myself," Innokenti replied. "I speak on behalf of others. You, William, belong in Krov in the vampire colony there. You have special abilities—you alone amongst our number can fight the kost."

"Are you being troubled by a kost at the moment?" William asked.

Innokenti gave William a mirthless smile. "No—not at the moment. But our kind grows thirstier. You know what that means."

Innokenti's pale eyes shifted to me. "And you, little one, you too, have a purpose. You are the Little Sun, and you are also destined to fight the kost. You owe us no particular allegiance, but your heritage confers certain obligations and responsibilities—ones that cannot lightly be ignored."

"Little Sun?" Anton said with a mocking lilt. "So you're the one. How about I call you 'Sunshine'?"

"It's true we can both fight the kost," William said, ignoring Anton. "What do you want from us?"

"I propose that you and Katie return with me now," Innokenti replied. "You can return to the colony, William, and Katie can live in the house that was vacated by her cousin, Odette. You can live near one another, and possibly even work with one another whenever a kost rears its ugly head. But I would recommend that you put an end to your romance. Such a relationship will not meet with much approval."

"And what if we refuse to go with you?" William asked.

Innokenti sighed. "I would advise against it. But in the event that the two of you refuse, I would return to the colony and explain to them, with a heart full of regret, that I was unable to make you see reason."

"You would not attempt to force us to return with you?" William asked.

Innokenti's eyebrows rose. "William, we are vampires. We are not barbarians."

William shook his head. "I don't understand what's going on here. You've admitted that the kost is not an immediate threat. And I can return to Russia any time I wish—you know that. And you've also admitted that Katie owes you no allegiance. So what does it matter to you where she lives? This must be about something else. There's something you're not telling me."

Innokenti fixed William with a piercing stare.

"William, you may not believe this, but you matter to us, and we know that this human girl here matters to you. Anton and I are here to help you both. Forces we don't entirely understand yet are gathering. And the two of you would make convenient pawns."

William was unmoved. "Then tell me what you do know. Give me all the information you have, and maybe I'll consider coming with you. Katie isn't to be involved in this—at all."

Anger flashed in Innokenti's cool eyes. "Katie will be involved in this no matter what you want. There's a price on the girl's head, and there are two separate groups after her. I am telling you that she is not safe."

"Who's after her?"

"I cannot tell you that, William. I am merely a humble servant of a greater power—and I have told you too much already. I have only been authorized to tell you that it's in your best interests to return with us."

"Then the answer is 'no,'" William said. "I'm not going with you and neither is Katie."

Innokenti's eyes flicked to me. "Perhaps you should let Katie decide for herself. After all, she is the one in the greatest danger."

William took a step toward Innokenti. "I won't allow Katie to be tricked into anything by you. That cousin of hers that you mentioned so cavalierly a few moments ago tried to kill her. If Katie goes back, her cousin may return, too, and try to finish what she started. Krov is far too dangerous for Katie. She's safer here with me."

"What do you say, little one?"

There was a strong hint of warning in Innokenti's voice, but I met his pale gaze unflinchingly.

"I want to stay here with William."

Innokenti suddenly seemed to radiate rage. He turned toward William.

"I'll give you one last chance. The girl doesn't really know enough of the world to make a reasonable decision, but you know something of the true darkness that exists out there. If you don't care about your own safety, then you should at least consider hers."

"We're not going with you," William said curtly.

Innokenti spread out his hands in a gesture of surrender. "As you wish, William. But remember this: I tried to help you."

He backed up a few paces, and his eyes flicked to me once more. "You cannot remain with him, little one. They will not allow it."

He melted into the woods. Anton gave me a wink and a smile, and then he, too, vanished into the trees.

I looked up at William. He was staring at the spot where Anton and Innokenti had just stood, and his face seemed set in stone.

After a moment, he looked around at me.

"We need to go to your house *now*. I need to be able to protect you."

Chapter Two

William and I walked through the trees in silence.
I was rattled, and I could tell he was worried.
Cursed, damned, outcast.

Those were words that William had used to describe himself on more than one occasion, and words that had floated through my mind back at the skating rink.

In a way, those same words could be used to describe me.

I let my mind stray to the words it had shied away from before.
Vampire. Sídh.

They were words that did not properly belong to this world. And yet I knew they were part of this world all the same.

William had been one of the Sídh once—a race of bright, immortal creatures of great power. And then he had been attacked by a vampire and turned—though how long ago this had occurred exactly, I didn't know. The Sídh had cast him out, taken his memories, left him to wander. He had found an unexpected home with the vampires of Krov, Russia—the village in which I had been born.

And I myself was a descendent of the Sídh. My grandfather had been sent to Krov to found a line of humans with Sídh blood—something the Sídh did every so many generations in fulfillment of an ancient treaty. The children of such unions were gifted with a unique

16

ability to combat evil spirits of great strength and age—particularly one known as the kost.

A kost was an evil spirit inhabiting—and animating—a human corpse.

My mother was the only child of this particular Sídh union, and like all those before her, she was known as the Little Sun. She was ordained by her birth to be the protector of Krov, and in this capacity she had fought and imprisoned a kost named Gleb Mstislav in his family's crypt. And he had worked in secret to poison and kill her.

My father had died shortly before her in an ordinary accident—he had died while hiking. And I had been left an orphan in the care of my grandmother, who knew nothing of my grandfather's true nature or my mother's purpose in life.

And then this past October, Gleb had escaped from his crypt, aided by his son, Timofei, and my own cousin, Odette. Gleb had come after me in Elspeth's Grove, hoping to kill me. My struggle with him took me to Russia, where William and I had worked together to destroy him.

On my mother's death, I had become the new Little Sun, though I didn't even know any such thing existed. And shortly after my sixteenth birthday I had begun to have visions, which I had learned were meant to help me in my battle against creatures like Gleb. But after Gleb had been defeated, and I had returned home to the U.S., the visions had stopped.

I had thought that it was over—that the darkness in Krov was something I had left behind forever. I had thought that I was free to live in Elspeth's Grove in peace with William.

But there were vampires from Krov in Elspeth's Grove now, and if they were telling me the truth, there was a price on my head.

I shivered as I thought of Anton and Innokenti. How long had they been following William and me? How long had they been watching us? Had they seen me at the house with GM?

I didn't want her to be in danger because of me.

"How did they find us?" I asked William.

He blinked as if I had startled him out of his train of thought. "What was that?"

"Innokenti and Anton," I said. "How did they find us? Only a few people knew that we were going ice-skating today, and I'm sure they wouldn't have told them."

William laughed—a strangely humorless sound. "No one had to tell Innokenti anything. He has ways of finding things out."

He lapsed back into silence.

"You and Anton appear to know each other," I said after a moment.

"Yes," William replied reluctantly. "He lived in the vampire colony in Krov at the same time as I did."

"The two of you don't get along?" I asked.

"No."

"Why not?"

"It doesn't matter now," he said quietly. "And I'd rather not discuss it. Please don't ask me to tell you."

There was a note of finality in William's voice, and I sighed.

"What do you think they really want from us?" I asked. "Did you believe Innokenti when he said that someone is after us, and that he wants to protect us?"

"No," William said. "It's a scare tactic. Innokenti's trying to trick us into doing what he wants. There's no one after us."

"Are you sure about that?" I asked. "One hundred percent sure?"

William paused for a moment before answering.

"No."

I felt a sense of dread settle over me. "So it's possible that Innokenti was telling the truth?"

"It is possible—but it's a remote possibility. You asked me if I was one hundred percent sure it's a trick. I can't be that sure. But I know Innokenti and the rest of them. They don't act in the interests of others—no matter what he says. They only act to help themselves."

"Why do you think they want us, then?"

William shook his head. "I think it's best if we don't find out."

We walked in silence again for a time before I asked the question that was weighing the heaviest on my mind.

"Do you really think they'll just take no for an answer?"

William looked at me, and a muscle worked in his jaw.

He did not reply.

Soon the trees we walked through began to thin, and we were in sight of my neighborhood. The thought of vampires lurking near my house left me feeling deeply uneasy.

I stopped and looked around.

"Do you think they'll leave like they said they will? Do you think they're watching us right now?"

William stopped beside me and placed his hands on my face. "They aren't nearby right now—I would know if they were. And I don't know what they're planning to do, but you and your grandmother will be safe. I'll see to that."

"William, if there really is a price on my head—if there really are two groups after me—"

He interrupted. "Have I ever let you down?"

"No, you've never let me down," I said.

"Trust me—I'll take care of it." William smiled. "Now, let's go see your grandmother."

He took my hand and started in the direction of my house.

"William, wait," I said. "I don't think we can spring your presence on GM like this. I don't have any idea how she's going to react."

"Katie, don't be ridiculous," William said, exasperated. "Our situation is serious—manageable—but serious. And I need to be around more. I need to have your grandmother accept and approve of my being here."

"I know," I replied. "That's why we can't just surprise her today. It won't do us any good if she throws you out of the house as soon as she sees you. Let me talk to her alone first. Come see me tomorrow at school, and I'll let you know when you can see her."

William started to protest, but I interrupted him.

"It will be soon—I promise. Who knows? Maybe she'll even invite you to dinner."

William gave me a tolerant look. "All right, but make sure it *is* soon. The sooner everything is out in the open, the better."

"I'll bring GM around," I said. "I promise."

We started walking again, and we paused at the corner of my street, like we usually did.

"At least I know now why you never let me walk you up to your door," William said. "I realize that I should have been more suspicious."

"What did you think before?" I asked.

He shrugged. "Humans are often uncomfortable around vampires—even incomplete ones like me. I thought maybe she didn't like to look at me, and you were tactfully not telling me."

"William," I said. "I can't imagine anyone not wanting to look at you."

He shook his head. But I thought I could see the ghost of a smile on his lips.

"I'll see you tomorrow at school, then, Katie," he said, turning to leave. "I'll be watching to see that you and your grandmother are safe tonight."

"William—I have one more question."

He turned back.

"What about that last thing that Innokenti said?" I asked. "What did he mean when he said that 'they' will not allow me to remain with you? Who are 'they'?"

William looked away from me. "As I said, I think this is all a trick. You don't have to worry about what Innokenti said."

"But you do have some idea of what he was implying?"

"I have an idea—but I can't be sure. In any event, you don't need to know. I'll see you tomorrow, Katie."

William gave me a small smile and walked off.

I stood looking after him with a familiar sense of disappointment. I wished he had trusted me with his suspicions.

Once William had disappeared from view, I walked up to my house and went inside.

I paused in the hall just by the door and tried to figure out how I was going to tell GM that William was in Elspeth's Grove and that I had been seeing him.

I knew it wasn't going to be easy.

To be fair to GM, I didn't know for certain that she disliked William. But the two times she had spoken to him had been difficult times, and William's entrance into our lives had coincided with the return of the past for GM. My mother, in her short life, had become deeply involved in the supernatural—she'd really had no choice. And the supernatural was something my grandmother had not believed in until it had burst into her house in October in a way that she couldn't deny.

Having the reanimated corpse of a man she knew to be dead break into her house was something even GM couldn't ignore.

But GM was stubborn, and she'd returned to her old ways once everything settled down. She'd been able to convince herself that all of the bizarre things she'd seen had a perfectly normal explanation.

GM still feared that I would fall under the spell of the supernatural and be consumed by it as my mother had been, and I had a feeling that she saw William as part of that supernatural threat. She didn't know what he was, of course—to her he was just an ordinary young man. But he'd been involved in events that she'd rather forget.

And I was afraid that she would prefer that William were forgotten, too.

I continued to stand by the door, trying to force my mind to work. I tried to come up with just the right words to convince GM that she had nothing to worry about—that William was beneficial and not a danger. After a few moments, I began to wonder if she would come out to see me before I'd come up with a plan—I knew she must have heard me come in.

But time passed, and GM did not appear.

After another few moments had passed, I decided to take GM on without a plan. I would just go in determined not to lose. After all, there was no good reason for me not to see William—he had already saved my life twice. Surely, I could make her see that I was better off with him than without him.

I walked through the house, but I didn't find GM in any of the usual places. Eventually, I found her in her office where I had left her earlier, which was odd—she didn't usually spend much time there on the weekends. She said she wanted to keep her home life and her work life separate—even if they co-existed in the same place.

As I entered the office, GM's head was bent, and I could see that she was poring over a letter. She had been receiving a lot of letters lately—letters that she wouldn't talk about but would hastily tuck away. I could see an envelope on the desk beside her. It had a number of colorful stamps on it—as if it had been mailed from overseas. I wondered—could GM be receiving letters from Russia?

"GM?" I said quietly.

She turned in her chair, clearly startled. She swiftly swept her letter back into its envelope, and deposited the envelope into a drawer.

"Oh, Katie! I didn't hear you come in. How was your first time ice-skating?"

"It was good," I said. "I didn't break anything, and I actually made it all the way around the rink several times." I paused. "Did you receive a letter from Galina?"

GM stood up. "Letter?"

"Yes," I said. "You had a letter in your hand when I came in, and the stamps seemed to be foreign. I was wondering if maybe you'd heard from Galina. I know you've been in contact with her."

Galina Golovnin had been a friend of my mother's. Although she was the same age as my mother, she had been a teacher of sorts to her—helping my mother to develop and hone her powers as the Little Sun. When I had encountered her in Russia, she had helped me, too. Galina's life was deeply steeped in the supernatural, something GM had resented bitterly. But since our recent trip to Russia, GM's attitude toward Galina had relaxed a bit. She was no longer determined to banish Galina to the past and pretend that she had never existed.

"Galina?" GM said. "Oh, no. No. I have not heard from her lately."

I waited expectantly.

GM, who was always so confident and self-possessed, suddenly seemed very unsure of herself. She wrapped her fingers around the silver cross she always wore and began to move the charm up and down on its chain in an agitated fashion. She looked around the room. Then she looked back at me.

"Enough about the letter. Forget about the letter. Solnyshko, I have something to tell you—to ask you, rather."

"Solnyshko" was a Russian term of endearment that GM often used for me—one that many people used. Oddly enough, the word literally meant "little sun." GM had been using it for me for as long as I could remember. She had no idea how apt it really was.

I took a deep breath. "I have something to tell you, too."

"Excellent. Then we have news to share with one another. Let's go in the kitchen. Are you hungry?"

"No, I'm not hungry," I said, as GM shepherded me out of her office.

"Some tea, then," she said. "It is always good to have tea when one talks."

I wasn't really keen on the idea of having tea. I'd lost my taste for tea and for hot drinks in general after I'd discovered that my mother had been poisoned by tea laced with vampire blood. I had been tricked into drinking some of the stuff myself, and the memory of it was an unpleasant one. But if drinking some tea would make GM happy, then I would go along with it.

In the kitchen, GM waved me to a seat, and she put the kettle on.

Soon the kettle was whistling, and GM poured out for us. I gazed into the golden depths of the tea reluctantly. I knew it was chamomile, and I knew it was untainted, but I couldn't help thinking again of the poisoned tea I'd been given.

I shivered.

GM sipped at her tea and gave me a look over the rim of her cup. Then she set it down with decision.

"Katie, I know we both have things to say, and I hope you don't mind if I go first."

"Go ahead," I said.

She paused for a moment. "Do you remember what I said to you back in October? I promised you that when that whole terrible business was over, that we would do some proper traveling?"

"I remember," I said.

She took a deep breath, as if she were gathering courage. "What do you think about spending Christmas in Russia?"

I didn't know what I had been expecting, but that wasn't it.

Several memories flashed through my mind—all of them terrifying.

"Christmas in Russia?" I said.

"Yes." GM nodded her head in an encouraging fashion.

"In Krov?" I asked.

"Yes."

My head began to spin a little. I loved Russia—I really did. It was the country of my birth, and I thought it was beautiful. But going back to Krov seemed dangerous at this point—especially since I had just met two vampires who wanted me to do exactly that.

"Why do you want to go to Krov for Christmas?" I asked. "Does it have something to do with all the letters?"

"Letters?" GM asked innocently.

"Yes," I said. "Letters like the one you were reading in your office just now. I've seen you with them before."

"Ah, yes. It appears you have sharp eyes, solnyshko. You don't have anything to be concerned about. The letters are not from anyone you know."

"Who are they from?"

GM shook her head. "Sometimes a grandmother needs to keep some things to herself. Do not distress yourself over the letters, Katie."

I decided to give up. Once GM decided she wasn't going to talk about something, she very seldom changed her mind. I stared back down at my tea.

"Katie, forgive me," GM said, "but you don't seem very excited about going to Krov. I thought you would be happy. I thought we might go to Moscow, too. You would love all of the beautiful buildings in the great square. St. Basil's Cathedral is a wonder in person."

I tried to think of how to put my thoughts into words, but what I wanted to say seemed to need more diplomacy than I was able to summon at the moment. I wanted to tell her that we couldn't go back to Krov because the village was crawling with vampires—and some of those vampires were eager for my return. But the right words just wouldn't come. How could I hint at a danger that I wasn't allowed to name?

GM leaned forward. "What is troubling you, solnyshko? Are you worried about not having a visa? If that is the case, then you need worry no longer. I have already obtained visas for both of us. We can fly directly into Russia."

I was startled. If GM had visas for us already, then she had been planning the trip for some time now and had never mentioned it to me.

"GM," I said, "why won't you tell me what's going on?"

"It's Christmas, Katie. I haven't spent a Christmas in Russia in many years. I miss my homeland."

I felt a twinge of frustration. I knew she was sincere when she said that, and to be fair, the reason she gave was a perfectly good one. But I couldn't shrug off a suspicion that that wasn't all there was to it. Then again, I wondered—what exactly was it that I suspected her of? I really didn't know.

"Where are you thinking of staying in Krov?" I asked. "Odette's house?"

GM gave me a sharp look. "So is that what's troubling you? Your poor cousin? I can understand that it must be hard for you. It's hard for me, too, solnyshko. You loved Odette and so did I. And hope is not lost entirely. People have been restored to their families after going missing for years, and Odette has only been gone for about a month. We may yet see her again."

Seeing Odette again was one of the things I was worried about—as William had told Innokenti, it was entirely possible that Odette would return. She *had* gone missing. But she was not lost in the way that GM thought she was—in the way that an ordinary human girl would be lost. Odette had become a vampire, and in October she had tried to kill me. She had disappeared after that, and her house in Krov had been left vacant. If we settled ourselves into her house at Christmas, who was to say that she wouldn't return and resent our presence? I had seen Odette when she was angry—it was a truly terrifying sight.

So, Odette might come for me, and so might Innokenti and Anton—in fact, I had a pretty definite feeling that the last two would. If I went to Krov for Christmas, would I ever be allowed to leave again? Would I even survive whatever Innokenti and his fellow vampires had planned?

"Do we have to go to Russia for Christmas?" I asked uncomfortably.

GM's face fell. "I am forgetting how hard that trip was for you, aren't I? Not only did you lose your cousin, but you were kidnapped by that madman who used to be your teacher. And then you were in the hospital. I am sorry, solnyshko. We don't have to go to Russia for Christmas."

I was sorry to see how disappointed she looked. I could tell that she'd really had her heart set on going to Russia—but such a trip would be dangerous, and there was no way I could explain that to her.

"I'm sorry," I said. "I just don't think I can do it."

GM reached across the table and patted my hand. "It is all right, solnyshko. I hadn't quite realized how difficult this would be for you. We won't go."

"Now," she said briskly, as if she'd completely banished the topic from her mind, "I believe you said you had something to tell me, too?"

Suddenly, I felt even worse. First, I'd ruined her Christmas plans. Now I was about to give her more bad news.

I had developed no clever plan of attack, so I decided just to plunge ahead.

"Please don't get too worked up over what I'm going to say."

GM raised one silver eyebrow. "Your tone doesn't inspire confidence, solnyshko."

"Do you remember William Sursur?" I asked. "He got us out of the house that night when we were forced to flee to the airport. And he got me out of the Mstislav crypt in Krov. He also came to see us at the house in Krov right before we left."

GM's expression grew carefully blank. I knew that look—it was one she wore whenever I brought up a topic she didn't want to discuss. It was as I had feared—GM didn't approve of William.

"I remember that he was very handsome," GM said.

"He meant a lot to me, GM."

"I also remember that he said the two of you couldn't be together. After all, he lives in Russia, and you live here."

"That's just it," I said. "William doesn't live in Russia anymore. He lives here."

GM was clearly startled. "He lives here in the United States?"

"He lives here in Elspeth's Grove."

Her eyebrows rose. "What is this that you are telling me?"

"GM, are you angry?"

"That boy lives here now? He has followed you?"

"Why don't you like him?" I asked.

GM's voice rose. "You cannot see him. I don't want him in this house!"

"GM, please!" I cried. "He saved both our lives!"

She fell silent.

"Why don't you like him?" I asked again. "What has he done?"

GM looked away. "I don't know anything about him. And he appears to be mixed up in some pretty dangerous things."

"Things he was trying to stop," I said.

She looked at me. "What exactly is it that you want me to say?"

"Please don't be like that. William is here in Elspeth's Grove. I like him. And he's really helped me. I want to see him. And if it's okay with you, I would like William to come over here, so you can talk to him and see that he's a good person."

GM looked down at her teacup, and she didn't say anything for a long time. I began to hope that she was wavering.

"There is something in what you say," she said at last. "You are a good girl. I suppose I can trust your judgment."

She looked up at me again. "I confess that I don't entirely know my own mind in this case. Perhaps the problem is that I just don't want you getting any older."

As I looked at GM, I felt tears stinging my eyes. "You don't have to worry that you're going to lose me. You have to know that I will always love you. Nothing will ever change that."

GM stood and walked around the table to me. She put her arms around me.

"I know, solnyshko. I will always love you, too. I have been both your grandmother and your mother. And it is sometimes hard for a mother to see her child grow up."

I hugged her back tightly.

GM straightened up and brushed a hand over my hair.

"When would you like your William to come over?"

I didn't want to rush things, but I knew the appearance of Innokenti and Anton had made it necessary for me to get William on good terms with GM as soon as possible.

"Is tomorrow okay?"

GM blinked. "Tomorrow?"

"I know it's sudden—"

She waved a hand. "It's all right. Invite him over for dinner. I will make pasta. Everyone likes pasta."

"Thank you, GM. Thanks for William and thanks about Russia."

She pressed a kiss to my forehead. "Anything for you, solnyshko."

She cleared away her cup and left the room.

I was left with my full cup of tea and a sense of relief. I was very happy that William would be able to come over tomorrow—though I realized that I didn't know if he actually ever ate anything or not. I supposed we would think of something if he didn't. And now that GM would allow William to be in the house, it made me feel a bit better about the fact that Innokenti and Anton were lurking out there somewhere. I wished William had told me how he knew Anton. Anton seemed much more dangerous than Innokenti—and Innokenti didn't seem safe.

I stood up and poured my tea into the sink. I had homework to do, but I wandered into the living room where I knew I would find a picture of GM and my grandfather.

The picture I was looking for stood on a table with other pictures of family and friends—a number of them featuring me. Some of the people were unknown to me, but the pictures of my parents and my grandparents sat side by side next to one another right in the center. The picture of my parents was from their wedding—my mother, pale and blond like me, my father just a little darker with light brown, curly hair. Both of them were beaming, and my mother was holding a single flower. It was curious that no one else seemed to be in attendance.

And then there was the picture of my grandparents.

I picked their photo up. My grandmother had been blond when she was younger, as had my grandfather. They looked like a perfectly normal couple—it was hard to believe that my grandfather had truly been one of the Sídh.

As I looked at my grandfather, I wondered what he was like. GM believed that he had died, but Galina had told me that he still lived and that he had gone back to his people. I wondered if he knew that GM lived in another country now, and if he ever saw her—even if she didn't see him. GM didn't talk about him very much, but I knew that she had loved him. And she'd told me that I would have loved him, too.

I set the picture down and walked up the stairs to my room.

I did have homework to do—if I could keep my mind on it. I told myself firmly to forget about Anton and Innokenti. They hadn't actually threatened me directly, and I knew William would watch over the house. Maybe he was right—maybe the presence of the two vampires in town was just a scare tactic.

I was still just a little too wound up to get to work, so I wandered around the room, straightening things up. As I walked past my dresser and the large mirror over it, I thought I saw something moving in the mirror—something that wasn't my own image.

I stopped, startled, and peered into the mirror. I saw only my own face and the room behind me.

I told myself I hadn't actually seen anything out of the ordinary.

I shrugged off my nerves and went to my desk, determined to finally get to work.

As I opened my books, however, I couldn't help thinking of the mirror, and an image flashed in my mind of what I had seen.

There had been a second image in the mirror.

I had seen a shadow walking behind me.

Chapter Three

I had seen shadows in the mirror before.

As I got ready for school the next morning, I stood looking into the mirror, thinking back to what I had glimpsed last night.

The shadows I had seen before had turned out to be miniature visions of William—I'd seen his face in the mirror before I'd met him. After I'd met him, the visions in the mirror had stopped. They had been replaced by full-fledged visions—images that appeared before my eyes with the sharpness and clarity of reality, blotting out what was actually in front of me while they lasted. But those visions had stopped now too—and I had no idea why.

As I thought back to it, the shadow from last night was not like any of the visions I had had before.

Of course, it was possible that my eyes had just been playing tricks on me. I *had* been a little wound up at the time, so I could have just imagined the shadow.

I resolved not to worry about it.

I looked down at the charm I was wearing—it was a gift from William, and I very seldom took it off. It was an iron cross, roughly hewn, but strangely pleasing to the eye and cool to the touch. William had given it to me for protection—but despite the shape of the charm, it wasn't any defense against vampires. The charm was actually a defense against the kost—it scrambled the creature's senses and made the person who wore it difficult to track.

I didn't actually fear being attacked by a kost on my way to school—I just liked wearing the charm. Something about it always gave me a sense of peace and calm. And it also reminded me of William.

I went down to the kitchen where I ate a quick breakfast with GM. Then I went out to begin my walk to school.

The morning was chilly and windy, and there was a light dusting of snow on the ground. I walked down the driveway past GM's red sports car, which nestled comfortably under a black cover and a thin layer of snow. I had to smile—GM was a speed demon, and I had a feeling that she was the only grandmother in town with such a high-performance vehicle.

I made my way to school, and as I reached the schoolyard, I could see that it was all but deserted. On days when the weather was warmer, the schoolyard was packed with students, many of whom had favorite spots that they had staked out—my friends Charisse Graebel and Branden McKenna had a picnic table that they'd been able to claim. But today only the hardiest students were out braving the wind and the cold.

As I entered the yard, I spotted a familiar blond head—two of them, in fact. Simon Krstic and his brother, James, stood with their shoulders hunched against the wind.

James turned and saw me first. He nudged Simon with his elbow and then nodded in my direction. Simon turned expectantly.

They had clearly been waiting for me.

James was the taller and older of the two, and his typically sullen expression had grown softer lately. James had been something of a troublemaker once, but this year he'd begun to turn things around. And then he'd been kidnapped by Timofei and Gleb Mstislav and dragged to Russia. Though James only seemed to have the vaguest memory of what had happened, the ordeal with Gleb actually seemed to have mellowed him even further.

Simon, by contrast, had always been good-natured and responsible. The two of us had been friends ever since I had moved to Elspeth's Grove when I was five years old. Except for Charisse, Simon was probably the best friend I'd ever had. But back in October, just before the trouble with Gleb had begun, Simon had revealed to me that his feelings for me had deepened into something more serious. Despite my affection for him, I had found myself unable to return those feelings.

But my feelings of friendship for him still remained and were strong.

Simon saw me and waved, and James turned and walked off toward the school.

It was clear that Simon wanted to talk to me alone.

As I reached him, Simon gave me a smile and a tolerant look. I began to feel a sinking sensation. Something about his expression made me feel defensive.

"Hey Simon," I said.

"Hey," he replied. He almost looked like a parent preparing to have a conversation with an unruly child. "Can I talk to you for a minute?"

"Sure," I replied. "Do you mind if we go inside? It's a little cold out here."

"Yeah, of course," he said. "Let's go in."

We went into the school, and I started toward the cafeteria, where most people went to hang out when it was cold outside.

"Uh, Katie?"

I stopped and looked back. Simon was not following me.

"Katie, let's not go to the cafeteria. I want to talk to you alone."

"Okay," I said. The feeling was growing on me steadily that the conversation we were about to have was going to be a chore.

"Let's go to the hallway by the library." Simon indicated the direction with a nod of his head. "It's usually pretty empty there."

He led the way, and we were soon standing in the library hallway. The library took up one full side of the hall, and its outer wall was glass, giving the two librarians an unobstructed view of everything that happened outside it. That last fact was why the hallway was usually deserted in the morning.

The other side of the hallway was taken up by display cases full of trophies and photographs. Simon drew me over to the display cases.

He stood for a moment, looking at me, and I could see uncertainty creep into his eyes—I could tell he was nervous now. His nervousness reminded me of my own anxiety when I had had something to tell him back in October. Back then, I had told Simon that a dead man named Gleb was after me, and that I needed his help to investigate what was going on.

Simon had been extremely skeptical of my story, but to his credit, he had agreed to help me. But shortly after that, GM and I had been forced to flee to Russia. Despite what had happened to his brother, Simon knew very little about what had taken place in Russia, and the two of us had never spoken about Gleb again. I wondered if he'd believed anything I'd said then—or if he'd thought I'd gone temporarily insane.

Simon continued to look at me nervously. Eventually, he looked down and scuffed a shoe on the linoleum floor, producing a sharp sound that echoed noisily in the empty hall.

He took a deep breath and gave me a resolute look.

"People are saying that you were out with that guy again this weekend."

"That guy?" I didn't want to be offended—Simon was my friend—but I couldn't help resenting the tone of his voice.

"You know—the one you were dancing with at Irina's Halloween party."

"His name is William—I told you that."

"Yeah—William. You were seen with him at the skating rink yesterday."

"I was 'seen'?" I said. "You make it sound like some kind of horrible secret."

I winced a little on the inside as I said the words. My meetings with William *had* been a secret from GM. I hadn't kept them a secret from anyone else, though.

Simon ran a hand over his hair. "Katie, please just listen. I didn't come here to offend you. I'm talking to you about this because I'm worried about you—I care about you. It's just that the guy has been seen all over town, and nobody knows much about him. He's even been seen here at school a couple of times, and I'm pretty sure he isn't actually a student."

He stopped and gave me a level stare. "How much do you actually know about this guy?"

"I know enough," I said.

I couldn't admit to Simon that I knew very little about William. William's stolen memories were partially to blame for my lack of knowledge, of course. But there was no reason why he couldn't tell me about his life since he'd moved to Elspeth's Grove. But as he had done yesterday, William always claimed that he was keeping me in the dark for my own protection.

"You know enough?" Simon was incredulous. "Katie, this guy—"

"William," I said firmly.

Simon sighed.

"William," he said, speaking the name very deliberately, "sounds like trouble."

I bristled. "William is *not* trouble. He's the best thing that ever happened to me."

A look of pain came into Simon's eyes, and I regretted having spoken so quickly. I didn't regret the words themselves—I meant them very sincerely. But I could have spoken to Simon more carefully—it hadn't been that long since he'd had his crush on me.

I glanced at him. I'd thought that he'd accepted that the two of us were better off as friends, but it seemed very possible at the moment that he wasn't completely over his crush.

"I don't think that he's good for you, Katie," Simon said. "He's been filling your head with crazy stories—telling you that there's a dead guy after you. It's like he's got some kind of hold on you."

I sighed inwardly. So Simon did remember what I'd told him back in October. There was a lot more I could tell him now. But I knew he wouldn't believe me, and none of it would make him like William any better.

Simon continued. "That—William has also been seen wandering around in the Old Grove. And you do know a girl was attacked there last night, don't you?"

"No," I said, startled. "What happened?"

The Old Grove was a grove of fruit trees in the middle of a large forest. It was the place where our town's founder, Elspeth Quick, had supposedly hidden from pursuers who had wanted to burn her for witchcraft. It was also a place that was reputed to be the site of hauntings and other supernatural activity.

"Some weird guy tore her neck up," Simon said. "Travis Ballenski told me—his dad's a cop. The police haven't released the girl's name yet, but Travis did tell me that she's going to be okay. She's still in the hospital right now. You know, you have to be really sick in the head to do something like that. They don't know who attacked her, but, Katie, I wouldn't be surprised to find out it was this William guy."

I suddenly felt chilled. I knew that William wasn't guilty. But what Simon described did sound like a vampire attack, and I had a pretty good idea who was behind it—either Anton or Innokenti—or possibly even both of them. I was glad the girl was okay, but I was alarmed by the attack—very alarmed. It meant that the vampires hadn't left—they were still hanging around town.

Simon continued. "Katie, you should take a warning from this. Like I said, how much do you actually know about this William guy? He kind of seems like a drifter. And drifters aren't usually good news."

"William is not a drifter," I said angrily.

He ran a hand through his hair in frustration. "I don't seem to be getting through to you. I don't know what I have to say to you to get you to be concerned about your own safety."

"I'm perfectly safe with William," I said.

He hung his head for a moment and then looked up at me. "What does your grandmother think of him?"

"GM has invited William over to dinner tonight," I said.

Simon threw up his hands. "Then I give up. Just promise me that you'll be very, very careful."

"I will," I said.

The warning bell rang, and he looked around.

"I guess we'd better get going," he said.

Simon really didn't look too pleased about the idea—he looked as if he would prefer to stay with me and argue about William.

"I'll see you at lunch, Katie," he said, and he looked so worried that I felt very genuinely sorry for him.

I wished I could reassure him, but I had a feeling that nothing I could say would make him trust William.

I went on to homeroom.

I sat through the announcements and then went on to first-period Social Studies. I tried to pay attention to the lecture, but I couldn't help thinking about the girl who had been attacked. I had a terrible feeling that she wouldn't be the only one. I was glad I'd asked William to come see me at school today.

I needed to tell him about the attack.

Eventually, the bell rang, and I moved on to second-period English. My friends Charisse and Branden were both in the class, and I spotted them as I walked in. Charisse had dark brown skin, and her black hair was arranged today in a cluster of curls on top of her head. Branden was pale, tall, and long-limbed, and his brown hair was, as usual, falling in his eyes.

It was unusual for the two of them to have arrived in the classroom ahead of me—they had a tendency to linger in the halls. Right now they were standing together and talking in low, serious tones. The two of them were dating and were really happy together—though they didn't look terribly happy at the moment.

I said hi as I walked past them—they looked like they didn't want to be disturbed at the moment—and Charisse reached out to grab my sleeve.

"We need to talk after class," she said.

"Okay," I replied, a little surprised.

Charisse smiled her thanks, and I moved on to my desk.

Mrs. Swinburne, our substitute teacher for the rest of the year, was seated at her desk, calmly sorting papers into neat piles. After our original English teacher, Mr. Del Gatto, had disappeared, a sub named Mr. Hightower had been brought in.

I felt a wave of revulsion wash over me as I thought of him.

Mr. Hightower had been sleek and superficially handsome. He had also been Gleb Mstislav's son Timofei, in disguise. And then, after Timofei had followed me to Russia and had met with his own death there, Mrs. Swinburne had been asked to take over the class until the year was out—and it was hard to think of someone who was more of a contrast to Timofei. Mrs. Swinburne with her permanently prim expression and cloud of fluffy brown hair was eminently respectable. Timofei had been all flashy disingenuousness.

I heard fierce whispering nearby, and I looked around. Irina Neverov, her glossy dark hair pulled into a smooth ponytail, was giving her friend Bryony Carson a sibilant harangue. I thought for a moment that Irina might be talking about me—she often was—but this time she didn't appear to be paying any attention to me.

I watched them for a moment. I wasn't surprised to see that Irina was doing all of the talking—Irina was clearly the leader and Bryony and her other friend Annamaria were her faithful followers. I seldom saw the three of them apart. But I was surprised to see that Annamaria was not in her usual spot at Irina's side, and both she and Bryony looked tense.

I had a feeling something was wrong.

As I watched the two of them, Irina glanced up and glared at me. I looked away quickly.

Irina and I had been friends a long time ago when we both were children. But as we'd entered high school we had most definitely grown apart—until we'd reached a point at which Irina wouldn't speak to me unless she absolutely had to. Things had thawed between us after Irina had been kidnapped and both of us had been trapped down in the tunnels that stretched under the Mstislav mansion. But our relationship had gone sour again shortly after that, and I wasn't entirely sure why. It seemed that we were once again not on speaking terms.

When the bell rang to signal the start of class, Mrs. Swinburne rose and closed the door. I happened to glance back at Charisse, and she gave me a significant look. I could tell something was going on with her—this wasn't a typical talk she wanted to have later.

After class, Charisse appeared at my desk and waved to Branden as he left the room.

I picked up my things quickly, and I stood up. "What's up?"

Charisse smiled and shot a glance around the room. "Not in here. Let's talk out in the hall where we'll be a little more anonymous."

I nodded, and we moved out into the hall.

With students chattering all around us, Charisse dropped her smile. She lowered her voice. "It's my mom."

"Your mom?" I asked. "Is she sick?"

"No."

Charisse seemed hesitant to go on, but she had said that she wanted to talk—so I waited patiently for her to speak as we walked.

"My mom is dating again," she said after a few moments, and her voice shook just a little bit.

I was startled. "She's dating? Already?"

"Shhhh!" Charisse hissed. "Not so loud. And yes."

"But what about the divorce?" I asked. "It can't be final yet."

"It isn't," Charisse replied. "But she said that the marriage is as good as over, and that the official end is really just a technicality."

"I suppose that's true," I said.

I was trying to tread very carefully here. Even though we were best friends, Charisse was not big on opening up to people, including me. Charisse's parents had separated in October just before all the trouble with Gleb had started. At the time, Charisse had claimed not to be bothered by the impending divorce—however, she'd also suddenly decided to run away to New York to become an actress.

Charisse had since called off her New York plans, but she'd continued to say very little about her parents and the divorce. I had a feeling that it troubled her a lot more than she would say, but I never said anything about it unless she brought it up. I hoped she knew that I would support her and not judge her.

Charisse lapsed into silence once again, and I could see signs of strain around her eyes. I wasn't entirely sure how to help her.

"Does your dad know?" I asked after a moment.

"I don't know," Charisse replied. "I don't know if it would make any difference if he did."

She stopped suddenly and closed her eyes tightly. Then she shook her head.

I stopped beside her, concerned.

Charisse opened her eyes and the look she gave me was full of fear.

"This guy my mom is seeing is strange—really strange. And someone needs to talk to her about him. She won't listen to me about him at all. She gets really stubborn. Once upon a time, my dad was the only person who could talk to her when she got that way. But now, of course, he's out of the picture. And even if they were on speaking terms, which they aren't, she would hardly take his advice on romance."

I suddenly felt chilled, though I didn't know why. Surely, it wasn't unusual for a child, even an older one, to feel uneasy when a newly single parent started dating—so Charisse's anxiety was probably perfectly normal. But all the same, there was something very convincing about her fear.

Charisse was genuinely worried.

"What do you mean this guy your mom is dating is strange?" I asked. "Strange in what way?"

"I don't know exactly." She gave me a glimmer of her usual smile. "Maybe it's nothing."

"Charisse," I began carefully, "you shouldn't force your feelings underground. If something feels off to you, you should talk about it."

Charisse frowned and then gave me an oddly desperate look. "I don't know what it is, Katie. I really don't. He certainly hasn't done anything wrong. And it's not anything he's said, either—in fact, he's very charming and polite. I can't actually pin anything on him, and yet—"

She paused. "Katie, I think this concerns you, too. I need you to—"

She stopped suddenly and drew back as if she'd been caught at something. She looked around and gave me a small smile. "This is my hallway. I'd better go. You should forget what I've said. I really shouldn't have brought this up at all."

She turned to go.

"Charisse, wait," I said.

She turned back and waved, but she kept going.

I had no choice but to hurry on to class.

I was growing increasingly anxious to see William. I never knew when or where he would show up when he came to see me at school. I just hoped he would appear soon. I needed to see him—I needed to hear his voice. I clutched my charm—it made him feel nearer somehow.

Third period and fourth period passed, and I didn't see William. I went to lunch, and I sat with Charisse, Branden, and Simon like I usually did. Charisse and Branden were talking quietly with one another again and didn't pay much attention to me. Simon, on the other hand, seemed to be working harder than usual to make me laugh, but I wasn't in a terribly humorous mood. I was beginning to worry that maybe William wouldn't show up today. GM would be really unhappy if she agreed to have him over for dinner and then he didn't show.

"So how about it, Katie?"

I glanced up. Simon was looking at me expectantly.

I realized that I hadn't heard anything he'd said in the last few minutes.

I blinked. "Sorry. What did you say?"

"I said, how would you like to go ice-skating with me this weekend? I thought it would be fun for you—especially since it seems to be something you're into now."

A familiar feeling of guilt settled over me—that always seemed to happen with Simon. It was beginning to be clear that what I'd suspected earlier was true—that his romantic feelings for me were returning. Perhaps they'd never really left. I really liked Simon—I really cared about him. But what I felt for him was nothing like what I felt for William.

"What about Irina?" I asked.

At the beginning of the school year, Irina had made no secret of the fact that she liked Simon. And as the weeks had gone by, she'd only seemed to like him more—and she'd been even more unpleasant to me than she usually was. After Irina and I had returned from Russia and our relationship had thawed, there had also been a warming up of the relationship between Irina and Simon. The two of them had seemed to be getting along well for a few weeks—they even seemed to be well on their way to becoming a couple. But lately, it seemed that they'd begun to drift apart.

I drew in my breath sharply—I should have seen it before. Irina had realized that Simon was interested in me again long before I had. That's why she was angry again.

For his part, Simon ran his hand over his hair. "Irina, yeah."

He looked away. I could see that he was trying to work out what he wanted to say. I wanted to tell him that he didn't have to explain anything about Irina to me—that I would actually be really happy if he liked her. But I had a feeling that telling him all that wouldn't make any difference. So I waited.

"Irina is a great girl," Simon said at last, "but she's not you. And I know you think you like this William guy, but Katie, I'm telling you he's not good for you."

I realized then that Charisse and Branden had stopped talking and were watching us closely. I suddenly felt very uncomfortable. Charisse and Branden didn't know much about William, but I had an unpleasant feeling that they disapproved of him, too.

Simon continued. "I'm sorry I've spent so much time with Irina lately. As I said—she's a great girl. I like her a lot, and I wanted to like her more—mostly because it seemed to be what you wanted."

I felt a little pang of guilt when Simon said that. I certainly hadn't meant to push Simon into a relationship that he didn't really want.

"But Katie, I soon realized that I could never feel anything more for Irina than friendship. And I also realized that it wouldn't be fair to her to pretend otherwise."

I sighed. I was certainly familiar with that sentiment.

"And I have to tell you," Simon said, "that it's almost like you're under some kind of spell lately. Things were going great between us until this William guy showed up. And you know, I blame myself for some of this."

"Simon, that's crazy," I said. "You have absolutely nothing to be sorry about."

He interrupted. "But I do. I really do. I was hanging out with Irina, but the whole time I was worried about you. I knew that you were in trouble with this—this William, and I did nothing. You needed me, and I wasn't there. And now you're in over your head with some shady guy from who knows where. I've failed you, Katie. And I'm sorry about that."

"You've got this all wrong," I said. "I don't want to hurt you, but I'm really happy with William—no one could make me happier."

Simon gave me a skeptical look. Then he shook his head and smiled.

"Okay, Katie. I'll humor you. For now."

I looked around at Charisse and Branden. Both of them were staring at me, clearly concerned.

"So what about you guys?" I asked, though I feared I knew the answer. "What do you think about William and me?"

Branden looked away.

Charisse pursed her lips. She started to say something then stopped. She was silent for a moment, and then her words started to tumble out.

"Katie, as much as I hate to say it, your situation is reminding me of my mom's. I wanted to say something before, but I couldn't. Some guy breezes into town out of nowhere and suddenly the two of you can't be separated. You don't spend time with your friends like you used to, and you seem to be in a dreamy fog all the time. And Katie, to be honest the few times I've been around William, I've gotten a really funny feeling around him. It's a lot like the feeling I have around my mom's new boyfriend. I think William is trouble, too."

"What can I do to reassure you guys that everything is okay?" I asked.

"Listen to your friends," Charisse said quickly. "Listen to the people who care the most about you."

I felt frustration welling up within me. That was not the kind of answer I wanted.

I looked around at the three sets of worried eyes that were turned toward me. "Can we change the topic, please?"

All three sets of eyes wavered—I saw disappointment and alarm flash across the faces that were turned toward me. Charisse, Branden, and Simon all became carefully polite, even conciliatory.

"Yeah, sure, of course," Branden said.

"If that's what you want, Katie," Simon said.

"Don't get angry, Katie. We're just trying to look out for you," Charisse said.

I told myself to be calm.

"I appreciate your concern, I really do," I said. "You'll all just have to trust me on this one."

In return I received three nods and three polite smiles. But I had a feeling this argument was far from over.

The rest of lunch was rather strained as we all made small talk, and I was relieved when the bell rang.

We all got up, and Branden and Charisse headed off together like they usually did. I turned to say good-bye to Simon, but instead of turning toward his hallway, he moved to follow me.

"I'll walk you to class," he said.

"Simon—" I began. I was suddenly nervous. I didn't want Simon following me. I was still waiting for William to show up, and I didn't want him to step out of the shadows when I was with Simon. Simon, though he pretended otherwise, still seemed pretty worked up. I feared what would happen if he saw William. I didn't want a confrontation—especially not at school.

He interrupted. "Katie, we're not done talking yet."

"Simon, please," I said. "I don't want to go over all that again—"

"Katie, you never answered my question."

I blinked. "What question?"

"Will you go ice-skating with me this weekend?"

I looked up into Simon's face. Despite everything I had said, he looked really hopeful. A terrible feeling of guilt settled over me once again.

"Simon, I like you. I really do. And we've been friends forever—"

"So, is that a 'yes'?"

I closed my eyes. "Simon, please just listen."

He remained silent, and I looked up at him again. "I want to stay friends with you, and I don't mind doing things with you as a friend, but somehow going ice-skating feels more like a date. And as much as I like you, I can't go out on a date with you."

"Because of *him*," Simon said.

"Because of William," I replied.

Simon nodded, then he looked up at me. "I'm not going to give up, you know. You think that he's right for you. But I *know* that I am. I'm in this for the long haul. You take all the time you need to moon over the wrong guy. But when he's gone—moved on to the next town or whatever it is guys like him do—I'll still be standing here. I'm the one you can depend on."

Simon backed up a few paces. "I'm not giving up, Katie. I promise you that."

Then he turned and was gone, disappearing into the crowd of students.

Chapter Four

After Simon had disappeared, I stood for a moment, feeling more than a little exhausted. Then I turned to go to class. As I did so, I found that someone was standing in my way.

I looked up and saw with relief that it was William.

"Was that guy bothering you?" He nodded his head in the direction of the now-vanished Simon. His tone was light, even joking, but I thought I detected an undercurrent of anger.

"Your hearing is pretty good, isn't it?" I said ruefully.

"Yes," William said, giving me his little half smile.

"How much did you overhear?" I asked.

"All of it," he replied.

"So you know that Simon is unhappy about you and me."

Simon and William had met on a few occasions—neither one had seemed to take to the other.

"Yes," William said, "and I think your friend has a lot of nerve. But because he's your friend, I decided not to make an issue of it."

"Thanks," I said. "Simon—"

I realized I didn't know quite how to finish the sentence.

"Simon means well," I said at last.

William didn't seem to like the topic very much.

"You have to get to class, don't you?" he said. "Lead the way."

We walked through the crowded hallway together, and I couldn't help wishing that William could actually go to school with me—then we could spend time together every day.

"Did you talk to your grandmother?" William asked.

"Yes, I did. She said you can come over for dinner tonight."

"Tonight?" William said. "Are you serious?"

"Yes, I'm serious. I wouldn't joke about something like this. Besides, it's not like she knows you're a—"

I stopped abruptly. The hallway was not the place for unguarded talk.

William gave me a wry smile.

"So can you come over tonight?" I asked.

"Of course. It's exactly what I was hoping for."

"GM said that she's going to make pasta or something like that. Do you—actually eat anything?"

"I can," William said. "It won't be a problem."

I realized that I'd never really asked William about his diet. I did know that he didn't drink human blood—he'd reassured me on that score—but I didn't know what he actually did consume—if anything.

"So what do you eat—drink—whatever it is you do?"

William glanced around. "I don't think this is quite the place for that discussion."

"Sorry," I said. "GM is going to ask you questions, too. She'll want to know a lot about you."

"I'll answer her questions," William said.

"You will?"

"Of course."

I was stunned. "But you almost never answer questions when I ask them."

William shot me an amused glance. "You're exaggerating."

"No, I'm not. You never tell me anything. Why will you answer questions for GM and not for me?"

"Don't you want me to answer questions for your grandmother?"

"Of course I do."

"Then you'll find out some of the things you want to know tonight."

Somehow that wasn't exactly an answer to my question.

My irritation seemed to amuse William further.

"What time is dinner?" he asked.

"Six-thirty."

"I'll be there then."

He smiled and turned as if he were about to leave.

I reached out and grabbed him by the sleeve. "William, wait. There's something else I have to tell you."

He turned back, and we started walking again.

I glanced over my shoulder and then lowered my voice. "I heard this morning that a girl was attacked last night in the Old Grove. From the description of the wounds, it sounds like a vampire attack."

William looked at me sharply. "You don't need to be worried, Katie. I'm keeping an eye on the situation."

"You already know about the attack?"

"Yes."

"Are Anton and Innokenti responsible for it?" I asked.

"I'm fairly sure it was one of them—but I don't know for sure which one it was."

"So they're going to hang around town?"

William was grim. "It looks likely."

"What are we going to do?" I asked. "If they stay here, there will be more attacks."

"*We* aren't going to do anything," William said firmly. "I'll take care of those two."

"What happened exactly?" I asked.

"The incident occurred around midnight. The victim was a girl from this school—her name is Annamaria."

I drew in my breath sharply. I realized now why Bryony and Irina had looked so worried.

"Do you know her?" William asked.

"Yes," I said. I felt light-headed.

"From what I hear, she's going to be okay."

"I know—I heard that too. It's just—"

I had to stop. A terrible thought had just occurred to me.

"Katie, I'm going to look out for you and everybody in this town."

William's tone was reassuring, but I was too rattled to be soothed.

William stopped walking. "If I'm not mistaken, this is your classroom. You should go in. The bell is about to ring."

I clutched at William's sleeve again.

"What about Annamaria?" I asked softly. "Is she safe from—"

I glanced around and lowered my voice further still. "Is Annamaria going to become a vampire?"

"No," William replied, "she isn't."

"Are you sure?" I asked. "Do you really know that, or are you just trying to make me feel better?"

"I went over to visit Annamaria this morning," William said. "That's why I was a little later meeting up with you than I intended to be. I asked her a few questions. She isn't in any danger."

"William, how does it happen? How does someone become a vampire?"

"Katie—"

I clutched his arm more tightly. "Don't put me off. I need to know. I won't go to class unless you tell me."

William didn't look happy, but after a quick glance around, he answered me.

"You have to be bitten by a vampire. Then you have to drink his blood in return. Then you have to die. Annamaria hasn't consumed any blood, so she should be safe. The vampire who attacked her is unlikely to be able to get her in the hospital—and I doubt he wants to anyway."

"So—"

"Katie, I've answered your question. Now go to class. I'll see you tonight. It really will be okay."

With that, he was gone.

I walked into class and sat down. I was really shaken up by the fact that it was Annamaria who had been attacked by a vampire. I tried to pay attention in class, but my thoughts kept wandering back to her.

What if she was only the beginning?

The rest of the day passed in a blur, and I felt a sense of relief when I heard the final bell ring. I hurried to my locker, and when I shut my locker door, Charisse was standing on the other side.

I couldn't help jumping a little. "You startled me, Charisse."

She was grim. "I want you to do something for me. This has gone far enough."

"Is something wrong?"

"Katie, I want you to come home with me right now."

"Ordinarily, I'd be glad to," I said. "But I have to get home. William is coming over for dinner tonight. GM and I have to get everything ready."

"Your grandmother won't mind if you're just a little late," Charisse said firmly. "I just need you to see something. Then I'll drive you right home. It'll only take a few minutes—I promise."

I was puzzled. "You want me to see something? Can't you just bring it in tomorrow and show me then?"

Anger flickered in Charisse's eyes. "I can't bring it in tomorrow. And I can't tell you what it is—you have to see it to understand. This is really important to me. And it's important to you, too."

I felt a flash of irritation. "Charisse, *tonight* is important to me. I want this dinner to go well. I want GM and William to like each other."

Charisse just stared at me steadily. She continued to look angry, but there was something else there too—it looked like fear.

"You're sure it'll only take a few minutes?" I asked.

"I'm positive," she said.

I sighed. "Fine."

The day had grown even colder since the morning, and as I followed Charisse out to the student parking lot, our breath rose up into the air as frosty white vapor. We got into her car, and I shivered in the car's frigid interior.

Charisse started the car and pulled out onto the road in silence.

I glanced over at her as we drove. There was tension in her hands as she gripped the steering wheel, and her lips were pressed into a grim line. I felt myself growing concerned for her. What could be at her house that had her so upset?

We pulled into her housing development, and she parked the car in a cul-de-sac. I glanced around—we were several streets over from her house.

"Why are we parking here?" I asked. "Is there any reason we can't park at your house?"

"Leave your stuff here," Charisse said. "It'll be safe. I'm just taking my keys."

She got out of the car, and I followed her.

"We're going to have to sneak up to my house" Charisse said grimly. "Just follow me and try to be quiet."

"Charisse, are you okay?" I asked. "You're acting really odd."

"I'm acting odd?" Her lips curled into a mocking semblance of her usual smile. "You should see what's going on at my house."

She led me across several streets and then into someone's backyard. She crouched down against the side of the house and motioned for me to do the same. We could see into Charisse's yard from our vantage point.

"Charisse, what are we doing?" I said. "Why don't we just drive up to your house like normal people?"

"I don't want my mom to know I'm home yet."

I was puzzled. "What's your mom doing home this early?"

Charisse's mother was an attorney, and I knew she usually worked long hours.

"Lately, my mother is home all the time," Charisse whispered. "It's really not normal. Just watch for a moment and don't say anything."

She held up a hand, and I waited silently. Just as my legs were starting to cramp, Charisse rose a little.

"It looks like the way is clear," she whispered. "Come on."

Charisse hurried over to her own backyard, still crouching down.

I hurried after her.

Charisse stopped just underneath a large window. I had been to her house many times, and I knew that that window looked in on her kitchen.

I crouched under the window beside her.

"I'm going to look in," Charisse said, and she lowered her voice so much that it was barely audible. "I'll let you know when it's okay for you to look, too."

Charisse reached up to grab the ledge, and inch by inch she raised herself up till her eyes were just high enough to look in.

"It's okay to look in right now," she said in the same almost-inaudible whisper. "But be ready to duck down if I give the word."

I reached for the ledge and pulled myself up slowly just as Charisse had done.

The scene that met my eyes was not out of the ordinary. Mrs. Graebel was seated at a table that I had sat at many times myself. Her black hair was pulled back into a ponytail, and she was wearing a pink turtleneck sweater. She held a mug in her hands, and I could see that she no longer wore her wedding ring. But there was nothing unusual about that—she *was* in the process of getting a divorce.

As I watched, Mrs. Graebel lifted her mug and took a drink.

I dipped back below the ledge.

Charisse frowned and slipped down beside me.

"What are you doing?" she hissed.

"What am I doing? What are *you* doing?" I whispered back. "I feel really weird spying on your mom like this. Was it really necessary to drag me over here so that I could watch her have a drink at her own kitchen table?"

Anger flashed in Charisse's eyes.

"*Look* at her," Charisse whispered. "*Really* look at her. Think about what you know about my mother, and then tell me what you see."

I started to raise myself up again, but Charisse pulled me back.

"Wait," she whispered. "I'll have to look to make sure the way is clear again."

I suppressed my irritation as Charisse slowly pulled herself up and looked into the kitchen once again. After a moment, she waved me up.

I was really anxious to be done with the whole thing, but Charisse was my friend, so I pulled myself up beside her.

Mrs. Graebel was sitting as before, sipping from her mug. I felt ridiculous, peering in at her without her knowledge, but I tried to evaluate the scene before me. Charisse seemed very sure that something was wrong. Had I missed something?

I examined Mrs. Graebel's expression as best I could. She certainly didn't look unhappy—in fact, she looked calm and peaceful—almost dreamy.

It was true that Mrs. Graebel wasn't the dreamy type—she was very energetic and no-nonsense. But perhaps the end of her marriage had taken some pressure off of her.

As I continued to look at Mrs. Graebel, I realized that there was something a little careless about her ponytail—and I had never seen her less than perfectly groomed. I had also never seen her wearing anything like the slouchy turtleneck she was wearing. I almost invariably saw her in suits, even on the weekends, and on the rare days when she took off and wasn't in suits, her taste was fashionable and somewhat severe.

I frowned. The turtleneck looked like it was too big for her. Had Mrs. Graebel lost weight?

"You see it now, don't you?" Charisse whispered. "You can see that she's changed."

"Your mother doesn't like pink does she?" I said.

"No, she doesn't," Charisse hissed. "Her favorite color is black—followed closely by gray."

"I don't know, Charisse," I said. "One pink turtleneck doesn't really seem like the end of the world to me."

Out of the corner of my eye I could see something move in the kitchen, and Charisse tugged fiercely on my coat sleeve.

"Duck!" she hissed.

We both dropped down below the ledge, and Charisse continued to stare upward as if she wished she could see through the wall.

"What is it?" I whispered.

Charisse gave another sharp tug on my sleeve and pressed a finger to her lips.

After a moment, Charisse motioned firmly for me to stay put. Then she crept slowly up toward the window, till she could see in once again.

I watched as her eyes narrowed.

"I knew it," she hissed.

I looked at her questioningly.

"I knew he was coming over to the house while I was gone," she whispered.

"Who?" I asked.

Charisse ducked down beside me, her eyes blazing. "It's Joshua—the guy my mom is seeing. He's never around when I get home, but I always have the feeling that he's only just left. I see now that I was right. This is what you really need to see."

She moved up to the window and watched again. Then she motioned for me to join her.

I peered into the kitchen, and this time I could see a man sitting at the table across from Mrs. Graebel. He was blond and good-looking, and he rested his chin on his hand as he gazed at Mrs. Graebel. For her part, Mrs. Graebel's expression had grown even dreamier. She had set her mug down, and she was leaning on her elbows, gazing back at the blond man.

I ducked down below the window ledge again. I didn't feel like watching any longer.

Charisse glared at me. "What are you doing?"

"This is weird," I said. "I don't want to do this anymore."

Charisse dropped down beside me.

"Katie, this is exactly what I brought you to see," she whispered fiercely. "You have to see the way the two of them interact. It's just not normal. It's like my mom's under a spell."

"I'm not going to spy on your mom and her boyfriend," I whispered back.

"But you have to see them."

"I've seen enough," I said.

"Well?" Charisse demanded.

"Well, what?" I asked. It was cold, and I was getting tired of crouching down below the window like some kind of criminal.

"What do you think about the two of them? Don't you think there's an unhealthy atmosphere there?"

"I think maybe it's—"

"Yes?"

I hesitated. I'd almost said "love," but that seemed a little too strong, and such a term would surely upset Charisse.

I tried again. "Maybe they're—happy."

Anger flashed in Charisse's eyes. "Happy? You call that happy?"

I tried to choose my words carefully. "I know it's hard to see your mom dating again—"

Charisse cut me off. "'Dating' is not the issue. My mom is home when she should be working. She's not acting like herself. And that man is with her when I'm not around. Something's not right."

"I don't know why your mom is home when she's usually at work, but—"

"Katie, you know, there's more than one reason why I wanted you to see my mom today, and I'm glad you got to see her with Joshua— that's the way you look when you're with William."

"You're really not helping your case with that," I said.

"It's true," Charisse hissed furiously. "That's the same dreamy, lost look you get when you're with William. William and Joshua are both the same. They're both trouble. And I heard William was seen with you at school today. He's got no right to be in our school."

I very nearly jumped to my feet, but I stopped myself in time— Mrs. Graebel and her boyfriend would surely see me.

"Charisse, I'm going back to the car. I'm not doing this anymore."

"Don't you dare leave!" Charisse hissed.

But I was already moving along the back of the house, still crouching down. I didn't care particularly if Charisse was following or not. I would wait by the car, and if she didn't show up, I would just walk home.

But as I reached the end of the wall, someone stepped into my path, and I was forced to stop short.

I looked up. In front of me was the blond man from the kitchen.

Charisse ran up beside me and grabbed me by the arm, pulling me back.

"You leave her alone!" Charisse shouted.

I turned to look at her. There was a look of genuine fear on her face.

"Hi, ladies," the man said pleasantly.

I turned back to look at the man before me. He smiled, and it gave him a youthful, boyish look.

He was wearing a coat, and he held out a gloved hand to me. "Charisse I know already, but I don't believe we've met. I'm Joshua Martin."

I reached my hand out automatically to take his, but Charisse grabbed my arm and pulled it back down.

Joshua gave Charisse a rueful look and pulled his hand back, brushing it over his hair.

"What are you doing out here?" Charisse asked. She continued to grip my arm and her eyes were wary.

"I might ask you two the same thing," Joshua said lightly.

The words were clearly intended as a joke, but I felt Charisse stiffen.

Joshua looked down and then gave Charisse another rueful look.

"Okay," he said. "I can see this isn't going too well. Let's start over again."

He turned to me and put a hand to his chest. "I'm Joshua Martin. I'm a friend of Charisse's mother."

"I'm Katie Wickliff," I replied. "I'm a friend of Charisse's."

"It's nice to meet you, Katie," Joshua said. He pointed a thumb over his shoulder. "It's pretty cold out here. Would you girls like to come inside and have something hot to drink?"

"No, we wouldn't," Charisse said sharply.

Joshua nodded his head and looked around.

"Just out of curiosity—what are you two doing out here?"

"Why do you want to know?" Charisse snapped.

Joshua spread out his hands. "Well, you know, it's just a little weird, Charisse. You and your friend here are hanging out beneath the window instead of coming into the house like normal people—"

"How did you know we were under the window?" Charisse interjected sharply.

"Water vapor, Charisse. We saw your breath rising up past the window. Your mom asked me to come outside and see what was going on. And then I see the two of you sneaking along the back of the house here."

Charisse bristled. "You have no right to ask me what I'm doing at my own house. You don't belong here. Come on, Katie. We're going back to the car."

She tugged on my arm and pulled me around Joshua, giving him a wide berth. She dragged me into the neighbor's yard.

I looked back.

I saw Joshua throw up his hands in frustration.

"I wouldn't do anything to hurt your mother, Charisse," he called after us. "I wouldn't do anything to hurt you, either."

Charisse continued to pull me along by my arm.

Joshua shouted after us again. "You know, it's not so terrible if your mother relaxes sometimes."

Charisse drew in her breath sharply. She broke into a run, dragging me with her.

We ran until we reached Charisse's car. She scrambled to pull the door open and jumped inside.

I hurried into the car. Charisse quickly locked the doors.

She twisted around and searched the street behind us. Then she fell back against her seat.

"He didn't follow us," she breathed. She closed her eyes.

I glanced back. The street behind us was indeed empty.

I turned back to Charisse. "What is going on with you?"

Her eyes flew open. "Are you serious?"

"Yes, I'm serious. You're acting crazy."

"You really didn't hear that?" Charisse demanded.

"Didn't hear what?"

"Katie, Joshua said it wasn't so bad if my mom relaxes sometimes."

"So?"

Charisse's eyes blazed. "So? Katie, he could hear us."

"When we were whispering beneath the window?"

"Yes. He heard me complaining about the fact that my mom wasn't at work like she should be."

"I don't see how that's possible," I said.

"Then how did he know?" Charisse demanded. "I never talk to him. I certainly never spoke to him about my mom's work."

"Well, of course you never talk to him," I said. "You told me he's not usually there when you get home. You can't talk to him if you don't see him."

"Katie, he comes back later in the evening to pick my mom up so they can go out. He tries to talk to me then. But I have absolutely nothing to say to him."

"Maybe you said something to your mom, and she mentioned it to him."

Charisse shook her head. "I don't talk to her these days, either. It's like she barely even knows I'm around."

"Okay, let's say he's weird and your mom's distant. I still don't see what your point is. What do you think is going to happen?"

"Joshua is not normal. He could hear us talking—I know it. And I think that's why he's gone when I get home—he can hear my car coming, so he leaves. He's trying to pretend like everything's normal, but it isn't."

I didn't reply, and Charisse lapsed into silence.

"I guess I don't know what my point is, either," she said after a moment.

She started the car.

"You probably want to get home."

Chapter Five

Charisse left me at my front door and then sped off.

I knew she was angry—she had maintained a stony silence during the drive to my house. But I didn't see that there was anything either one of us could do if her mother liked Joshua Martin. Maybe Charisse had noticed something strange about him—but I hadn't.

And it seemed to me that if anyone could recognize trouble, I could.

Just as I was getting out of the car, I had asked Charisse to tell me if anything new developed—anything truly out of the ordinary.

Charisse had not replied to that.

I supposed I couldn't really blame her.

So feeling out of sorts, I watched Charisse's taillights disappear. Then I went into the house and on into the kitchen.

A pot of water was boiling vigorously on the stove, and GM was sitting at the kitchen table reading a letter. The letter seemed to absorb her completely—so much so that I could tell she didn't know that I had come into the room.

I stood for a moment watching her.

My eyes dropped from her rapt face to the piece of paper in her hand. I squinted at it, and I realized that I could just make out the dark outline of the words she was reading. I wondered if I could read the words backwards.

GM looked up suddenly and jumped when she saw me.

"Oh, Katie! I didn't know you were home."

She folded the letter up swiftly and swept it into an envelope that had been lying facedown on the table. Then she hurried out of the room.

It was pretty clear to me that she was going to her office to hide her letter.

Sure enough, when GM returned a moment later, her hands were empty.

"Sorry I'm later than usual," I said, as GM moved to the stove. "I stopped by Charisse's house."

GM was measuring orecchiette pasta into the boiling water and looked around at me.

"It is of no consequence, solnyshko."

She turned back to the boiling water and threw in a pinch of salt.

It was unusual for GM not to require me to account for all of my time.

"Who was the letter from?" I asked.

GM waved a hand airily. "No one."

She smiled at me and moved to the refrigerator.

I felt a flash of frustration, but I tried to keep my voice even. "A letter can't come from no one. Someone has to write it and send it."

GM shut the refrigerator door and turned back to me. "It's not from anyone you know."

I persisted. "Is it from the same person who sent you all the other letters?"

"What other letters?"

"GM, please. You know I've seen you with the other letters."

Her face went carefully blank.

"This is my private correspondence, Katie. It has nothing to do with you."

I decided to drop the topic. GM was clearly getting ruffled, and I didn't want her to be in a bad mood when William arrived.

"Is there anything I can do to help with dinner?" I asked, changing the subject.

"The sauce is made already," GM replied. "You can chop up this basil."

She handed me a bunch of the herb. "When you're done with that, you can cut some slices of bread."

GM and I worked on dinner after that, and before long, I was running up the stairs to get ready myself.

I changed my clothes quickly and pulled a brush through my hair. Then I stood before the mirror surveying my reflection.

I was starting to get nervous now, and I ordered myself to be calm.

I really wanted this evening to go well.

As I turned away from the mirror, I thought I saw a flutter of movement out of the corner of my eye.

I turned back quickly and searched the mirror, but there was nothing in it that shouldn't have been there.

I turned away again, but as I did so, I got the strangest feeling that someone in the mirror had turned away also.

I resisted the urge to look at the mirror again and shrugged off the feeling—surely it was just my nerves getting the better of me. Or was it just nerves? A horrible thought occurred to me, and I resolved to ask William about it.

I hurried downstairs.

I found GM in our seldom-used dining room, lighting candles. The table was set and all the food was out—GM had made a few extra dishes that she hadn't told me about.

"It looks beautiful," I said.

"I used to do a lot of entertaining once," GM murmured, almost more to herself than to me. "I gave a lot of big parties. I know how to turn out a good table."

I was caught by the tone of her voice—it was faraway, even wistful. I was on the verge of asking her a question when there was a knock at the front door.

I glanced at GM nervously.

"You will give William a chance, won't you?"

"Of course I will give him a chance. I've done all this, haven't I?" She waved a hand at me. "Now, go. Say hello to your young man."

I hurried to the door and opened it.

William gave me his crooked smile.

I stood for a moment just looking at him—I had a strong desire to throw my arms around him, but I figured that really wouldn't help my case with GM.

GM walked up behind me.

Suddenly I felt strangely shy.

"Katie, aren't you going to invite your friend in?" GM said.

"Won't you come in?" I said to William.

"Thanks." He stepped in, and there was a bottle in his hand.

GM glanced disapprovingly at the bottle—I imagined she thought he was sixteen as I was. I supposed I should have warned him not to bring something like a bottle of wine.

"GM, you remember William Sursur from Russia," I said.

"Yes, I remember him," she replied shortly.

"It's good to see you again, Mrs. Rost," William said. He held the bottle out. "This is for you."

She accepted the bottle and glanced at the label. The corner of her mouth quirked up.

"Sparkling apple juice. Thank you."

The three of us went into the dining room. William held GM's chair out for her. Then he did the same for me. GM seemed amused.

William sat down, too, and we started on dinner.

"So, William," GM said, "do you attend school with my granddaughter?"

"No, I don't."

GM seemed surprised. "Where do you go to school, then?"

"I don't go to school," William replied simply.

GM shot me a disapproving glance. "I see. What do your parents think about that?"

"My parents are no longer with us."

I glanced at William sharply. GM, no doubt, would assume from that that William's parents were dead—I wondered, though, if he actually knew anything about them. It seemed to me that William might not know where, or even who, they were.

But I could hardly question him about that in front of GM.

GM herself seemed momentarily stunned by William's reply and something like sympathy flickered in her eyes.

She soon shook off the emotion and returned to her questioning.

"Do you work?" GM asked.

"Yes."

"What do you do?"

"I work freelance. I'm a software engineer."

"You are quite young to have a job like that."

"A lot of computer geniuses started young."

GM's eyebrows rose. "So, you are a genius, then?"

William's face was suffused with color. "No, that's not what I meant at all."

"Why are you here in Elspeth's Grove?" GM asked. "Is it for work?"

"No," William replied.

"You came here to see my granddaughter?"

"Yes."

GM was holding a fork in her hand. In that moment I wouldn't have been surprised to see her snap it in half.

"You sound to me like a reckless, irresponsible young man," she said in a voice of iron.

"GM—" I began.

"Hush, Katie," GM snapped. "You stay out of this."

She turned her attention back to William, and her eyes blazed. "You *admit* that you came here to stalk my granddaughter?"

"I can appreciate your concern, Mrs. Rost," William replied mildly. "And I'm very grateful that you invited me over here tonight. I wanted you to see me, and I wanted you to know more about me. I did move here to be near Katie—I admit that. But I can assure you that I haven't come here to stalk her. I only want to see Katie as long as she wants to see me."

GM seemed incredulous. "So, if Katie were to ask you to go—to leave Elspeth's Grove entirely, what would you do?"

"I would leave," William said.

"Just like that?" GM demanded.

"Just like that."

GM stared hard at William for a long moment, and he calmly returned her gaze.

William was the one who eventually broke the silence.

"I hope you'll forgive me for saying this, Mrs. Rost, but I am much happier here. Things are difficult for me in the town of Krov. I believe that is something you can understand."

GM seemed to consider William's words. After a moment, she sighed.

"It is true, what you say. I love Krov, but I could never live there again. I, too, am happier here. Krov is hard on her children."

GM didn't seem entirely sold yet, but the tense lines in her face had relaxed.

"Where do you live, William?" GM said.

"I have a house in the Old Grove."

I gave him another sharp glance. He had already told me that he would answer GM's questions—even though he wouldn't answer mine—but somehow the fact that he had answered this particular question so easily rankled.

I felt for just a moment as if the two of them were united against me.

"Do you rent or do you own?" GM asked.

"I own the house."

"And your freelance work—is it full time?"

"Yes."

"It is strange," GM said. "You are almost like a full grown man, dating a high school student."

William didn't have an answer for that.

GM was suddenly fierce. "I want it to be clear that I will allow nothing and no one to harm my granddaughter. Neither you, nor anyone else, will jeopardize her future. Katie will finish high school and go on to college. She will have a flourishing career in whatever field she chooses. She will not run away with you and elope. The two of you will not decide that you can 'live on love.' And if you were to attempt to abscond with my granddaughter, I would hunt you down and murder you myself. Do you understand that?"

William blinked and sat back in his chair. I had never seen him look intimidated before.

He was intimidated now.

"Yes, ma'am. I understand that," he said.

GM nodded. "Good."

Something in William's answer must have satisfied GM, because her sudden anger seemed to subside. After she had regained her composure, her attitude became less confrontational. She began to ask William about the company he was currently freelancing for. When GM discovered that she had done projects for the same company, the two of them began to talk pleasantly.

I was relieved that the grilling was over.

The rest of the evening seemed to go well, and GM was almost friendly when she said goodnight to William.

As William left, I followed him outside and closed the front door behind us. I'd been turning something over in the back of my mind, and I had to ask him about it.

I glanced back at the window in the front of the house uneasily. I knew I wouldn't have much time, and I knew GM would be watching. I just hoped she couldn't overhear us.

"I think this went well, don't you?" William said.

"It does seem like this was a good idea," I replied.

"I'd kiss you good night, but I have a feeling that your grandmother would storm out here and forbid me ever to return."

"William," I said quickly. "I have some questions that I need to ask you."

"More questions?" William was amused. "I would have thought we'd both had enough of those at dinner."

"I need to ask you about Anton and Innokenti," I said.

"You don't need to know about those two," William said.

"I know you've said that before," I replied, "but there's a lot I don't know about—about—"

I stumbled over my words, afraid that GM was listening.

"I need to know about *them*," I said at last.

"Katie, they aren't nice—'people.' I'll call them that for lack of a better word." William glanced up at the window as if he, too, feared that GM could hear him. "You really don't want to know about them."

"I don't mean that I need to know about those two as individuals." I dropped my voice nearly to a whisper. "I mean I need to know about vampires."

William winced and shot another glance at the window.

I expected another protest from him, so I went on quickly.

"I have a specific reason for wanting to know," I said. "I've been seeing strange things, and there *are* two of them in town. I don't know what I can believe about them and what I can't. For example, in popular folklore, crosses can ward off vampires, but in actual fact, crosses have no effect on them, right?"

"That's true," William said.

"Those are the kinds of questions I have."

"What do you want to know?" William asked quietly.

"Are they hurt by garlic or holy water?"

"No."

"What about sunlight?" I remembered that Odette had disappeared during the day. "Will sunlight kill them?"

"No. Like many night creatures they're sluggish during the day— it's when they're most vulnerable. They *do* tend to hide from sunlight. But it won't kill them."

"Can they enter a house without being invited?" I was getting closer to the question I wanted to ask the most.

"Yes," William said.

I was a little startled by his answer. "Yes?"

"Yes."

"But I invited you into my house."

"You didn't need to. And if you'll recall, I entered your house when Gleb broke in. You didn't invite me in that time."

"So, Anton and Innokenti can walk into anyone's house any time they want to?"

"They can. But I'm watching your house. They won't get past me."

Suddenly an image flashed in my mind of Anton walking around in my living room, his eyes alight with malice. He picked up one of my family photos and examined it. Then he turned expectantly, as if someone had come into the room.

The image faded quickly, and I staggered.

William reached out a hand to steady me.

"Katie, are you all right?"

I wasn't sure if what I'd just experienced was a vision or not, but the image that I'd seen had been unnervingly clear. Somehow, however, it didn't feel like a vision. Maybe it had just been my subconscious fears bubbling up to the surface.

I knew one thing for certain—no matter what I had seen, Anton wasn't in my house right now. William would have known if he were, and he would have rushed in to stop him. So I took a few deep breaths and decided to ignore the image and focus on what was bothering me the most—the topic I hadn't brought up yet—my mirror.

"I'm okay," I said to William. "They—people like Anton and Innokenti—they're fast, aren't they?"

"Yes, they are." William searched my face as if he still feared that something might be wrong with me.

"Can they be seen in a mirror?" I asked.

"Of course," William replied.

I felt a chill spread through me.

"I've been seeing things in my mirror again," I said.

William knew all about my history with mirrors and visions. He also knew that my visions had stopped.

"But what I'm seeing now is different from what I've seen before," I said. "Now I see something fluttering—just a little motion out of the corner of my eye. Could I be catching glimpses of a vampire? Could they be hiding in my room, but moving so quickly that all I see is a little flash in my mirror?"

"I don't know what you've seen in your mirror," William said firmly, "but neither Anton nor Innokenti has been in your house. I know that for certain."

"They're fast," I murmured. "They have keen senses, too, don't they? And they have the power to control people's minds—to persuade their victims to do what they want. Odette used that last one on me."

I shivered.

"You shouldn't think about things like that," William admonished gently. "You're going to upset yourself, and you'll have trouble sleeping tonight."

"How can I not think about things like that when Annamaria was attacked, and I've been seeing strange things in my mirror?" I asked.

"Annamaria will be okay. She's safe in the hospital. And like I said, neither Anton nor Innokenti has been in your house. I promise you that you haven't been seeing them in your mirror."

William paused. "You do believe me, don't you?"

"I believe you," I said. "I just wish there was something I could do to get the two of them out of town. I won't feel really safe until they're gone."

William ran a soothing hand over my hair. "I'll worry about them. You don't need to."

"How do you kill them?" I asked suddenly. "Will a wooden stake work?"

"Katie, I'm not sure a discussion like that will do you any good."

"Will a wooden stake work?" I repeated.

"Wood has some effect, especially if the vamp—"

He stopped and glanced over at the window. "Especially if one of them is already weak. But it won't work on all of them. Typically, the older they are, the stronger they are. Sometimes all that will work is beheading and fire. And it wouldn't hurt to scatter the ashes, too."

"That doesn't sound very easy."

"It isn't."

"If they're so hard to kill, why aren't we overrun by them?"

"They aren't completely invulnerable," William said. "And fire *is* effective—especially, as I said, when combined with a beheading. Also, there aren't very many of them—humans outnumber them by a wide margin. And most humans have a natural aversion to them and do tend to attack them—you know, crowds with pitchforks and torches and all that. And they fight amongst themselves a great deal."

"What about—"

"Katie, please," William said. "This conversation is getting a little dark. You won't need to destroy any of them tonight. This house is safe, and I mean that. You should go inside now. Before your grandmother gets too anxious and runs me off."

I still felt uneasy. "Will you come to see me at school tomorrow? I still have some questions to ask you."

"I'll come to see you tomorrow if you'll go inside now and stop worrying."

"I'll go inside now," I said.

William gave me his little half smile. "Then I will see you tomorrow."

As always, I was reluctant to see William go.

I sighed unhappily. "Good night."

"Good night, Katie. And no more thoughts of dark creatures. You can always call me, you know." He disappeared into the night.

William wasn't talking about an ordinary call on a cell phone or a landline—I didn't actually know if he had either one of those, though presumably he did since he ran a business. The type of call he was talking about was something different—it was an incantation—something he had granted to me that would summon him to me from wherever he was. He could be at my side instantaneously from anywhere in the world.

All I had to do was say the right words, and he would appear.

So I supposed I was safe enough.

I turned and went into the house.

GM met me at the door.

"You were out there with him for quite a long time." GM wasn't angry, but there was something very stiff about her posture. Her face was carefully blank.

I was a little confused by her manner—she had seemed to warm up to William during dinner.

"Do you like William, GM?"

She folded her arms. "He seems pleasant enough—it's not a question of liking him."

"But something about him bothers you?"

"I'm allowing you to see him, aren't I?"

"But something *does* bother you?"

GM shrugged, her arms still crossed. "It's just that he seems to have appeared out of nowhere. Despite his readiness to answer questions, he remains mysterious. I don't like that."

GM's pointed comments from earlier in the evening suddenly came back to me. She had mentioned eloping. She had mentioned living on love and giving up a promising future. I thought of the photo in the living room of a young couple in a bare room with a single flower.

"Did you like my father?" I asked suddenly.

GM blinked at me in surprise. "Your father?"

"You're wearing that expression," I said. "The expression you wear when you don't want to discuss the past. Does William remind you of my father?"

GM threw up her hands. "I suppose that's possible. Your father seemed to come out of nowhere, too. He just appeared in our little town."

"Did you like him?" I asked again.

GM pressed her lips together.

"You shouldn't ask me a question like that."

I felt alarm rising within me. "Why not?"

"Oh, Katie, don't look at me like that. I'm sorry—I don't want you to think I didn't like your father. I did like him. But I'm not sure I trusted him."

"Why?" I said. "What reason did you have not to trust him?"

"Please don't be upset, solnyshko. Your father was a good man. He meant well. But his head was full of superstition. Your mother seemed to attract people like that. I think sometimes he might have influenced her the wrong way."

GM reached out and touched a lock of my hair. "Such a pale gold," she murmured. Her eyes roamed over my face, and they tightened at the corners. "You are so like your mother."

"But I'm not my mother," I said quietly. "And William isn't my father. He knows all about the superstitions of Krov, and he wants me to stay away from them."

William's insistence on my staying out of everything was typically something that bothered me, but in this case I knew GM would find it reassuring.

"Well," GM said, looking mollified. "That's certainly a point in his favor."

I felt again for a moment like they were united against me.

GM turned as if she were going to go into the kitchen, and I knew I had to stop her. She was in an unusually talkative mood—perhaps because the evening had been a little unsettling for her. It seemed to have shaken her usual control.

"GM," I said quickly, "you said it seemed like my father appeared out of nowhere, but he came from the UK, didn't he?"

She turned back. "Yes, he did."

"Then why did you say he came out of nowhere?"

GM shrugged. "It was never clear to me exactly why he had come to Russia, or how he had found our little town of Krov—it's an isolated place in many ways. We certainly never received many visitors. He didn't seem to be there for work or family, and he seemed to have come there specifically to find your mother. It was an unusual situation to say the least."

"I can see now why William reminded you of him," I said. "What explanation did my father give of himself when you first met him?"

"He didn't give any account of himself when I first met him. He was presented to me as a fait accompli," GM said curtly. "My daughter introduced him to me as her husband."

I was startled. "They were already married when you met him for the first time?"

"Yes," GM said. "They married without telling a single soul beforehand. I never did find out how long they'd known each other before they came to that decision."

I knew now why their wedding photo was so spartan—apparently my mother, like her mother, was fond of her secrets.

I felt myself growing concerned about the mother I'd barely known. "Did my father have job?" I asked.

"No," GM replied. "But he did seem to have a lot of money. He said he'd inherited it. He never said from whom."

"And my mother didn't have a job, either?" I said.

"No," GM replied shortly.

"If my father had a lot of money, why did you all live together?" I asked.

"We lived in my house. I insisted on it. To my surprise, they agreed. I don't know that I could have prevailed upon them if they hadn't—they were both so willful. But they weren't interested in a home of their own—or in material goods in general. Their minds were all full of their spiritual quest. They believed they were both put on this earth to fight the powers of darkness."

A note of despair had crept into GM's voice.

"It was all nonsense, of course," she said. "And they both paid for it in the end."

I looked at GM sharply. "What do you mean?"

She shrugged—not so much as if she didn't care, but as if she were pushing away difficult emotions. "Your mother, you know, exacerbated her fever chasing after phantoms. And she didn't survive."

I nodded. That was the version of the story that GM knew. I knew the reality—that she had been systematically poisoned. But the truth was something that she would never believe.

GM continued and some acidity crept into her tone. "Your father supposedly died in a hiking accident. But your father never had any interest in hiking or any other kind of outdoor sports. I think he was doing something else—chasing after some foolish fantasy. And whenever one of your parents went chasing after a fantasy, they seemed to run afoul of criminals like Gleb Mstislav and others of his ilk. I think your father upset someone he shouldn't have upset. And then that someone had him killed."

I felt a chill run through my body—a chill that ran so deep it seemed to freeze my heart.

An accident was a terrible thing.

But a murder was even worse.

GM caught sight of my face. "I see I have upset you, Katie. This is exactly why I don't like to talk about the past. Perhaps it is best if we end this conversation."

I felt suddenly as if an important opportunity were about to slip away—that as painful as the topic was, I had to keep GM talking or I would lose the chance to find out something very important.

I felt frozen, though. I couldn't think of anything to say that would keep her talking.

As I continued to struggle, GM ran a hand over my hair.

"I am sorry about what I said, solnyshko. I shouldn't have said those things about your father's death. It was tragic, but I'm sure it was nothing it shouldn't have been."

I pushed myself to speak. "No—no—you should say what you think. I don't want you to keep things from me—even if they're painful."

GM shook her head. "I spoke out of turn. And speculation about your father's death will change nothing—he is gone regardless. All this discussion will do is hurt you. I will say nothing more about it."

I tried to think of a way to counter that—to come up with the argument that would change GM's mind and keep her talking, but I could tell from her expression that the topic was closed.

"Your parents were good people," GM said softly. "Dreamy, yes, but good. I didn't mean to say anything that would tarnish their memory."

She smiled sadly. "It must be hard for you—very hard. You barely knew your parents. I am sorry about that, solnyshko."

GM brushed a hand over my hair once more, and then she left the room.

I had let the moment slip away.

Chapter Six

The next morning, I was up before my alarm went off. William had promised to meet me at school, and as far as I was concerned, I couldn't see him soon enough.

I'd told him I still had questions for him, but that wasn't really the case. I just wanted to see him—to be reassured by his presence. And I needed that more now than I had last night when he'd left. GM's revelation that my father's death might not have been an accident had left me feeling shaken, and I had passed the night in broken dreams.

I needed to see William.

As I quickly got ready for school, I was startled to see a tiny pile of ash on my dresser, just in front of my mirror.

I bent close to it, and even dipped an experimental finger into it, but I couldn't figure out where the ash had come from. I swept it into a trashcan and then hurried downstairs.

GM, as usual, had no interest in discussing anything that had happened last night, and I hurried through breakfast.

I left the house as quickly as I could.

The morning was clear and cold, and as I walked, I could see that many of my neighbors had already put their Christmas decorations up. The bright colors, however, did little to lift my spirits.

Despite the warm coat that I wore, I was cold—as if the late fall air had worked its way under my skin and chilled me from the inside out.

I reached the schoolyard and noticed that just one hardy soul was braving the cold out in the open air.

Branden was standing alone by the picnic table he and Charisse had staked out, and he looked up expectantly as I approached.

When he saw who it was, his face fell.

"Oh, hi, Katie," he said.

"Hi, Branden," I replied. "You don't look very happy to see me."

"Sorry," he said. "I thought you might be Charisse. She said she was going to get here early today so that we could talk about what we're going to do for winter break. She isn't usually late when she says she'll be early. And she hasn't called me or sent me a text or anything to let me know where she is."

He gave me a sudden, hopeful look. "She hasn't sent you a text, has she?"

I pulled out my phone just to double check. "No." I looked back up at him. "Maybe she's inside."

Branden shook his head. "She said to meet out here—she wouldn't forget. And she always calls me when she's going to be out sick."

He glanced around the schoolyard anxiously and then looked back at me. "Charisse told me she was going to meet up with you yesterday after school. How did she seem then? Was she okay?"

I thought back to the look on Charisse's face as she had driven away yesterday—she had clearly been angry. She'd been very upset, both with me and with her situation at home. I wondered for a moment if she could have run off—Charisse, I knew, could be impulsive.

I glanced at Branden. No matter how angry Charisse might be with her mother or with me, I knew she wouldn't take off without telling Branden—if anything, the two of them were likely to run off together.

"Charisse was pretty angry with me," I admitted. "She wanted me to see the guy her mom is dating."

Branden looked at me sharply. "Did you see him?"

"Yes," I said. "We did. Charisse was acting a little weird, actually. She got me to help her spy on him through the kitchen window. Then he came out and talked to us."

Branden made a face. "That Joshua guy's a creep."

"I don't know," I said. "He didn't seem so bad."

"He's a creep," Branden said firmly.

"That's what Charisse thinks, too. We ran off after Joshua came out to talk to us, and Charisse was furious that I didn't quite feel the same way about Joshua that she did."

"But that's all that happened?" Branden asked anxiously. "Nothing else happened with the creepy guy?"

"No—Charisse just drove me home."

Branden looked relieved. "The guy was probably gone, then, when she got back. He doesn't stick around much when she's home."

"So, you don't like Joshua, either?" I asked.

"I think I've made my feelings pretty clear," Branden replied. "I believe I've used the word 'creepy' quite a few times."

"Creepy, you say?" Another voice broke in on our conversation. I turned to see Simon standing behind us.

He turned to me. "I assume you're talking about your dinner with what's-his-name last night?"

"You know his name is William," I said to Simon. "And dinner went pretty well."

Branden shook his head. "I don't know, Katie. I don't like William, either. He's not quite as bad as Joshua, but I'd say he's the same type."

I turned on Branden. "Why? What has William done to you? What has Joshua done to you for that matter?"

"Joshua has freaked out Charisse pretty badly," Branden said. "That's a big deal to me. And William gives all of us a bad feeling. We can't all be wrong."

"Well, you are all wrong," I said. "And having a bad feeling isn't enough to condemn someone."

Branden shrugged. "All I can tell you is what I think."

Simon reached for my arm. "Let's go inside, Katie. We can talk there."

"I'll stay out here," Branden said.

"We'll tell Charisse you're out here if we see her," I said as Simon steered me toward the school.

"She's not in the cafeteria," Branden called after us.

Simon and I went inside and headed toward the cafeteria. I noticed that Simon was looking pretty grim. I had a feeling we were in for yet another difficult conversation.

We reached the cafeteria and stood in the doorway, as Simon surveyed the room. Most people were concentrated on the side of the cafeteria that was closest to the kitchen, leaving the other side largely empty. Simon led me to a round table on the less-crowded side, and we sat down.

There was no one near us, but I couldn't help but notice that Irina, who was sitting on the crowded side of the cafeteria with her friend Bryony, was watching us intently. Even from across the room, I could see anger in her dark eyes.

I looked around for Charisse. Branden was right—she wasn't in the cafeteria.

"So, this dinner last night," Simon began.

I turned back toward Simon, but I didn't quite look at him. Instead, I focused my attention on his backpack, which sat on the table by his elbow. I wasn't really in the mood for an interrogation this early in the morning—especially not when the person I really wanted to see was William.

"What really happened?" Simon asked.

I did look at him then.

I was struck by the realization that a few short months ago, Simon had been the person I had most wanted to see. I had always found his presence to be soothing.

Now, we were still friends, but Simon's presence could sometimes be exhausting. The person who really gave me a sense of peace was

William—even when he didn't say anything—even when things were bad. And William did all of that just by being near me.

Simon leaned forward. "Katie, you aren't listening. I've asked you the same question about three times now."

I shook my head. "I'm sorry. What did you say?"

Simon gave me a searching look. "I'm trying to get you to tell me what really happened at that dinner last night. Why are you avoiding my questions?"

"The dinner went well," I said simply.

I could hardly tell him that GM didn't entirely trust William, in large part because he reminded her of my father. Nor could I tell him that she believed my father had been chasing imaginary monsters and had gotten himself killed as a result. I had tried to confide in Simon about supernatural things before—and to his credit he had tried to be open-minded. But ultimately, Simon couldn't believe in the things I had seen and experienced, and he could never understand who William was or why I had such trust in him.

Simon couldn't know that his suspicions were unfounded.

Simon sighed heavily. "The dinner can't possibly have gone well."

"It did."

He gave me a level stare. "You're telling me that your grandmother likes this drifter without any doubts or misgivings, and that nothing he said or did during dinner gave her pause?"

"Simon—"

"Just answer the question, Katie."

"GM is letting me see him."

"That's not what I asked."

I looked away.

"Katie?" Simon prompted.

I looked back at him. "GM is not one hundred percent sure of him."

"Thank you for admitting that."

"But it's not for the reasons that you think. She doesn't think he's a 'drifter.'"

"Then what are her reasons?"

Simon continued to look at me steadily, and I found I didn't know how to answer him.

"She thinks—"

I stopped.

"Yes?" Simon said.

I shook my head. "Simon, any concerns GM has don't matter. What matters is that she's letting me see William. If she really mistrusted him, she wouldn't do that."

"Unless she was afraid you'd see him behind her back. This way she gets to keep an eye on you."

I shot Simon an angry glance—I really resented his tone. And yet, I *had* been seeing William without GM's knowledge.

Even so, she had had nothing to worry about.

"Why are you so sure William's a terrible person?" I demanded. "Why are you so sure that GM dislikes him?"

Simon ignored my questions, and he countered with one of his own.

"I asked this before, but you still haven't actually answered it. What really happened last night?"

I sighed in exasperation. "William brought sparkling apple juice. We had pasta. William left. That's what happened."

"He didn't try to get you to follow him out to his shack in the woods?"

"No," I said firmly.

It was funny how little Simon understood about William. He had originally been unwilling to let me know where his house was—let alone try to lure me to it.

It was Simon's turn to look angry. "Well, it may interest you to know what your friend was up to last night after he left you."

"What do you mean?" I asked.

"Another girl was attacked last night, like Annamaria was—her neck and shoulder torn up and bloody. She's in the hospital now, but she'll be all right."

A ripple of shock ran through me. "Who was it?"

"I don't know the girl's name," Simon said. "She's from another school district. Travis Ballenski told me. His dad's a—"

"A cop," I said. "I know."

"The police found her wandering around in the Old Grove. They also found your friend what's-his-name nearby. Apparently, he was having an argument with two other men—probably they're all in this together."

"Two other men?" I asked sharply. That had to mean Anton and Innokenti. "Do you happen to know what they looked like?"

"No," Simon said. "They took off when they saw the cops. Your friend stuck around and answered some questions."

"So William cooperated with the police," I said. "Just like any innocent person would."

Simon rubbed a hand over his hair. "Katie, you're impossible. This William guy is found at the scene of an attack, and you make excuses for him."

"I haven't made any excuses," I protested. "Innocent people cooperate. William cooperated."

"Unless he's just that bold," Simon said. "Killers have bluffed their way out of trouble before."

"No one has died," I said. "And William's not guilty. If anything, he probably tried to help the girl."

I stopped abruptly, realizing that that was probably exactly what had happened. Anton or Innokenti had attacked the girl. William had shown up just in time.

"Amazing," Simon said. "Absolutely amazing. The way you can just twist facts around until they mean what you want them to mean."

"I haven't twisted anything," I said. "I know William, and you don't."

Simon stood up. "Fine. I give up. But watch yourself. Be very careful. I really care about you, Katie, and I don't want anything to happen to you."

He picked up his backpack. "I've got to get to homeroom."

I watched as Simon walked out of the cafeteria. A moment later, the warning bell rang, and I rose also. As I made my way out with the rest of the students, I felt someone plucking on my sleeve.

I turned to see Bryony walking beside me.

She tucked a lock of light brown hair behind her ear, and smiled at me shyly.

"Hi, Katie."

"Hi."

"I'm sorry to bother you," she said, "but I have something to tell you. My grandmother told me it was important."

"You're not bothering me, Bryony."

I felt eyes on me, and I glanced around. Irina was standing at a table alone, glaring at both of us.

I turned back to Bryony. "You can tell me anything you want."

A faint blush crept up her cheek, and she bit her lip. "It's a little strange."

"That's okay," I said. "I've gotten used to strange things."

Bryony hesitated for a moment and then plunged ahead in her quiet voice. "My grandmother lives in the Old Grove. She has a ghost in her house. I know you heard me say so once in class."

Bryony glanced at me, and I nodded.

She continued. "My grandmother told me the ghost has a message for you. She—the ghost that is—she's worried about you and wants you to be careful."

I was startled. "The ghost has a message for me?"

"Yes."

"What's the message?" I asked.

"The ghost said, 'don't let him sing to her.'"

"'Don't let him sing to her'? 'Her' meaning me?"

"That's right," Bryony said.

"Who is 'he'?" I asked.

Bryony looked rueful. "I don't know that—I'm sorry. My grandmother said ghosts aren't very good communicators. But she also said that if they make an effort to contact you that it's important to listen."

"And you're sure the 'her' the ghost mentioned was me?"

"Yes. My grandmother has saved every issue of the *Elspeth's Grove Gazette* she's ever received—she has decades and decades' worth of newspapers. She said the ghost flipped through her newspapers till she came to that story they ran about the three of you who were held captive by Mr. Hightower in Russia. The ghost stopped on a picture of you."

The image that rose up in my mind at Bryony's words made me shiver.

"Was that the entire message?" I asked.

"Yes."

I was stunned by Bryony's news—but I didn't doubt her. I knew that Bryony was sincere—she certainly wasn't playing a trick on me. And having a ghost send me a message was no odder than any of the other supernatural things that had happened to me in the last few months.

"Thanks for telling me, Bryony," I said, feeling more than a little light-headed.

"You don't think I'm crazy?" she asked.

"No—I don't think you're crazy. I appreciate your giving me the message. Please tell your grandmother thanks, too. I'll try to be careful."

Bryony gave me another shy smile and moved off into the crowd.

I felt a tap on my shoulder, and I turned to see Irina standing just behind me.

"Stay away from my friend," she hissed, her dark eyes flashing.

She stormed off, and I walked to homeroom, scanning the crowd. I didn't have time to dwell on the fact that Irina had found a new reason to be angry with me. I had to keep an eye out for William. As usual, I had no idea when he would appear.

I didn't see William on the way to homeroom, and I didn't see him on the way to first-period Social Studies. For the most part, I listened attentively to the lecture and took notes. But I couldn't help thinking back to Bryony's ghostly message.

Don't let him sing to her.

Who could 'he' be?

I wondered if William knew about the ghost. Since he lived in the Old Grove now, too, maybe they had run across each other.

I didn't see William on the way to second-period English, either, and though I knew there was plenty of time left in the day, I began to feel uneasy. I really hoped I would see him before lunch.

In English class, however, I was met by an unusual sight—Branden was the only one in the classroom, apart from the teacher, Mrs. Swinburne, and he was standing by my desk.

"Katie, where is she?" Branden whispered as I walked up to him. He shot a glance over at Mrs. Swinburne—Branden wasn't her favorite student, and she had given him quite a few detentions—often for reasons that seemed to bewilder him. I wasn't surprised that he didn't want her to overhear him.

"You mean Charisse, right?" I asked.

"Of course I mean Charisse. I've called and texted her about a million times, but she doesn't answer. I called her mom, too, and got through to her once. She doesn't know where Charisse is, and she doesn't seem to care. I've called her again and again, but she doesn't answer now, either. Katie, what kind of mother stops answering her phone when her daughter is missing?"

Branden's voice had risen hoarsely, and Mrs. Swinburne shot us a disapproving glance.

He lowered his voice again. "I have half a mind to skip class and go looking for her."

"Branden, I don't know where Charisse is," I whispered. "And I agree that it's strange about her mother, but I don't think we should panic yet. I'm sure Charisse would call you if anything were wrong."

"If she was able to call me, you mean," Branden interjected fiercely.

"Maybe Charisse had a doctor's appointment this morning, and her mom just didn't want to tell you about it."

"Charisse always tells me about those things," Branden replied. "Sometimes in agonizing detail."

"Just give it some time," I said. "You know I care about Charisse, too, and I think things are a little tough for her now that her mom has started dating again. Maybe she just needed to be alone—maybe she even went to talk to the school counselor."

Branden looked at me sharply. "Why did you bring up her mom's dating? Do you think that Joshua guy has something to do with this?"

"No, I—"

Branden interrupted. "And you said he was at her house yesterday?"

"Yes, but—"

His hands were resting on the straps of his backpack, and they tightened involuntarily. "That's it. It's that guy. This is all his fault. Charisse is gone because of him."

"You think she ran off?" I asked, looking around. The room was filling up with students, and I was glad that their talking was masking our conversation. Branden was growing more and more agitated, and I was glad that no one seemed to have noticed. "I thought about that, too, but I can't believe that she would ever leave you."

Branden was grim. "She didn't leave me. Not voluntarily. Joshua's behind this."

"What are you saying, Branden?"

"I'm saying that Joshua's going to be sorry."

He started to move away, and I held out a hand to stop him.

"Branden, wait. Don't do anything that's going to get you in trouble. Don't leave school. Just give it till the end of the day. Charisse may still show up."

Branden gave me a mirthless smile. "I'm not going anywhere yet. I have to plan out what to do first. After all, I have to find out where Joshua lives."

He turned away and went to his seat. The classroom was full now, and I sat down at my desk as the bell rang. I turned in my seat to steal a glance at Branden. He had his head down, and his hair fell over his face, shielding his eyes. He was working busily on his phone. Branden was typically not someone who thought things through before he did them—the fact that he was planning now made me nervous.

My uneasiness continued to grow throughout the day, and it wasn't made any better by the fact that I still hadn't seen William by lunchtime.

But I told myself not to worry—that William would probably be waiting for me as soon as lunch was over. I'd seen him yesterday after lunch, so there was no reason for me to be anxious.

In the cafeteria, I found Simon sitting at a table by himself—and Branden was nowhere to be seen. I had a sinking feeling as we both started on our lunch.

Simon was unusually quiet.

"So, I'm guessing Charisse hasn't shown up, and Branden still doesn't know where she is," I said.

Simon nodded.

"Where's Branden?" I asked.

Simon gave me a small smile—without looking at me—and kept eating.

"Simon, I know you heard my question," I said. "Where is he?"

He remained silent.

"Branden can get in a lot of trouble by skipping school," I said.

Simon shrugged. "You could get into a lot of trouble by hanging out with a drifter, but that doesn't seem to be stopping you."

My first instinct was to defend William, but I checked it—I knew it wouldn't do any good. Pleading William's case to Simon hadn't produced any effect on him so far—he seemed to be determined to believe terrible things.

"Is Branden going to call you and let you know what he finds out?" I asked.

"Maybe," Simon replied.

"Simon, Charisse and Branden are my friends, too, and I want them to be okay. It's not like I'm going to tell on them."

Simon gave me a rueful smile and actually looked at me for the first time since I had sat down.

"Yeah, I know," he said. "I really don't know if Branden is going to call. We didn't talk about that. Maybe he will. Maybe he won't. I guess it depends on what happens. Maybe he'll call the police instead."

I figured that that was as close as I was going to get to an admission that Branden had skipped the rest of the school day to look for Charisse. The truth was that I was starting to get worried myself. It wasn't like Charisse not to keep in touch with both Branden and me, even when she was sick. And though I had texted her several times, I had received nothing from her in return.

Branden's insistence that something was wrong worried me, too. He wasn't easily upset, and he certainly wasn't overly emotional. I thought back to the story Simon had told me earlier in the day about the second girl who had been attacked in the Old Grove. Charisse had been angry yesterday—had she driven around, too angry to go home, and decided to stop somewhere and go for a walk? Could Charisse have gone to the Old Grove herself or to some other place that Anton and Innokenti were haunting? I pushed the thought away—it was too horrible to contemplate. But I decided I would go over to Charisse's house after school. I had to be sure she was all right.

When lunch was over, and Simon and I parted ways in the hall, I drew apart from the crowd to wait for William. I watched the faces that passed me anxiously, and the minutes ticked by. Eventually the warning bell rang.

William did not appear.

The rest of the day seemed to fly by, and there was no sign of William. Before I knew it, the final bell rang, and I was headed out of the school along with everyone else. I lingered in the schoolyard, hoping that William would appear at the last minute. But as I watched, the crowd of students slowly thinned out, till there was only me and a handful of others. A strange sense of abandonment welled up within me.

William had not come.

The weather was very cold, so I figured I had better start walking. Charisse's house was in the opposite direction from mine, but it was only about a fifteen-minute walk from the school. I started off slowly, looking back over my shoulder every few moments to see if William had suddenly shown up in the schoolyard. He did not appear.

I forced myself to walk more quickly—I was anxious to see Charisse to make sure that she was okay. I told myself that it really wasn't so terrible that William hadn't shown up—he'd probably had something important to do. There were, after all, two vampires in town.

But, at the same time, William always did what he said he would do—and he'd never failed to meet me before. I tried again to convince myself that his absence didn't mean anything, but my uneasiness kept growing.

I had a feeling something wasn't right.

I pushed myself to move faster, and eventually I broke into a run. By the time I reached Charisse's house, I was actually pretty warm, and the exertion had made me feel a little less anxious. I saw with relief that Charisse's car was parked in the street just in front of the house. So Charisse was home. Maybe she'd been sick and just hadn't felt well enough to answer the phone.

I walked up to the house and pulled the screen door open. I was just raising my hand to knock on the wooden door behind it when I realized that the door was already open. I pushed on it gingerly, and it swung open a few more inches.

"Charisse?" I said. "Mrs. Graebel?"

There was no answer, and I nudged the door open a little more and peered inside. The small foyer was empty. I could see into the living room and dining room—both were dark and unoccupied. The house had a profoundly still feeling, as if no one were home. I glanced back at Charisse's car. Surely she was home if her car was. Of course, I couldn't see into the garage, so maybe Charisse had been driven somewhere by her mother. I figured I should lock the door properly and then pull it shut.

I stepped inside and turned the lock on the doorknob.

"Katie," came a soft whisper.

I looked up. The sound seemed to have come from a darkened hall off the foyer.

I'd just decided that I'd imagined the sound when the whisper came again.

"Katie."

This time I was sure—the sound had definitely come from the darkened hall.

"Charisse?" I said.

"Katie, help me," said the whisper.

I hurried forward and switched on the light in the hall. The hall was empty, and several dark doorways opened off of it on either side.

"Katie," said the whisper again.

I walked down the hallway, glancing into each one of the doorways. "Charisse, where are you?"

I reached the end of the hallway, and I was faced with a set of stairs and another dark doorway. I knew the stairs led up to the bedrooms. The dark doorway led down to the basement.

"Katie, down here." The voice was a little louder.

I was struck by a horrible thought. What if Charisse had fallen down the basement stairs and hurt herself? What if she'd been lying there all day while we were all at school wondering about her?

The basement door was standing open, and I reached for the light switch on the wall. The light overhead blazed to life, illuminating bare white walls and a set of wooden stairs.

"Charisse, are you down there?" I asked. "Are you okay?"

"Katie, help me," said a soft voice.

I hurried down the stairs.

"Charisse, where are you?" I said. "Help me to find you."

I heard a soft rustle and glanced around sharply. There was a curtain near the stairs that partitioned off a small room where I knew Mrs. Graebel had a large freezer and several shelves full of cans and other nonperishable goods.

The rustling came again. The sound seemed to be coming from behind the curtain.

I pushed the curtain aside, and I reached up for a slim chain that hung down from a naked light bulb that was mounted on the ceiling. The light clicked on, and I could see a large pair of shoes sticking out past the edge of the freezer.

The shoes were clearly too big to be Charisse's, and I hurried forward. Branden was lying on the floor next to the freezer, his eyes closed, and his arms arranged in an X across his chest. Charisse was lying next to him, arranged in the same position. Charisse's mother was lying next to Charisse.

Quickly I dropped to the floor to examine them. Their hearts were beating steadily, and they were all breathing comfortably. I gave each one of them a shake and called out their names, but none of them stirred. They were clearly deeply unconscious, and I had a feeling that they had been that way for quite some time. Who then had called my name? Who had made the rustling sound?

I stood up. I took a few steps backward, and as I did so, I stumbled against a solid body.

I turned. Joshua Martin was standing behind me.

"Joshua, you're here just in time." I realized I was shaking. "Something's happened to Charisse, Branden, and Mrs. Graebel. We've got to help them.

"They're okay," Joshua replied calmly.

I stepped aside. "Have you seen them? Maybe you didn't notice that everybody's unconscious."

"They're all right," Joshua said. His composure was unnerving and somehow out of place.

I started to feel strangely light-headed.

"Do you know what happened to them?" I asked.

"They're sleeping. Like I said, they're all right."

"How did they all fall asleep? All at the same time? All in the basement?"

Joshua gave me his boyish smile. "I did this. I have certain—talents."

I stepped backwards—away from him. My hand brushed against the metal shelving that held all of the canned goods.

Joshua was between me and the curtain that led to the stairs.

"You said you'd never hurt Charisse or her mother," I said. "I heard you say that only yesterday."

"They're okay. I'm not after them. I'm after you."

"Me?"

Joshua flashed his boyish smile again. "Yes, you. There's a price on your head. And I intend to collect."

I was startled. Innokenti had said there was a price on my head—but there was no way Joshua Martin could know about that.

"I'm just a high school student," I said. "No one would be interested in me."

Joshua tilted his head on one side and gave me a look as if I were missing something obvious. "No one human."

I felt a stab of fear run through me. "You're a vampire?"

Once more, Joshua smiled.

"Are you with Anton and Innokenti?" It was hard for me to force the words out.

"I haven't had the pleasure of meeting them, but it doesn't surprise me that there are others. The reward for catching you is a very attractive one."

"What is it? Who's after me? Why would someone offer a reward for me?"

"You're starting to sound hysterical now," Joshua said. "There's no need for you to be afraid."

He held out his hand. "Just come with me."

I tried frantically to think of something to say that would get rid of him, but my mind refused to work. My body was as frozen as my mind. I wanted to run for the curtain, but I couldn't make myself move.

"I see you eyeing the doorway there." Joshua's tone was pleasant. "You know you won't make it, right? It's much easier if you just come with me."

Don't listen to him, cried a voice in my head. *Block him out. Do something.*

Anything.

"Now, I see you're still hesitating to come with me. Let me explain the situation. I've planned this all out—and you'll understand that it's in your best interests just to come with me. Do you watch any sports?"

"What do mean?" I asked. *Don't listen to him*, cried the voice in my head. *Don't answer him.*

"Basketball? Football? Hockey?"

"Sometimes, I guess."

"Well, then, you know." Joshua sounded pleased, approving. "There are two ways you can play just about any sport. You can be a power player or a finesse player. Do you understand the distinction?"

"Yes," I said, though I was unwilling to answer the question. I just couldn't stop myself somehow.

"I knew you'd know," Joshua said. "Me, I'm a finesse guy. I use skill rather than force. That's why I came to your friend's house to find you. You see, if I'd been seen hanging around your house, and you went missing, I'd be a suspect. On the other hand, if I spend time at your friend's house, and you go missing, no one will even think to look at me. Who's going to make the connection? I'm willing to bet that no one even knows you're over here. Am I right?"

"That's not true," I blurted out. "My grandmother knows I stopped by. If I don't come home soon, she'll be right over here."

The corners of Joshua's eyes crinkled. "You're lying. That's why I'm so good at the finesse game. I'm really good at reading faces. You're trapped, and you can't get away from me. That's why it's best if you just come with me."

I felt panic well up within me, and I forced myself to move. I reached behind me and grabbed a can. I threw it.

The can hit Joshua squarely in the face. I threw another and another.

Anger flashed in Joshua's eyes. "Katie, I'm really going to have to ask you to stop that."

I threw more cans and then I heaved a bottle of some kind of oil at him. He reached out to catch the bottle, and he grabbed it out of the air with such force that it burst, dowsing him in oil.

He lunged for me then, and in a panic, I grabbed onto the shelves. I tugged on them as hard as I could, and the shelving tipped forward. As Joshua reached me, I pulled the whole structure down toward us. I managed to scramble out of the way, but Joshua was caught by the full weight of the shelves.

I ran for the stairs.

I had just reached the top when something like an iron band wrapped around my ankle and pulled my feet out from under me. I fell to the floor heavily, and I cried out in pain.

"Hello? Who's there?" A voice floated down the hall to me. "Is that you, Charisse?"

"In here!" I screamed. "In the basement! Help me!"

Footsteps hurried down the hall, and I soon saw a familiar face.

"Simon!" I cried. "Simon!"

Simon rushed forward and grabbed at my hands. As he did so, a large, dark shape vaulted over my head and hit Simon in the chest.

Joshua and Simon rolled down the hall.

I scrambled to my feet and ran after them, my mind racing. Holy water, garlic, sunlight—all no use. That left wood or fire. And fire was best.

The two of them stopped rolling, and Simon stared, dazed, into his attacker's face. "It's Joshua, right? What are you doing?"

In lieu of an answer, Joshua stood, picked Simon up, and threw him against the far wall in the living room. Then he turned toward me. I ran toward a small table and picked up the lamp that rested on it. I threw the lamp at him, but the electrical cord pulled taut and the lamp smashed harmlessly on the floor. I threw the table at him next, and Joshua hit it, splintering it into pieces.

"Leave her alone!" Simon shouted.

He jumped up and caught Joshua by the shoulders and spun him around. Simon punched Joshua solidly in the stomach and then in the face. Joshua simply smiled, baring his sharp teeth.

Simon took a step back in shock.

"Fire or wood!" I cried. "We've got to use fire or wood to stop him. But fire is best!"

Before Simon could react, Joshua lifted him up and threw him against the wall again.

I picked up a vase and smashed it against Joshua's head. Then I hit him with a big pillar candle.

"I found a lighter," Simon cried.

Joshua ignored him and kept coming for me. I pulled a picture off the wall and broke it over his head. The glass splintered and left jagged cuts all over his face. The frame itself rattled around his neck.

Joshua grabbed me by the throat, and I clawed desperately at his hands.

"I did try to do this nicely," he said.

Joshua's thumb pressed firmly against a spot on my throat. My vision began to swim, and I felt myself slipping into unconsciousness. Suddenly there was a flash of metal, and a heavy kitchen knife slashed across Joshua's wrist. With a cry of rage, he let me go.

As I fell to the floor, I thought I saw fire leaping up in front of me. A moment later, Simon wrapped a burning coat around Joshua and heaved him into an even brighter blaze.

Simon hauled me to my feet. "Come on, Katie, we've got to get out of here."

As Simon dragged me toward the door, Joshua pushed ahead of us and ran outside, his entire body engulfed in flames.

We followed him outside.

Joshua's blazing figure soon vanished, but his screams continued to echo in my ears even after he had disappeared from my sight.

Chapter Seven

A re you okay?"

Simon had asked me that question about ten times so far. We were sitting in plastic chairs in the emergency room, waiting to be seen. We had already talked to the police, and the fire department had put out the fire at the house. Charisse, Branden, and Mrs. Graebel had been removed from the house, and they were currently resting in rooms in another part of the hospital.

I smiled at Simon, who was without his coat, and tried to sound reassuring. "I'm fine, really."

"You're sure?"

"Yes," I said. "Are *you* okay? You had a really rough time back there, and your hands don't look so good."

Simon glanced down at his hands. "The burns are pretty superficial. I'll be fine."

He reached out then and touched my neck gingerly. "Those bruises look bad."

"My neck's a little sore," I said. "But I'm still breathing. Thanks to you."

Simon frowned. "You know, oddly enough, I don't think Joshua was trying to kill you—at least not right away. I think he was just trying to put you out. If you press on that group of blood vessels there, you can induce unconsciousness. I think that's what he was trying to do."

I shivered. "He may not have been trying to kill me, but I can't imagine that what he had planned would've been any good for my health. I don't know what would've happened if you hadn't shown up when you did. I'm really lucky you were there."

"Yeah, well, I was there because of you. I knew Branden had gone over to Charisse's house, and when you asked if he was planning to call, and I had to admit that he wasn't, I figured that I'd better go over and check things out myself. And I'm really glad I did."

"You're out of your mind if you think I'm going to take any of the credit for that," I said. "This all belongs to you. No one would ever have seen me again if you hadn't shown up. You saved my life. You're a hero. You'll have to accept that."

Simon smiled and looked down at his hands again. As he did so, his smile faded. "Do you think Joshua's okay? I had to stop him, but I didn't want to hurt him seriously. Burns can be dangerous, even fatal, and if he knows the police are after him, he may not—"

I interrupted him. "Joshua will be fine. Trust me. His wounds will heal quickly. He's not a normal person."

Simon looked at me sharply. "He wasn't normal, was he? I hit him, and he just stared at me. And his strength. He threw me around like a rag doll. It was like nothing could stop him. That's why I did what I did after you said to use fire. I found a lighter and lighter fluid in the kitchen, and I just reacted."

He paused.

"How did you know fire would work on him?"

I took a deep breath. I wanted to tell Simon the truth, but I doubted he would believe it. I stared at the floor and tried to think of what to say.

"Katie?" Simon prompted.

"Did you happen to notice his teeth?" I asked.

"Yeah. They were super sharp."

I gave Simon a significant stare.

"And you said to use wood or fire against him," Simon said slowly. "Wood as in a wooden stake."

He ran a hand over his hair. "You think Joshua's a vampire."

I made no reply, and Simon sighed heavily.

"You know, Katie, your imagination has really begun to run riot over the last few months."

I was glad now that I hadn't said anything outright. Even allowing Simon to work things out for himself hadn't convinced him. He couldn't even trust the evidence of his own senses.

But Simon wasn't finished. "Katie, there are people—weird people—but regular human beings nonetheless, who get their teeth filed down to give them a vampiric appearance. Sometimes there are perfectly normal explanations for things that seem out of the ordinary."

"Then what about his strength?" I asked. I couldn't help pointing that out, though I doubted it would do any good. "You said yourself that he was unstoppable. And you were right—no normal measures would have stopped him. And how did he put three people into a trance? You saw them when they were carried out—that wasn't normal."

"Katie, it's possible to drug people. Don't make this out to be more than it is."

"But you did notice he wasn't normal—you just said that."

Simon shrugged. "Maybe that was drugs, too. I've heard people can do crazy things when they're whacked out. I've heard sometimes bullets won't even stop them."

He gave me a serious look. "Please don't mention vampires to the doctor. I don't want you to get committed."

I sat back in my chair. Every time Simon seemed about ready to listen, he pulled back. I supposed I couldn't really blame him. I had been forced by circumstances to accept a lot of unusual things. Simon simply hadn't seen all that I had seen.

Not long after, Simon and I were both called to be examined, and we were swept into separate curtained-off compartments.

I had some cuts and bruises, but basically I was fine. I could hear Simon's doctor talking to him and asking him questions. Simon had some burns that needed to be treated, and the doctor warned him to be alert for signs of concussion, but I was relieved to hear the doctor say that once he had spoken to Simon's parents that he would be free to go.

GM and Mrs. Krstic showed up soon after that.

GM rushed into my compartment, sweeping back the curtain. She sat down next to me on my creaking cot and gave me a hug.

"Oh, solnyshko. You have not had much luck these past few months. Tell your grandmother what has happened."

I had a feeling the police had already filled her in on the facts, but it was something of a relief to tell her myself. The horror of the whole situation and the knowledge of just how close I had come to being Joshua's victim overwhelmed me as I spoke. I felt tears running down my cheeks, and GM ran her hands over my hair.

"That's all right, Katie. You have every reason to be sad. I don't know what this town is coming to."

I was careful, of course, not to mention anything about Joshua Martin's true nature.

When I was finished with my story, and I was feeling calmer, GM patted me on the shoulder.

"They told me that your friends are upstairs, and that they're awake now. Would you like to go up and see them?"

"Yes, I would." I thought of Charisse, Mrs. Graebel, and Branden lying strangely motionless on the floor. It would be a relief to see for myself that they were okay.

Simon and Mrs. Krstic were still talking with Simon's doctor, so GM and I decided not to disturb them and to just go ahead without them. We left the emergency room and went into the main body of the hospital.

The whole place was highly polished and smelled strongly of antiseptic.

As we waited at a bank of elevators, GM turned to look at me. To my discomfort, she continued to stare.

"GM, please," I said, after some time had passed, and the elevators had stubbornly refused to put in an appearance. "You're making me nervous."

"You know, Simon Krstic is a remarkable boy," she said. "And he has certainly proved today that he cares about you. Perhaps he even loves you."

"I know," I said.

"And yet that is not enough for you to love him in return," GM said ruefully. "I'm sure you think I'm being a busybody. But I know something of these matters."

"I suppose you're thinking of William and my father again," I said. "But William's not a bad influence. He really isn't. Like I said, he wants me to stay away from danger—not go out and look for it."

GM gave me an odd little smile. "Actually, I was thinking of my own life. I loved your grandfather very much. But sometimes I wonder if I made the right decision. It's easy to fall for the man who is exciting and mysterious. Sometimes it's just as easy to overlook the man who is quiet and dependable. His love is no less strong just because it's not showy."

There was a chime, and an elevator finally opened up for us. We stepped inside, and I looked at GM in surprise.

"What do you mean?" I asked.

She shook her head. "It doesn't matter any longer. I have to keep reminding myself of that."

GM refused to say anything further, and when our elevator came to a stop, she led me on through the hospital's highly polished halls.

We stopped by Branden's room first, but he was already surrounded by a crowd that consisted of his divorced parents, both of their spouses, and an assortment of siblings and half-siblings. We decided not to interrupt, and we moved on.

In the room next door, we found Charisse and Mrs. Graebel, who were separated by a curtain just as Simon and I had been down in the emergency room.

GM stopped to talk to Mrs. Graebel, and she waved me over to Charisse.

"Go and talk with your friend. I'm sure the two of you would rather not have me hovering over you."

I walked over to Charisse's side of the room, and GM pulled the curtain out further so that we were shielded completely. I had a feeling that GM was actually more interested in talking to Mrs. Graebel herself rather than in giving Charisse and me privacy.

They probably wanted to discuss how better to protect us. Unfortunately, that was likely to mean decreased freedom for both of us.

I sat down in a chair next to Charisse's bed, and she gave me a wan smile.

"Hey, Katie."

"How are you feeling?" I asked.

Charisse shifted a little and yawned. "Honestly, I'm fine. I'm just really, really tired. I don't seem to be able to shake off this sluggish feeling."

"When did you wake up?"

"I was here in the hospital when I woke up. I don't know when it was exactly."

"What happened back at the house? How did Joshua put you guys out?"

Charisse frowned. "I don't know. I don't remember being put out. The last twenty-four hours are kind of a blur. The last thing I remember clearly is dropping you off yesterday and then driving home. Then it's all a blank. I only know Joshua was involved in the whole thing because the police told me."

She made an effort to focus on me. "The police told me you and Simon came to check on me, and then there was a fire. Are you guys okay?"

"Simon and I are fine," I said. "It looks like I should have believed you. Joshua really was trouble."

Charisse shook her head. "It's not your fault. You know, I was actually starting to believe that Joshua had powers—like he was superhuman or something. But he was really just a run-of-the-mill psycho. I shouldn't have let my imagination run wild like I did."

I sighed inwardly. Charisse's instincts had been right, of course, but there was no way I could tell her that.

"How is your mom?" I asked.

Charisse turned her head involuntarily toward her mother, even though the curtain blocked her from view. She took a deep breath and then turned back to me. "I think she's okay at the moment, but she's still pretty groggy. When she's more herself, and she realizes what almost happened, I think it's going to hit her pretty hard."

Charisse gave me an agonized look. "Katie, I didn't like Joshua, and I didn't like having him around, but I never wanted my mom to be hurt. I never wanted anything like this to happen."

"I know you didn't," I said. "And your mom knows that, too."

I could see tears welling up in Charisse's eyes, and I came over to sit beside her on the bed.

"Don't think about it," I said. "You're both safe now. This wasn't your fault, and it wasn't your mother's, either. People like Joshua are really good at what they do." Unfortunately, I knew from personal experience that this was true. "Plenty of smart people have been tricked by him—trust me. Your mom didn't really have a chance against him."

Charisse looked down at her hands. "He's still out there, isn't he? He wasn't caught."

"No, he wasn't."

"We aren't safe then, are we?" Charisse said. "He could come back for us."

"I don't think he will," I said. "I think he's wise enough to stay away from you and your mother."

Whether or not he would come back for me was a different matter.

"I hope you're right," Charisse said. She frowned. "You know, I really *don't* remember what happened, but I have a feeling that there was something important I needed to tell you—something you needed to know."

I already knew that Joshua had set up the whole thing to trap me—the details didn't matter.

"Don't upset yourself," I said quickly. "I'm sure if there's anything I need to know the police will tell me."

"No—it's important—it really is. Give me a minute. I'll think of it."

Charisse closed her eyes. In the silence I could hear GM and Mrs. Graebel murmuring on the other side of the curtain.

Charisse remained still for such a long time that I thought she had fallen asleep. Then her eyes flew open.

"Someone else was there."

"What was that?" I asked.

"That's what I needed to tell you," Charisse said. "I knew it was important. Someone else was there with Joshua—someone who had a connection to you."

"Are you sure you actually remember that?" I asked. "You said you didn't even remember Joshua. And Simon and I didn't see anyone else."

"I'm sure of it, Katie. Something was pushing at the back of my mind—something that mattered so much that it pushed through whatever drug it was that Joshua gave me."

Charisse frowned again and struggled to remember. GM stepped around the curtain and came to stand beside us.

"How are you, dear?" GM asked Charisse. "You've had quite a trying time."

"I'm fine, Mrs. Rost. I really am." Charisse gave her a small smile, but her brow remained creased in thought. "I don't really remember much, but I'm trying to remember something now. Someone else was there with Joshua."

"Someone else?" GM looked concerned. "Who was it?"

Charisse rubbed her temples. "I'm sure it has something to do with Katie."

She paused for a long moment.

"It was William," she said suddenly.

GM blinked in surprise. "What did you say?"

"William was there," Charisse said, staring at me defiantly. "I'm sure of it."

"Charisse, that's crazy," I said. "There's no way William was there. If he had been, he would have stopped Joshua himself."

"Have you told the police about this?" GM asked sharply.

Charisse ignored what I'd said and addressed GM. "Not yet. It's only just come back to me. But I will."

I was horrified. "Charisse, you can't do that."

"Why not?"

"Because you never saw him. You told me you didn't remember Joshua. If you didn't remember him—and both Simon and I saw him—how can you possibly remember that William was there? Neither one of us saw him. And as I said, William would have helped you."

"I'm positive William was there," Charisse said. "I told you William reminded me of Joshua. That's probably because subconsciously I knew they were working together."

"You can't let your dislike of William cloud your judgment," I said angrily. "You're imagining things now. It would be irresponsible of you to tell the police you saw William at the scene. You can't be sure."

"I'm sure," Charisse said stubbornly.

"Charisse, what's wrong?" Mrs. Graebel called out.

GM pulled the curtain back. Mrs. Graebel was getting out of bed.

"I just remembered something that happened back at the house," Charisse said.

"Charisse, you didn't—"

Mrs. Graebel interrupted me gently. "Katie, Anna, would you mind leaving us? I think my daughter and I need to talk."

"Of course. We will go." GM put an arm around my shoulder. "Come along, Katie."

I allowed myself to be steered out of the room and down the hallway.

"William was *not* at the house," I said to GM as we waited for the elevator. "Charisse was unconscious when I found her. I was wide-awake. She doesn't know what she's saying."

I was really worried that Charisse would actually go ahead and tell the police her crazy story. From what Simon had said earlier in the day, William had already been questioned in connection with the attack on the second girl in the Old Grove. If he were also identified as being present in Charisse's house, he really would be in trouble.

"We need to talk," GM said firmly.

And talk we did. By the time we reached home, it was established that I wasn't allowed to go anywhere in town alone—not even to school. GM would be driving me to and from school just as she had back in October when people had begun disappearing.

And I was no longer permitted to see William.

I had argued and argued against that, but eventually I had to give up. I realized that no amount of arguing on my part was going to change GM's mind—at least not at the moment.

I was worried about what William would say when he found out. Would he want to abide by GM's rules and not see me?

He would certainly be worried by Joshua's attack. Would he think that avoiding me was safer for me?

That was ridiculous, of course. In fact, I realized now that I should have used William's call and summoned him to me. William would have appeared in an instant, and he could have stopped Joshua and prevented the fire from ever happening.

Things would have been different if I had just called William.

As GM and I got out of the car, I couldn't help but wonder what had gotten into Charisse—she seemed so positive that William had been at her house with Joshua. Her dislike of him must have been stronger than I had realized.

GM went into the house ahead of me, and I paused outside on the step as a disturbing thought occurred to me. What if Charisse *had* seen something and misinterpreted it?

What if there really had been someone with Joshua? What if there was yet another vampire lurking in town?

GM looked back at me. "Is something wrong, solnyshko?"

"No—it's nothing," I said. I went into the house and closed the door behind me.

GM and I had a quiet dinner, and then I went upstairs to do my homework, wishing all the while that it were already tomorrow, and that I was already back at school.

I *had* to see William tomorrow.

And once again, before I went to bed, I passed by the mirror and could have sworn that a shadow moved within it—a shadow that shouldn't have been there.

GM drove me to school the next morning, and I was nearly frantic to see William. I knew that I could use his call to summon him, but that was something I felt I should only use in an emergency. I hoped he would show up right away.

Maybe he'd heard about Joshua and would even be waiting for me outside the school.

I hurried into the schoolyard and scanned it quickly. There were a few students standing out in the yard huddled against the cold, but William was not among them. I'd already had a text from Charisse telling me that neither she nor Branden would be in school today. But I did spot Simon standing by the usual picnic table—he was clearly waiting for me.

I hurried over to him.

He turned at my approach. "Hey, Katie. How are you? Did you sleep okay last night?"

"Yes, thanks," I said. "How are you? How are those burns?"

Simon pulled off his gloves to show me his bandaged hands. "They're good. I know all this wrapping looks bad, but it should heal well. There probably won't even be any scarring."

He gave me a smile. "That last part is too bad. I hear girls like a few scars." He pulled his gloves back on. "Would you like to go inside? It's freezing out here."

107

I took one last look around the schoolyard and felt disappointment rising within me.

"Sure," I said. "Let's go in."

We went into the school and made our way to the cafeteria.

"So, your grandmother is shepherding you to school again, is she?" Simon asked as we sat down at a round table.

"Yes, she is," I said. I scanned the cafeteria for William. He usually chose to appear at busy times when he was less likely to be noticed, but I hoped to see him anyway—I didn't care if Simon saw him and wondered why he was there. I looked over each face carefully, but William clearly wasn't in the cafeteria anywhere. Disappointment welled up within me again.

Simon continued. "That's probably for the best that you have a chaperone." He took a deep breath. "I heard about Charisse—I heard that she saw William at the scene of the crime."

"Charisse doesn't know what she saw," I said, my anger flaring. "She also told me she didn't remember much of anything at all."

"She seemed pretty sure about William. Katie, I hope you don't take this the wrong way, but I really think you should stop seeing him."

My anger faded as quickly as it had come—Simon was just onto his favorite topic. There was no point in arguing with him.

"You've been saying that a lot lately," I said wearily. "And as it happens, GM agrees with you."

"Oh, does she?" Simon did a poor job of concealing a smile.

We talked a little more, but my heart wasn't really in it. I was relieved when the warning bell rang, and Simon and I streamed out into the hall with everyone else.

Shortly after Simon waved goodbye and disappeared into the crowd, I felt a tap on my shoulder. I turned around expectantly, but it wasn't William who was standing behind me.

It was Irina.

Her dark eyes were blazing. "You almost got him killed. Are you happy?"

"What are you talking about, Irina?"

"I'm talking about Simon. It's all over the school. He was nearly killed in a fire last night. All because he was trying to save you."

"That's not exactly what happened."

"Do you even care about him?" Irina demanded. "You take everything so calmly. Like the world owes you something. Like everyone's supposed to be in love with you. And you can't even be bothered to care about anyone in return."

I felt my anger flare up again. "You don't know anything about Simon and me. We've been friends for years—and during most of those years you didn't even seem to know he was alive. Do you actually care about him? Or is he just something you can't have?"

"Do *I* actually care?" Irina's voice rose hysterically, and several people in the crowded hall turned to stare at us. "Do I care? I care more than you ever have or ever will."

I was startled to see tears welling up in Irina's eyes. "Irina—"

"Your family has always been trouble," she said suddenly. "My father told me all about it."

I was thrown off by the sudden shift in topic. "My family?"

Irina's lips twisted into a bitter smile and a tear spilled down her cheek. "My father told me that your family tried to ruin us back in Russia. He told me about what your grandmother did. And you— you're no different."

Irina stormed off, and I was left staring after her in shock. What could my friendship with Simon possibly have to do with anything that had happened in Russia?

And why was she attacking my grandmother?

I shook off my shock and hurried on to homeroom.

As the day wore on, I looked anxiously for William. I lingered in the hallways and was very nearly late for several classes. I had lunch with Simon, and though I tried to be sociable, I had a hard time paying attention to anything he said.

The second half of the day passed all too quickly, and though I did receive a series of unexpected glares from Irina—who suddenly seemed to be everywhere—I didn't see any sign of William.

At the final bell, I went to my locker slowly and lingered in the halls, searching the faces that passed me. With reluctance, I left the school and stood outside in the cold, watching the crowd as it swelled at first and slowly dispersed.

As the minutes ticked by, the cold seemed to seep under my coat and into my skin. I waited as long as I could, knowing that GM was probably growing anxious.

I was alone in the schoolyard when I finally got out my phone with shaking fingers and called home.

Once again, William had forgotten me.

Chapter Eight

Two more days passed without any word from William. When the final bell rang at the end of the day on Friday, I went to my locker and pulled out my books without looking around. I'd reached a point at which I no longer scanned the crowd for William—I actually avoided looking as much as possible.

I didn't want to see that he wasn't there.

I knew I could use the call to summon him, but I kept telling myself that I wanted to keep that for emergencies.

In reality I was afraid that he wouldn't appear.

I had realized with a pang that I couldn't call William the regular way either—since I didn't have a phone number for him. It hadn't mattered very much before—he'd appeared of his own volition often enough that we stayed in regular contact—even if our meetings tended to be brief. I supposed it had been part of his plan to keep some distance between us.

I tried to tell myself that there was nothing to worry about, that William had something important he had to do, and that he would come back when whatever it was was finished.

Somehow, I felt as if William were still nearby, still watching over my house at night so I could sleep in safety.

If that is the case, whispered a dissenting voice in my head, *then why didn't he protect you from Joshua Martin?*

I pushed the thought away—I didn't have an answer for my own question.

All I could do was wait—and hope.

I closed my locker door, and I was surprised to see Charisse standing on the other side of it.

Things had been awkward between the two of us since that day in the hospital when she had accused William of being at her house with Joshua, and though she had returned to school, we hadn't really spoken much.

So as I looked at her now, I wasn't sure what to expect from her.

"Hey," she said.

"Hey," I said warily.

"I don't want things to be weird between us," she said.

"Neither do I," I replied.

"I want you to know that I didn't tell the police that I saw William at the house with Joshua," Charisse said slowly. "Ultimately, I couldn't be sure it was him. My memory of the whole incident is very, very hazy."

She frowned and looked down in thought. "It's really weird. Like I said, my memories are hazy, but the part about William stands out really clearly—that's partly why I don't trust it now. It's almost like I imagined it."

Charisse looked up at me. "Maybe it was just my dislike of William bubbling up to the surface. I *did* tell the police that I saw someone. But I didn't ID William—I didn't think it was fair to malign him when I couldn't be sure."

She held out a warning finger. "I don't want you to think I like him now. I don't. And I'm still not entirely sure he's not guilty. But I couldn't really come up with a motive for him—he certainly wasn't dating my mom."

Relief flooded through me. "You don't have to like him. I'll settle for your not having him thrown in jail."

"So are we friends again?"

"We were always friends," I said.

Charisse smiled. She looked relieved, too.

"Do you have any plans this weekend?" she asked conversationally.

"No, not really," I admitted. "GM hasn't really let me go anywhere since the incident at your house."

I didn't mention that GM had forbidden me to see William after what Charisse had said at the hospital. It seemed ungenerous since she was starting to thaw a bit, and at any rate, it didn't really matter now that he had disappeared. At the moment there was no need for GM to forbid anything.

"My mom won't really let me go anywhere, either," Charisse said. "But on the plus side, she does seem to be back to normal. She's taking everything seriously again and not brushing off work. Of course, she's coming home a lot earlier now to keep an eye on me. So she brings home a huge stack of papers, and we both sit together working—she does her stuff, and I do my homework. It's only been two days, but it's driving me slightly crazy."

"What about your dad?" I asked. "Have you heard from him?"

Charisse shrugged. "He called, but I think he thinks my mom is being melodramatic and is exaggerating the danger we were in. I don't think he actually thinks it was a big deal. He told her to be more careful about the men she dates."

She shook her head wearily. "You know, my dad seemed really distracted when I talked to him. I think something's up with him. I just hope it's not something as bad as what was up with my mom. Parents are a lot of trouble sometimes."

There was a polite cough behind me, and I turned to see Bryony standing nearby. She gave me a smile and tucked her hair behind her ear.

"Hi," she said.

I wondered how long she'd been standing nearby before she'd worked up the nerve to speak.

"Hi, Bryony," I said.

She handed me a small, square envelope. She gave one to Charisse, too.

"They're invitations to my birthday party," she said in her soft voice. "It's tomorrow, out in the Old Grove. Sorry for the short notice, but we only just got the permits we needed. Annamaria will be there, too. She's out of the hospital now."

"The Old Grove?" I asked. "Won't that be cold?"

"It will be a bit cold, but we've booked a gazebo, and we'll have fires and portable heaters. That's what we needed the permits for. I just really wanted to have a cookout. I love cookouts."

"I'd like to come," I said. "I'm just not sure if I'll be allowed to."

"I'm not sure if I can go either," Charisse said.

Bryony looked deeply disappointed, and I had a feeling she thought we were brushing her off.

"I'll come if I can," I said quickly. "I really will. I just have to make sure it's okay with my grandmother. I'll send you a text tonight to let you know."

"Same here," said Charisse. "My mom hasn't let me go anywhere lately."

Bryony brightened up and gave us her number.

Then she gave us a thoughtful look. "Things must have been pretty hard for both of you this past week. My parents will be there if that helps. And you can bring your friends Simon and Branden, if you want."

"Thanks," I said.

A dark-haired girl passed by, and I glanced up, thinking that Irina—who had continued to stalk me during the week—had found us and was about to pounce. I relaxed when I realized it was actually someone else.

I turned back to Bryony. "I'm sure you invited Irina, too. Will she mind if I'm there?"

A distant, defiant light went on in Bryony's eyes. "Irina is my friend. But I'd like to be friends with both of you, too. Even if Irina doesn't approve."

I smiled then. "Okay. I hope we both can go."

Bryony smiled her thanks and left us.

"Would you like a ride home?" Charisse asked.

"Thanks, but I don't think I can accept. I'd better let GM pick me up—especially if I want to go to Bryony's party tomorrow. I think it'll make her feel more secure."

"With any luck I'll see you tomorrow, then," Charisse said. "Send me a text to let me know."

"I will."

Charisse turned to go off to the student parking lot, and I headed toward the front of the school. As I stepped out into the schoolyard, I called GM.

I made a point of not looking for William.

As I waited in the cold December air, I realized—almost against my better judgment—that if I was able to go to Bryony's party that I would also have an opportunity to search the Old Grove for William's house. I didn't know what it looked like, but maybe someone at the party would know.

I wondered, if I succeeded in finding William's house—would I find him at home?

And if he was, in fact, home—what would he say when he saw me?

I realized that I was afraid of how he would react.

But I had to know.

GM's red sports car soon glided to a graceful stop in front of the school, and I hurried over to it. I settled into the warm interior of the car, and GM took off at an unholy pace like she always did. It never failed to amaze me how she could drive as swiftly and expertly as she did, racing up to red light and stop signs, and then braking so smoothly that you barely felt the deceleration. And on country roads she really flew, negotiating hilly roads and tight turns with remarkable ease.

Of course, not everyone appreciated her driving skills—she had a desk drawer full of speeding tickets at home.

I decided not to tackle GM on the subject of Bryony's party right away. I figured I would wait until the right moment presented itself. In the meantime, I was content to ride along with her in silence.

As GM drove, I glanced at her profile. It struck me that I hadn't told her about the things that Irina had said earlier in the week—that our family had injured hers and that GM in particular had done something terrible. There was probably nothing in it, but I did want to ask her about it. I hadn't even realized that our families had known each other back in Russia, but "Neverov" was a Russian name, and I supposed an acquaintance wasn't impossible.

I would have to wait for the right time to ask about that, too.

After dinner that night, GM seemed to be in a good mood, and I decided to broach the topic of Bryony's party. I ran up to my room and grabbed the invitation. Then I ran back down and handed it to GM in the kitchen.

I watched anxiously as she opened the envelope and read it.

She looked up at me. "You would like to attend this party, Katie?"

"Yes, I would."

"I suppose there will be a lot of other people?"

I nodded. "Bryony invited Charisse, Simon, and Branden along with all of her other friends. She also said her parents will be there."

"I imagine you will be safe enough, then, solnyshko. You may go."

I was relieved.

"Thanks, GM."

"But call me when you want to come home."

"I will."

"I hope you will have fun at the party," GM said. "There have been too many terrible things lately. It's time you had some good things, too."

She turned back to the dishes she'd been clearing away, and I sensed that Bryony's invitation had in no way dampened her good mood. I decided to risk bringing up the other topic I was interested in.

"GM, I have kind of a strange question to ask you."

"What is it?"

"It has to do with something Irina Neverov said a few days ago."

GM looked around with a good-natured smile. "How is Irina? It seems like I haven't seen her in a while."

"What Irina said actually wasn't very pleasant. She that our families knew each other back in Russia, and that our family has always been trouble. She said that she knew all about what you had done."

GM's eyebrows rose in shock. "Irina said that?"

"Yes, she did."

"I cannot understand it. The two of you have been friends since you were children. Is she angry with you for some reason?"

"Yes, she is—it's a bit complicated. Did our families really know each other in Russia?"

"Yes," GM replied. "Both families once lived in Krov."

I was startled. "We did? Why didn't you tell me this before?"

GM shrugged. "It didn't really seem important to tell you. And you two have always been such good friends that it seemed likely that you would find out on your own."

She frowned. "What's wrong between you and Irina?"

I didn't want to lose sight of my real objective, which was to find out about our relationship with the Neverovs, but it seemed best to go along with GM's questions for the moment. Maybe I could get my questions in without her noticing.

"Like I said, it's complicated," I replied. "But at the moment, the problem is that she likes Simon."

GM drew in her breath sharply and put a hand to her mouth.

"So, she thinks you have stolen him from her."

"I suppose so," I said. "Though that's kind of a strange way of putting it. He was my friend for years before she ever paid any attention to him."

"That would explain it," she said softly, but she was speaking more to herself than to me.

GM lapsed into silence. After a moment she seemed to shake off her reverie. "How about dessert, solnyshko? Would you like dessert?"

"What about what Irina said? She seems to think that our families are enemies. And she seemed to be accusing you of doing something terrible."

GM waved a careless hand. "Irina is a young girl. Young girls often say things they don't mean—no offense to you, solnyshko. I am sure the two of you will be friends again very soon. I will go get dessert."

She walked around me, and I was resigned to the fact that—for the moment, at least—she wasn't going to tell me anything more about our past with the Neverovs.

But I was relieved that I would be able to go to Bryony's party—at least I had managed that. After GM and I had both had dessert, which was actually just fruit—GM didn't approve of sweets—I ran up to my room and threw myself on my bed. I texted both Bryony and Charisse to let them know I was going to the party. And then I texted Simon to let him know about the party, too.

He called me immediately.

"Hey, Katie."

"Hey, Simon."

"So there's a party for Bryony tomorrow?"

"Yes. I'm sorry about the short notice. It's in the afternoon, so I hope it won't interfere with any plans you have for Saturday night."

"No, it's no problem," Simon said. "I'd love to go."

He paused. "Is *he* going?"

"You mean William?"

"Yes."

I felt a sharp stab of pain. "No, William's not going."

"Oh, okay."

I could hear relief in Simon's voice.

I gave him the rest of the details, and he sounded happy and excited as he said good night.

Afterward, I sat for a long time just holding the phone.

What I'd told Simon about William was true—as far as I knew, he wasn't going.

But I did hope to find William out in the Old Grove.

I didn't know why he'd disappeared. I still had some hope that there was a very simple explanation for why he was gone, but that hope was a little shaky.

If I managed to find William tomorrow, would he be happy to see me?

Would he send me away?

When I'd come up to my room, I hadn't turned the light on, and I continued to sit, watching the daylight dying through my window. Eventually, darkness stole over the room, and night was fully upon me. There was something soothing about the darkness, and I found that I wanted to breathe it in.

I went to the window and opened it. Then I pulled the chair from my desk up to my window, and I sat down, leaning on the windowsill and letting the cold night air wash over me.

There was something soft and inviting about the night. It seemed as if I were listening to a melody that I could almost hear—a melody so beautiful that it didn't belong to this world. I saw myself wandering out into the night, out into the delicious cold to find the source of the melody.

I remembered that I'd felt the night calling to me once before— right before I'd met William. But that feeling had been feverish and disturbing—it had clouded my mind. This feeling was serene and inviting. It occurred to me that if I could find the source of this almost-heard melody, that along with it I would find peace.

A car drove down the quiet street below, and I stirred. I remembered vaguely that someone had given me a warning—it was hard for me to force it forward in my thoughts, and I decided it didn't matter. I wasn't going anywhere anyway. I was just going to sit by the window and listen to the night.

And so I listened.

I couldn't tell how long I had sat by the window, or if I might even have fallen asleep, but suddenly my vision was flooded with light, and I felt warm hands on my shoulders.

"Katie, what are you doing?"

I turned in my chair, blinking. Someone had turned the light on in my room.

GM was leaning over me.

"Solnyshko, you are absolutely frozen. Come away from the window."

It seemed to me that GM sounded alarmed. I allowed her to pull me out of the chair, and I jumped when she shut the window forcefully.

I was suddenly alone—bereft of the beautiful music I could almost hear.

The lovely spell of the night had been broken. I held my hands to my head.

"I am surprised at you," GM was saying. "You won't make it to the party tomorrow if you make yourself ill. Surely you have better sense than that."

I looked around at GM. She seemed angry.

"Come now," GM said, pulling me toward the door. "You're going to take a warm shower to bring your core temperature up, and then you're going to bed. If you are sick in the morning, you're staying home. No argument."

She steered me into the bathroom, and she turned on the water in the shower. After a moment, she drew her hand back.

"There. That should be all right. Keep the shower warm, not hot. I'll bring you some nightclothes."

GM left the room and returned a moment later. She handed me a small pile of clothing.

"Now, take a shower like I said and get to bed." She stared at me for a long moment. "Sometimes, Katie, I swear I don't know what gets into you. You really scare me. You remind me of your—"

She broke off. "Just take your shower, Katie. And no more foolishness tonight."

GM left the room, closing the door behind her.

I watched as the mirror slowly fogged up, and as the air filled with steam, my mind began to clear.

I looked down at my hands, which were bright red and starting to sting. My throat was sore too, and the warm, damp air was soothing. Like GM, I wondered what I had been doing.

I undressed and got into the shower, and the water seemed to wash the remaining cloudiness from my mind. I figured I had just let all my worries overwhelm me.

I stayed in the warm water until I felt myself thaw completely, and then I dressed for bed. I went back to my room.

My room was still a bit chilly, but I could see that GM had put the heat on. I was about to climb into bed when I realized that I wasn't wearing the cross William had given me.

I found it and held it in my hands for a moment. Looking at it always made me feel calm—perhaps because it made me think of William. The iron charm was cold to the touch, but I knew that it would warm up after I had worn it against my skin for a little while.

I put it on and went to the window, but I wasn't going to open it again—I just had a sudden idea that I might glimpse William.

I supposed it was unlikely, but he had said that he would watch the house and make sure that it was safe. Once again I realized that although William would no longer see me, I did indeed feel safe—I did believe that he was watching over me.

I had a feeling that William still kept his lonely vigil.

I peered into the night, but I didn't see any sign of him.

As I turned away from the window, I thought I saw a figure out of the corner of my eye—a figure of a man—tall and starkly white.

I turned back quickly, but there was no one outside.

121

I shook my head to clear it. I seemed to be catching things at the edge of my vision all the time now—I figured I must have imagined it.

I climbed into bed and turned out the light. I curled my fingers around my cross and thought of William until I fell asleep.

I woke up early, dressed quickly, and hurried downstairs. Every nerve in body was tingling at the thought of seeing William again. The days I'd spent without him had felt like an eternity. I didn't care at the moment why he'd disappeared—I just wanted to see him.

GM was in the kitchen when I came down, and she was just pulling something out of the oven.

"Brownies?" I asked in surprise. GM was always very vocal in her disapproval of sweets, and I hadn't actually realized that we had all the ingredients necessary for brownies in the house.

GM set the pan of brownies on the stove and shut the oven door. She looked at me searchingly. "How are you feeling this morning, Katie?"

"I'm fine. I slept really well—after I warmed up."

"You really are well? Really and truly?"

"Yes, really and truly," I said.

"Well, then." GM waved a hand clad in an oven mitt toward the brownies. "I know parties are not the same as they were when you were very young, but I still thought it would be nice for you to have something to take with you this afternoon."

I gave GM a hug. "Thank you. I'm sorry about last night. I don't know what came over me."

GM pulled off her oven mitt and brushed the hair off my forehead.

"Don't think about it, solnyshko. You have had a very trying week. I am very grateful that you got away from that horrible man unscathed. You have actually taken everything that happened very well. I suppose something like this was bound to happen—it must have been a reaction to the trauma."

I wondered if GM was right—had my odd frozen trance of the night before been a delayed response to the attack by Joshua? I supposed it was possible.

But something tugged at the back of my mind—something I was forgetting. I tried to force the thought forward, but it was elusive. I figured it would come to me if it were important.

After breakfast, I worked on homework until it was time to leave for the party. As I went out to the car with GM, cradling a container full of brownies in my arms, I felt a pang of nervousness. I was going to be able to search for William soon.

I scolded myself then and told myself to think of Bryony first—she was the real reason I was going out to the Old Grove. Seeing William would have to come second—after all, a few more hours would not change whatever reason he had for avoiding me.

Silently, I told myself to relax.

But I was nervous all the same.

I glanced over at GM as she drove us swiftly over to the Old Grove. Despite my best efforts, William kept breaking into my thoughts, and I realized that I hadn't told her that Charisse had changed her mind about seeing him with Joshua. In fact, GM and I hadn't spoken about William since she'd forbidden me to see him. I wondered if she thought she had put an end to our relationship for good. It was always hard to tell with her.

"GM," I said carefully. "There's something you should know. Charisse didn't report William to the police. She said she couldn't be sure she'd seen him with Joshua Martin."

GM's hands tightened on the steering wheel, and she glanced at me sharply. "Is that your way of telling me that he's going to be at the party?"

"No. William wasn't invited." I realized suddenly that I was actually on pretty shaky ground. If GM got upset, there was a very good chance that she'd turn the car around and take us straight home.

"I am relieved to hear he wasn't invited," she said. "We'll discuss his status in our household later."

I looked out the window and watched the scenery flying past us. I decided once again just to focus on Bryony and the party.

Before long we reached the Old Grove, and GM insisted on walking with me until we found the party site. Once we spotted a large gazebo full of people, she allowed me to go on alone.

The day was cold, but I could see several bright fires up ahead, and some of the party guests had removed their coats already. The grove itself was a pretty place, and laughter from the party drifted over to me.

It was hard to believe that anything terrible had happened here, but I thought suddenly of Anton and Innokenti and the two girls who had been attacked in the Old Grove. I felt a momentary panic that the two of them might put in an unwelcome appearance. But I looked toward the crowd ahead of me, and I told myself not to worry about them—surely Anton and Innokenti would not risk attacking such a large group.

And there appeared to be plenty of fire around.

As I reached the party, Bryony spotted me and waved, and I walked up to her.

"Thanks for coming," she said, smiling.

"Happy birthday," I said, holding out my plastic container. "I've brought you some brownies. My grandmother made them."

Bryony accepted the container from me. "Thank you. My grandmother couldn't come today—she said it was too cold for her. She did ask me to tell her how you were doing. She's been concerned about you ever since the ghost in her house gave her the warning for you."

I drew in my breath sharply. *Don't let him sing to her.* Was that what had happened to me last night when I had sat by the window in a trance-like state? Had someone been singing to me?

Bryony was staring at me in concern. "Are you okay? You went awfully pale all of a sudden."

I shook off my fears. Whatever had happened last night, I was in no danger at the moment.

I would just have to be careful from now on to keep the warning from Bryony's grandmother in mind.

"I'm fine," I said, in what I hoped was a reassuring tone. "And please tell your grandmother that I'm doing well." I looked around. "It looks like you've got a good crowd here."

Bryony smiled. "I've been really lucky. A lot of people were able to come even with the short notice."

I glanced around again, and I happened to catch Irina's dark eye. She quickly looked away.

"I've asked Irina to be nice," Bryony said quietly. "She said she would."

I resisted the impulse to smile. I was sure that that request had not gone over well with Irina.

"Come and meet my parents," Bryony said.

I met Mr. and Mrs. Carson and Bryony's older sister, Eva, a tall, slender senior with the same long, light brown hair that Bryony had. I had seen Eva in the halls at school before—she looked like the cover of a magazine.

Bryony's father was busy manning a barbeque, and there were several tables laden with food nearby. Bryony deposited my brownies with a number of other desserts, and then we went to talk to the other guests. I said hello to Annamaria, who was just taking off her coat and scarf because of the heat. As she did so, she revealed a series of angry red scars on her neck.

Between the heaters and the fires, it was actually quite hot in the gazebo, and I found myself peeling off my own winter things.

As I was folding my coat over my arm, Simon came up to me.

"Thanks for inviting me to this," he said with a smile.

I smiled back. "I can't take credit for that. Technically, Bryony invited you. I just passed the message on."

"Well, thanks for doing that. My brother thanks you, too."

Simon nodded his head, and I followed his gaze. Simon's brother, James, was now talking with Eva.

Simon continued. "James insisted on crashing when he heard where I was going today. He's been scheming for ages to get a chance to talk to Eva. This was a perfect opportunity for him."

I watched the two of them talking. James's expression—typically harsh and closed—was open and friendly. Eva smiled at something he said, and James smiled in return. His smile was shy and uncertain, but it was a smile nonetheless.

"He's doing really well, isn't he?" I said, turning back to Simon. "You can see the difference in him."

"Yeah. His grades are way up this quarter, and in January he's going to begin applying to colleges. He'll probably have to go to community college for the first year or two, but he may be able to transfer to one of the state schools after that."

"I'm really happy for him," I said. "It's amazing how he's turned his life around."

"Yeah. I'm proud of him." Simon paused and then gave me a serious look. "One thing that really helped him was getting rid of bad influences—people he thought were his friends but really weren't. It was hard watching him back when he was younger and he first started going down the wrong path. Those bad influences were working on him then, dragging him down. I don't want to see you go downhill, too."

"You're talking about William," I said wearily.

"I'm talking about—him, yes. This is a good first step—not having him here. Isn't this much better? Just you and me, like old times."

Simon looked at me steadily, and there was something pleading in his eyes.

I didn't know what to say, and I was spared from having to come up with a reply by the arrival of Charisse and Branden.

I found a paper plate with grilled chicken and a can of soda suddenly pushed into my hands.

"I noticed you two didn't have any food," Branden said by way of greeting.

Simon's hands were soon similarly laden.

"It's good to see you two together," Charisse said.

It was clear to me that she was hinting at the same subject that Simon had just been pursuing—she was also happy that William wasn't here.

Before I could respond, Branden swept us all of us away.

"Come on. There are some seats over here."

I sat and talked and ate and mingled, and as the afternoon wore on, I spied an opportunity. Simon had been collared by Irina, Charisse and Branden were completely absorbed by one another, and I was between groups. I walked around slowly but purposefully until I was on the edge of the party. Then, when no one seemed to be watching, I slipped off into the woods.

I was going to look for my own personal bad influence.

Chapter Nine

I walked until the lights and sounds from the party had disappeared. I soon felt the cold, and I pulled my coat back on.

I didn't really have a plan. I'd intended to ask around at the party to see if anyone knew where William lived, but somehow I'd been unable to bring the topic up.

Simon's near-constant presence had probably contributed to my difficulty.

So I wandered through the trees, hoping that something would stand out—something that would point the way to William.

I knew the woods of the Old Grove well, and I knew there were houses around its perimeter, as well as houses dotted all throughout it. I had a feeling that William's house would be in the woods, rather than around the outer edge—the houses inside the woods themselves seemed to be more secluded. That seemed like something he would prefer.

I'd never paid a lot of attention to the houses within the woods, so I didn't know which way to turn exactly to start searching. So I simply continued to walk.

Even without a plan, the motion made me feel as if I were accomplishing something.

As I walked, a sense of calmness and well-being stole over me. The nervousness I'd felt before about the possibility of seeing William again melted away completely.

I breathed in the cold air deeply. There was something soft about the atmosphere—something strangely warm and inviting.

I continued to walk.

Eventually, I found myself standing in front of a cave. It was actually the same cave I had gone into back in October while I was searching for Gleb Mstislav. And I had actually found him inside it—though at the time I hadn't realized who he was.

I stared into the cave mouth for a long moment, entranced by the soft quality of the dark within. It seemed to me that the soothing, inviting feelings that I'd detected were emanating from the cave. I was just beginning to wonder if perhaps I should head into it, when I saw a white light moving toward me out of the darkness.

The light came closer and grew larger—it lit up the interior of the cave. Soon I could see a man walking toward me. When he was close enough that I could reach out and touch him, he stopped.

I stared up at him—not in any way alarmed—just curious.

The man was entirely covered in a thick layer of ice, which seemed to be giving off the white light that illuminated the cave. Though he'd walked toward me purposefully, I could see that his eyes were tightly closed, and I had the impression that he hadn't opened them in a very long time.

His face was a ghostly, blurry white, and through the thick ice, I could see that his matted hair was black. His clothes, from what I could see, had once been ornate but were now in an advanced state of decomposition, hanging in tatters in some spots. Despite his ragged appearance, a sense of warmth and well-being rolled off of him in waves. I felt safe in his presence—secure and happy to be near him.

I closed my eyes, imitating the man before me, and I could hear a faint sound—a melody that called to me, asked me to follow. I opened my eyes and stared at the man in front of me. I wanted to know more about him.

Still with his eyes closed, the man raised his ice-covered hand and held it out to me.

I raised my hand to take his.

I was wondering vaguely how he could bear the cold when I heard a sharp snap behind me, and I turned quickly.

The vampire Anton was standing just a few feet from me, two halves of a broken stick held in his hands.

"Hello, Sunshine," he said.

I looked back toward the cave. The man covered in ice had disappeared and along with him had gone the sense of warmth and well-being that had enveloped me. I stared for a moment, wondering if I had imagined the strange, ragged white figure.

Slowly, I turned back to face Anton. I was hoping that I'd imagined him, too.

But Anton was still standing a few feet away—still holding the broken sticks just as he had been a moment before. I felt my breath coming quickly, and a sharp stab of fear lanced through me.

I tried to think of what to do. But it was hard for me to form coherent thoughts, and the smug, self-assured look on his face didn't help matters. I forced my eyes away from his face. I glanced at the sticks in his hands.

"What are you doing?" Even to my ears my voice sounded high and shaky.

"What are *you* doing?" Anton countered. "You seemed to be in a trance. I had to make some noise to wake you up. Just out of curiosity, what did you think you were reaching for?"

I tried to force my voice to be steady. "There was a man—here—in front of the cave. He was deathly pale and covered in ice. He held out his hand to me."

I glanced quickly over my shoulder again, but the mouth of the cave remained empty. "Didn't you see him?"

"No."

Suddenly, I realized just how far I had wandered from the party. I was uncomfortably aware of the fact that Anton and I were in an isolated spot. I looked around again—this time to see if we were truly alone.

Unfortunately, we were.

Anton continued to look at me steadily.

"I have a party to get back to," I said. "People are expecting me."

I turned and started to walk away.

Anton stepped into my path.

I was forced to stop.

I could feel my breathing becoming more labored, and my heart began to beat painfully. I fought the impulse to run—I knew I couldn't outrun him. I'd have to stay calm to have any chance of getting away.

"How's William?" Anton asked.

"He's doing well," I said.

Anton took a step toward me. "When did you last see him?"

I thought of lying, but I had a feeling that would be a mistake. "It's been a few days."

Anton smiled. "Would you like to know where he is?"

"I'll see him soon," I said.

"Are you sure about that?" Anton's tone was mocking.

"Yes," I said. "Actually, I came out here to meet him at his house. I've just gotten turned around a bit."

Anton's smile deepened. The expression on his face was not a pleasant one.

"I see where I am now," I said firmly. "I've got to be going—William is expecting me."

My heart was now beating wildly, but I tried to appear confident as I walked away from both Anton and the cave.

I felt a little flutter of hope as I continued to walk and heard no following footsteps.

I resisted the temptation to turn around and look back at Anton to see if he were truly not following me. I resisted a further temptation to break into a run. I was headed back toward the party, and I told myself that I would make it there safely if I remained calm and just kept moving.

I had not gone very far when I felt a breeze rush past me, and suddenly Anton was standing before me, blocking my path once again. He was so close that I had to stop short to avoid running into him.

I quickly took a step back.

"It might interest you to know," Anton said, "that you're going the wrong way."

"I know where I'm going," I said defiantly.

"William's house is that way." Anton pointed.

I glanced swiftly in the direction he indicated and then looked back at him. His eyes were still mocking, and I wished I knew if I could believe him.

It was entirely possible he was showing me the correct way. But it was also possible that he knew I didn't know, and he just wanted to run me around in circles for his amusement.

I shut my mind firmly against what the end of that amusement might be.

Stay calm, I told myself. *Continue to think. You can get out of this.*

"I know where I'm going," I repeated.

With a boldness I didn't really feel, I stepped around Anton and started to walk toward the party again.

Anton followed me, and we walked along side by side for a little while in silence—almost as if we were friends.

After a few moments, Anton reached over and lifted a lock of my hair.

"Just like sunshine," he murmured.

My breathing grew even more ragged.

"You still haven't answered my question," Anton said, releasing the lock of hair.

I forced my voice to come out evenly. "What question was that?"

"Would you like to know where William is?"

"I know where he is," I said.

Anton draped an arm over my shoulder casually, and I felt fear wash over me. His arm was heavy, and I imagined that I could feel the wintry coldness of his skin through the cloth we both wore. My heart began to hammer painfully.

Keep thinking, I told myself. *Keep thinking.*

"The thing is," he said, giving my shoulder a little squeeze, "that William's house is back that way, like I told you, so I don't really believe that you're heading there to meet him. However, it's possible that you were so dazzled by my good looks when you saw me that you completely lost your head, and in your confusion, you started off the wrong way. As I told you once, I have a devastating effect on women. In fact, I can hear your heart pounding right now, you know."

Anton tilted his head and peered into my face, and my eyes lifted involuntarily to meet his. He smiled then.

I looked away.

Anton continued. "So, that is a possibility—I concede it. But I confess that I don't actually think that's what's happening here. I don't think you and William arranged to meet at all. I think you wandered away from that party up there at the gazebo—keep in mind that I can hear them—and you were hoping that you would run into William by chance out here. And right now you are hoping desperately to make it back to the party before I drag you away. Am I right?"

I was feeling dizzy and light-headed, and I found that I was completely incapable of making any reply.

Anton tilted his head and stared into my face again, and this time I studiously avoided looking into his eyes.

"That's what I thought," Anton said.

He gave my shoulder another squeeze—a gesture that was almost affectionate. "Like I said, I can hear them up at the party. Several of them are starting to wonder where you are. But though I can hear them, they wouldn't be able to hear you if you were to cry out now. We're still too far away."

I looked at him then, even though I didn't want to, and I saw that his eyes were alight with malice.

"Let go of me," I said, wincing at how reedy and thin my voice sounded. I shrugged off his arm and kept walking—with the blood pounding in my ears.

Anton stepped out in front of me and turned to walk backward so he could continue to look at me. Though there were trees all around us, he never came close to hitting one—something I noticed with bitterness.

"I find this intriguing," Anton said. "And don't worry, I won't let you get close enough to the party to escape. But since I've met William here again, he's seemed very protective of you. However, he hasn't told you where he lives, and he hasn't told you where he's gone. That's very neglectful of him, if I may be so bold as to comment on your relationship."

"William hasn't gone anywhere," I said, but a new fear was beginning to steal over me.

Anton seemed very sure that William wasn't anywhere nearby.

What if he was telling the truth?

You can still call William, I told myself. *Anton probably doesn't know that William has granted you that power. He'll come to you just like he did in the Mstislav crypt.*

But what if he didn't? I glanced at Anton involuntarily, and another sharp pang of fear ran through me.

His eyes glittered. "Oh, but William has gone, Sunshine."

"You're lying," I said.

Anton was triumphant. "William left with Innokenti."

I stopped, startled. "What?"

"I knew you didn't know." Anton's smile was superior.

"He wouldn't leave me," I said. "He wouldn't."

Without warning, Anton grabbed me by the collar and pulled me close. "He *has* left you. He did exactly what Innokenti wanted and went back with him to Russia. William isn't here to save you."

Anton began to drag me back the way we'd come. "I told you I wouldn't let you get close enough to the party to escape."

I struggled ineffectually in his grasp. *Keep thinking*, I told myself.

"What about Innokenti?" I said in desperation.

"What about him?"

"He said that he wanted me to go back to Russia, too," I said quickly. "Innokenti wouldn't like what you're doing right now."

"Innokenti isn't here," Anton said.

We were moving much faster now, and the landscape around me began to blur. Unfortunately, I had been dragged by a vampire before—I knew that they could reach terrifying speeds.

I had a feeling he was dragging me back toward the cave. I didn't want to get dragged down into the darkness.

I had to stop him.

The speed at which we were traveling made it unsafe, but I reached out and tried to tear a branch off a tree—I thought maybe I could strike him across the eyes with it—but I came away with nothing but twigs. Digging in my heels certainly wouldn't work, and I knew that beating on that solid, preternatural body wouldn't work, either. I decided just to go limp—I hoped that Anton would be surprised enough to stop.

I closed my eyes and just dropped, relaxing all of my limbs.

Anton continued to drag me along for a moment and then stopped. He let me fall to the ground, and I opened one eye. I saw a large rock lying on the forest floor nearby—it appeared be the best weapon I had to hand.

Anton touched me on the shoulder. "What's going on, Sunshine?"

I grabbed up the rock and swung it around quickly, hitting Anton on the temple as hard as I could. He blinked, looking startled.

I jumped to my feet and started to run.

As I did so, I spoke the words William had given me.

"Katie Wickliff summons you."

I was suddenly bathed in golden light. A tall form stood before me, his face obscured by the brightness that surrounded us.

"William!" I cried.

Hope rose in my heart. He hadn't deserted me.

I ran toward the figure in the light, but when I was close enough to see his face, I stopped.

The man standing before me was not William.

I looked back, panicked, to see where Anton was.

I was startled to see him standing, frozen, at the edge of the golden aura that surrounded me. He was caught in mid-stride, clearly moving to go after me, and a bright red trickle of blood sat motionless on his pale skin, arrested in its descent down the side of his face.

I turned back to the strange man in the center of the glow.

"Is he—he was chasing me—is he—"

I found myself unable to speak clearly.

"You are safe," the man said. His words were perfectly clear, but he had a strange accent that I couldn't quite identify—although something about it was familiar. "He won't move until I allow him to do so."

"How—what—" I took a deep breath and tried to control the beating of my heart. "You did this?"

I gestured vaguely at the golden light that surrounded us.

"Yes."

"Then, you saved me from—from him."

"Yes."

"Thank you," I said.

A smile quirked at one corner of the man's mouth. "You're welcome."

I stepped closer to the man and looked at him closely for the first time. His hair was a dark gold—an unusual color that I couldn't remember having seen on anyone else before. His eyes were a very bright blue, and he was wearing clothes that were somehow both simple and ornate. I didn't know quite what to make of him.

"Did you come in response to my call just now?" I asked.

"Yes."

"But I don't even know your name," I said.

"You may call me Cormac."

He held his hand out to me. "Come with me. Quickly."

I looked at his hand—the broad palm, the long fingers—there was something strong yet light about it. I felt a longing to go with him—to go wherever he and the golden light had come from.

I raised my hand to his and then pulled it back, reminded unpleasantly of the strange, ice-covered man I had seen coming out of the cave.

"Was that you?" I blurted out.

Cormac looked at me in surprise. "I don't know what you mean. What is it that you wish to know?"

The whole situation was making my head spin. I glanced over at Anton. He still stood motionless at the edge of the golden circle of light, his face contorted in anger with a frozen drop of blood on it.

I turned back to Cormac. "I saw a man coming out of a cave in this forest. He was completely covered in ice. His skin was white, and he seemed to glow. He never once opened his eyes. He held his hand out to me just as you did now, and I felt compelled to go with him. The man disappeared when Anton showed up."

Cormac's gaze shifted to the frozen vampire. "That, I take it, is Anton?"

"Yes."

"I don't know who it was you saw. I wasn't in the cave. I suspect the man was part of a trap the vampire set for you—he may even be a vampire himself. Do not think of them. You're safe from them while you're with me."

I glanced at Anton again. "Won't someone notice him standing there like that?"

"No. No one can see any of us in here. We are completely shielded from human eyes."

"Human eyes," I murmured. Cormac was clearly not human—what human being could freeze a vampire like that? And he had come in answer to the call William had given me. I realized with a start that I was probably looking at one of William's people—I was looking at one of the Sídh.

"Did William send you?" I asked.

"No. He didn't send me." Cormac's words were even, but there was something like distant anger in his eyes.

"But you do know him, don't you? William Sursur? It was his call that I used. You must have come in answer to it."

"I did come in answer to your call. And I do know of him."

Hope leaped in my heart. "Have you seen him? Can you take me to him?"

"I haven't seen him. And you won't see him, either. He's gone."

I was puzzled. "But you're like him, aren't you? You're one of William's people."

"I am not like him." Cormac's voice was harsh.

"But aren't you—"

"The one you speak of—William—suffers from a contagion." Cormac seemed to stumble over the name. "His condition is permanent. He can never return to us."

I felt anger flare up within me. I had heard talk like this from William—that he was cursed because of the vampire attack that had altered his nature. I disagreed with William's assessment of the situation, and I disagreed with Cormac's just as much. I was about to tell him so, when I stopped, arrested by the obvious anguish in his face.

I decided my outrage could wait for the moment. I focused instead on what was most important—finding out what was going on with William. Cormac seemed to know something of his whereabouts.

"Why did you say that I wouldn't see William again?"

"Because you won't."

"Why did you say he's gone?"

"Because he is. William—" Once again, the name seemed to come out with some difficulty, "will trouble you no longer."

"William doesn't trouble me," I said. "And he wouldn't leave me. He couldn't. He loves me, and I love him."

Cormac's expression softened then, and I could see sympathy register distantly in his eyes.

"You love the remnants of what William was. I am sure some small part of his original personality still survives. But he is altered now forever. These creatures cannot help what they are."

Cormac glanced briefly at Anton. "But that doesn't change their nature. They're predators, and their tempers are uncertain. They are often seized by violent urges—violent whims. William could kill you at any moment. If any shred of goodness remains to him, if any part of him is indeed capable of loving you, then it is for the best that he will never see you again."

Once more, William's own words were echoed by Cormac. But Cormac couldn't possibly know William well if he could believe he was anything like Anton.

I realized once again that I had to put my indignation aside—I had to focus instead on getting information about William from Cormac.

"Cormac," I began, "I have to—"

I stopped when Cormac suddenly turned his head sharply—he was looking at something in the golden light that I couldn't see.

"I don't have much time," he said urgently. "Come with me, quickly now."

I hesitated, unsure of what to do.

"Don't waste what I have done," Cormac said pleadingly. "Why do you think I came here to rescue you today when it is so hard for me to break through? Why do you think I planted that memory in the girl's mind?"

"What memory?" I asked.

Cormac held out his hand again.

"Come with me, Katie. I know who you are. I know what your purpose is, and I can help you to realize it. I can take you to a place where creatures like him," he nodded curtly at Anton, "will never trouble you again."

I felt a strange longing to find out what lay beyond that golden light—a light that seemed to promise warmth and happiness. But I felt an even stronger pull toward William.

"No, I can't," I said. "I can't go with you."

"Katie, please. We have to hurry."

"No."

Cormac looked stunned. "You are refusing? You choose to remain in a world of danger and death?"

"I'm choosing to remain with William."

Something I couldn't define flickered in Cormac's eyes. "Very well. At least I can take you to safety—for the moment. Do you have friends nearby?"

"Yes. There's a party in these woods. I have friends there."

I looked around in the golden glow, intending to point the way, but it was impossible for me to tell which way we were facing.

Cormac closed his eyes. "I have located them."

Without warning, the golden light that surrounded us intensified. The glare became so bright that I was forced to close my eyes, and when I opened them again, I was startled to see that I was no longer standing with Cormac in amongst the trees. Instead I was now back at Bryony's party, standing in the gazebo, surrounded by Bryony's party guests.

I turned around frantically. My first thought was of Anton—I figured that if the glow were gone that he might be free now, too. But like Cormac, Anton was nowhere to be seen. I continued to look over the crowd. All of the partygoers looked relaxed, happy, unconcerned.

I felt a certain measure of relief—I figured I was safe from Anton at the moment, even if he were free of the golden glow. He was unlikely to risk attacking me in the midst of the party—he had said himself that he intended to keep me away from it.

I knew I was safe for now, but I also knew I had to go home again.

And I knew that nightfall was inevitable.

I couldn't fend off an involuntary shudder, and I wrapped my arms around my body and closed my eyes.

"Katie! There you are!"

I opened my eyes to see Simon pushing through the crowd toward me.

I made an effort to smile as he came to stand beside me.

"Hey," he said. "Where have you been? It was like you disappeared completely."

I struggled to come up with a plausible excuse for my absence, but Simon rushed on without waiting for an answer.

"Are you okay?" he asked suddenly. "You're really pale. And you're shaking. Are you cold?"

I wasn't cold at all, but I could well imagine that I was pale.

"I'm fine."

"Are you sure?"

I knew there was no way I could possibly explain to him what had just happened to me—I wasn't entirely sure I understood it myself.

I looked into Simon's face—his expression was both good-natured and worried, and I felt cheered for a moment by his obvious concern.

"I'm fine. I really am."

"I'm not sure I believe you when you say that," Simon said. "Come and stand over here by one of the fires."

He bundled me over to a bright orange blaze, and I stood before it, until beads of perspiration formed on my forehead. Eventually Simon relaxed his vigilant watch over me and began to talk with other partygoers again.

Only then did I allow myself to face the harsh truth that had just been revealed to me—the truth that I'd been afraid to test before.

William hadn't come to me at school during the week as he'd said he would. In the forest, Anton had told me that William was gone. Cormac, who had clearly despised Anton, had also said that William was gone. And when I needed him, and I had called to him with the words he'd given me, he hadn't come to me—even though he'd promised me he always would.

Tears ran down my face, and I wiped them away quickly. I hoped that anyone who saw me would think that I was just blotting my overheated skin and wouldn't recognize that I was crying.

The truth was that William had abandoned me.

Chapter Ten

When GM picked me up after the party, I gave her a quick smile and turned my face to the window. I hoped that she would assume I was tired and wouldn't notice that anything was wrong.

I was to be disappointed. The questions started as soon as we pulled away from the Old Grove.

"Are you ill, solnyshko?"

I opened my eyes and glanced over at GM. She was watching both me and the road, and her eye when it rested on me was suspicious. I looked away quickly.

"I'm fine, GM. I'm just a little tired." I tried to sound sleepy.

"No, no—I think you're ill. Your face is pale with red blotches."

I raised a hand to cover my face. The crying I'd done had left its mark, and GM had noticed—though she didn't quite recognize what it was. Simon had noticed my crying also, and I had told him that cinders from the fire had gotten into my eyes.

He'd insisted on rinsing them with bottled water—and the coolness of the liquid had had an oddly calming effect. At the very least it had helped me to stem the tide of my tears back at the party.

"You are ill," GM said firmly. "Or you will be very shortly. You spent too much time out in the cold. I should have foreseen this."

"I'm fine," I protested.

But GM went on with her interrogation.

She asked me a series of questions—whether I felt too hot or had the chills—whether I felt achy all over.

GM continued her questions until we reached home. I understood why she was so concerned that I might be ill—it was always the same reason. She believed my mother had died of a fever—exacerbated by overexertion—so she always became nervous whenever she thought I was sick. She didn't want illness to claim me, too.

GM sent me up to my room to rest, and I was alone with my worries.

I sat on my bed and looked around my room. The objects in it were the same as they had always been. My favorite things were still there—my old coverlet, my picture of my parents and me, my lamp with the sunburst shade that reminded me of my mother—they were unchanged. But my world had shifted dramatically.

Gone was my feeling of safety from last night.

I knew now that William was well and truly gone, and that no one was watching the house. I also knew that at least two vampires were after me—if not more. Anton and Joshua Martin had both attacked me, and as far as I knew, both of them were still in town. I tried to remember exactly what Innokenti had said about there being a price on my head—but my memory refused to work, and my mind was clouded by fear. I sat for a long time overcome by an unusual feeling.

I was in the unique and terrible position of knowing that my house was a target for creatures that drank human blood.

After the first wave of shock had worn off I thought of GM—I realized with horror that she was in danger, too. Vampires could come into our house at any time of the day or night, looking for me. And I knew they wouldn't hesitate to kill her if she got in the way.

A fresh wave of panic washed over me.

I wanted to warn GM, but I knew she'd never believe me—and why should she? She'd seen some strange things over the last few months, but she had no idea that she'd actually seen a few vampires.

And I certainly didn't have any evidence to offer her that would convince her.

I let my thoughts run down this gloomy track without my seeing any solution. The longer I let my thoughts run, the more William began to crowd into them.

Soon the tears began to fall again, and I turned my face into my pillow. I didn't want GM to hear me crying.

I cried until I had no more tears left, and then I was left with a deep, horrible ache.

Why would William leave me? Why would he leave without saying a word?

Why was he gone?

I lay on my bed watching the rest of the daylight fading away. And I seemed to sink into insensibility. It dulled the pain.

As shadows fell across the room, GM came in to check on me.

She turned on the light and clucked at me disapprovingly.

"You should be under the covers."

Once she had me settled in to her satisfaction, she stood with her hands on her hips.

"Your face is still pale with red blotches. It is as I feared—you are ill, Katie."

I began to protest that I was fine, but GM waved my protestations aside.

"You need to rest tonight. If you're still ill in the morning, I'll take you to see the doctor. Doctor Lundin has Sunday hours, I believe."

I tried again to tell GM that I wasn't ill, but she interrupted me.

"I don't like the blotchiness," she said emphatically.

Then she left me to rest until dinner.

My thoughts immediately returned to William. I felt the terrible pain returning to me—the pain of losing him, of never seeing him again—the pain of knowing that he didn't want me and that my love didn't matter to him. Hurt continued to wash over me in waves.

He had abandoned me completely, without even bothering to say goodbye. I didn't even matter enough for him to tell me he was going. I sank deeper and deeper into the pain.

I wanted to be angry with him, but I found that it just wasn't possible. All I felt was sadness and a hurt so profound that I thought it would tear me apart.

The same question kept running through my mind.

Why had he left me?

Then something came to me through the haze. I still had GM to consider—I'd have to come up with a way to keep her safe. Despite my doubts about her reaction, I would have to try to warn her. And I'd have to come up with a practical way to protect the house. I made an effort to pull myself together. I had to get myself into some kind of state where I could think properly.

I figured it was nearly time for dinner, so I went to the bathroom, and I washed my face. Then I pulled a comb through my hair. Pain still surged through me, so I made an effort to compartmentalize it—to push it into one corner of my mind and build a wall around it. It was easier to shut the feeling out completely than it was to try to cope with it directly.

I made a point of going down to dinner before GM could come up to check on me.

GM gave me a disapproving look as I entered the kitchen—I imagined she thought I should have stayed in bed—but I knew I wasn't ill, and I figured that the sooner I was able to prove that to her, the better.

GM kept an eye on me as we ate, and I was sure she noticed that I didn't have much of an appetite. But she didn't comment on it, and she didn't object when I helped her clear up after dinner was over.

As I loaded the dishwasher, I cast an eye over the kitchen. I wondered if there was anything that I could use in the event of a vampire attack. I knew that the bottom drawer to the left of the sink had several boxes of wooden matches—as well as a lighter that we used for our outdoor grill. I spotted a broom in a corner, and I wondered if I could wrap towels around the brush and light them—thus giving myself a makeshift torch with a long reach.

I figured fire would be the most effective weapon. I'd heard wooden stakes didn't always work, and they seemed like a risky option anyway—especially against an opponent who was faster with much sharper reflexes. Unfortunately, I knew from experience that both of those things were true of Joshua and Anton.

As I continued to glance around the kitchen, I remembered that GM had once had an oil lamp with a cloth wick. I wondered if I might make use of that.

"GM, do you still have that old oil lamp?"

She blinked at me in surprise. "Oil lamp?"

"I remember when I was about eight years old you had a lamp with green oil that you used to light in the winter."

"Yes, I remember now. I think we still have it. But I don't think we have any oil for it anymore."

"Do you know where it is?" I asked.

GM thought for a moment. "I believe it's in that small cupboard over the refrigerator. What made you think of that old lamp?"

"It just popped into my head, that's all," I said.

I was disappointed to hear that we probably didn't have any oil, but I figured I might think of a use for the lamp anyway. I resolved to include it with my supplies—I would come back down after GM had gone to sleep and gather up everything I could possibly use to fend off vampires. I knew they could attack during the day, but I had a feeling that any attacks would come in the middle of the night—they did seem to be stealth hunters.

As GM wrapped up some leftovers, I thought again about warning her.

Maybe I could give her a warning about something she would understand.

"The police haven't caught Joshua Martin yet, have they?" I asked abruptly.

GM looked surprised by the sudden switch in topic. "No, no they haven't. Does that worry you, solnyshko?"

Of course, I knew that the police hadn't caught him, and I had a feeling that they never would. But bringing him up seemed like the best way to put GM on alert.

"It does bother me," I admitted. "I think he might try to come after me. GM, what would you do if he showed up here suddenly?"

"Here at our house?" she asked incredulously.

"Yes," I said. "I think it could happen. And I think we need to be prepared."

"No wonder you've been looking ill today if that's what you've been thinking about," GM murmured.

"What do we do if Joshua shows up here?" I said with a touch of impatience. GM didn't seem to be as concerned as I'd hoped she would be. "I'm serious about this."

She reached out and touched my cheek. "These last few months have been very difficult for you, haven't they? I confess that I hadn't considered the possibility that Joshua Martin could come here. I would think that Charisse and her mother would be in far greater danger."

I felt a sinking feeling—GM's reaction was entirely normal. To her, I had really been a minor—even incidental—participant in Joshua's attack. She didn't know that he'd set the whole thing up to trap me.

She continued. "But it's true that that horrible man did go after you. I suppose that we should be prepared. I will think on it."

"What if he shows up tonight?" I asked urgently. I could hear the rising panic in my own voice. I wanted GM to be safe. I wanted her to look out for her own welfare. But I was afraid again that I wouldn't be able to convince her of the danger. The proofs I had to offer her she would never believe in.

"Do not distress yourself," GM said soothingly. "I am aware that this is a serious situation. I will call the police tonight and ask them to keep an eye on our house. And I will keep my cell phone next to my bed in case I need to call."

It didn't seem like enough to me, but I supposed it would have to do.

"Thanks, GM. But if you have a strange feeling at any time that tells you that you need to get out of the house right away—I want you to promise me that you'll do it—even if it seems like a silly thing to do."

GM smiled at me then. "You are a good girl, Katie, to worry about your grandmother. I will promise to do what you ask. And I also promise that I won't go without you."

I started to object—I knew that she would actually be safer without me, but GM interrupted me.

"Hush now, and don't protest. I can look after myself and you better than you think. After all, I've kept you alive all these years, haven't I?"

"Yes, you have," I said, and I couldn't help smiling a little myself.

"It is settled then. I will take the precautions I have mentioned, and you will stop worrying. This Joshua Martin is only a man—no, 'man' is not the word I want. He is only a thug. And I am more than a match for any average thug."

I shivered then—I couldn't help it. If only the creatures that stalked our house were ordinary mortals.

GM noticed the tremor that ran through my body and misinterpreted it. "I see you have a chill. No doubt the cares that have lain heavy upon your mind have worn down your body's defenses. And I'm still convinced that all that time you spent out in the cold today did you no good. Go back up to your room and rest. I'll finish here in the kitchen."

I did as she asked and went up to my room—but I knew that real rest would be out of the question.

I sat on my bed, and my worries welled up within me, threatening to overwhelm me. My mind kept spinning as my fear grew and reached a fever pitch. I was alone now—vulnerable to every monster that stalked the night and wanted to collect the price on my head.

I seemed to fall into a sort of trance—my mind remained busy, working on problems I couldn't possibly solve, while my body remained still and my breathing slowed.

I waited, watching the clock that sat near my bed.

When it was finally late enough for me to go to sleep, I forced myself to stir. I got ready for bed like I usually did, so that GM would hear all of the usual sounds and wouldn't notice that anything was different. But instead of changing my clothes for the night, I kept my day clothes and my shoes on—that way I could be prepared if it became necessary for me to flee the house with GM.

Then I climbed under the covers—just in case GM should stop in.

I turned out the light and settled in to wait until she went to bed.

Time seemed to crawl by as I waited in the dark, but there was no danger of my falling asleep.

I was far too worried for that.

After what seemed like an eternity, I heard GM come up the stairs and head to her room. She typically went to bed late and slept for only a few hours each night—but when she did sleep, she slept heavily, and it could sometimes be hard to wake her. I knew that once she fell asleep, I would be able to go downstairs and collect my supplies.

GM would be unlikely to hear me moving around in the kitchen.

I realized then that GM's having her cell phone next to her bed probably wouldn't help her very much. Anyone who broke into the house could attack both of us before she ever woke up.

I pushed that gloomy thought aside and listened to GM as she moved around, getting ready for the night. Eventually, the sounds of her activity stopped, and the house settled into silence.

But no house is truly silent, and soon I began to hear little creaks and other sounds that I couldn't quite put a name to. As I thought about what I had to do, my heart began to beat so hard that I imagined it was audible in the room.

I wondered if that was how human hearts always sounded to vampires.

Once I thought that enough time had passed for GM to be fully asleep, I switched on my light and walked quietly to my bedroom door.

I eased it open.

I had a half-formed idea that a vampire might be standing on the other side, but the hallway outside my lighted room was dark and apparently empty.

Somehow, I wasn't relieved.

I stepped out into the hall, and I pulled the door closed until just a narrow sliver of light was visible.

Then, leaving the hall dark so as not to risk any chance of disturbing GM, I crept down the stairs to the bottom. Using the wall as a guide, I walked through the darkness to the kitchen. Only then did I risk turning on the light.

Once again, I half-expected to see a vampire standing in the kitchen waiting for me—but the room was empty. Quickly, I gathered up the matches, the automatic lighter, the broom, and a bunch of kitchen towels for my makeshift torch. I even found GM's oil lamp, and though she was right that there was no oil, I took the lamp anyway, grabbing a bottle of olive oil just in case that would work instead.

Balancing everything carefully, I shut off the light with my elbow. Then I crept down the hall, brushing my shoulder against the wall to help me find my way in the dark. When I reached the end of the hall, I felt with my foot for the stairs and began to climb gingerly.

I managed to make it to my room, and I set everything on my bed. I remembered something about hairspray being flammable, and I went to the bathroom. I found two cans of hairspray there, and I returned to my room, closing the door.

I got everything ready, and then I lit a small candle that sat on the table by my bed. After that, I shut off the light. I hoped that having the light off would encourage any invaders to come to my room first— with any luck I could keep them away from GM entirely.

Then I settled down to start my lonely vigil.

I sat on my bed next to my supplies and stared at the flame on the candle. I began to listen again to the tiny sounds that the house made in the night, and each sound that my ears caught filled me with fear. I was afraid to look anywhere but at the candle—it seemed somehow like the only safe thing in the room.

Eventually the light from the candle began to hurt my eyes, and I was forced to look away. I began to adjust to the gloom, and dark shapes, which I knew would appear familiar and innocuous in daylight, seemed to me now suspicious and menacing—every dark mass seemed to hide a vampire.

Though I knew there was nothing to be afraid of in my room, I couldn't shake off my fear. I told myself repeatedly that none of the shapes could possibly be vampires—if they had been, they certainly wouldn't have waited to attack.

As time passed, the sounds in the house seemed to get louder—every noise seemed to be someone breaking in.

I continued to stare around my darkened room, and time seemed to lose all meaning. After what felt like an age, I heard a loud creak. I had fallen into something like a daze, and I snapped into alertness. I heard another loud creak, and I fumbled for my covered broomstick and the lighter. My heart began to hammer painfully, and I waited, listening for yet another creak.

I was sure a vampire was coming up the stairs.

Silence ensued, and I strained to hear, my breathing shallow.

Come on, I thought. *Don't make me wait.*

I just want this to be over with.

But there were no more creaks, and no one battered down my door.

But maybe that wasn't my stalker's style—Joshua, for example, had said he believed in finesse.

I looked toward my door, which was heavily shrouded in shadow, and I watched it, expecting to see it ease open.

But the silence in the room continued to stretch on uninterrupted, and the door remained closed.

I couldn't have said how much time passed, but I began to relax again despite myself, and I loosened my grip on my broomstick. My breathing began to grow deeper and more comfortable.

I was pretty sure that GM and I were still alone in the house.

I tried to force myself to remain alert to all sounds, but my mind began to wander despite my best efforts. And even though I told myself that I didn't need distractions, my thoughts began to dwell on William.

I was suddenly hit by a wave of loss, and unwelcome tears sprang to my eyes. I scrubbed them away fiercely and ordered myself not to cry—I couldn't allow myself to give in to tears when I had to protect the house and my grandmother.

I closed my eyes tightly and concentrated on the tiny sounds in the house, but William crowded into my thoughts again so easily that I didn't have any chance of keeping him out.

William, where are you? I thought. *I want to see you. It hurts me to be apart from you.*

William, why did you leave me?

And that was really the important point. William had left me—had vanished completely. He'd abandoned me, and he'd never said a word to me before he'd disappeared.

According to Anton, William had gone back to Russia with Innokenti. It was clear I meant nothing to him.

And yet, I still missed him. I knew I still loved him.

Suddenly there was loud creak out in the hallway, and I looked around, startled. I fumbled once more for my broomstick and lighter, berating myself for my inattention. There was a second loud creak, and I flicked the lighter on, watching its tongue of flame flicker to life. My heart began to hammer.

This is it, I thought. *Get ready.*

But as before, the house settled back into silence, and my bedroom door remained closed. Soon, all I could hear was the crackle from my lighter.

I allowed my finger to ease off the lighter's trigger, and the bright flame at the end was extinguished. My room was plunged back into its greater gloom, and I felt the dark to be oppressive—I longed suddenly for daylight.

I wondered if it was possible for this night and this darkness to go on forever—could some supernatural element slow time so that dawn would never come?

I told myself I was just being paranoid, and I worked to slow my breathing and my pounding heart.

Once I was calm again, my thoughts began to wander—and they wandered right back to William.

This time I began to berate myself over him.

William knew you were in danger when he disappeared, said a fierce voice in my head. *He left you to this. He left you to darkness. He left you to danger. And you still love him?*

I closed my eyes, completing the darkness.

I thought only of William.

Even though I knew it probably shouldn't, thinking of him made me feel calmer.

I gave into the feeling and allowed myself to picture his face in every particular—the shade of his eyes, the slope of his brow, the line of his jaw. I pictured his odd half smile. I felt peace growing within me, and my fear began to subside. I knew that I would give up just about anything to see him one last time—even if he hated me.

I answered my own question.

Yes, I still love him. Even if he left me to this.

I tried to banish William then, to concentrate solely on the sounds in the house again—and the danger around me—but his image was persistent.

I decided to let him stay with me.

I imagined that he was in the dark beside me—and my fear that the house was going to be attacked began to fade. I was still alone—I knew that, but somehow I felt different. I could find strength in my love for William.

The night wore on. There were more creaks, more alarms. At one point I seemed to see GM in my bedroom. She stared at me without saying anything, but there was reproach in her eyes. Behind her stretched a forest of pure white trees.

She turned and walked away.

I followed her, but she moved so quickly that I couldn't catch up with her. I ran after her through the trees and soon found myself in a clearing.

GM had disappeared, but before me loomed a castle keep—a round stone tower of a building.

I felt a presence behind me, and I turned quickly.

A tall figure walked toward me, and for just a moment, I thought the figure was William.

I soon saw to my horror that it was Anton.

I ran toward the keep.

A door on the far side of the building stood open, and I plunged inside quickly.

I ran up a spiraling stone staircase until I found myself standing at the very top of the keep in the open air.

Anton soon appeared on the roof along with me.

I tried to run, but my feet suddenly refused to move.

The floor beneath me gave way, and I felt myself falling.

My eyes flew open, and I gasped for breath. I was lying back against my pillows, clutching my broomstick, with all my other supplies scattered around me. Sunlight was streaming into my room. I glanced over at the candle on my nightstand.

It had gone out.

I sat up, alarmed. I couldn't believe I had allowed myself to fall asleep.

I wondered in a panic if my sleep had been assisted—I knew that vampires had power over the human mind.

I dropped the broomstick and ran my hands over my neck. My skin was smooth and unbroken, and I quickly examined my wrists and arms. I seemed to be free of bite marks. My thoughts flew to GM. Had my falling asleep left her prey to night invaders?

As if in answer to my panicked thoughts, there was a gentle knock on my bedroom door.

A voice filtered through to me. "Are you well, Katie? It's not like you to sleep so late."

"GM, are you okay?" I asked. She sounded all right, but I wasn't reassured.

The door opened and GM entered. Her eyes opened in surprise when she saw me.

"GM, are you okay?" I said again. She looked perfectly healthy, but I needed to hear her say the words.

"Yes, of course I'm okay." She stepped closer. "The question is, are you?"

She stood by my bed, surveying the matches, the towels, the broomstick, and all the other things I had scattered around me.

"Katie, what on earth are you doing with all of these things?"

I tried to come up with a reasonable explanation for my odd collection, but nothing came to me.

GM picked up the lantern. "Is this why you were asking about my old lantern last night? Because you wanted to place it in your bed?"

I tried to come up with a reason for my having the lantern, but I floundered again, unable to come up with a response.

GM's eyes darted to the grill lighter. "You have my lighter, matches, towels. You weren't planning on burning the house down, were you?"

I found my voice then. "No, of course not. No."

"Then what were you doing with all of this stuff?"

I realized that I could tell her at least part of the truth.

"I was afraid that Joshua Martin would attack the house at night. I thought I could fight him off with these things."

GM sank onto the bed. "Oh, Katie. You poor child. I hope you didn't sit up all night."

"I tried to," I admitted. "But I didn't quite make it."

GM reached over and ran a soothing hand over my hair. "You must not worry like this. I'm perfectly capable of looking out for you. As I said, I've kept you alive all this time, haven't I?"

"I know you said that," I replied. "But I wasn't just worried about me. I was worried about you, too. I don't want Joshua to come after you, either."

Fire flashed in GM's eyes. "I am more than capable of looking after myself." She leaned forward and her eyes bored into mine. "More than capable. There are things about your grandmother that you don't know. So no more worrying."

She stood up then. She looked over my supplies once again and shook her head.

"First, the open window on a freezing-cold night, and now you're preparing for a firefight. Sometimes I wonder about you, Katie. Please promise me that there will be no more shenanigans of this type."

Now that GM had caught me, I knew that I wouldn't get another chance to sneak in supplies from the kitchen—I knew she would put locks on the cupboards if she felt she had to.

I would have to come up with something else.

"I promise, no more shenanigans," I said.

"You are a good girl," GM said. "I have always known that. You are a little strange, but nonetheless, you are good."

She turned to go.

"GM," I said sharply, "you've said that you can protect us, but that wasn't true that one night, was it?"

She turned back. "To what night are you referring?"

Since GM and I had returned from Russia, neither one of us had spoken of Gleb Mstislav's attack on our house in October—an attack that had forced us to flee the country. GM hadn't spoken of it because she wished to pretend it had never happened. I never spoke of it because I knew it was taboo.

"I'm talking about that night in October," I said, "when Gleb Mstislav broke into our house and tried to kill us. And you recognized him. You said you did. You weren't able to stop him then. What if something like that happens again?"

I expected GM to be angry, but instead her expression softened.

"Yes, that was a frightening night, wasn't it? I confess that I didn't react as I should have done. For a time, I accepted Galina's nonsensical explanation that Gleb had returned from the dead. I, like many, had believed that he was dead. But then I came to my senses. I realized that he'd been in hiding—that he'd allowed us all to believe he was dead so that he could continue his criminal activities without interference. And I now believe that he must have been under the influence of drugs that night—hence his ghastly appearance. You need fear him no longer, solnyshko. He's gone. He's in the family crypt now. The police even opened it up to look."

She became brisk. "Now get up, get ready, and come downstairs for breakfast. There will be no more time for fears today."

She turned and left the room, closing the door firmly behind her.

I found GM's attitude toward Gleb Mstislav to be curious. She believed that Gleb had been walking around alive and well in October, but had not been surprised when the police later opened the crypt and found him lying in it dead. She didn't seem to have wondered how he had gone from one state to the other without interruption. Perhaps she thought his son Timofei had killed him—though that was not one of the crimes he had been accused of. But I supposed, ultimately, that GM didn't wonder about it because she didn't want to.

I couldn't really blame her for that—reanimated corpses were not a pleasant topic.

And she was right. Gleb was gone now. I had seen him wrestled back into death with my own eyes.

I stood up and stretched. I looked down at my supplies and wondered if I could try stashing just a few things in my room for my next vigil.

I was relieved that GM and I had survived the night, but I was far from easy in my mind.

Why hadn't I been attacked?

And who had placed a price on my head?

I could think of only two people who could possibly want me dead—Gleb and Timofei Mstislav.

And both of them were dead themselves.

But I knew only too well that the dead could come back.

Chapter Eleven

I showered and dressed and then returned to my room, where I sat for a long time just staring at a patch of sunlight on the floor. I knew I had to move—I had to think. I had to come up with a plan for guarding the house. But I just kept staring at the sunlight. It seemed so normal, so safe.

Everything my life was not.

Eventually, I forced myself to move. I got up and took all my things downstairs where GM supervised me as I put them away. Then I ate breakfast.

After that, I worked on homework, cleaned my room, ate other meals—the rest of Sunday passed quickly.

All too soon it was night again—and I didn't have a plan to fight what waited for me in the dark.

I lit my candle and sat up as I had the night before, waiting to hear footsteps on the stairs, watching my door to see if it would be opened by an intruder. But despite my best efforts, I fell asleep again, and I was awakened on Monday morning by the insistent beeping of my alarm.

I looked around my room in groggy surprise. I had survived another night.

I should have felt relieved, but instead a new fear settled over me. The house was no longer protected—I knew for a fact that no one watched over it.

But there was a price on my head, and at least one of the would-be collectors—Anton—knew that I was now alone.

So what was stopping any of them from coming in?

Were they planning something worse than the attack that I already feared?

I shivered.

I supposed I would be safe enough at school—there would be too many witnesses around for someone like Joshua or Anton to attempt anything. But I had to be alert all the same.

I got ready for school quickly, and as I crossed the room to go downstairs, I was seized suddenly by a sharp pain as William crowded into my thoughts. Now that the reality of his abandonment had truly sunk in, I was left with an agony that seemed to grow worse each day. And along with that deepening hurt went the continuing realization that I still loved him—that I would always love him.

I felt emptiness stretching before me, as if I were falling and would fall forever.

William did not love me.

Pain continued to wash over me, but I knew I had to find a way to get on with the day. I worked to contain the hurt, to force it into a confined space and make it manageable. There were still other people in my life to think of—and I had to look out for GM.

I reined the pain in and resolved again not to think of William.

As I went downstairs, I happened to catch sight of some downy white flakes fluttering past the window.

I felt momentarily cheered—I always loved to see snow.

I didn't eat much at breakfast, and I didn't protest when GM insisted on driving me to school once again.

She set off quickly, and the world outside my window turned into a white blur. I closed my eyes and leaned back against the headrest.

After a second night of waiting up to guard against intruders, I was tired.

I must have fallen asleep briefly, for when I opened my eyes we were already gliding to a stop in front of the school.

GM eyed me closely. "Are you well, solnyshko? You didn't look well yesterday, and you don't appear to have improved any this morning. Perhaps you haven't recovered yet from your day out in the cold on Saturday."

I gave her a smile and attempted to appear cheerful. "I'm fine. I really am."

"You will call me if you start to feel worse?"

"Yes, I will. Thanks, GM."

I moved to get out of the car.

"And call me when school is over, so I can pick you up."

"I'll give you a call," I said.

She nodded approvingly. "Now hurry into the school. Don't linger out in the cold air."

I couldn't help but smile a little at GM's fussing, and as I got out of the car, I gave her a little wave to reassure her that everything was all right. Once GM realized that I was, in fact, headed into the school, she sped off.

As I walked across the schoolyard, I carefully avoided glancing over at the picnic table where Charisse, Branden, and Simon tended to gather, just in case they were there. I realized that I wasn't really in the mood to see any of them. They'd been set against William, and now that I knew for sure that he was gone, I didn't feel up to talking to them. They didn't know he was gone, of course, and they certainly hadn't made him go, but I still didn't want to see them.

I knew that if they found out that William had left me, that they'd be happy.

And I realized right after that that I'd thought of William without meaning to. I resolved not to let it happen again.

I drifted through the first half of the day, hardly hearing anything that was said in any of my classes, and I felt little except for a distant dread that lunch was coming—I wondered if I should skip lunch and avoid seeing my friends altogether.

When lunch arrived, I decided I had better face them and get the worst of seeing them over with.

They don't know what happened with William, I told myself, *and you don't have to tell them.*

I bent my steps toward the cafeteria.

Simon smiled when he saw me, and we went through the line together. I didn't really notice what was being served, and even though Simon kept up a cheerful line of conversation, I couldn't really focus on what he was saying.

All I could think about was how happy he would be if he knew that William was gone. I realized I couldn't blame Simon for that—especially considering what he thought William was like—but I couldn't help but feel something angry and unpleasant toward him. It felt a lot like resentment.

Simon and I sat down at a table with Charisse and Branden, and even though Charisse smiled at me, and Branden started telling a story about something funny that had happened in one of his classes—I couldn't help but feel some resentment toward them, too.

At one point during Branden's story, I looked up to see that Charisse was staring at me. Her eyes were searching and concerned.

I looked away quickly.

"So what do you think about that?"

I blinked. Branden was staring at me now, smiling.

Simon was looking at me also, but he seemed to be worried like Charisse was.

"Katie," Branden said, still grinning, "how about it? What do you think?"

"I'm sorry, Branden," I said. "I didn't really hear what you were saying. My mind's been somewhere else."

"I'll say. You missed a great story, even if I do say so myself. I was explaining why there are so many Russian immigrants in this town."

"What's that about Russian immigrants?" I asked.

Branden laughed. "You really have been checked out. I was telling you that this area was a hotbed for the Russian mob a little over ten years ago—that's how families like yours and the Neverovs and others came to be here."

"Branden, that's terrible," Charisse said. "Katie's grandmother is no mobster. And I'm sure Irina's family isn't full of criminals, either."

Branden shrugged. "You thought it was funny a minute ago."

"No, you thought it was funny a minute ago," Simon said. "We weren't quite so amused."

"Whatever," Branden replied. "It's a funny story no matter what you say."

Branden and Simon continued to argue, but I was struck by what Branden had said. It had never occurred to me to wonder how GM had come to settle here in Elspeth's Grove, and now that I knew Irina's family was from Krov like we were, it seemed to me an odd coincidence that both of us should have found our way to the same small town.

"What do you mean the Russian mob was here?" I asked abruptly.

Both Simon and Branden turned to look at me.

"He doesn't mean anything," Simon said.

"I mean moonshine," Branden replied, grinning. "Illegal hooch."

"Like during prohibition?" I asked. "What would the point of that be? It's not like alcohol is illegal."

"No," Branden said. "But you do have to have a license to sell it, and a lot of people don't like to go to the trouble of getting one—especially not college kids."

An image of my grandmother selling bottles of homebrewed alcohol out of the trunk of her car flashed through my mind, and I had to work really hard to suppress a sudden laugh. I couldn't think of anything less likely.

I shook my head. "Even if people were selling alcohol illegally around here, how would that attract the Russian mob? I would imagine it's too small a business. It wouldn't attract criminals on an international level."

Branden looked smug. "You see, I'm being clever."

"You? Clever?" Simon snorted.

"Yes, me," Branden replied. "I'm giving the story to you in pieces, just like the cops got it. The illegal hooch operation was actually a front."

Simon snorted again. "You don't know what you're talking about. You're supposed to use a *legal* business as a front—the point is to *not* attract the attention of the police. If your business is illegal to begin with, the police are going to come looking for you. That's exactly what you don't want."

"That depends on what it is you're trying to do. The mob wanted to attract the attention of the police."

"That doesn't make any sense," Simon said.

"Sure it does," Branden said complacently, as if he'd been dying to make exactly that point. "You set up something illegal but minor, let the police find it and shut it down, and then you settle down to be good, law-abiding citizens, and people stop wondering why there are so many immigrants from the same part of Russia here. And it doesn't seem so strange when they start bringing more and more relatives over—because they've been assimilated, you know. And what's more natural than that families should come over so they could all be together?"

"So what are you saying?" Simon asked.

"I'm saying that they wanted to lull the cops into a false sense of security—the cops think they've taught them a lesson, but the cops were really just fooled by a blind. Now the mobsters are free to pursue their real plan."

"Which is?" Simon asked.

"Mining."

"Mining?" Simon repeated scornfully. "I think someone would notice that."

"You don't know what they're mining for," Branden said.

"What are they mining for?" Simon asked. "And where are they keeping all their equipment? It's pretty hard to hide one of those shaft jumbo drills."

"No one knows what they're mining for—it's something they want to keep secret. And apparently they don't need any equipment—at least not other than the old-fashioned kind. They're digging."

"Digging," Simon said.

"Yes."

"Then why did you say mining?"

"Because they're digging for something that's buried very deep," Branden said.

"Like buried treasure?" Simon asked.

"Exactly."

"But no one knows what it is?" Simon asked.

"That's right."

"Where did you hear all this genius stuff?"

"I already told you way back at the beginning."

"Well, remind me."

"I heard it in Social Studies class."

"And this was presented as fact—that members of the Russian mob moved here to search for buried treasure?"

"Well, it wasn't presented as fact exactly—more as an example of the types of rumors that spring up around groups of immigrants."

"So, it was presented as something that wasn't true?"

"Yeah," Branden said. "You know you're taking this way too seriously. This was supposed to be funny."

"It's offensive," Simon said.

"Katie doesn't seem to be upset," Branden replied. "So I think you should relax."

"Maybe Katie isn't offended, but I am," Simon said.

"On Katie's behalf?"

"On Katie's behalf."

Simon and Branden continued to quarrel.

I knew the argument wasn't serious, and I saw Charisse looking on in tolerant amusement, so I just let them keep talking. Simon and Branden typically didn't listen to me when I tried to interrupt one of their arguments anyway.

I didn't really believe Branden's tale about the Russian bootleggers, but once again I was struck by the odd coincidence that both my grandmother and the Neverovs had found their way from Krov, Russia to the small town of Elspeth's Grove. And according to Branden's rumor, there were others. I didn't know of any other Russian families in the area, but that didn't mean they weren't around. I wondered if those families had come from Krov, too—and if so, how did they all find our town?

I thought suddenly of the letters GM had been receiving, and a half-formed suspicion rose in my mind—could GM be up to something that involved the Russian families in Elspeth's Grove? She was certainly up to something that she didn't want me to know about.

I pushed the thought away quickly—the very idea that GM would be involved in something illegal was ridiculous.

I agreed with Simon that an illegal mining operation was as unlikely as a moonshine operation—he was right that there was no place to hide the equipment. But the idea that there could be something of value underground gave me pause.

I thought back to the strange, frozen man I had seen emerging from the cave in the Old Grove after I had wandered away from Bryony's party. I thought back to October, too, to my own journey through that same cave in the dark when I had followed the twisting white smoke and found Gleb Mstislav. Gleb and his son Timofei had been taking shelter there during the day when Gleb was most vulnerable, but I wondered now if there had been any other reason for their presence there. Could they have been looking for something?

I remembered with a sudden jolt how William had found me in the cave, spying on Gleb and Timofei, and had pulled me out to safety. I remembered his face as he had stood in the forest, blocking my path to the cave, determined not to let me go back down into it.

I could see him so clearly that it was almost as if he were standing before me. I felt a sharp pang of loss once again, and the feelings I had been holding at bay all day welled up within me, threatening to overwhelm me. Why had he left me? Why had he gone back to Russia without saying a word? The pain was so fierce that I felt tears stinging my eyes. Though I tried to block it out, I wanted to see William again more than I wanted anything, and there was no way I could do that. I could never, ever see him again.

Or could I? It suddenly occurred to me that GM had asked me to go to Russia over Christmas—and I had refused back when William was still with me. But maybe I *could* go. The idea seized me strongly. If I could see William one last time—hear his voice one last time—even if he turned away from me—it would be worth it.

"Katie, are you okay?"

Charisse was staring at me now, as were Branden and Simon, who had apparently stopped arguing.

"Are you okay?" she asked again.

"Yes, I'm fine," I said. My cheeks felt warm, and I could feel that my heart was racing. I made an effort to be calmer. "Why would you think I wasn't okay?"

"It's just that you suddenly got this crazy look on your face," Charisse said. "You kind of looked like you might go running out of the room. It wasn't a normal look."

"I'm fine. Really." I hadn't realized how unguarded I had allowed myself to be. "I—"

I tried to come up with an explanation, but nothing came to me. "I'm—just fine."

Simon and Charisse exchanged worried looks, and I felt a flash of irritation—no doubt they thought my strange mood had something to do with William. They were right, but it didn't make the situation any less irritating.

Branden shot a glance at Simon and Charisse. "Lighten up, you two. If Katie says she's fine, she's fine." He turned to me. "I make weird faces all the time, too. You go ahead and make the faces you need to make. Don't worry about it."

Branden's support was unexpected, and he made a face that was so ridiculous that I couldn't help but laugh.

"Katie," Simon said ominously, "you'd better be really careful if you're doing anything that Branden thinks is normal."

After lunch, I waited anxiously for the day to end. I even considered skipping the rest of my classes and just heading home—something I would never do under ordinary circumstances. But I knew GM would likely be at home working and would be furious that I had skipped both school and her escort. And that would hardly help me when I made my case for going to Russia.

GM had been eager and excited about the trip before, but what if she no longer wanted to go? What if she demanded an explanation for my changing my mind? I certainly couldn't tell her that I was going to look for William. If she wanted a reason, I'd have to hope that a good one came to me.

At long last, the day ended, and I called GM. She picked me up, and we rode home in silence. I figured I would wait until we got home to spring my request. For her part, GM seemed to have something on her mind.

We reached home, and both of us went into the kitchen—I was in the habit of having a snack when I came home.

Today, however, food could wait.

"GM, I need to talk to you," I said breathlessly.

"And I need to talk to you." Her tone was formal, and her expression had gone carefully neutral—I knew that meant trouble.

"Is there any chance I can talk to you first?" I asked.

"No," GM replied. "Have a seat, please."

I sank into a nearby chair, and I felt my chances of going to Russia slipping away. If she was already angry, then—

I didn't allow myself to complete the thought. I waited uncomfortably to hear what she had to say.

"It's that boy, isn't it?" GM asked, her voice clear and cold.

I felt a flash of panic run through me. "How did you—"

I stopped before I could say anything incriminating.

"How did I know? Of course I knew. I see you moping around here. I see you start at every sound. And you've been acting strange at night—especially the night you sat up with the matches—and it's been getting worse lately. That boy has done something, hasn't he?"

I relaxed a little—she didn't know that William had abandoned me and gone to Russia. But I was still on dangerous ground.

"William's been a bit distant lately," I said slowly.

"What's happened?" GM asked sharply. "Has he broken your heart? I don't want you to be unhappy."

Pain lanced through me. I wished she hadn't assessed my feelings quite so accurately.

"You said you would give him a chance," I said.

"A chance is not a pass for everything."

I made an effort to smile. "I'm fine, really." It seemed to me that I'd been saying that a lot lately. "I'll be all right—I promise."

GM stared at me for a long moment, and then she sighed heavily. "I suppose you have to go through things like this. We all do. So I'll step back for now. But I did warn that boy. If he does the wrong thing, I will have my revenge on him."

GM's tone was so menacing that I couldn't help smiling for real.

"You laugh, but I am serious," she said.

"I know," I replied. I didn't doubt GM's mettle for a moment.

She took a deep breath.

"Now, what was it that you wanted to talk about?"

I felt my nerves coming back. I tried to think of a good way to broach the idea of a trip to Russia. But nothing was coming to me.

GM eyed me closely. "What is it, Katie? You look uneasy. Is this about that boy? You just said you were fine, but you fill me with doubts again."

Her perceptiveness was starting to unnerve me. I wished she wasn't so close to the truth.

"Is it okay for me to change my mind?" I blurted out suddenly.

GM brightened. "About the boy? Is that what has been troubling you? Yes, of course, solnyshko. You are perfectly free to leave him."

"No, that's not what I meant. Can we still go to Russia?"

GM stared at me in surprise. "What are you saying? You would like to go to Russia?"

"Yes—I would like to go to Russia."

GM's face lit up. "For Christmas?"

"Yes. For Christmas."

GM stood up and pulled me into a hug. "Yes, solnyshko. Of course we can go to Russia for Christmas."

I was stunned. GM was seldom so effusive. She took a step back and beamed at me. "I will make plans at once."

"You're not upset?" I asked. "This is kind of last minute."

"No, no, my dear child, I am not upset at all."

My heart leaped. GM had really said yes. We were going to Russia. I was going to see William again. Nothing was going to keep me from him—even if he no longer loved me.

GM continued. "Christmas in Russia is just the thing for you. I have no doubt that it'll bring you out of the melancholy mood you have fallen into. And it'll be wonderful for you to finally see Russia without that horrible cloud of superstition hanging over it. This trip will be different from the last one." She waved her hands. "Go, have some food now. Refresh yourself. I have arrangements I must make right away."

She hurried out of the room.

As I sat at the kitchen table, eating a snack, I thought over GM's words. Unfortunately, I knew that the cloud of superstition that she thought had lifted was still to be found hanging over the town of Krov.

It suddenly occurred to me that I had just volunteered myself for something very dangerous.

Innokenti had wanted me to return to Krov, and I knew that if he discovered I was in town, that he would most definitely come to find me. I also knew that the price on my head would attract other vampires to me—vampires that might even be worse than Anton or Joshua Martin.

There was even a chance that my cousin Odette would come after me.

But then I thought of the delight in GM's eyes when she'd realized that I wanted to go to Russia. She was really, truly happy to be going back. She wanted this trip, and now, so did I.

I realized that I would have to be very, very careful in my quest to see William.

I was happy to be going, I really was. But I had to wonder.

What had I just done?

Chapter Twelve

That night I sat on my bed, far too wound up to sleep.

GM had purchased our plane tickets to Russia after dinner. We were going to leave as soon as my winter break started, and we were going to fly into Moscow before heading on to Krov.

I had sat with GM in her office as she'd purchased the tickets online, and she'd chattered to me effusively both during and after the purchase. She was excited about taking me around Moscow and showing me the sights, I knew, but there had been another light in her eyes that had made her appear feverish and overexcited.

GM was clearly happy—perhaps a little too happy.

And so I was left to wonder if I had made the right decision. I would get a chance to look for William, but I was also taking GM with me into a potentially dangerous situation.

And, of course, there was still the night to contend with. Though my vampire attackers hadn't materialized so far, I knew that they were still out there.

So, GM and I would go to Russia—*if* I lived long enough.

With that cheerful thought, I put out the light and slipped under my covers.

I didn't have any plan to deal with intruders if they did come, but so far staying awake prepared to fight hadn't accomplished anything apart from leaving me exhausted in the morning. So I decided to try to sleep and trust to luck. I hoped that if I were attacked, I would be able to improvise—something.

I closed my eyes and tried to clear my mind, but relaxation eluded me.

I got up and crossed the dark room. I went to my window and pulled back the curtains. The street below was quiet, and the night seemed innocent. But I knew that there were more mysteries lurking in the night than most people dreamed of.

I thought of the man encased in ice, who had emerged from the cave and then vanished.

I thought of Cormac, who had appeared out of nowhere and saved me from Anton.

I wondered for a moment if I had imagined them both—but I knew the puzzle they presented wouldn't be solved that easily. I had been through too many strange things to truly doubt what I had seen.

So what did the two of them want?

I had never heard any tales of a man encased in ice. I wondered if he could be after me like Joshua Martin and Anton were. And what of Cormac? Could he be after me, too?

But Cormac had come in response to my call—the call that used to bring William to me. That didn't seem like the action of someone who meant to harm me.

Would the call work if I tried it again? Would it bring Cormac to me if I used it?

The idea took hold of me very strongly, and I decided to try it out. If I could see Cormac again—talk to him—maybe I could find out something about what was going on.

I hesitated to call him in my room. His presence, should he appear, would be very difficult to explain to GM. So I decided to wait until she went to bed and then try to call him outside in the yard behind the house.

That was the same place where I'd called William to me for the very first time.

My heart fluttered a little at the thought of him, and a tiny hope sprang up that this time William might appear instead of Cormac.

Maybe there had been some kind of interference the last time I'd used the call. Maybe I wouldn't have to go all the way to Russia to look for William.

Maybe he would come here.

Don't get too excited, I warned myself. *You'll only feel worse if William doesn't show up.*

But once the possibility of seeing William had occurred to me, it proved to be a difficult idea to shake. So, I waited anxiously, my ears straining to hear every sound the house made, until I heard GM come up the stairs and settle in for the night.

Then I slipped downstairs as noiselessly as I could and let myself out the back door. I felt a flash of panic as I stepped out into the starless night. I realized suddenly that going outside unprotected when I was the prey of vampires was unwise. But I would risk it to see William again.

William won't come, I told myself sternly, as I walked across the backyard, feeling the chill of the night wrap itself around my body. *Don't even think about him.*

But think about him I did. I stood still in the frozen night, my heart beating wildly. And as I whispered the words, "Katie Wickliff summons you," I felt my breath quicken, and a sharp stab of nervousness that wasn't entirely unpleasant ran through me.

What if I was about to see him again?

I waited for the rush of air that preceded his arrival. I waited for William.

I searched the dark for his long, lean form.

But nothing stirred in the night.

I told myself not to panic—perhaps I had whispered too softly. I spoke the words again, my heart beating even more wildly than before.

Time passed, and I felt the cold biting more deeply into my skin.

William was not coming.

I whispered the words a third time, and I felt tears stinging my eyes.

No William. No Cormac, either. No one listening in the night, no one watching over me—no one was there to keep the creatures who were after me at bay.

But worst of all, there was no William.

Tears began to fall, and I brushed them away. I felt my hand shaking, and I tried to tell myself that it was only the cold that caused it. I had known that William was gone—I had *known* that he wouldn't come when I called, and yet I had allowed myself to believe—

The tears began to fall more fiercely, and I could feel them hot and burning as they ran down my cheek and neck. A cry escaped from me, and it sounded unnaturally loud on the night air. I quickly pressed my hand against my lips. My other hand I wrapped around my waist.

I wanted him to come back. I wanted to see William again, even if he didn't want to see me. But more than anything, I wanted to see him as he'd once been—I wanted to see the William who looked at me with love in his eyes.

Was it possible that William—the one I loved and the one who loved me—still existed? Or was I going to Russia to search for someone who'd grown cold inside?

He'd vanished without explanation. What if I found him, and he finally said the terrible words to me that I feared? Could I bear to stand before him and have him tell me he didn't love me and he wanted me to go?

The tears continued to fall, and I knew that I would risk fresh hurt to see him again.

I would find him. I would see him one last time.

I went back into the house and locked the door behind me.

I climbed into bed, shivering and grateful for the warmth of my covers. I had redoubled my resolve to see William again. I just hoped that those who stalked the dark for me would let me live until that day arrived.

In the morning, I was restless, eager to leave for Russia—eager to start my search. But I still had ten days of school left.

I didn't know how I'd get through it.

I hurried down to breakfast, and as I ate, I noticed that GM was watching me carefully.

"You don't look well, Katie."

I had barely glanced into the mirror before I'd come down, but I had a feeling that my eyes probably showed signs of the crying that I'd done last night.

"I'm fine, GM," I said in the most reassuring tone I could muster, "I really am."

"You're not ill?"

"No."

"Are you worried about school? I know your mid-term exams will be soon."

GM was right—I did have exams coming up. And I hadn't been working as I hard as I should have been. I would make an effort to keep my mind clear of distractions and focus on my schoolwork.

"Is it school, solnyshko?" GM prompted when I didn't answer right away.

"No, I'm not worried about school."

GM sighed. "Still that boy," she murmured.

She stood up and began to clear her dishes away. "I think it's good for you that we'll be going away soon. You'll find that the air of Russia can be healing. And there isn't so much urgency this time."

GM paused, a dish held in her hand. She seemed to lose her train of thought for a moment.

I wondered if she was thinking back to our first visit together. And I wondered once more what she allowed herself to remember about it.

"You'll have a good time on this trip," she said at last, her voice dreamy and distant.

She blinked and seemed to come to herself again. "You may walk to school this morning if you wish. I think you'll be safe—these last few days have been quiet. And I have some errands to run today—things I have to pick up before our trip."

She gave me an apologetic smile. "I may not be home when you get back from school today."

I couldn't help but smile myself—GM was always there when I got home from school. Coming home to an empty house would be a novelty.

"I think I'll be fine," I said. "A few hours alone won't hurt me."

GM waved a hand at me. "Just leave your things on the table. There's no need for you to clear up this morning."

I finished breakfast and hurried out into the cold morning. I wasn't looking forward to ten more days of school—but I'd get through them.

Once at school, I walked quickly through the yard without looking around—I didn't want to catch sight of Simon or Charisse or Branden. I'd feel obligated to stop and talk to them.

And I didn't want to talk to anyone right now.

I hurried to my locker and then hurried to the cafeteria, where I buried my nose in a book. I would throw myself into studying and focus only on my exams. Time would pass more quickly, and I would fulfill my responsibilities. I really liked my classes anyway, and my grades were important to me. I'd been guilty of letting things slide lately.

I became immersed in my reading and was startled when the warning bell rang.

I did more studying in homeroom, and when I ran into Branden and Charisse in second-period English, I smiled and waved and went to my desk to do more reading. I felt bad, but I genuinely did need time to catch up.

I realized it might be best for me to study at lunch for the next few days, too.

So, when it was time for lunch, I hurried through the line and took my tray to a table in the corner. Then I opened a book and read as I ate.

A short time later, there was a crash that shook the table. I looked up, startled.

A dark green backpack had suddenly appeared in the middle of my table. The backpack was swept off the table and onto the floor with surprising swiftness, and Branden sat heavily in the plastic chair next to me.

"So, why are you avoiding us?" he asked without preamble.

"What was that?" I was a bit dazed after being jolted out of my reading so abruptly.

Charisse took a seat next to Branden. Simon sat down on my other side.

"Simon thinks you're angry because of what I said the other day," Branden said. "About the Russian immigrants in this area and the bootlegging and so on and so forth. Are you angry about that?"

"No," I said. And it was true—I wasn't.

Branden held out a hand triumphantly. "See? I told you."

Simon ignored Branden. "Katie, you can't get hung up on the crazy things Branden says. You know he doesn't know what he's talking about half the time—or ever, for that matter."

"Hey," Branden said.

"Simon," I said, "I'm not upset about anything Branden or anybody else said. Really. Honestly."

Simon looked at me searchingly. "Then why have you been avoiding us?"

"I'm not. I need to study. I haven't—"

I felt a little stab of regret as I looked at the concerned faces ranged around the table.

Truthfully, I had been angry with them, and I knew it. I still resented the fact that they would be happy if they found out that William had left me. I'd told myself before that my friends were not responsible for what William had done. But the resentment had remained.

I really did need to study, but it was also a way to escape from them—and from thoughts of William.

Ultimately, though, they were my friends.

I would try to stop blaming them for a situation they couldn't help.

"You're right," I said. "I'm sorry. I guess I've been trapped in my own head lately."

"I understand that you may need to study," Simon said, "but too much studying can be a bad thing, too. You should at least take a break when you're eating."

Branden reached over and shut my textbook. "Time to relax. A little. It's not like we get nearly enough time for lunch anyway."

"Have lunch with us like you usually do," Charisse said. "You can at least give us that."

"I will," I said.

And I did make an attempt to be sociable, but I found that my thoughts kept drifting back to my trip to Russia.

I wanted—needed—to get back to studying—if only to keep myself sane.

Mercifully, lunch ended at last, and I picked up my books, relieved to be free to lose myself in them once again. I felt bad about avoiding my friends—I really did—but I could never explain to them what was bothering me. I couldn't tell them that danger stalked me in the night—they'd never believe that. And I certainly couldn't tell them that I was planning to search for William.

As I went out into the hallway, I felt a soft tug on my sleeve. I turned to see Bryony walking beside me.

"Can I talk to you for a moment?" she said quietly. "I wanted to ask you something—without the others around."

"Yes, of course," I said.

Bryony and I drew apart from the crowd.

She looked around, hesitating. "I was wondering how you—how you've been doing—with the ghost's message and everything. I know it's weird for me to keep bringing it up."

I was quick to reassure her. "It's okay. I didn't mind the message. Really."

"Did anything—"

She looked around again and lowered her voice. "Did anything happen? Did you hear the singing she warned about?"

I realized that I didn't know how to answer her. Had I heard singing? I'd felt a strange, enchanting softness in the night air and an intense longing to draw nearer to it. And I'd felt that feeling again when I'd seen the strange man encased in ice emerging from the cave.

Had he been singing to me? I'd wondered that before.

"Honestly, Bryony, I'm not entirely sure. But I did see something—or actually, someone—strange. It was on the day you had your birthday party."

Her eyes widened in alarm. "What happened?"

"I saw a man with tightly closed eyes who was entirely covered in ice. He came out of the cave in the Old Grove, and I felt the strangest feeling—I felt like he was drawing me to him."

No sooner had I finished speaking than I began to feel foolish. Bryony would think I'd imagined the whole thing.

I didn't know why I had said anything.

But Bryony didn't laugh or look shocked—she just looked more concerned. "Did you recognize the man?"

"No, I didn't," I said. "Have you heard of something like this happening before?"

"No."

I began to feel foolish again. "It was probably nothing. I can't be sure what I saw."

"No, I believe you," Bryony said. "I know you're level-headed and smart. I don't think you're making anything up. Besides, I've learned that when the ghost sends a message it's important to pay attention to everything that happens—no matter how bizarre those things are."

"I'm glad you don't think I'm crazy."

"No," she said. Then she looked away in thought. I realized now why I had spoken so easily about the strange man—why I had told Bryony something I would never tell any of my other friends. There was something deeply calm about her—it really was a unique quality.

"Katie," Bryony said after a moment, "if you don't mind, I'm going to tell my grandmother about what you saw. Maybe she can find out something further from the ghost. But doing so is a little tricky."

"Yes, sure. Go ahead. I need all the help I can get at this point."

"I'll go over to her house tonight, then. Hang in there, Katie. And try to ignore any more strange feelings or 'singing' if you hear it. I'm sure it can't be good for you."

Bryony moved off again into the crowd, and I went on to class.

It seemed to me that my conversation with Bryony should have left me feeling more worried—she *had* said she was going to consult a ghost about me—but I actually felt a little relieved. It was good to speak to someone who would actually listen.

I thought then of Galina—someone else who had listened to me. I wondered if I would get to see her once we reached Krov. I was under the impression that GM's attitude toward her had thawed—and it occurred to me that she might know something about the vampires who were after me.

And she might even know where I could find William.

I spent the rest of the day absorbed in my schoolwork as much as possible. Any spare moments I had I spent reading or going over my notes. I resolved to spend the rest of the night studying and working, and I realized I was looking forward to being current with my schoolwork again. When the final bell rang, I jumped up from my seat and hurried to my locker. I didn't want to run into anyone I'd have to talk to.

A light snow had just begun to fall as I exited the schoolyard, and I paused just outside the fence to watch it fall. I held out my palm and let a few flakes settle there. The snow was cool and damp against my skin, and I watched as it dissolved, soaking in.

I'd always liked snow and the peaceful atmosphere that came with it. Snow seemed to make the whole world quieter. As I continued to watch it fall, I felt my own internal turmoil subside. I walked home slowly, enjoying the snow, allowing the stillness of it to soak into my skin like the snowflakes had.

When I reached home, I noticed that GM's red sports car was missing from the driveway. So her errands had kept her out late, just as she had anticipated.

I let myself into the house and went to the kitchen. I set my backpack down and got myself an apple and a glass of milk.

I was seldom in the house alone, and the solitude was something of a relief—I didn't have to pretend anything for anyone at the moment. I could be completely myself.

I ate leisurely and then just sat for a moment, listening to the quiet, occasional creaking of the house. But as much as I enjoyed the peace, I knew I had homework to do. With a certain degree of reluctance, I got up.

As I rinsed out my glass, I thought I heard a sound in the hall. I turned to look, but no one was there. I realized I must have just heard the house give an unusually loud creak. I'd heard enough of those in the night to know it meant nothing.

I finished clearing up, and as I picked up my backpack, I thought I heard another sound—like someone moving around. This time it seemed to be coming from the living room.

"GM, is that you?"

Maybe I'd just been so lost in my own thoughts that I hadn't heard her come in.

I walked into the living room.

Anton was standing by the table, picking up picture frames and examining my family photos.

I realized with horror that I was seeing my brief vision from about a week ago come to life.

I felt my backpack slide off my shoulder.

Anton turned to look at me.

"Hello, Sunshine."

I felt a strong desire to run, and I decided to indulge it.

But Anton quickly moved to block my way, forcing me to stumble backward. I tripped over my backpack and fell to the floor.

Anton was soon beside me, reaching out a hand.

I shied away from his hand and found my feet again.

"What are you doing here?" I asked. My voice sounded high and frightened.

"I was trying to help you up."

I backed away from him. "I meant what are you doing in my house?"

"I came to see you." He waved a hand toward the photos. "Nice pictures."

"You have to leave," I said.

He smiled. "No, I don't."

"My grandmother will be home soon."

"She won't be home soon enough." Anton sat on the couch. "Let's have a little talk."

He patted the cushion next to him.

I ran into the kitchen, hoping to reach the back door, but Anton blocked my way before I reached it.

I turned, trying to get away from him, but no matter how I moved, he remained in front of me, blocking my escape.

I stood still.

"What do you want?" I tried to keep my voice from shaking.

"I told you I want to talk."

"What would we talk about? You tried to kill me."

"I did *not* try to kill you. I was just trying to kidnap you. Then I was going to turn you over to some other people—who probably *would* have killed you. But I wasn't going to do it myself."

"That's not really any better," I said.

"No, I suppose from your perspective it wouldn't be."

"Is that what you're here for this time? To kidnap me?"

"No. I've already told you why I'm here. No offense, but you're a little slow on the uptake today."

Anton continued to stand solidly in my way, staring at me.

He wasn't going away.

"You said you wanted to talk," I said after an uncomfortable moment.

"Yes."

"What do you want to talk about?"

"I don't want you to go."

"What does that mean?" I asked.

"I don't want you to go to Russia for Christmas."

I felt a fresh stab of panic. "How do you know about that?"

"I've got pretty good hearing."

"You've been spying on me?"

"Yes. And let me tell you, it was a good thing. There are a *lot* of people after you. It's been a chore keeping them away from you."

I was stunned. "You've been keeping them away?"

"Yes."

"Why? Why would you do that?"

Anton simply smiled at me. "Don't go to Russia."

"But you were with Innokenti when he practically ordered me to go back. And now you don't want that?"

Anton shrugged. "I changed my mind."

"What's wrong with my going to Russia?" I asked.

Anton shook his head. "I know you think that you'll find William, and he'll come back to you. But you're wrong. He's not who you think he is."

"You don't know William," I said.

"On the contrary, you're the one who doesn't know William."

"I trust him." I said the words before I even thought about them— but I realized they were true.

"You trust him?" Anton asked. "Even though he's left you? Even though I told you he went off with Innokenti?"

"I don't know why William's gone," I said. "But I'll see him again."

Anton tilted his head to one side. "What if I told you that I knew why William had left?"

Suddenly I felt panicked, and my heart began to beat wildly. I stood, speechless, afraid of what Anton might say—but I'd just said myself that I trusted William.

What could Anton possibly say that could be worse than what had already happened?

"Why did he leave?" I asked at last.

"William left because Innokenti brought him an offer."

I stared into Anton's eyes unflinchingly.

He continued. "The offer was from the Sídh. They told him they could remove the—as they put it—'vampire contagion' from his body. They could make him fully Sídh again. They would take him back. But only if he gave you up forever."

I suddenly felt like I couldn't breathe. I knew how much William hated the part of himself that was a vampire. I knew how much he wanted his old life back.

Anton leaned closer, placing his lips next to my ear. "There's a lot you don't know about William. Memories are important to creatures like us. They're one of the few things that can be used to bribe us, and anyone who can manipulate them can command us. William will have his memories as a vampire erased and his memories of his life with the Sídh returned. And for this he gave you up."

My vision began to swim, and it was even harder for me to breathe.

William's memories meant everything to him.

Anton's voice seemed to come from a distance. "Are you all right, Sunshine?"

I felt light-headed.

"Sit down," Anton said, steering me toward a chair. His fingers were shockingly cold—so much so that the touch of them forced me to draw in my breath sharply.

"You understand about William now, don't you?" Anton asked quietly. He kneeled beside me.

"You—you're trying to help me?" I asked cautiously.

"Yes. Like I said, William isn't who you think he is. Besides, there are rumors someone's building an army over in Krov, and that destroying you is one of their aims. Stay here. You'll be safe here."

"Safe?"

"Well, safer."

"Why would you want to help me? You said yourself that you were going to turn me over to—to—"

I looked at him. "Who were you going to turn me over to?"

"You know, the reward for turning you in is pretty good," Anton said, ignoring my question. "Remember what I said about memories? Well, the Sídh aren't the only ones who can manipulate them. I was offered a chance to blot out everything I've done over the last few centuries—and that was an offer I fully intended to take advantage of. But that day in the forest when I caught you, I changed my mind."

"Why?"

"You tried to face me—not very successfully I might add—but you *did* try. Most people do a lot of begging and crying. You did do your share of running, but no crying. And just now, you did it again. No crying. In fact, you even tried to order me out, even though you were clearly scared and in no position to give me orders of any kind. You're different from any other victim of mine."

"Victim?"

"Well, potential victim. Now past tense."

Anton was staring at me steadily. His dark eyes were mesmerizing.

"You're oddly intriguing," he said.

The front door slammed, and the spell he was weaving was broken.

"GM!" I cried. "GM, I'm in here!"

I stood up quickly, stumbling over my chair.

There was a rush of air, and I spun around.

Anton was gone.

Chapter Thirteen

W hat's wrong, Katie?"

GM rushed into the kitchen. "Katie, are you okay?"

Several shopping bags she was carrying tumbled to the floor.

"I—I'm glad you're home," I said, glancing around to make sure that Anton was truly gone. "I didn't mean to scare you. I'm just—really excited to see what you bought."

The words sounded inadequate to me, but GM seemed to accept them.

She beamed at me and deposited all of her bags onto the kitchen chairs.

"I don't blame you for being excited, solnyshko. It's only natural."

She began to pull out her purchases.

"Oh, Katie. We're going to have a wonderful Christmas in Russia. Wait till you see what I've bought."

I was still shaken after the scene with Anton, and I tried to put it behind me. I told myself that and GM and I were safe.

Or at least I hoped we were.

I made an effort to focus on GM and what she had bought—and what she had bought was quite a lot of clothing—all of it well made and chic, with names on the labels that I'd only seen in magazines.

"Wow," I said.

The piles of clothes continued to grow.

"Do we really need all this stuff?" I asked abruptly.

GM looked at me in surprise.

"Sorry," I said. "I didn't mean that to sound so blunt. The clothes are beautiful—really beautiful. I've never seen anything like them before."

GM laughed. "Yes. I have excellent taste, don't I?"

"But I imagine that the trip to Russia itself must be expensive," I said, "and our social calendar isn't so glittering that we typically wear clothes like these. Do we really have this kind of money to spend?"

GM laughed again. It was a little odd to see her in such high spirits. "Practical girl! My dear, thoughtful, Katie. You need not worry. Your grandmother is a clever woman—this you know. But I am cleverer than even you realize. I have a good head for business. And yes, I'll say it—I am a financial genius. We'll always have money when we have need of it. Never fear."

She held a dress of a storm-colored blue under my chin and studied the effect. "Just as I thought—it brings out the color of your eyes. You will be beautiful in this."

She tilted her head and gave me a contemplative look. "We are Rosts, you know. Yes, your father's name was Wickliff, but you are a Rost, too. At one time Rost was an important name in our part of Russia, and though circumstances have changed, Russians have long memories. The name 'Rost' will not soon be forgotten. And as we have ample time to prepare for this trip, we shall go in a style that befits our name. I have shoes, too. Also, hats, coats, and gloves."

I was reminded for just a moment of the missing Odette, who had once gone on a similar shopping spree. I very nearly mentioned it, but I stopped just in time.

I knew how much Odette's disappearance had hurt GM.

She began to gather all of her purchases back into their bags. "I'll put your things in your room. When you pack, you should take all of them. Don't leave them here for fear of ruining them. Such clothes are meant to be seen."

GM left the room, and I had to wonder about our finances. GM was much in demand as a graphic designer, and I was sure she did pretty well. But I was also sure that we weren't well-to-do. We *had* gone on a last minute trip to Russia via Georgia in October, which I'm sure had been expensive. But that had been an emergency.

We had literally been chased out of the house—by someone who had wanted to kill us.

But now, GM's purchases seemed extravagant, and Branden's remarks about Russian moonshine in Elspeth's Grove suddenly popped into my mind. Of course, it was ridiculous for me to think even for a moment that GM was involved in anything illegal. She was very proud and lived by a strict moral code. I knew she would go after something fiercely if she wanted it. But she would see criminal activity as the wrong route—and she would never take it.

I bent down to pick up a silvery chiffon blouse that GM had dropped. As I ran my fingers over the fine fabric, it occurred to me that, taken all together, the clothes she'd bought were at least as expensive as the entire trip to Russia—if not more so.

I didn't doubt GM's boast that she was adept at handling money. All the same, I couldn't help wondering as I went to take the blouse back to her—how had GM found the money for so many expensive things?

The rest of the evening passed in a bit of a blur as I tried hard not to think of Anton's visit to the house earlier in the day. I ate dinner, I did my homework, I talked with GM about our trip.

But as I lay in bed that night, the feelings that I had kept carefully bottled up since Anton's terrifying visit suddenly broke free, overwhelming me.

I had avoided thinking about it—but I had to face it now.

Anton had done the worst thing possible.

He had at last given me the one thing I was missing—he'd given me a good reason for why William had left me. And I believed him.

Horrible coldness, horrible emptiness swept over me. I drifted through wave after wave of pain. I knew I cried because I felt tears running down my face, but the realization of it came to me distantly.

I was only dimly aware of myself, of my body—I had become nothing more than raw hurt.

Now there was no longer any chance of my seeing William one last time. There could be no reunion, no matter how brief. Seeing me would deprive William of what he wanted most, and he would never let that happen.

William could have what he dreamed of now—he could have his memories back. He could return to his old life. He'd had a choice to make. And he hadn't chosen me.

William was lost to me.

I was lost to myself now, too.

I wasn't sure how to go on.

The night passed, and then it was day once more. The world went on around me as if nothing had happened. I managed to pull the hurt in, to bind it, suppress it. I went on with my usual routine. Day after day, I went to school. I ate meals with GM. We talked about the trip. I took my exams. Nine more days went by.

Before I knew it, my last day of school had arrived. Our bags were packed and waiting in the hall that morning when I came downstairs for breakfast. GM and I were leaving for Russia that evening. All I had to do was complete one more day, come home, eat dinner, and then we were off.

GM beamed at me across the breakfast table and then gave me a hug as I turned to leave the house. I was glad to see her looking so happy, and I was relieved that she didn't notice my abstraction. GM's thoughts were clearly far away—in her mind she was surely in Russia already.

I stepped out into the cold, clear air to begin my walk to school.

My final day to decide had come at last.

I'd avoided thinking about the topic, but I was forced to confront it today. Now that I knew for certain that William had given me up—why was I still going to Russia?

The trip, of course, was obviously making GM very happy—even through my mental fog, I had seen how her excitement had grown day by day. And then, too, my canceling at this point would mean that GM would have spent a lot of money for nothing.

Those were two very good reasons still to go.

However, there was one major argument against going—the trip would be dangerous. And now that there was no longer any hope for me to see William, was the risk worth it? I would be heading back into the midst of all the supernatural terrors I had fled from—and I'd be taking GM into that danger along with me.

Innokenti had wanted me to go back to Russia—he'd said it would be safer for me. But William had disagreed at the time, and now Anton rather astonishingly wanted me to stay home, too. Despite the attacks I'd suffered from him, I was inclined to believe that I was actually safer in Elspeth's Grove.

It seemed to me that I would be surrounded once I was back in Russia.

Of course, GM would be scornful if I tried to tell her about the danger to her. And if by some miracle, I did manage to make her understand, I knew she'd want to charge out to meet it—with me safely stashed away somewhere else, of course.

And what about William? Did I believe, despite what I knew, that there was a chance that I could see him again?

The answer was no. By now William would be in possession of what he wanted, and he would be long gone. He would have gone back to the Sídh—he would be in a place I could never go.

So I would go to Russia for GM. And I would try to keep us both out of trouble.

I felt a twinge of the vast loneliness and hurt that I'd been keeping locked away. I quickly pushed the feeling back into its prison.

I knew that if I let it out that it would overwhelm me.

When I reached school, I spotted Simon, Branden, and Charisse standing outside by their usual picnic table, despite the chill. I'd been avoiding the three of them in the mornings so that I could study, but now that exams were over, I didn't really have an excuse not to be social.

I suddenly realized that depending on what happened in Russia, I might not ever see the three of them again.

It was a disturbing thought.

Charisse caught my eye and ran over to meet me.

She slipped an arm through mine and began to walk determinedly toward the school.

"You're coming with me," she said. "No arguments."

"Charisse—I—"

I began to protest, but then stopped when I realized I didn't know why I was doing it. Was I planning to argue with her simply out of habit? I *did* want to talk to Charisse. I'd missed her—and there was something more.

I wanted to say goodbye.

Just in case.

Charisse steered me to the cafeteria and pushed me into a chair.

"All right, Katie. Talk."

"Charisse—"

"I know, I know—you're always saying that you have to study. Well, you don't have to study today. And I'm not your best friend for nothing. Something's wrong. Something's been wrong for a while. And you're going to tell me what it is."

"Okay," I said.

Charisse blinked in surprise. "Okay?"

"Okay," I said again.

Charisse sat down.

I considered telling her everything. It would be a relief to finally tell someone. I thought about telling her that there was a price on my head. I thought about telling her that there had been attacks. I thought about telling her that William had abandoned me when I needed him most. And I thought about telling her that I would never see him again.

I thought, too, about telling her that I had been forced to make myself feel nothing—to go completely numb so as to control a pain that was so strong that it threatened to tear me apart.

I looked into her clear brown eyes and thought about telling her.

"We're going to Russia for Christmas," I began. "We're leaving tonight. And things there aren't quite right yet."

Charisse's eyes widened. "To Russia? To your grandmother's hometown again?"

"We're going to Moscow first. But then after that, yes, we're returning to Krov."

She stared at me.

I decided to plunge ahead. "Like I said, there's a lot that's still wrong in Krov—some of it might be hard to believe—"

Charisse interrupted. "Oh, Katie. No wonder you've been so closed off and jumpy. Your grandmother wants to take you back there? Where a murderer kidnapped you and imprisoned you in a crypt? Why didn't you refuse?"

"I did, at first—"

"Oh, Katie, I understand now. I understand everything."

Charisse hugged me impulsively, and I realized that the moment for confession had passed. She'd latched onto the wrong reason for my being distant and had given me a way out.

With an odd twinge of regret, I decided to go with it. Ultimately, it would be easier for both of us.

Charisse would never have believed the truth anyway.

She sat back in her chair. "Katie, the memories must be horrible. Why is she making you go?"

"She's not making me go. I said no at first, and then I changed my mind."

"Why? Why did you change your mind? And why does she want to go?"

"I honestly don't know why GM wants to go. But she seems really happy about it—really excited."

Charisse frowned. "She doesn't have a new boyfriend, does she? I'd say it's pretty uncharacteristic of your grandmother to take you back to a place where your life was threatened. I'd hate to see another Joshua Martin situation developing."

I was startled. "A boyfriend? GM? She's never had a boyfriend. No—I'm sure it's nothing like that."

Charisse eyed me again. "You're really and truly going?"

"Yes."

"I don't blame you for acting weird. Promise me you'll stay safe."

"I'll try."

I felt a sudden rush of affection for Charisse. We'd been friends since we were both small. And now that the trip to Russia was actually upon me, the fear that was at the back of my mind was steadily growing. What if today truly was the last time I would ever see her?

"Charisse," I said seriously, "you're my best friend. I just wanted you to know that."

"Katie, don't talk that way," she said sharply.

"What way?"

"Like you're saying goodbye."

I shifted uncomfortably in my seat and tried to make my voice sound light. "I *am* saying goodbye. I'm leaving tonight."

"That's not what I meant. Promise me you'll come back here. Promise me I'll see you again."

"Charisse, of course—"

"Promise me. And don't say you'll try."

"I promise," I said.

The warning bell rang, and Charisse sighed.

"Sorry I'm acting so crazy," she said. "It's just—I have a bad feeling about this trip of yours." She stood up. "But it's probably nothing. You know what—just forget what I said. I'm sure you'll be fine. I hope you have a good time."

She gave me a wan smile. "I guess we'd better get to homeroom."

As Charisse and I went our separate ways, I wondered if I would be able to keep my promise to her.

In second-period English, Branden came up to me and wrapped me up in an all-encompassing hug.

"I heard you're going back to the crazy town where the crazy dude tried to kill you," he said from somewhere over my head.

He stepped back and pressed a compact red object into my hand.

"It's a Swiss Army knife," he said as I looked down at it. "Take it with you. If you run into another crazy dude, just give him a good stabbing. You can't take it in your carry-on, but you can take it in your checked luggage."

"Thanks, Branden."

"Remember, a good stabbing."

"I'll remember."

Charisse walked over and wrapped both her arms around Branden. "He insisted on giving that to you as soon as I told him about your trip."

"It's very thoughtful," I said. "With any luck, I won't need to use it."

"Does Simon know you're going yet?" Charisse asked.

"No," I said.

"No? I would have thought that Simon would be the first person you'd tell."

"Why? I told you first. Like I said, you're my best friend."

"You're my best friend, too, but I would have told Branden first."

"Charisse, Simon and I aren't dating."

"Yes, Katie, but Simon—"

She stopped.

I sighed inwardly. I knew all about how Simon felt. He meant a lot to me, but I just couldn't feel for him what he felt for me.

I was saved from further conversation by the entrance of Mrs. Swinburne.

But later in the day, as I was walking into the cafeteria, Simon drew me aside.

"Do you mind if we have lunch alone—just the two of us?" he asked. "I already talked to Charisse and Branden about it. They don't mind."

"Uh, sure," I said. "Does this mean that they told you?"

He blinked at me. "Told me what?"

"I guess that's a no."

Simon smiled. "So, you have something to tell me, then? Well, I have something to tell you. This should be fun."

I wasn't so sure about that.

The two of us went through the line together, and then we sat down at one of the smaller round tables.

As I bit into my pizza, Simon looked at me eagerly.

"Do you mind if I go first?"

"Sure. Go ahead," I replied.

"Okay. So, Christmas Eve. I'm sure you and your grandmother have your own traditions and everything, but my family and I would be delighted if the two of you would join us at our house for dinner. James is having Eva over—do you remember how he got to meet her at Bryony's party? Well, he invited her over, and she said she could go. And I would just really love it if you could be there, too. What do you say?"

"I—oh—"

I stopped. I felt a familiar sinking sensation. It was a feeling that came to me more and more often when I was talking to Simon these days. Why did our friendship have to be complicated?

"Simon, this kind of leads into what I have to tell you."

"What is it?"

"GM and I aren't going to be here for Christmas."

"Where are you going?"

"We're going to Russia."

Simon looked stricken. "What?"

"We're leaving tonight."

"You're—"

Simon stopped and took a deep breath.

"You're leaving tonight for Russia, and you never said a word about it until now? Did you just find out today?"

"No," I said simply.

There wasn't really anything else I could say. I couldn't begin to explain to Simon what was going on. I'd tried to tell him before about the strange turn my life had taken.

He hadn't believed me.

I glanced at him now. His jaw was working in a familiar angry way.

"I'm sorry, Simon. I'm sorry I can't have dinner with you and your family. I'm sorry I didn't tell you sooner that I was going to be leaving for Russia."

"Where in Russia are you going?" he asked in a low voice.

"We're going to Moscow first and then to Krov."

"Is Krov where you were—"

He broke off and looked away.

"Yes. That's where I was kidnapped by the guy who was pretending to be a substitute teacher here."

"Why is your grandmother allowing this?"

"GM wants to go—she's the one who first suggested it. She's really excited about it."

"Katie, it can't possibly be safe."

Despite the fact that I understood the dangers of the trip far better than Simon did, I felt myself bristling.

"Why wouldn't it be safe?" I asked. "Timofei Mstislav is dead—buried in his family's crypt. And Krov isn't entirely peopled with criminals."

Simon brushed a hand over his hair. "I know that. That's not what I meant. It's just—I would think there would be some bad memories associated with the place—for both of you."

I paused. I had known Simon for as long as I had known Charisse, and my affection for him ran deep. I was struck once again by the terrible feeling that this might be the last time I would ever see one of my closest friends. This time I could feel tears stinging my eyes.

"There are bad memories," I said quietly. "And I'm not as excited about going on this trip as I once was. But it means a lot to GM. Simon—let's say goodbye on good terms."

"Goodbye?" Simon reacted with horror, much as Charisse had done. "You're saying goodbye? You're talking like you're not coming back."

I backtracked quickly. "I just meant goodbye for now. I want us both to be happy when we go on winter break. We are friends, right?"

"Katie, we're more than friends. I wish you could see that."

An uncomfortable pause ensued, and I turned back to my pizza.

"Of course we're friends," Simon said dully after a moment. "If that's what you want. I thought since I hadn't seen what's-his-name around lately that maybe you'd changed your mind."

Simon looked so forlorn that I had a sudden urge to hug him. I pushed the urge away and tried to think of something soothing to say.

Nothing came to me.

Mercifully, our conversation soon turned to small talk—incidentals about my trip and about his plans with his family. At the end of lunch, Simon smiled at me and wished me a good trip, but I could see that he was miserable.

As he walked away with his backpack slung over one shoulder, I could see him hunch his shoulders and bow his head, shoving his free hand into his jeans' pocket.

Simon's feelings for me were obviously very strong. He was good and smart and dependable—he would risk a lot for me. And he would never disappear without saying a word.

He would never abandon me.

For just a moment, I wished that I could be in love with Simon.

Chapter Fourteen

When the final bell of the day rang, I couldn't help but feel relieved.

I rushed to my locker and then hurried through the halls. I knew that if I lingered, there was a chance I might run into Charisse or Simon, and I couldn't say goodbye to them again—it would be too hard.

As I moved quickly toward the exit, however, I happened to find myself walking alongside Bryony.

I was glad that I would get a chance to say goodbye to her, too.

I wondered then why I was feeling so fatalistic. I had a definite feeling that this could be the last time I would ever speak to Bryony. But there was no real reason why I should feel that way. The trip would be difficult, but I could get through it, couldn't I?

"Hey, Katie," Bryony said.

"Hey," I said.

"I hope you have a good winter break."

"Thanks. You too."

"Are you going away for Christmas?" Bryony asked. "Or are you staying here?"

"I'm going away. Actually, my grandmother and I are going to Russia. How about you?"

"We're staying here. My whole family lives around here, so we very seldom go anywhere for the holidays. Sometimes I wish we could go somewhere else."

Bryony paused, and she seemed to have something on her mind. After a moment, she spoke again in a lower voice.

"I talked to my grandmother about the ghost's message like I said I would. She's tried to contact the ghost to get more information, but unfortunately, she's been unsuccessful."

Bryony looked at me sheepishly. "It's not really that unusual that she hasn't heard from the ghost again—she very seldom sees or hears it at all."

"I guess ghosts are elusive by nature," I said. "Thanks for trying."

"My grandmother did say not to forget about the warning. It's *really* hard for the ghost to communicate. The fact that it did so means it's a matter of life and—"

Bryony stopped abruptly. "Sorry. That sounds terrible. I'm sure you can look out for yourself. And maybe you'll be safe from the singing once you're in Russia."

She stopped again. "You know, I probably shouldn't have brought this up at all. I'm sure you don't want to hear any of this crazy supernatural stuff before you go on break."

"It's okay," I said. "I'm glad you asked your grandmother—even if she didn't find out anything else. I appreciate it. I really do."

"I'm glad I didn't freak you out," Bryony said with a shy smile. "Have a good trip. And a good Christmas."

"Thanks. You too."

We were outside the school fence, and Bryony turned toward a waiting car.

I hurried home.

GM was waiting for me, and she spun me around as I walked through the door.

"Can you believe it, Katie? The day has finally arrived, and we're almost on our way. Dinner will be ready in about an hour. Will that be too early?"

"No, that's not too early."

"Put your books away—rest, relax. There will be nothing but happiness for us from now on."

I went up to my room, kicked off my shoes, and lay down on my bed. My luggage was all downstairs, and GM had taken care of everything else. Some vague instinct told me that I should try to get some sleep.

Sleep eluded me, however, and GM soon called me for dinner.

We had lasagna, which was one of my favorites. And despite the fact that she hated raisins and disapproved of sweets, GM had made raisin bread—another one of my favorites—for dessert.

After dinner, we began to take our luggage out to the car.

Taking out the luggage was going to require at least two trips, and after the first one, I stopped by the car and looked around, suddenly wary.

It occurred to me that Anton might put in an appearance at the last minute and try to stop us from going.

But GM and I managed to get all of the luggage out of the house and into the car without incident. I wondered where Anton was, though, and if he'd been watching us. If so, was he still keeping all would-be attackers away from me?

It was strange to be both afraid that Anton was watching me and afraid that he might not be.

After GM and I had filled up both the trunk and the back seat of her little car with our luggage, we got in ourselves.

As we pulled out of the driveway, I glanced back at the house. I loved my home.

I wondered if this would be the last time I would ever see it.

I told myself once again not to be so fatalistic.

GM drove on with her usual expert speed, and I watched the scenery flying by as time passed and the light slowly faded. GM didn't play music as she had on our previous trip to the airport. On that other, terrifying trip, she'd played Mussorgsky's *Pictures at an Exhibition*, a favorite of my mother's, to give me a measure of comfort.

Such a thing wasn't necessary this time around.

Eventually the day gave way completely to night, and we continued on through the dark. I lost track of time—possibly I dozed a little—but I grew alert when the airport materialized in front of us, large and luminous in the night.

GM found long-term parking, and then we took a shuttle to our terminal. As we checked our luggage and went to our gate, I was surprised to see how many people were flying to Moscow with us. I stood, surveying the crowd. People sat talking, reading, and tapping away on cell phones. Everything seemed very normal.

Even so, I started to feel nervous.

I was at a point at which it was still possible for me to turn back. I could run from the airport—run back to the car, and GM would be forced to follow.

Neither one of us would go on the trip, then, and I would never have to find out what waited for me in Krov.

But I knew that I wouldn't leave.

I would wait quietly for the plane, and when the time came, I would board it.

I was going to Russia now—no matter what. I felt as if I were being pulled along inevitably by an invisible cord.

I wondered for a moment if this trip was truly a choice I'd made, or if it were something that would have happened no matter how hard I'd tried to avoid it.

GM pulled on my sleeve, and my reverie was broken. She'd been surveying the crowd too, and she'd just spotted two empty seats next to each other.

We sat down, and GM looked around the waiting area with sparkling eyes.

"Well, here we are," she said. "From now on all we have to do is sit back and let others get on with their work. We can truly relax now."

She glanced over at me. "Dinner was some time ago. Are you hungry, Katie?"

I could feel my stomach tying itself into knots. "No—I don't think I could eat anything right now."

GM beamed at me. "Neither could I—I am far too excited."

I had brought a book to read, but I found myself unable to focus on the words. My mind was suddenly full of images that I'd tried to bury forever—images of underground tunnels in Krov where I'd been trapped. Images of a man named Gleb Mstislav, whose lifeless body had been resurrected. Images of Timofei Mstislav, who'd freed his cursed father so that he could kill me.

I jumped up from my seat suddenly, unnerved by my own memories. I walked to the huge windows nearby that looked out on the runway. There I watched the planes take off and land while I fought to banish the nightmares from my mind.

At long last, boarding for our plane was announced, and GM positively glowed as we walked down the narrow tunnel into the body of the plane and found our seats.

"So very different," GM murmured as she settled in. "Such a very different experience from last time."

I looked over at her. She was right about that. There was none of the urgency, none of the terror. And yet I felt uneasy, and my uneasiness was steadily growing.

Had I made a terrible mistake? And had I dragged her right into the middle of it along with me?

For her part, GM seemed completely happy—she saw only a good trip ahead of her. I hoped she was right.

"We should speak in Russian from now on," GM said to me in that language. "I'm very glad that you kept your Russian up. But then, you're a very smart girl, and I'm sure that it's easy for you."

I couldn't help but smile at this little speech of GM's. And I told myself to reign in my feelings of panic and to focus on being normal. I told myself further that if I stayed alert, we could both survive this trip.

"Russian it is," I said.

GM searched in her purse then and produced a small, slim object, which she pressed into my hand. "This is for you. I have one, too. I bought us cell phones that will work in Europe. This way we won't be stuck by the side of the road again without a working phone. How lucky we were last time that Aleksandr and Odette happened to be driving by."

I thought back to our rescue by Aleksandr and Odette—it was yet another instance in which I would never be able to explain to GM what had truly happened. The whole incident hadn't come about by luck—it had been engineered.

Aleksandr wasn't who he'd seemed to be.

To all appearances, Aleksandr was the son of my mother's childhood friend, Galina. He was, in fact, the Leshi—a Russian spirit of the forest who was impersonating the kidnapped Aleksandr in an attempt to help combat Gleb Mstislav. The Leshi had actually caused the flat tire that had marooned us, and then he'd doubled back to pick us up.

So Aleksandr had most definitely not been what he'd seemed to be.

And Odette hadn't been who she'd seemed to be, either.

GM continued, unaware of my abstraction.

"We'll be staying in a very nice hotel in Moscow," she said. "I think you'll really enjoy seeing the capital. It's a beautiful city. A city of dreams."

"When we get to Krov, will we see Galina and Aleksandr?" I asked, my mind still lingering on the Leshi.

A slight look of strain tightened GM's eyes, and I wondered if she'd say no. GM's relationship with her daughter's friend hadn't been a positive one for many years, but by the time we'd left Krov in October, it had begun to thaw, and I knew that GM had been in contact with Galina since then.

Despite the thaw, was GM still wary of her?

She remained silent for several minutes, and I realized that even if she said no, I would still go to see Galina and the now-restored

Aleksandr on my own. I would also seek out the Leshi in the Pure Woods. Looking for William was out of the question now, but I could at least try to find out who had placed a price on my head—and maybe I could find out how many vampires were actually after me. And I would avoid Innokenti at all costs.

Eventually GM sighed. "Yes, I suppose we should go see Galina and Aleksandr. Galina isn't such a bad woman, really—she's just a bit misguided."

The seat belt light came on, and we lapsed into silence. Our plane taxied down the runway and took off, and I stared out the window as the plane climbed into the sky. We reached cruising altitude, and a flight attendant came by and offered us drinks.

After the flight attendant left, GM reached over and patted my hand.

"We're going to have a wonderful Christmas in Krov. We'll be in our old home again."

Our old home. I thought of the house in Krov with its apple tree and its roses. I had lived there with my mother, my father, and GM until my parents' death when I was five years old. A year before they had died, my cousin, Odette, had come to live with us. Beautiful, red-haired Odette was five years my senior, and I had adored her.

I'd been happy in that house in Krov, and it had existed for me only as a pleasant memory. I'd never expected to see it again.

But back in October, GM and I had found our way back to that house. It had been both strange and wonderful for me to enter a house I'd believed I would never see again.

And now, only two months later, we were going back yet again.

Krov, it seemed, was unwilling to let us go.

GM continued. "I'll be sure to find us a Christmas tree for our house in Krov."

"A Christmas tree?" I thought back to the decorated house that we had left behind in Elspeth's Grove. "We'll have a Christmas tree in Krov, too?"

"Yes, of course," GM said. "The traditions of Christmas are a little different in Russia than they are in the U.S., but we can add anything we wish to our celebration."

She paused and then went on wistfully. "Christmas is beautiful in Russia. Possibly more beautiful there than anywhere else in the world."

Something about GM's dreamy tone suddenly reminded me uncomfortably of Charisse's suggestion that GM might have a Joshua Martin of her own.

"Are we going to Russia to see someone?" I asked abruptly.

"No, no, of course not." GM looked startled. "This trip is just for us."

"But people usually travel at Christmas to see loved ones," I said. "If we're just traveling to Krov so the two of us can sit around a Christmas tree, then—"

I stopped.

"What, solnyshko? Go on."

"Well, then, we might just as well have stayed at home. We have a nice Christmas tree there, too."

"You're still worried about the expense, are you?" GM patted my hand again. "You have nothing to worry about on that score—truly. And there will be only the two of us at Christmas. And it will be wonderful in Russia—you'll see."

I had a strange feeling that GM was avoiding something, but I decided not to pursue the topic any further.

I had thirteen hours to spend on the plane, and after some time had passed—and the lights had been dimmed in the cabin—I tried to sleep. But relaxation of any kind escaped me, and I remained wide awake and jittery, watching a small graphic on the screen in front of me of our plane's progress over the ocean. I knew we were going hundreds of miles an hour, but on the map the plane barely appeared to be moving at all.

I glanced over at GM. She appeared to have fallen into a deep sleep.

On impulse I pulled out the charm William had given me.

Though he was lost to me forever, I couldn't bear to part with the charm. I stared at the roughly hewn cross, turning it over and over in my fingers. It had, I knew, special properties that gave its wearer some protection against the kost—that's why William had given it to me.

I'd thought once that perhaps the charm had had some other significance to him—something that had nothing to do with its protective properties. I'd thought that maybe William had given it to me for that reason, too. It seemed now as if I'd been wrong about that.

As I continued to stare at the charm, I felt calmer and less jittery.

Before I knew it, I'd fallen asleep.

I awoke with a start some time later—the cabin was still dark—and it took me a moment to realize where I was.

I'd had disturbing dreams—just images flashing by. All my worst memories had been replayed for me.

I'd seen Gleb and Timofei hiding in the cave in Elspeth's Grove. I'd seen Gleb advancing on me in the tunnels in Krov. I'd seen Joshua Martin snarling at me in Charisse's basement. I'd seen Anton lunging for me in the Old Grove.

I had a terrible feeling that new images of horror would be added to this list.

I tried to shrug the feeling off, but as I sat in the dark cabin listening to the steady hum of the plane's engines, the feeling only increased.

As the moments crawled by in the darkness, an unpleasant idea took hold of me.

What if the next image to be added to the list would be the last one? What if I wasn't destined to survive this trip?

Maybe Krov would be the end for me.

I closed my mind firmly against the thought and tried to sleep again.

After several long hours, the lights came on once more, and the flight attendants began to serve breakfast. Then, after several more hours, our plane touched down in Moscow.

I was relieved to finally be off the plane, and I hoped desperately that I was wrong about what this trip to Russia held in store for me.

When GM and I reached baggage claim, we discovered that all the luggage from our flight had been heavily wrapped in plastic. It took us some time to identify which bags were actually ours.

After that, we spent a lengthy time going through customs. But eventually we got through the line, and we were free to enter Moscow.

It was early evening, and GM and I took a cab into the city. We checked into our hotel and had dinner at the hotel restaurant.

GM gave me some Russian money then—colorful ruble banknotes, ruble coins with a double-headed eagle on them, and kopek coins which were worth one one-hundreth of a ruble. I was fascinated by the new money, just as I had been on our trip to Georgia.

After dinner, we went for a walk, just to look around. Strangely enough, I was in a good mood by the time GM and I returned to our hotel that night. The novelty of the new city and all its sights and sounds had gone a long way toward lifting my fatalistic gloom. Back in our room, I fell into a dreamless sleep.

In the morning, GM and I went out to go sightseeing. We were going to spend two days in Moscow before heading on to Krov.

The sense of fatalism that had troubled me before returned suddenly with full force. I couldn't help but think that I had only two days left to live.

And yet the morning was sunny, the air was clear and cold, and I felt excited despite my fears.

GM and I had breakfast at a little restaurant not far from our hotel, and then she took me to Red Square. I had seen the square and its ornate buildings many times in the movies, and I was excited to realize that I would actually get to see it all in person.

We went first to St. Basil's Cathedral, and as I gazed up at its fantastic, colorful domes, I felt myself transported—the church was surely something from another world.

"What do you think of St. Basil's?" GM asked quietly. "People have varied opinions on it."

"I think it looks like something from a dream," I replied. "It's wonderful."

GM smiled. "A good answer, solnyshko. As I said before, this is the land of dreams."

"It's hard to believe this is all real," I said, looking around the square. "It's hard to believe I'm here."

"I haven't forgotten my promise to you—the one I made back in Georgia. I mean for us to take proper vacations in the future. Would you like to see Paris next year? Or maybe London? Your father was born in London, you know."

I felt a strange sort of pang. I'd known that my father was born in the UK, but I'd never known where. "No—I didn't know that."

"There is much that you don't know about the past—though for the most part that's for the best. But you've been deprived of a normal childhood. I wish you could have your mother and father back. I wish you could have a normal family like your friends have."

"I have you," I said.

GM gave me a small smile and brushed a hand over my hair.

We went into the cathedral and explored its small, brightly-colored chapels. Every available surface in every narrow room was painted with portraits, fantastic patterns, and other embellishments. St. Basil's was truly amazing inside and out.

We went back out into the square and then spent the rest of the day exploring the Kremlin, including the building I most wanted to see there—the Armoury. The Armoury housed fantastic treasures—diamonds, gold and silver objects, imperial carriages, and ten Fabergé eggs. The eggs interested me particularly—there was one I was very much drawn to. It was red and gold—its colors reminded me of the clear fire I had once been able to summon.

We took the Metro into another part of the city for dinner—to a restaurant GM had loved years ago. She was delighted to find that it was still open.

GM then took me to the ballet as a surprise, and it was marvelous and magical—a really amazing evening. Without knowing it, GM had succeeded in taking my mind off my worries. By the time we got back to our hotel, I was happily exhausted, and I fell asleep very quickly.

And yet, when I woke up the next morning, a terrible thought popped into my head—that I had one day left to live.

I quickly pushed the thought away.

GM and I had breakfast in the hotel restaurant, and she read a newspaper named *Vremya* as she drank her tea. We'd been sitting in companionable silence for some time when I realized that the quality of the silence had changed.

I looked up at GM. Her shoulders had gone rigid, and her face was pale.

"What's wrong?" I asked.

"Nothing."

She folded up the paper quickly and set it on her lap, out of sight.

"Was it something in the paper?"

GM waved a dismissive hand. "Newspapers. They can be so sensational."

I sighed inwardly. Obviously, something in the paper had upset her—something she didn't want me to know about. And I knew from long experience that once she'd made up her mind to be silent, nothing would convince her to speak.

I decided that if I got a chance to have some time alone that I would go and buy a copy of *Vremya*.

"I'm a little tired of museums," GM said, by way of changing the topic. "Do you mind if we go shopping today?"

"Sure. Anything you'd like, GM. It's your trip, too."

We made our way back to Red Square, and as we were crossing to a huge department store named GUM, GM stopped and pulled out her phone.

She read a text, and something flickered in her eyes that she quickly masked.

"I have to make a phone call, solnyshko. I think it may take a little while. Would you like to go off by yourself for a little while? We could meet back in front of GUM in an hour, if you like."

"Who are you calling?" I asked. "Is it something to do with your work?"

"It's nothing you need to worry about, Katie. I'll see you soon."

She turned and walked away.

I wanted very much to know what GM's phone call was about. But at the same time, I realized I now had a chance to get a copy of *Vremya*. I hurried off into the crowd.

Finding a newspaper in Red Square, however, was no easy task. I wandered around the buildings, looking for a bookstore or a newsstand. When nothing like that materialized, I scanned the crowd, hoping to spot someone carrying one. As I did so, a man passed in front of me. His eyes were a bright, unnatural brown, oddly reminiscent of cinnamon.

I recognized those eyes.

"Aleksandr!" I cried.

The man turned away from me and hurried off.

"Aleksandr!" I cried again. Of course, with those eyes the man wasn't really Aleksandr Golovnin, Galina Golovnin's son. He must actually be the Leshi—in disguise as a mortal man again. But I could hardly call out the name of a Russian forest spirit in the middle of a crowd. I didn't want to appear crazy.

The man began to move faster, and I hurried after him. Soon I broke into a run.

But no matter how fast I ran, the man remained just ahead of me.

I watched as he headed toward one of the Kremlin's buildings—a museum—one I hadn't visited yet.

"Aleksandr!" I called after him. "It's me! Katie Wickliff!"

The man disappeared into the museum.

I ran in after him.

The man pushed his way through the crowd inside, hurried around the front desk, and went up a staircase, taking the stairs two at a time. I ran after him and was just in time to see him run down a corridor and disappear behind a door. The door slammed closed behind him.

I ran up to the door—a sign on it read in Russian "staff only"— but I went through the door anyway.

Once inside I found myself in a long, dimly lit room that stretched on into shadow. There was no sign of the man I'd followed.

I ran my hand along a nearby wall, searching for a light switch, but I couldn't find one. I took a few tentative steps into the room.

"Aleksandr?" I whispered. "Aleksandr?"

There was no answer.

I walked further into the room. There were several desks and then a long line of shelves. The shelves were laden with objects of varying shapes and sizes, all of which bore tags with serial numbers. Between the shelves were a number of strange shapes draped in cloth and several large crates. I opened the lid of one of the crates, and two marble, sightless eyes looked back at me. I was staring into the face of a statue.

I was clearly in a room where the museum stored exhibits when they weren't on display.

I let the lid of the crate fall back into place, and the statue was returned to its slumber.

Just then a slamming sound from the dark end of the room drew my attention. If the man I'd followed truly was the Leshi, then I had to talk to him. He just might know something about who and what was after me.

With his help I might even survive my trip to Krov.

I edged toward the other end of the room. Through the gloom, I could see that there was another door—I figured that the sound I'd just heard was the sound of this door closing.

I went through it into the next room. The new room was also dimly lit and apparently devoid of light switches. This room had more desks and tables and was lined by glass cases.

Even in the gloom I could see something glittering in the cases, and I went closer.

On thick red cushions lay row after row of ornate, intricate jewelry—necklaces, rings, bracelets, earrings—even a tiara. In the next case were small icons—beautifully rendered portraits of saints and holy figures. Such things were common fixtures of Russian churches. Labels underneath each icon identified the individual who was depicted.

I reached the end of the case and started on the next one.

The next case also contained icons, but this group of icons was like nothing I'd ever seen before. The images were rendered in the usual fashion, but the subjects were clearly not saints. The eyes staring back at me were malevolent, not serene. The faces were pale and unhealthy, and there was something cruel about the mouths. The names listed underneath the icons were names I didn't recognize.

When I reached the end of the row, I saw a face I did recognize, and I froze. The final icon depicted a man of extreme pallor. His eyes were closed, and his face was covered by a filmy substance with sharp edges—he was covered in ice. Though the image was stylized, I had no doubt that I was looking at the same man who had appeared to me at the cave in the Old Grove.

I read the inscription below the icon. It was one word.
WERDULAC.

Chapter Fifteen

Stumbling, I made my way out of the dark room as fast as I could. I was no longer interested in finding the Leshi. I just wanted to get back out into the sunlight again.

I was badly rattled.

As I hurried back out into the museum corridor, I nearly ran into a woman who began to berate me loudly.

"What were you doing in there?" she cried in Russian. "Those rooms are off limits to tourists. Be off, or I will call security."

I needed no encouragement to leave.

I ran along the hall and down the stairs. I kept running until I was back out in the square. I drank in the cold air gratefully, and the sunlight felt like an embrace.

I had enough presence of mind to glance at my watch—it was just about time for me to meet GM at GUM.

I turned in the direction of the department store.

I couldn't help shivering as I walked, and the image from the icon rose up in my mind again. I had no doubt that that was the same man I had seen emerging from the cave.

Werdulac.

I wondered how old the icon was. I had a terrible feeling it was from a span of time that greatly exceeded the life of an ordinary human being. This Werdulac had appeared to me in Elspeth's Grove, but it now appeared that he was known in Russia. Was he one of the creatures that was after me?

And just what was he?

Cold fear suddenly washed over me in a wave. Now that I was back in Russia—would he come for me here, too?

Even in the open square I felt surrounded—trapped.

I spotted GM on the other side of the square, and I began to move toward her, pushing my fears aside. But a moment later, I spied a man with a newspaper. He was preparing to throw it away.

I hurried over to him.

"Excuse me! Excuse me!" I said.

The man stopped, arrested in the act of dropping the newspaper into a trash can.

"Sorry," I said. "May I have your newspaper? Since you're about to throw it away anyway?"

I didn't know for sure if it was the same paper GM had been reading, but even if it weren't, it still might have a story that would stand out to me.

The man looked surprised, but he smiled and held the paper out to me.

"Thank you." I glanced at the paper. I was in luck—it was *Vremya*. "Really. Thank you very much."

The man gave me a bemused look, and I ran off to the cover of a nearby building. I stashed the newspaper in my bag and then hurried over to meet GM.

I was curious about her phone call, but she, of course, said nothing about it. As we walked into GUM, I glanced furtively at her face, looking for any sign of emotion—good or bad—that might tell me how her phone call had gone. But her expression was unreadable—it might have been a routine call about work after all.

GM had a wonderful time shopping at GUM, and I did, too, at first—all of the activity helped to take my mind off the bizarre discovery I'd just made. But GM's passion for looking at clothes and jewelry far exceeded my own, and after about two hours, I was ready to be done with shopping for the day. GM's interest, however, didn't abate in the least, and I tagged along after her as she discovered one fresh delight after another. She bought quite a few things—for me as well as for herself—and after a few more hours we were forced to go back to our hotel to drop off our purchases.

We took a break from shopping for lunch, and then we were off again—this time we took the Metro to TSUM, the Central Universal Department Store on Petrovka Street. We spent several hours there—once again, heading back to our hotel when our purchases became too cumbersome to carry.

Back in our room, I looked over all the bags that were strewn over our two beds in bemused horror.

"How are we going to get all of this stuff to Krov?" I asked.

GM waved a dismissive hand. "I have rented a car to drive us—a much better car than we had on our last trip. It will be no problem for us."

We rested a little while at the hotel, and then GM had us dress up in some of our new clothes so we could head out to a fashionable restaurant for dinner. The restaurant was beautiful, the crowd was well dressed, and the food was delicious, but I was growing anxious again, and despite my best efforts, I was distracted.

The trip to Krov was almost upon us, and I was overcome once more by the terrible feeling that I was going to die there. Seeing the icon of the Werdulac at the museum had only deepened my fear. Now that I knew that he—whatever he was—was known in Russia, I realized that coming on this trip truly was a mistake. The Werdulac had appeared to me in the Old Grove for a reason—he had drawn me to him there. Surely here it would be even easier for him to get to me. I wrapped my fingers around the iron charm William had given me. I wondered if it had any power to repel the Werdulac.

After dinner, GM surprised me by taking me to a nightspot named Serebro that was even more fashionable than the restaurant had been. I was unsure if the massive bouncer at the door was going to let us in or not, but GM looked fabulous and was, as usual, supremely confident as she addressed him, and we sailed in as easily as if we'd been regulars.

As GM and I settled in at a clear, tiny table, lit from below, I looked around. The crowd inside was definitely hip, and there was a palpable atmosphere of wealth. I was not drinking, of course, and neither was GM, and the pretty waitress who attended us raised an eyebrow at our decidedly innocent order.

"Are you sure we belong here?" I whispered to GM.

She looked at me in surprise. "Of course we do, solnyshko. I am a Rost and you are, too. I've been to places much more sophisticated than this."

"Places like what?"

GM shrugged. "It's not important at the moment. Right now we should just have fun. Now is the time to relax."

I wondered again about the life that GM had led in Russia before I was born—there were hints, shadows—but nothing concrete, and nothing GM would actually tell me about outright.

I sipped on my cranberry juice and club soda and wished I knew what was going on with her.

GM eventually pulled me onto the dance floor, and despite my gloom, I began to have a good time.

GM and I returned to our hotel at a respectable enough hour, and tired out from shopping, dancing, and worrying, I fell asleep right away.

I awoke in the early hours of the morning to see GM standing in our darkened room with her hands on her hips, surveying our luggage. Somehow, magically, she'd packed up all our new things, and we appeared to be ready to go. The only suitcase that was still standing open was one of mine—I had a feeling it had everything in it that I would need to get ready for the day.

"Good morning, Katie. Did you sleep well?"

I pushed my hair away from my face. "Yes, thanks. Is it time to go already?"

"We should leave as soon as possible. Do you mind if we have breakfast on the road?"

"No, I don't mind," I replied.

"I'll go downstairs and have breakfast boxed up for us, then. Please try to be ready by the time I get back."

GM left the room, and I couldn't help sighing to myself. She was clearly in a hurry—and I was suddenly hit by a strong sense of dread.

I remembered then the newspaper I'd found in Red Square. I quickly grabbed my shower stuff and my bag. Then I locked myself in the bathroom.

I was a little slower at reading in Russian than I was at speaking it, and I pored over the paper carefully, looking for the story that had upset GM on the previous morning. It was possible, of course, that she'd reacted to something that I knew nothing about—after all, her past in Russia was much longer than mine. But GM would typically talk to me about neutral topics—she was only completely silent when the subject was something she thought would upset me.

I was beginning to think I was wrong about what GM must have seen in the newspaper when I spotted the word "Krov." Right above it was an ominous headline: GHOULISH GRAVE ROBBERS PLAGUE SMALL TOWN. What followed was a story about a rash of thefts from area cemeteries—more specifically, graves had been opened and the bodies had been stolen from them. There was a rather lurid description of empty, yawning graves and sobbing, frightened families discovering that their loved ones' remains had been taken. A wave of fear washed over me as I read on. Amongst the plundered graves was the crypt of the Mstislav family. Though other bodies had been left undisturbed, the body of Timofei Mstislav had been stolen. The article went on to note that before his recent death, Timofei Mstislav had been wanted for kidnapping and murder. Authorities had no motive for the robberies.

The newspaper slid from my fingers to the floor, but I was only dimly aware of it. When he was alive, Timofei Mstislav had come after me, intending to kill me in retribution for my mother's imprisonment of his cursed father. He was dead now—I knew that for a fact.

But I also knew that the dead could come back.

I heard GM come back into our room, and I hurriedly turned on the water. I forced myself to shower and dress quickly. Then I gathered up my things and placed my hand on the doorknob.

I didn't know if I could walk through the door.

I wanted to hide myself away forever. What could I tell GM that would make her turn back? Maybe I could get her to agree to stay in Moscow for the duration of our trip. A chill spread through me as I realized that GM already knew that Timofei Mstislav's body had been stolen, and she still wanted to go on.

She was taking me right back to him.

Of course, GM didn't believe in the supernatural. She didn't believe that Timofei's father, Gleb, had been resurrected as a kost, or that he'd stalked the living until he'd been wrestled back into his tomb—and back into quiet death.

She thought Timofei could do no more harm now that he was dead.

And I realized that there was no way I could hide from him anyway. In October Timofei and Gleb had left Russia and had found me in Elspeth's Grove. And now according to the paper, Timofei was out of his grave. If somehow he returned to an unnatural life, he could certainly find me in Moscow.

A cold, heavy feeling settled on me—I might as well go to Krov. Whatever was waiting for me there couldn't be avoided now.

It would come for me no matter where I went.

I pulled the door open and stepped out into the room.

GM turned. "Good. You're ready. Breakfast has been packed up for us." She gestured toward the dresser where two paper bags and two paper cups sat. She turned back to me. "You should—"

She took a step forward. "What's wrong, solnyshko?"

I held the newspaper out. "Why didn't you tell me?"

"What do you mean?"

"I saw you reading the newspaper yesterday, and one of the stories shocked you. But you wouldn't tell me what it was. I know now what you saw."

"Oh, Katie. You saw the article about—"

"The grave robberies in Krov," I said. "The article that says Timofei Mstislav's body was stolen. Doesn't that sound like something that I should know about?"

GM was suddenly unnervingly calm. "I don't see why."

"What?"

"I don't see how it affects you."

"How could it not affect me?" I asked. "He nearly killed me."

"But he's dead now himself," GM said reasonably. "It's disturbing that his body's been taken from its proper resting place. But Timofei Mstislav no longer has the power to hurt you. The news affects his family, I'm sure, but it's nothing to do with us."

"I can't believe how calm you are about this," I said, my voice shaking. "I can't believe you think I should have no feelings about this at all."

GM's expression softened. "I've upset you now, and that's not what I intended. Yes, of course, this affects you. It must bring back terrible memories—memories that are all the more terrible because they're recent. I'd hoped you wouldn't find out. Not just to spare you the memories, but also because—"

She stopped.

"Because?" I prompted.

"Because of the things you said at the time," GM replied. "Because of the strange things that happened—things that were hard to explain. Because, like your mother, you seemed to believe in the supernatural— at least while all of that was going on. I didn't want to stir up ideas in your mind."

She gave me a serious look. "I didn't want you to start to thinking that something mystical was going on. I didn't want you to think, as your mother once did, that a dead man could come back to life."

Unfortunately, that's exactly what I did believe. As GM continued to look at me, I found that I could summon up no words of comfort for her.

"I'm sure everything will be fine," I said at last.

"Oh, Katie. I can see that you don't mean that."

GM brushed a soothing hand over my hair. "We'll have a good Christmas. You have nothing to fear. As I told you once, there is nothing in the dark. Now, quickly, pack the rest of your things up. We need to be on our way."

I did as she asked, and then, with the help of several hotel employees, we got all of our luggage out of the hotel and into our rental car.

"I may have to ship some of these things home," GM murmured as we settled in.

Despite my new worries, my spirits had lifted a little when I'd seen the rental car GM had selected. I didn't know much about cars, but I could tell that this was a high-performance vehicle—it reminded me a lot of the one she had at home, except this one was a bright, blazing purple.

If there was one thing GM really loved, it was speed.

Unfortunately, now that GM had a car to match her temperament, that also meant that she'd be able to drive with her usual eerie speed and finesse. She'd be able to rush us toward a place I wasn't eager to get to.

As we set off, it was hard for me not to dwell on the fact that "Krov" was the Russian word for blood.

Neither one of us ate the breakfast that GM had brought with us, and when we stopped for lunch, I was still in no mood for food. GM insisted, however, that I eat something, and I tried to, even though my stomach remained in knots.

All too soon we were back on the road, and I stared out the window, watching the countryside flying by.

The longer I watched, the heavier my eyelids grew. Eventually, despite my worries, I fell asleep.

I awoke with a start some time later, and I was surprised to see how dark it was.

GM glanced over at me. "You slept a long time, Katie. You must have needed the rest."

"Where are we?" I asked.

"We're almost in Krov. It won't be long now."

I sat up in my seat and stared out the window. It was so dark that I could see nothing of the scenery, and the only light seemed to be that which came from our own headlights.

As I continued to gaze out into the darkness, straining my eyes for a sign of something familiar, I caught sight of a light flickering far out in the night.

I blinked, and the flickering disappeared.

A moment later, the light flickered again. This time it blazed up brighter than before, and I saw an orange-gold ball of fire light up the dark. It went out as quickly as it had come.

There was another blaze after that, and then another and another.

Fires continued to spring up and then disappear, illuminating the area immediately surrounding them for a moment. I could see that the fires were flaring up in the midst of a thick wall of trees.

"GM, someone's trying to set that forest on fire," I said in alarm.

As I spoke, I could see several more blazes springing up beyond her window.

GM glanced to the side and shrugged. "It's just local farmers burning brush. It's nothing to worry about."

It was a plausible explanation, but I wasn't entirely convinced she was right. I had to admit, however, that the fires didn't appear to be harmful—they continued to flare up and then go out, and the trees themselves didn't appear to be catching on fire.

All the same, it was strange.

Eventually we moved beyond the fires, and the lights of Krov came into view. After another few minutes, GM stopped the car in front of our old house—a house with a now-barren apple tree and rosebush.

GM and I got out of the car, and I stood looking up at the house in the light from our street's two working streetlamps. I had assumed all along that we'd be staying at our old house, and GM had always indicated that that would be the case. But I realized now that there was no reason I should have assumed that. After GM and I had left Russia when I was five years old, ownership of the house had gone to Galina, and she, in turn, had made the house over to Odette when she was old enough. The house actually still belonged to my cousin, Odette—who hadn't been seen since the night Timofei Mstislav had died back in October.

Now that she was gone, I had no idea who owned the house—most people assumed that she was dead.

Only I knew that Odette had actually disappeared of her own accord.

"Let's just take in what we need for tonight," GM said. "We'll get the rest of the luggage in the morning."

We walked up to the house, and GM pulled out a set of keys.

"Where did you get the keys to the house?" I asked. "Are they from our last trip?"

GM seemed to stiffen a bit, but she answered me. "Galina sent them to me back when I first thought of coming here for Christmas. She's looking after the house until Odette returns."

She said the words with such conviction that I felt a rush of sympathy for her. GM believed very firmly that Odette would come back.

I wasn't so sure about that—in fact, it would probably be safer for us if she didn't.

"Does Galina know we're here now?" I asked.

"No, I don't believe so," GM said shortly.

I said no more, but I decided to visit Galina in the morning—if I could get some time away from GM.

And if I survived the night.

I would see Galina first tomorrow, and then I would go looking for the Leshi. Maybe one of them could tell me more about who was after me and why. And maybe one of them could tell me about the Werdulac.

GM and I went into the house, and GM suggested trying to find some shelf-stable goods in the pantry. But I really wasn't in any mood to eat. Instead, I went up to my old room.

I was struck once again—just as I had been back in October—by how little my room had changed since I was five years old. Neither Galina nor Odette had done any redecorating. The rocking horse rug my mother had made still lay on the floor, its bright colors undimmed. The painting of the yellow bird that I had been so fond of still hung on the wall. And my full first name, EKATERINA, still defaced the wall by the door in my own childish scrawl.

As I sat on my bed, I expected to be overwhelmed by fear—I was now back in Krov, there was a price on my head, and I fully expected that the house would be attacked tonight. But somehow I felt all my dread slipping away from me.

I felt safe in the house. Back in October when I'd first come back to the house after many years, I'd felt safe then, too. And I'd thought to myself in amusement that there were no monsters in the house. But I'd been wrong—there had been a monster in the house—my cousin Odette.

Whether my current sense of security was false or not, it was still a relief. I wasn't tired at the moment—not after my long sleep in the car—and I resolved to stay up and watch over the house. If someone or something did come for me, I would lead it away from the house and GM.

I looked out my window. The yard was empty, and no obvious threat stirred in the dark. I would have to stay alert for any tiny sign of movement out in the night.

Despite my best efforts to remain awake, I found myself lapsing into short spells of sleep. I remembered fragments of dreams—happy ones in which I saw my family and myself the way we used to be when I was a child. When I finally shrugged off the last of the sleeping spells, it was dawn.

I was very much alive, and the house had apparently gone completely undisturbed all night. I was eager to see GM again, just to be sure.

I showered and dressed and then quickly hurried downstairs.

As was her custom, GM was already up and drinking a cup of tea.

I shuddered inwardly, remembering how Odette had used tea to poison me, but I knew that all of the tainted tea had been removed from the house. I'd disposed of it myself.

Even so, when GM offered a cup to me, I found that I had to refuse.

"I hope you do not mind, solnyshko," GM said, as she drank the last of her tea, "but we'll have to go out for breakfast. There is, lamentably, very little food in the house. I should have foreseen this, but I didn't. I'm sorry."

"That's no problem," I said. "I don't mind going out for breakfast."

GM looked down and began to fuss with her empty teacup—an uncharacteristically nervous gesture.

"There is something else I need to ask you," she said.

"Sure."

"After breakfast, do you mind spending some time on your own today? We could meet up again here at the house at say, four o'clock? And then we could go shopping for a Christmas tree, if you would like."

I was excited about the prospect of having most of the day free—I could go looking for Galina and the Leshi, and I wouldn't have to come up with any excuses to get away. I tried not to sound too eager.

"Sure. That would be great."

I was curious about what GM was planning to do, but I didn't want to jeopardize my own freedom by asking her too many questions—that was the quickest way to put her in a bad mood.

She gave me a searching look. "You truly don't mind?"

"No, of course not. Like I said before, this is your trip, too."

GM smiled. "Thank you, solnyshko. I'll make up for my absence later on today. We'll have a very good Christmas, I promise you."

"It's okay, GM, really."

I remembered from our last trip to Krov that there was a small row of shops nearby, and GM drove us over there to a little combined bakery and restaurant for breakfast.

Our waitress was a girl not much older than myself, who seemed to recognize GM. The girl said everyone in Krov recognized the Rosts.

GM was greatly pleased at first, but our talkative waitress soon turned the conversation toward the fiery blazes that had begun to appear in the neighboring forests at night. She said that the locals had termed the blazes "witch-fire" and believed that they were supernatural in origin.

The girl herself agreed with local opinion and predicted with a great deal of cheerful gloom that the witch-fire would bring about disaster.

GM grew stiff and formal and tried to shut the girl down, but she chattered on undeterred. GM and I had certainly seen some strange fires in the forest on our drive into Krov, and I wondered if we'd witnessed the witch-fire ourselves.

At the end of breakfast, GM drove me back to the house and then went in with me to give me a copy of the house key so that I could come and go as I liked.

She turned to leave, and then stopped and turned back, giving me a long look.

Before we'd left for Russia, GM had looked excited, eager—happy. And after we'd arrived in Moscow, her excitement had only seemed to grow—I knew that she was delighted to be back in Russia.

But as GM looked at me now, I could see signs of strain in her face and a flicker of doubt in her eyes.

"I'll see you soon, solnyshko. Enjoy the day."

I thought I heard a tremor in her voice, but it was so slight that I might have imagined it.

She turned away from me and left the house.

I had the strangest feeling that GM was nervous.

Chapter Sixteen

s soon as GM had driven away, I walked back to the shops where we'd just had breakfast. I'd noticed a bicycle shop there, and I was hoping to be able to rent a bicycle for a few days.

It would be nice if I didn't have to walk everywhere while I tried to figure out what was going on.

Luckily, the woman in the shop didn't mind letting me have a bicycle for several days—she said it was her slow time of year, and there wasn't much rental business at the moment.

I thanked the woman and began my ride to Galina's house. The weather was warmer than it had been in Moscow, but it was still pretty cold, and as I rode along, the breeze made me even colder.

I rode on to the square in the center of town, which was dominated by the Mstislav mansion—once the home of the now-deceased Gleb and Timofei Mstislav. As I remembered, a tree-lined path led up to the imposing white building, which was actually quite pleasing to the eye in the winter sunlight. The last time I'd seen it—on the night of Timofei Mstislav's "surprise" ball—it had been hung with bright red banners. The banners were gone now, and the mansion's face looked clean and innocent. It appeared to be unoccupied, too. I wondered about the Mstislav family—how many of them there were, where they were—what they thought about Timofei and what he had done.

227

I thought next of the Mstislav crypt that Odette had lured me to on the night of that same ball—the same crypt from which Timofei's body had recently been stolen. I'd feared that that crypt would become my own final resting place.

I moved on quickly.

I continued on past the mansion to the vast, empty expanse of desolated fields that stretched beyond it. Galina had told me that a village had occupied this space once—bounded on the other side by a monastery that was now abandoned.

And I knew all too well that a network of tunnels ran under the ground from the mansion to the monastery. I'd been trapped in those tunnels once, just as I'd been trapped in the Mstislav crypt. And Timofei Mstislav's father, Gleb, had almost killed William and me down in those tunnels.

For the most part, I had only seen this part of Krov at night. Now that I looked over the empty space, locally termed the "Wasteland," in the daylight, I realized that it stretched far off into the distance away from the road.

I wondered how far those underground tunnels really ran.

Something about the Wasteland was very depressing, and I was relieved when I finally caught sight of the abandoned monastery up ahead. Beyond the monastery lay the petrified forest of the Pure Woods, so-called because of its stark white color.

And nestled up against the edge of the woods was the house where Galina Golovnin lived with her son, Aleksandr.

After a few minutes, I spotted the house. I pulled off the road and stood for a moment just looking at it. The house seemed quiet and watchful somehow, as if it were waiting for something.

I told myself that that was just my imagination.

I went up to the front door and knocked, but there was no answer. I knocked again and again, but silence reigned in the small house, and no one came to open the door.

On impulse, I reached out and tried the doorknob.

The door swung open at my touch.

"Galina?" I said.

There was still no answer.

I pushed the door open a little further and went inside.

"Galina? Galina, are you here? The door was open."

There was no reply.

I went further in.

Galina's house was much as I remembered it—cluttered but scrupulously clean.

I went through the whole house, but there was no sign of Galina or Aleksandr. I had no way of knowing if they'd just stepped out for a moment, or if they'd be gone all day.

I went back to the kitchen to see if I could find an errand list or something similar hanging on the refrigerator. There was nothing of that nature in the kitchen, so I went to the study where Galina had first told me about my mother—it was an overstuffed room with a desk and a lot of books. Perhaps I would find an appointment book or a calendar in there.

In the study, I found a pile of papers on the desk, covered in a tiny, cramped script. As the writing was in Russian, it was a bit difficult for me to decipher, but it all seemed to be hastily scribbled notes that Galina had written about a long list of towns and villages. Unfortunately, there was no hint as to where she might have gone on this particular day. I began to worry that perhaps she'd gone on a long trip and wouldn't be back for days or even weeks.

I continued to sift through the papers, and I saw nothing that was significant to me until I caught sight of one word.

Werdulac.

The word was on a small scrap of paper by itself, and it had been underlined three times. I searched through the papers more carefully after that, hoping to find information about what the Werdulac was. But all I found was even more notes about various towns and villages.

Had Galina gone in search of the Werdulac?

I looked around the room in resignation. I was unlikely to find the answer to that question in here. And I figured that wherever Galina and Aleksandr had gone, they were unlikely to be home soon.

I decided to go out into the woods and search for the Leshi.

I was leaving a note for Galina in the kitchen—just in case she did return—when I heard a door slam.

"Galina?" I said.

I hurried toward the front of the house.

No one was there.

I opened the front door and looked around—the road in front of the house was empty.

I went back inside.

I was heading back to the kitchen to finish my note when I heard another sound, like someone was pulling a chair back from the table.

I froze.

"Galina? Aleksandr?"

There was no answer, and I was suddenly overcome by panic. I ran out of the house and plunged into the Pure Woods. I had the strangest feeling that I would be safe there—even though I knew that the woods were home to just as many dark creatures as light ones.

At the very least, I wouldn't be trapped in the woods the way I would be inside the cramped house.

I glanced back in the direction of Galina's house. There was no sign of anyone following me.

All the same, I was glad I'd left. I was sure that I'd heard someone in the kitchen, and I'd learned it wasn't a good idea to ignore my instincts in a town like Krov.

Once I was certain that there was genuinely no one pursuing me, I wandered through the woods, trying to feel the spiritual energy around me, trying to let it lead me to the Leshi. It was possible, too, that the Leshi might happen to see me while I was wandering and come to me on his own. But whatever connection I'd once had to him or to the woods seemed to have disappeared. I wandered, concentrating, but I came upon nothing, sensed nothing.

Eventually, I had to give up—I wasn't going to find anything this way. I decided to come back later tonight to try searching the house and the woods again. Maybe Galina would come back. Or maybe I'd be able to connect with the energy of the woods once the sun had gone down.

I started back toward Galina's house.

When I reached the house, I was struck by how peaceful it now seemed—the alert, watchful quality it had given off before was now gone.

It appeared to be nothing more than an ordinary, empty house.

All the same, I didn't want to risk going back inside, even though my note to Galina wasn't finished—I hadn't even signed it. I hoped it would be enough to make her curious. Maybe she'd go into town looking to see who could have written it.

I rode my bicycle back into the center of town and decided to stop at a little café I'd passed along the way for lunch.

As I neared the café, I spotted a familiar, slim figure with a long, silver braid. GM was standing in front of the café with a tall man in a black overcoat. The man had thick white hair and a handsome, weathered face. As I watched, the man took GM's hand and executed a courtly bow over it. Then he straightened and offered her a single blossom—a lavender iris.

GM smiled, and the smile suffused her face with a youthful light. I suddenly felt like I was seeing her as she had looked as a young girl.

The two of them stood for a long moment, just gazing at one another.

Then they must have felt my eyes on them, for they both turned to look at me at the same time.

GM looked dismayed. The man looked back at me with a good-natured, puzzled expression.

I froze, completely unable to move or look away.

Eventually, GM beckoned me forward, and I suddenly wished that I could disappear. But there was no way I could slip away—they had both seen me.

Feeling a blush rising to my cheeks, I wheeled my bicycle up to them.

"Hi, GM," I said uncertainly. "I just saw this café earlier and thought it looked like a good place for lunch."

"We had the same idea," the man said politely. His voice was rich and full of good-humor.

He glanced over at GM. "Am I correct in assuming that Dame Fortune has arranged a meeting I'd believed impossible? Is this charming young lady your granddaughter?"

"Yes, Maksim, this is my granddaughter, Ekaterina Wickliff," GM said. There was more than a touch of stiffness in her tone. She turned to me. "May I present Maksim Neverov."

"Neverov?" I said.

Maksim took my hand and bowed over it as he'd done with GM. "Enchanted, Miss Wickliff."

I felt strangely light-headed. "Please just call me Katie."

"Well, then, I insist that you call me Maksim. Would you be agreeable to joining us for lunch, Katie?"

I glanced at GM. She seemed to be angry with both of us, but she also appeared to be resigned to her fate.

"Yes, Katie, you should join us," she said.

I hurried to lock up the bicycle, and then I went into the café with GM and Maksim.

After ordering, we waited for our food in strained silence. I tried to cover up my discomfort by sipping on a glass of water.

"I suppose I should begin with a word of explanation," Maksim said at last, addressing me and breaking the silence. "You see, I am in love with your grandmother, and I have been for many years."

Maksim looked over at GM, and I was surprised to see a rosy glow color her face. Once again, she looked years younger—and really beautiful.

"Maksim, you must not say such things," she said.

He turned back to me. "Your grandmother and I haven't seen each other for a very long time, and I feared when she left Russia years ago that I would never see her again. Losing her was the great tragedy of my life."

Though Maksim was looking at me, I had a feeling that he was actually talking to GM. I glanced at over at her—she was wearing an unusual expression. She seemed both pleased and uncertain—or was the second emotion shyness? It was hard for me to be sure. GM was seldom anything less than completely confident.

Maksim continued. "As a matter of fact, I fully intended to marry your grandmother, until your grandfather got in the way."

I looked at him in surprise. So did GM.

Maksim looked away from both of us.

"I see lunch has arrived," he said pleasantly.

After the waitress had set down our food and departed, GM leaned forward.

"Maksim, you must be careful what you say around my granddaughter," she said in a low voice. "Katie is young and impressionable."

Amusement flickered in Maksim's eyes. "You think I may be a bad influence on our young lady here?"

He switched his gaze to me. "Tell me, does your grandmother still drive as if she has to outrun the end of the world?"

I couldn't help smiling a little. "Yes. That's a pretty good description, actually."

GM looked at me in shock. "Katie!"

"It's true," I said. "You have a desk drawer full of speeding tickets."

"I am an excellent driver," GM said emphatically.

"Yes, yes you are," Maksim replied. "I'm merely making a point—what constitutes a bad influence to one is perfectly harmless to another. And I see nothing wrong in discussing the past—especially not if the past concerns true love."

"Oh, Maksim," GM said.

"So, Katie, what do you plan to do during your stay here in our humble town?"

"GM and I were going to get a Christmas tree this afternoon."

"How *au courant* of you," Maksim said. "Though it's not traditional here, the Western-style Christmas with a tree has become very popular. I, myself, have never put up a tree. But Russians do love an excuse for a celebration. Our traditional Christmas is actually on January seventh, according to the old Julian calendar, and it's a much quieter day—some might to go church, but that's about it. What we really celebrate is New Year's. We have a tree then, and our Grandfather Frost comes. There's also a lot of food—and drink."

He shot a glance at GM. "But here I must be careful what I say. I don't wish to be a bad influence."

Suddenly a little spark of mischief leapt up within me. "Would you like to come with us?" I asked Maksim. "To pick out a tree today?"

Maksim and GM both looked at me in surprise.

"Since you've never put up a tree before," I said. "Maybe you could even help us decorate it."

GM suddenly looked murderous.

Maksim's good humor seemed to desert him for a moment.

"Thank you for the invitation, Katie. But your grandmother doesn't appear to be too pleased by the prospect."

As she looked at Maksim, GM's expression softened. "Nonsense, Maksim. We'd both be happy to have you accompany us."

Maksim gazed at GM for a long moment, as if trying to gauge her mood.

"Thank you," he said at last. "I would be delighted."

He turned to me once again.

"So, Katie, what else do you have planned beyond tree-shopping and decorating?"

I found myself at a loss for words. I could hardly tell Maksim that there was a price on my head and that I was trying to find out who was behind it. And I could hardly tell him that I was searching for information about a supernatural creature known as the Werdulac.

My mind, however, remained firmly fixed on inappropriate topics—I couldn't even come up with a good cover story.

"I hadn't really thought about what I was going to do," I said after a pause.

"Well, you might enjoy the Firebird Festival," Maksim said. "That'll be in two days on the twenty-third. There will be a market during the day, and games for the children. And then at night there will be dancing and food and drink. As I said, we Russians love our celebrations."

He glanced over at GM, and the flicker of amusement I'd seen in his eyes before suddenly gleamed there again.

"Of course, if you do go out in the evenings, I must caution you to be wary of the witch-fire."

I was instantly alert. I'd remained curious about the blazes GM and I had seen on our way into Krov, and if the witch-fire was indeed something supernatural, then I needed to know about it—anything supernatural could turn out to be a threat to my life.

"What do you know about the witch-fire?" I asked.

"A local phenomenon of recent origin," Maksim replied. "Mysterious fires have been flaring up in the forests in and around Krov—fires that burn brightly, but somehow don't seriously burn anything. These fires began around the same time that a series of unpleasant grave robberies began here in town. The more superstitious amongst the villagers say the fires are evil spirits being summoned from realms of darkness—spirits that will use the stolen bodies to walk the earth."

A wave of fear washed over me—such a story might sound like nothing more than local superstition to most people.

But I knew that such things could actually happen.

"Nonsense," GM said firmly. "Nothing but nonsense."

Maksim smiled. "You don't believe in witch-fire?"

"I certainly do not."

"But we saw it last night," I said. "On our drive in—fires flaring up in the forest."

"Farmers burning brush," GM said dismissively. "I thought that last night, and I think that now."

"Yes, I recall that you never had much use for the supernatural," Maksim said. "You dislike it almost as much as you dislike raisins."

Maksim was rewarded for this recollection by a small smile from GM. But she was warming up her arguments and didn't seem to notice that Maksim was simply teasing her.

"First of all, why is it called 'witch-fire'?" GM asked belligerently. "That doesn't make any sense—not if the fires are caused by evil spirits."

"Ah, yes, but it's witches who are summoning the evil spirits," Maksim said. "Witches are instigating the entire operation. Evil spirits can hardly summon themselves."

"And what of these 'realms of darkness'?" GM said. "Can anyone identify positively where one of these places actually is?"

"I assume the witches know."

I thought then of Galina. On my last trip to Krov, I'd heard that some of the villagers called her "Baba Yaga"—it was the name of a witch from Russian folklore. Was it possible that some of the locals thought she was behind the witch-fires?

Galina's door had been unlocked—had she been forced to flee her home for her own safety?

"Have the villagers identified any witches?" I asked, alarmed. "I hope no innocent people have been accused of being witches."

"That is an excellent point you make, Katie," GM said approvingly. "Superstition can lead to all kinds of bad behavior, including violence. I hope no citizens of Krov have engaged in any rash acts."

"No, no, of course not," Maksim said, sounding ruffled. "There are whispers, rumors, talk against this person or that one, but there is no persecution here. Krov is not a medieval village. It is a thoroughly modern place. And I am proud of it."

GM's stern expression softened again. "I am proud of Krov, too. That's why I wish the superstition would disappear. There's nothing wrong with folk tales. There's nothing wrong with studying them, honoring them. But there is something wrong with believing them as literal truth."

"You are wise as ever, Anna."

GM and Maksim exchanged a long look. At the end of it, GM smiled.

Krov was certainly a dangerous place in some ways. But at the moment, I was truly glad we'd come.

After lunch was over, Maksim did indeed go with us to select a tree at a small farm. Choosing a tree was an activity that drew an unusual amount of laughter from GM, and she and Maksim spent a lot of time smiling at one another. Eventually, we found a tree, and Maksim and the young man who sold it to us attached the tree to the top of GM's rental car.

GM, Maksim, and I drove home then, and Maksim helped us get the tree into the house and into a stand that GM discovered in a closet. Maksim declined to stay after that, and GM walked him to the door.

After he'd gone, GM went up to her room and brought down a box of ornaments and decorations. Vague memories of Christmases I'd spent in this house stirred in my mind. The Christmas I remembered most clearly was the last one—it was the year that Odette had spent Christmas with us. I remembered that I'd thought she looked just like the angel that had sat at the top of our tree.

As GM and I got to work on the tree, she explained that when I was a child celebrating Christmas had been my father's idea. Most of the ornaments were actually his.

I was suddenly hit by a wave of longing—I wished my mother and father—and Odette—could be here as they all had been once.

But I knew those days were gone for good.

I looked over at GM—I realized it was likely that the last time she'd seen these ornaments that her daughter had still been alive. I wondered how seeing the ornaments again made her feel, but I knew she didn't like discussing the past—especially not when it was painful.

So I said nothing about it.

But part of the past had come back today, and I felt I had a right to discuss it.

"So, that's who the letters were from," I said. "Maksim. He's why we're really here, isn't he?"

GM stopped working and gave me a despairing look. I was surprised to see so much raw emotion in her face.

"Yes. That's why I wanted to come here," GM said quietly. "But I also wanted to keep this from you. You shouldn't have met Maksim today."

"I honestly don't mind if you have a boyfriend, GM. In fact, I think it's wonderful. It was nice to see you looking so happy."

She sighed heavily and threw up her hands. "Grandmothers don't have boyfriends. It's just not right."

"There's nothing wrong with it," I said. "Were you really going to marry him once?"

"Yes, we were engaged to be married," GM said simply. "Until your grandfather appeared—out of nowhere, it seemed—a distant cousin of the Rosts. I fell in love with him so thoroughly that nothing else seemed to matter—and that included Maksim."

My grandfather, of course, had been one of the Sídh, though GM had no knowledge of that. I wasn't surprised that she'd been overwhelmed by him. From what I'd seen of the Sídh, they were a pretty dazzling group.

"Is Maksim related to Irina back home?" I asked. "It sounded like you said his last name was 'Neverov.'"

"Yes. Maksim is Irina's grandfather."

"Is that what she meant when she said you tried to ruin her family?"

The words came out before I could stop them. I realized too late that it was too personal a question to ask. I waited for GM to erupt.

Instead, she just sighed again.

"That's the trouble with the past. People's memories get colored and corrupted by later events—and the opinions of others. I'm sure that's part of what Irina meant. But there was nothing untoward about my relationship with Maksim—it was never inappropriate or scandalous. Maksim was from a prominent family, and he'd been betrothed at a young age to a girl from another prominent family—that girl was to become Irina's grandmother."

GM paused and drew herself up. "Of course, my family was more prominent than either one of theirs. But Maksim was never in love with the girl, and when he was old enough to know his own mind, he broke off their engagement. That was before I even met him."

GM had grown a little heated during this speech, and she paused to draw breath.

"Maksim was a free man when I met him. And he was a free man when we became engaged to be married, and if your grandfather hadn't appeared when he did—"

GM broke off suddenly and gave me an apologetic look. "Your grandfather was a good man, and I loved him very much. I don't want you to think I regret marrying him, because I don't. Not for a moment. But I loved Maksim once, too."

She frowned. "It's all so confusing. Emotions can become a terrible tangle. But the end of it is this: I fell in love with your grandfather, I broke off my engagement with Maksim, and I married your grandfather instead. Maksim eventually went back to Irina's grandmother and married her."

GM gave me a level look. "I wouldn't be surprised if Irina's grandmother remembered things differently, but I can assure you that I'm telling you the truth. I try always to keep my mind clear—to look at the facts unclouded by sentiment. Everything about my relationship with Maksim has always been proper and correct."

She put her hands on her hips and gave me a defiant stare. Then, as she looked at me, a hint of worry, of fear, crept into her eyes.

"So, what do you think?" she asked.

"I think you should have dinner with Maksim," I replied.

Chapter Seventeen

G M did indeed go out to have dinner with Maksim. And once she was gone, I walked back into town to retrieve my bicycle. I'd forgotten about it in all the excitement that was attendant on meeting Maksim.

On my way home, I stopped at the small grocery store that GM, the Leshi, and I had stopped at back in October—it was in the little row of shops near the house. I bought a few things there and then went home and cooked dinner.

After dinner I settled down in my room to wait for night. I sat by the window, watching the sky darken and the stars emerge. I would try Galina's house again after GM went to bed, and I'd also go back to the Pure Woods to look for the Leshi.

And if I didn't find Galina or the Leshi, I might find someone else. Vampires and other dark creatures were always more active at night, and since they were after me, I would prefer to meet anything that was stalking me far away from GM. I didn't want anything to happen to her.

GM came home around eight o'clock. I wanted to ask her if she knew where Galina was, but I was afraid to admit to her that I'd gone looking for Galina without her knowledge. I had a feeling that she'd disapprove. I also didn't want GM to think I was keeping track of her and Maksim. So I came down to sit with her for a little while, but I didn't ask too many questions. We sat together and gazed at our newly decorated Christmas tree, and GM looked relaxed and happy. I excused myself early and went back up to my room to wait till she went to sleep.

GM surprised me by retiring early—for her—at around eleven. I waited for about an hour to be sure she was asleep. Then I slipped out of the house to go look for Galina and the Leshi.

The night was cold, but it was no colder than it would have been back in Elspeth's Grove, and I was perfectly comfortable bundled up as I was.

I rode my bicycle through town and past the Mstislav mansion, which loomed pale and ghostly in the dark. The floodlights that had lit up the house at night when I'd been in Krov back in October had been removed. Krov as a whole was not well lit at night, and the general gloom only added to the air of unreality that surrounded the mansion. Its outline was dim and indistinct—I had the strangest feeling that the house might waver and vanish right in front of me. But I knew that the house was real enough—I had been inside its walls and had been trapped in its crypt. I knew just how solid it was.

The darkness beyond the mansion was solid, too. I would have to cross the Wasteland to get to Galina's house, and I had nothing with which to light the way.

I stopped not far from the mansion, and tried to think of where I could get a light at this time of night.

I knew that all the shops were closed. Krov wasn't the kind of place that had twenty-four hour stores. I figured that I could go back to the house, but I wasn't entirely sure if we had anything I could use there, either. GM had brought flashlights on our first trip in October, but I was pretty sure she hadn't brought them with us this time around. The circumstances of the two trips were very different—the first trip had been panicked, this trip was supposed to be a vacation. And GM's idea of a vacation most definitely did not include wandering around a forest at night with a flashlight.

I glanced back at the Mstislav mansion. Timofei Mstislav's body had recently been stolen from its crypt, and I knew from personal experience that the crypt locked rather solidly. Whoever had broken in must have done a lot of damage, and if someone was still maintaining the mansion, then the crypt might be under repair. Maybe there would be something lying around that I could use as a light.

I didn't like the idea of going anywhere near that crypt in the dark, but it seemed like my best option, and the night would certainly not get any easier as it went along. I figured I might as well give the crypt a try.

I rode up the tree-lined drive to the mansion and then followed the drive around to the back. My memories of the night Odette had led me into the crypt were a little hazy, but I definitely remembered that she'd brought me out of a back entrance to get to the crypt.

I left the bike leaning against the mansion itself, and I squinted into the vast lawn that stretched behind it. There were no lights on at the mansion, but there was a little moonlight, and the whiteness of the sprawling building seemed to reflect what little light there was. I could make out several large shapes out on the back lawn.

I knew that none of those shapes could be the crypt—the crypt entrance was actually in the ground like a cellar door. But if the crypt were being repaired, the shapes might be work sheds—I might find what I needed inside them.

I crept forward slowly, lest I stumble into the crypt entrance in the dark. It occurred to me that if the crypt were being worked on, it might have been left open.

I would have to be very careful.

I walked up to the smallest and closest of the shapes. Then I took off my gloves and ran my hands along it—it turned out to be a wooden shed. I tried the door, but it was firmly locked.

I crept toward the next shape until I could touch it—it was another shed, and it was locked, too. I crept forward again, and my feet struck something smooth and solid. I crouched down to run my fingers over it—it was a door, lying on its side. I felt a stab of fear run through me as I realized that I had found the crypt—it was indeed open as I had feared. I jumped back quickly.

As I did so, I stumbled over something solid on the ground and fell on the hard earth. I felt around for what I had tripped over, and my fingers closed around a handle. I was holding a tool that looked something like a pickax. Someone was clearly working to repair the crypt and had left a few things lying around—since the sheds were locked, I would have to go down into the crypt to see if I could find what I needed.

I got to my feet, and I found that I was shaking. I forced myself forward until I could feel the crypt door again, and using the door as a guide, I crept along until my hands reached out and touched only open air.

Unpleasant as it was, I'd found the entrance to the crypt.

Before plunging into it, I searched around in front of the entrance, and I found a wheelbarrow, a large stack of square, stone blocks, and a big heap of rubble. I also found a table that was laden with tools.

I felt a rush of excitement as my fingers closed around the barrel of a flashlight, but I pushed on the switch and the light failed to come on. I tried it several times, but the batteries were clearly dead. My heart sank.

I kept searching, and I came upon a cardboard box that turned out to be full of wooden matches. I hoped that meant there might be something lying around that needed to be lit.

I continued searching outside the crypt, but I didn't find anything else that might help me.

I would have to search inside the crypt itself.

I walked over to the yawning darkness that was the opening of the crypt, and I stepped shakily over the threshold.

Trailing one hand along the wall as a guide, I walked slowly down the stairs into the crypt, toeing ahead of me with my boots. I knew from my experience with Odette that there was one flight of stairs, and then a brief landing and another flight of stairs. The second flight of stairs led to a long hallway that led first to the crypt itself, and then to the tunnels that reached under the Wasteland. There were no electric lights in the crypt—only cold stone and the Mstislav dead.

I soon descended into complete darkness. I reached the bottom of the first set of stairs and searched the landing. I continued to toe ahead with my feet to investigate, since I couldn't use my eyes. And occasionally, I bent down to examine objects that I stumbled against with my hands. I encountered more tools and a water bottle. Then my boot struck against something that clanked. I picked it up—it felt like a lantern.

I hurried up out of the crypt and discovered that I was indeed carrying a lantern. I quickly grabbed up a handful of the wooden matches, and then I retrieved my bicycle. I moved across the grounds as fast as I could. Once I was clear of the mansion, I would use the lantern and the matches.

But at the moment, I just wanted to get far away from the crypt.

After I reached the road, I glanced back once at the mansion, and I thought I saw a light flicker in one of the windows on the ground floor. Of course, there was nothing strange about that. If someone was having the crypt repaired, then the house was probably still occupied by the family.

All the same, the flicker of light had startled me.

I rode away from the Mstislav mansion until there was just enough light to see by. Then I stopped and lit the lantern, which I'd hung from my handlebars.

With the lantern throwing out a small golden arc in front of me, I continued on across the Wasteland. I couldn't see very far ahead, and I feared what I might come upon in the dark. I worried, too, that I might go past Galina's house without noticing it.

I strained my eyes into the darkness, trying to catch sight of anything sinister before it could jump out at me, and I listened for any sound of pursuit.

Just as my ride across the Wasteland was beginning to seem endless, I caught sight of the white glow of the Pure Woods up ahead of me. I hurried on to Galina's house, and I unhooked my lantern.

I approached the house cautiously.

The place was dark, and the door was still unlocked. I pushed it open and held the lantern up, illuminating a small portion of the dark hall.

"Galina?" I called.

It was possible that Galina was home but just asleep—it was, after all, after midnight by now—but I hesitated to go in. Something didn't feel right. I gave up on the house and turned toward the Pure Woods.

The trees in the woods gave off a faint phosphorescent glow, which I remembered was adequate to see by, so I extinguished my lantern and left it near Galina's house. I figured it would be a good idea to conserve fuel, just in case.

I walked in amongst the trees and tried to quiet my mind, tried to sense any spiritual energy that might be around me. But the energy of the woods eluded me, and I began to feel deeply uneasy. It seemed to me that there were eyes upon me, and that at any moment I could be attacked.

I thought then of the clear fire. I had first learned to summon it in these woods—it was an ability I had inherited from my mother. The clear fire had great power over the dark creatures that lived in the Pure Woods—the kost was particularly vulnerable to it.

The clear fire, however, wasn't very effective against vampires, but they didn't like to be around it all the same. If I could summon it, it might help to protect me while I searched for the Leshi.

And I remembered that the clear fire had always given me a profound sense of calm.

I began to walk in the direction of the stone circle where I'd first summoned the clear fire. I reached out with my mind as I did so, searching for the fire, searching for its energy.

I sang the melody my mother had taught me, the one that unlocked the spiritual door behind which the clear fire was hidden.

I tried to draw it to me, tried to will it to appear.

As I walked, I began to feel calmer—I sensed something soft and soothing in the night, like a song I couldn't hear but could only feel. I had assumed when my visions left me that my connection to the clear fire had been severed, too. But perhaps I'd been wrong. Perhaps I could find it again.

I followed the softness on the air, concentrating on it. Soon, I spied a glow up ahead.

I hurried toward it.

As I drew near the glow, I saw that it was emanating from a figure that was tall and starkly white—it looked very much like the figure of a man. As I watched, the man began to sink into the ground, disappearing inch by inch. I ran forward, trying to catch him before he disappeared completely.

The man's head sank into the ground and vanished just as I reached the spot where he'd stood only a moment before. I was surprised to see that a wide swath of snow now stretched in front of me. I kneeled beside it and brushed the snow away with my fingers. The snow was cold, but something underneath it was even colder.

Soon I could see that there was ice under the snow, and something white gleamed at me from beneath the ice. I kept scraping the snow away, and before long, I found myself staring at a figure that was entirely buried in the ice—it was the man I'd seen emerging from the cave in Elspeth's Grove and the face I'd seen in the icon in Moscow. It was the Werdulac—dressed in his tattered clothes, his skin an unnatural, glowing white, his hair matted, his eyes closed.

His face was mesmerizing, and I found myself unable to look away. As I continued to stare at the Werdulac, his eyes opened.

His eyes were a solid blue-gray with no pupil, as if he were some kind of sightless deep-sea creature, and as I gazed into them, I felt myself falling forward. I crashed through the ice, and I began to plummet through empty space. I could no longer see the Werdulac— everything was black. I continued to fall. I no longer knew where I was, and I reached out blindly, grasping for something to break my fall.

Suddenly, I felt a sharp pain in the back of my head.

My eyes flew open.

I was still in the Pure Woods. I had left the patch of snow and ice far behind and had apparently been walking through the woods with my eyes closed.

Had I been in a trance? I tried to remember what I'd been doing exactly.

I had a vague memory of a song—something that had tried to lead me on—just like in Elspeth's Grove.

I caught sight then of a flicker of flame in amongst the trees ahead of me. The flickering was faint, and as I watched, it disappeared. A moment later, I glimpsed it again—and then a thin ribbon of smoke passed in front of it, and it vanished once again.

I wondered if the flickering could be the witch-fire.

I hurried toward it.

As soon as I saw the source of the flickering, I skidded to a halt, my feet slipping on the forest floor.

There was a small clearing just in front of me. In the center was a pit with a small fire—it was far too small, in fact, to have generated the types of blazes that GM and I had seen earlier. The fire before me was obviously not witch-fire.

But that wasn't what had given me pause. Swirling slowly around the fire was smoke—smoke of a kind that I'd seen before. It was writhing and twisting, turning in on itself in tormented shapes. It was black where it touched the light and white where it touched the darkness. It was the distinctive smoke trail that was generated by a kost—a trail that only I could see.

And lying in front of the fire was a body in a shroud.

The smoke was twisting around the body.

I was clearly looking at an active kost.

All around the fire were figures swathed in furs, their faces hidden by hoods. They were whispering—a sinister, ugly sound. I'd heard whispering like it once before—back in the cave in Elspeth's Grove when Gleb and Timofei had hidden there.

As I watched, the smoke twisted faster and faster, and then rose up in a ghostly column toward the dark sky.

The figure in the shroud twitched.

Then it sat up.

The shroud fell away to reveal a face I knew all too well.

It was Timofei Mstislav.

His face was handsome as it had been in life, but now his skin was the horrible, bleached-bone white of the dead. He opened his eyes, and I saw green flame blazing in them—the same green flame I'd seen burning in the eyes of his father.

Those eyes, full of malice, full of hatred, shifted.

And looked right into mine.

Before I could react, one of the figures surrounding the fire surged forward and latched onto Timofei's neck.

The figure appeared to be biting him.

The other figures surged forward next, shielding Timofei from my view, and the air was torn by his screams.

I did react then—stumbling backwards and running through the trees. I had no thought in my mind other than getting away from the horror behind me as fast as I could.

I ran back to Galina's house and grabbed up the lantern, which I lit with shaking fingers. I looked around frantically for the bicycle, but I couldn't see it.

So I ran.

I ran away from the house and the Pure Woods. I ran along the dark, deserted road that cut across the vast and empty Wasteland. I ran until my lungs burned and my sides were sore.

The only sound I could hear was my own ragged breathing, which sounded dangerously, unnaturally loud in the quiet.

Something made me glance over my shoulder, and I saw a white figure behind me, following me.

A cold wave of fear washed over me.

I ran harder, but when I looked over my shoulder again, the white figure was even closer.

I felt tears stinging my eyes.

The white figure was going to catch me.

Soon I could hear the heavy sound of pursuit—it sounded like approaching thunder.

There was a rush of wind, and the white figure shot past me. It wheeled around sharply and came to a stop right in front of me on the road.

I cried out as I ran into the huge, solid body in front of me.

I fell to the ground. My lantern landed beside me and went out.

I lay on the road for a long time before I dared to look up. I waited, bracing my body for an attack. But an attack didn't come. I listened, but once again, all I heard was my own breathing.

I didn't want to look up. I had the strange idea that if I didn't look at the creature in front of me that it couldn't hurt me—I would just have to stay as I was forever. But as time passed, and silence continued to reign, my eyes lifted involuntarily.

I found that I was looking up at a horse.

I shuffled backward and got to my feet, rubbing at my eyes. When I opened them again, I was still looking at a horse.

It just didn't seem possible.

For its part, the horse stared back at me placidly. It might have been my imagination, but I thought I saw amusement in its mild, dark eyes. The animal was beautiful—silver pale, finely molded and delicate in its lines, and its smooth, well-muscled body gave off a faint sheen.

It wasn't what I'd expected. It wasn't Timofei Mstislav returned from the grave to destroy me. But a feeling was growing on me that the animal wasn't what it appeared to be.

Clearly, it looked like a horse.

But something told me that it wasn't a horse at all.

The beautiful creature lifted its head, and I had the strangest feeling that it wanted me to climb on its back.

I quickly retrieved my lantern from the road—it was lying on its side with one of its glass panes broken. And though I'd never ridden a horse in my life, I managed to climb onto its back and twine my free hand into its thick, glossy mane.

For one disorienting moment, I'd actually imagined that the horse had shrunk in size while I'd climbed onto its back, making it easier for me. And then I'd imagined that it had grown larger again once I was safely seated.

That, of course, was impossible.

The horse started forward, and though I could no longer see where we were headed now that my lantern was extinguished, I knew that we were headed in the direction I wanted to go.

I sensed that we moved swiftly, but I barely felt the motion at all.

It was almost as if we were flying rather than galloping.

I hugged the broken lantern to me and closed my eyes, resting my head against the horse's neck.

I felt myself relax. I knew that if Timofei or any of the other figures from the clearing were pursuing us, that they would have no chance of catching us. I had a strange feeling that someone had just told me this, though I couldn't remember actually having heard a voice of any kind.

I let myself float along, and when I opened my eyes again, we had stopped. The horse and I were standing in front of my house. Still clutching my lantern, I slipped down easily off the horse's back.

I stood for a moment, looking up at the creature before me in the feeble light from our street's two streetlamps. The horse truly was a magnificent animal, and something like sympathy showed in its dark eyes.

I had the impression that it had just rendered me a great service.

I lifted a hand to stroke its shining neck.

"Thank you," I said.

The horse gazed at me for a moment longer and then turned and trotted off into the night. I went into the house, and after making sure that the door was locked securely behind me, I went up to my room.

I knew I should be afraid. I'd just seen Timofei Mstislav out in the Pure Woods—and he was supposed to be dead. And dead he actually had been. I knew that for a fact.

But I had witnessed his restoration to a cursed, unnatural life.

He'd been reborn as a kost. An evil spirit was now animating his lifeless body—a spirit that existed only for revenge and destruction.

Timofei would come after me—in fact, he was no doubt after me this very moment. I should have been afraid. I should have feared for GM and for myself. But once I reached my room I just set down my lantern, changed my clothes, and climbed into bed.

I felt peaceful. I felt serene. I felt secure. I also felt very, very tired.

So I turned out the lights.

And within moments, I was fast asleep.

I found myself in a dream then—or was it a dream? I felt as if I had slipped through sleep and had landed on solid ground. I suddenly felt very aware of being conscious. I walked through a room that was heavily shrouded in shadow, and though I couldn't see well, I was sure that the walls around me were made of stone.

Through the darkness, I saw a light glimmering up ahead of me.

I ran toward it.

I didn't know where the light was coming from, but I felt no fear in connection with it—instead I was eager, expectant. I was excited to see what was waiting for me.

Without really seeing it, I knew I was running down a narrow hall. At the end of the hall, I felt, rather than saw, that the space around me had widened, and I had entered a stone-walled chamber.

The source of the light was right in front of me.

Before me was a long mirror that covered the length of an entire wall. Shining out from the surface of the mirror was a single, golden point of light.

I walked closer to it.

I stared into the mirror but couldn't see what was causing the light—it was as if a star had been trapped inside the mirror itself.

I continued to stare into the mirror, but apart from the light, I could see only my own face.

And then there was a flicker—from the light—as if something had passed in front of it.

I saw a shadow move in the corner of the mirror, and I turned to look at it.

The shadow disappeared.

Another shadow moved at the opposite end of the mirror, and I turned toward it.

This second shadow didn't disappear, and soon another shadow joined it. Then there was another and another.

I peered closer.

The shadows were actually human forms.

More shadow forms joined the first ones, and soon I could see an entire crowd of people on the other side of the mirror.

I didn't fear them—instead, I was overcome by an intense longing to know them.

I placed my hand on the mirror right over the light. I saw the light shining between my fingers, and I marveled when the light suddenly grew brighter.

I felt the world melt away.

Chapter Eighteen

I awoke some time later, and the darkness of the room told me that it was still night.

I knew someone else was in the room—I knew instinctively that it wasn't GM. And yet I wasn't afraid.

I sat up in my bed and turned blinking toward a small, flickering light in the room. The frame of my bed was large and square, and the piece at the foot of it was thick and flat, like a ledge. A candle sat on the ledge, and its lone column of flame seemed unnaturally bright in my dark room.

I blinked again.

Someone was sitting in front of me.

A girl was leaning on the ledge next to the candle, resting her head on her forearm. She wasn't looking at me—instead she was staring into the candle's flame. Her expression was dreamy and faraway, as if she wasn't even aware of my presence.

The girl sat so still and was so pale that I wondered for one panicked moment if I was looking at a ghost. But as I continued to stare at the silent figure at the foot of the bed, I realized that I recognized the beautiful, alabaster face before me.

I was looking at my cousin Odette.

Involuntarily, I flinched backward, hitting my back against my headboard. For one brief moment, I thought about running for the door, but I quickly discarded the idea.

Odette was fast—too fast. I would never get past her.

I knew that from experience.

"What are you doing here, Odette?" I asked. I tried to sound confident, but my heart was hammering so hard that I was sure she could hear it.

In fact, I knew she could hear it. I knew just how keen her senses were.

She didn't stir, and I began to wonder if I was dreaming again—at the very least I hoped I was.

Perhaps I was revisiting a nightmare—Odette and a candle in the dark. I looked her over searchingly, trying to determine if she were real, or simply a figment of my tortured imagination. Her red-gold hair looked dark in the light from the lonely candle, and the look in her eyes as she stared at the flame was soft and contemplative.

Odette seemed real enough, but the dream that had only just passed—the one with the mirror and the stone walls—had seemed real, too.

Maybe if I waited long enough, she would disappear.

Odette continued to sit still, and as the silence stretched on, I felt myself relax. I glanced around my dark room—nothing else was creeping out of the shadows to threaten me. I was safe. Surely this was all another vivid dream. All I had to do was wait for it to fade away.

"I'm the one who stopped you, you know."

I glanced back at Odette sharply. She was still gazing at the candle, and she didn't appear to have moved at all. I thought she'd spoken, and perhaps she had. Imaginary people in dreams spoke all the time—the bare fact that they spoke didn't make them real.

Odette sat up then, and a flash of panic ran through me.

"I've been watching you since you arrived."

Odette spoke, but she didn't look at me. Instead she continued to stare into the candle flame.

"Is this a dream?" I asked.

Odette looked at me then. "What did you say?"

"Are you really here? Am I dreaming?"

She blinked at me, and a faint look of scorn crept into her eyes.

"Don't be ridiculous. Of course I'm really here. And, no. You aren't dreaming."

She shifted her gaze back to the candle.

I tried to control the panic that was rising in me. Odette looked calm, but then again she usually did—even when she had murder in her heart. Beautiful and cold, Odette had remained calm back in October when she'd plotted against me, serenely poisoning me and luring me out of the house to what she believed would be my death.

The fact that she'd later saved my life told me that she wasn't entirely without compassion. Perhaps she wasn't here to kill me.

But I couldn't be sure of that.

"Odette, what are you doing here?" I asked again.

Maybe I could talk her out of whatever it was she was planning to do—and I knew she had to be planning to do something. She certainly hadn't shown up in my room in the middle of the night just because she missed me.

Odette continued to stare at the flame, and she answered my question in a tone tinged with irritation.

"As I said, I've been watching you since you arrived. I came here to tell you that you have to leave. I think you were a fool to come back."

I was inclined to agree with her, especially after what I'd just seen in the forest. I drew in my breath sharply as the memory of Timofei's ghastly face came flooding back. I looked around then—I half-expected to see him come crashing through my bedroom door at that very moment.

"What is it?" Odette asked sharply. "What's wrong?"

"What about Timofei Mstislav?" I asked.

"I'll get to that. I'm trying to explain what's going on, but you have to be quiet and stop acting like an idiot."

I forced myself to be calm. Apparently, vampires didn't like to be rushed.

"I saw you go to the Mstislav mansion tonight," Odette said. "I also saw you go out to Galina's house and then into the Pure Woods. It's very dangerous there at the moment. You shouldn't go there again."

She returned to contemplation of her candle as she continued.

"But even though it wasn't wise for you to be there, you were behaving normally in all other respects. You were searching the woods for something, I assume. And then you seemed to go into a trance. You froze and lifted your hand like you were brushing something away. And then you started running. You ran and ran, and I followed you—you're surprisingly fast for an ordinary mortal. And then you reached a point at which I had to stop you. I knew what you were running toward."

"I was running?" I asked.

"Yes."

"So you didn't see him?"

"I didn't see anyone but you," Odette said.

"He was right there—under the snow and ice," I said. "Maybe you didn't look down to see him."

"Who?" Odette asked impatiently.

"The Werdulac."

She looked up at me, startled.

"Did you say the Werdulac?"

"Yes," I replied. "He was there under the ice like I said. I'd felt him calling to me. When I touched the ice, I fell through it. I was falling and falling until I felt a sharp pain in the back of my head."

"That was me," Odette said. "I hit you. I couldn't let you get too close to what was happening out there. They would have killed you."

I felt a chill steal over me. "The Werdulac was luring me there, wasn't he? He wanted to lead me into the middle of—all that."

"How do you know that name?" Odette demanded. "Why do you keep saying you've seen him?"

"The Werdulac?"

"Yes!" There was a note of hysteria in her voice.

"Because I have seen him. And not just here. He appeared to me back in Elspeth's Grove—before I came here—but I didn't know his name then. And then I saw him on an icon in Moscow—that's when I learned what his name was. Who is he?"

"You are foolish to ask such a question," Odette said angrily. "He's too powerful a creature for you to deal with, no matter what you think."

"Who is he? What is he?" I said.

Odette's agitation seemed to subside, and she shrugged. "I suppose it can't hurt to tell you. And maybe it'll even help to convince you to leave."

She gave me a piercing stare, and her eyes glittered in the candlelight. "The Werdulac is a vampire. But he's not just any vampire. Long ago, when the world was young, he crossed the Black Sea and came to Russia, where he founded a great line of vampires. He's the father of all of our kind here. Long ago, too, he was killed by his enemies—turned to ash and encased in ice."

"So he's dead?" I asked.

"Technically, we're all dead," Odette replied. "But I know what you meant. The Werdulac was supposed to be gone—gone for good—consigned to oblivion. But his power was great, and his life force was strong. The rumors are that he continued to exist under the ice with his ashes. They say that over the centuries he has reconstituted himself—knitted his ashes back together. They even say he'll soon be strong enough to rise again, and break out of his prison. His strong will is whole already, and he has sent it out in advance of his body, drawing creatures to him, giving them orders. He's building an army. That's what you saw in the woods."

"An army?" I said. Anton had said something about an army once, too.

"An army of hybrids—kost and vampire. Evil spirits combined with blood-drinkers—both with superhuman strength. You may be the Little Sun, but you'd better leave. There's nothing you can do here."

"What does the Werdulac want with an army?"

Odette shrugged her slim shoulders. "In ancient days he enjoyed a blood-soaked reign over this region. Perhaps he wants to revive it. I don't know exactly. Whatever it is, I'm sure it isn't good for any of us."

"Where is the Werdulac? Can he be stopped before he's whole again?"

"Well, *we* aren't going to stop him. So put it out of your mind. All we can do is get away from here. And no one knows where the Werdulac's icy tomb is. His final resting place was purposefully kept a secret. He was supposed to disappear forever."

"If no one knows where the Werdulac is," I said, "then how does anyone know that he's the one who's actually behind everything?"

"You're not the only one who's seen him," Odette said. "And many of those others who have seen him are far older and more knowledgeable than you. They can understand things that you never will."

"Why is the Werdulac after me?" I asked.

"I don't know that he is," Odette replied shortly. "But if he is, you'd better pray that you never find out why. If he truly is calling to you, you should make sure that you're never alone again—someone should always watch over you. His will is stronger than yours. In the end, if he wants you, you'll go where he tells you to go."

Odette's words made my blood run cold, and for a moment, my mind froze in fear. But I knew I had to push on—I had to find out what I could from Odette. She was the only link I had to the forces that were threatening me.

"So the Werdulac has people working for him," I said. "People he has called to him?"

"Yes—he has both ordinary humans and vampires. There might even be other creatures involved, too, for all I know. The woods are full of spirits—and other things I can't see."

I thought back involuntarily to the horror I'd witnessed earlier in the Pure Woods.

"And all those people and creatures working for him—tonight I saw some of them creating kost-vampire hybrids? Timofei Mstislav is now a hybrid?"

"Yes."

"What does the Werdulac want with Timofei Mstislav?" An involuntary shudder ran through me. "Why bring him back?"

"I don't think he cares particularly which bodies he uses," Odette said with some distaste. "Any bodies will do, so long as they are free. People here will soon find themselves menaced by their own loved ones."

"I know exactly what that's like," I said ruefully. As soon as I'd spoken the words, I regretted them.

"What do you mean?" Odette demanded.

"I—"

I knew I was on dangerous ground.

"It's just that when I first returned to this house back in October," I said slowly, "I was surprised to see how little my room had changed. And I remembered that as a little girl I'd accidentally locked myself in my closet here once. I'd been trying to see if there were any monsters in the closet when the door was closed. And then I laughed, telling myself that there were no monsters in the house, but I was wrong because there was one—there was you—you were a—"

I stopped.

"So I'm a monster, am I?" Odette said.

I tried to salvage the situation. "I just meant that I thought I was safe in this house."

"You *are* safe in this house," Odette said shortly. "And I suppose as offensive as it is, I can't entirely blame you for your opinion of me. I did come very close to getting you killed."

I had a feeling that that was as close as Odette would ever come to an apology.

She continued. "But as I said, you're safe in this house. That's why I had to lure you out of it. I could give you poison to weaken you, but I couldn't actually let Gleb in to kill you. And he wanted to kill you himself."

"What do you mean? Why couldn't Gleb enter the house?" I asked.

"Your mother sealed this house in a protective way—Galina told me about it. If you don't believe me just look out the window."

I got out of bed and went to my window, pulling back the curtains. Since my room wasn't on the side of the house that faced the street and the streetlamps, it was dark. But I could just make out a figure standing in the backyard.

I stumbled back away from the window when I realized who the figure was.

It was Timofei Mstislav.

"Odette," I whispered. "Timofei is out there."

"I know."

"You know?" I said.

"I know," Odette replied impatiently. "That's why I told you to look."

"What are we going to do?" I asked.

Odette shrugged. "Nothing. I told you the house is safe. You can go look at him again. He won't come in."

I didn't really want to look at Timofei Mstislav again, but I had to see what was going on.

I crept back to the window and peered out. Timofei was still standing in the backyard—he didn't appear to have moved. I could see his eyes now—two tiny points of green flame in the dark.

He appeared to be staring fixedly at the back door. White smoke twisted and swirled around him—it was very much like the trail given off by the usual kost, but as I watched the smoke move, I could see a difference. The trail of an ordinary kost made sinuous, tortured, almost voluptuous patterns in the air. The trail of the hybrid, while equally tortured, had an impossible linear quality to it—the smoke turned back in on itself at sharp angles, creating geometric shapes. The bizarre way it twisted fascinated me, and I found myself watching it, entranced.

An impatient sound from Odette broke the spell, and I turned back to her.

"What is he doing here?" I asked.

"I believe he's waiting for you to come out. He can't get into the house. He can't even touch it. Creatures of evil like vampires and kosts can't come in. I could come in because I was part of your mother's original enchantment—I was one of the 'safe' people who could always come in. You don't need to worry about Timofei right now—like I said, he can't get in."

I touched the charm William had given me. "Why didn't my charm work?"

"What do you mean?" Odette asked.

"It's made of iron," I said. "Iron is supposed to scramble the kost's senses. It's supposed to keep him from following my trail."

"I don't think he had to follow your trail," Odette said. "He saw you. And he knows where you used to live in this town. This house was likely to be the first place he would go to even if he hadn't seen you. The kost is usually born with a strong desire for revenge—it will go after anything its host hated. And Timofei Mstislav certainly hated you."

"Thanks," I said.

"It's just the truth," Odette replied. "Besides, Timofei is a hybrid now—part kost, part vampire. The senses of a kost are typically rather dull—apart from their sense of smell—but the senses of a vampire are terrifyingly sharp. It's possible that iron has less effect on hybrids."

"So are GM and I trapped in this house?" I asked. "You're fast—you might be able to get past him. But the two of us will never get out with him standing guard over the door."

"Your grandmother should be fine," Odette replied. "Timofei's not after her. And in any event, he'll go after you first every time. He won't even glance at her until you're gone."

"But doesn't he need to drink blood?" I asked. "Wouldn't he attack her for that reason alone—even if I'm not around?"

"She's safe on that account, too," Odette said. "They will have supplied him with blood. The Werdulac's people have thought of everything. Besides, Timofei will be gone at daybreak. Like vampires and kosts, the hybrids don't like sunlight. It won't kill them, but they are weak and sluggish during the day—it's the time when they're most vulnerable. Timofei will seek shelter."

"Do you know where he'll hide?" I asked.

"No," Odette said. "And I suggest that you don't go looking for him. I'm sure he'll be protected. If you really want to help Annushka—and yourself—you should leave in the morning. And you should convince Annushka to refuse to see her new gentleman caller."

Annushka was the name by which Odette knew GM, and as for her gentleman caller—

"Do you mean Maksim Neverov?"

"Yes."

"Why should GM stay away from him?"

"Because I've seen him in some strange places," Odette said. "And because he's a Mstislav."

"Maksim's a Mstislav?" I said. "But he can't be—his last name is Neverov. And he's the grandfather of a girl I know back home. There's no way he's a Mstislav."

"It's entirely possible because it's a fact," Odette said. "Maksim's father was a Neverov. His mother was a Mstislav."

I was stunned.

"Maybe it doesn't mean anything," I said. "Just because Maksim's related to the Mstislavs doesn't mean he's like Gleb or Timofei."

"Perhaps not," Odette replied. "But I'd still advise you both to be careful."

I started to feel like I was sinking. A resurrected dead man was waiting in my backyard, hoping to kill me. A vampire was sitting at the foot of my bed. And now my grandmother's sweetheart turned out to be related to the monster outside.

I sat down on my bed again. I wished there was someone I could talk to.

"Do you know where Galina is?" I asked.

"Galina and Aleksandr both disappeared a few weeks ago. I don't know where they went."

"What about the Leshi?"

"I haven't seen him since that night we were all in the Mstislav crypt," Odette said. "He seems to have disappeared, too. I wish he'd come back. I know I said I wasn't very interested in him once, but I've found now that I miss him. Or at least I think it's the Leshi that I miss. I'm not entirely sure where Aleksandr ended and the Leshi began."

I was surprised to hear the mournful note in her voice.

"I think I saw him," I said.

Odette stared at me. "The Leshi?"

"Yes—in Red Square. He looked like Aleksandr, but his eyes were overbright like they were when the Leshi was impersonating him. The Leshi told me once that you can always tell one of his disguises by the eyes. I spotted him in the crowd, and he ran off, so I followed him. He led me to a back room in a museum, and then he disappeared completely. But it was there in the museum that I stumbled across the icon of the Werdulac. It was because of the Leshi that I found out the Werdulac's name. I think he was trying to warn me."

"So he was trying to help you," Odette said bitterly. "Just as I'm here to help you. Everyone is always trying to help you."

"Timofei Mstislav isn't trying to help me," I said. "He's trying to kill me."

"That's true enough." Odette gave me a sidelong glance. "Just out of curiosity, how did you get out of the woods so quickly tonight? Did the Leshi come for you?"

I blinked at her in surprise. "No—it wasn't the Leshi. You didn't see the horse?"

"I saw a white flash, and then you disappeared," Odette said. "It was a good thing, too, because Timofei ran after you as soon as he was free of the ritual. He surely would have caught you if you hadn't just vanished."

"That white flash was a horse," I said. "I climbed onto its back, and it carried me home. I don't know where it came from, or where it went. It was almost like I dreamed it."

"It was a nightmare," Odette said.

I looked at her in surprise. She'd spoken the last sentence in English. "What did you say?"

Odette looked a little self-conscious.

"Was that not right?" she asked in Russian. "I learned the English word 'nightmare,' and I thought I'd make a play on words. It was night, and you met a mare—or a horse, anyway—that seemed like a dream. I thought the word fit."

"A nightmare," I said in English, before switching back to Russian. "I see what you mean. That's clever. Where did you learn those words?"

"I've been studying English on my own. I never had time for studies before," Odette said ruefully. "I have nothing but time now."

"Have you ever heard anything about a horse like the one that helped me?" I asked. "Do you know what it was?"

"It sounds like one of the creatures of the light that inhabit the Pure Woods," Odette said. "After all, it did come to save you. That's all I can tell you. I know more about the creatures of the dark—that's really my area of expertise."

Unbidden, William suddenly came to mind. One of the creatures of the dark—that's what he thought he was. And he'd left me because he believed the curse could be lifted. I hoped for his sake that such a thing was truly possible—I knew it was what he wanted most in all the world.

Odette also didn't seem too happy with her current status, even though, unlike William, she'd actually chosen it. I wondered if there was a way back for her, too—if she wanted it.

"Odette, I heard that it was possible for a vampire to—"

I tried to choose my words carefully. "To return to his previous state. Is that really possible? Would it be possible for you?"

"There is a legend about the Firebird," Odette said wistfully. "It is said that the Firebird can heal anything—any kind of malady. I've wondered if the Firebird can even heal me—there are old stories that say it can. The Firebird Festival is coming soon—that's the time when the Firebird is most likely to make itself seen. It's funny about fire— it's the best way to kill us, but according to the folktales, the right kind of fire can actually purify us."

I watched Odette's face in the candlelight, and her expression grew softer as she spoke. She looked very young—and lost.

"Creatures of the dark have to be careful of themselves, you know," she said. "I thought I'd be laughing at the night and at everyone else, too—I thought I'd have everything I ever wanted. No wrinkles, ever! Clothes would always look good on me! And I would have powers, yes! I would be glittering and fearless and above all earthly cares. But all of this means nothing to me now—there are many dangers from my own kind, and there are even worse dangers from even darker creatures. And now I creep around, hiding myself, wishing I was something other than what I am."

"Where do you live?" I asked. "Where do you go when you hide yourself away? You could come back to this house. You could live here again. You could come back to us."

Odette stiffened. "It isn't possible. I can never come back. The Firebird is just a myth—a pretty folktale. And I can't come back as I am. I can never rejoin the human world. I can never feel its warmth and love again." She paused, and her mouth twisted in a bitter smile. "I sought to place myself above you, only to find that once again you end up with everything, and I end up with nothing."

Odette stood up suddenly, and I moved back in fear.

"I have just enough affection left for you to tell you to leave," she said fiercely. "Get out of this village before you get yourself killed."

She extinguished her candle, and the room was plunged into darkness. In a panic, I fumbled for the lamp by my bed.

By the time I had the light on, Odette had gone.

Chapter Nineteen

After Odette left, I tried to force myself to sleep—that was all I could really do—I could hardly tell GM that a vampire had come to visit me.

So I passed in and out of troubled dreams.

I knew that I needed to sleep—even though the horror that was Timofei Mstislav was standing outside.

I needed to have a clear head in the morning.

The situation I found myself in was getting worse by the moment, and I knew that I wouldn't be able to fight off Timofei on my own. I'd only defeated Timofei's father with the help of William and the clear fire—and I didn't have either one of them any more. And leaving Russia, as Odette had suggested, wasn't an option. I knew from past experience that Timofei would follow me wherever I went.

If I were to survive, I would have to have help.

William, of course, was long gone. Galina and the Leshi had both disappeared. Odette was clearly not inclined to be cooperative. And GM wasn't equipped to deal with the supernatural.

I had only one option.

I would have to seek out the vampire Innokenti.

I was sure he was dangerous. But he'd also told me to return to Russia for my own safety. Perhaps he could help me to ward off Timofei—or at least help me to get GM out of the country unharmed.

Odette had said that GM was safe from Timofei, but I was still uneasy about her.

I didn't want anything to happen to GM because of me.

So I did the best I could to sleep, and to a certain extent, I succeeded.

When the first gray light of dawn crept into my room, I decided to give up struggling with my dreams.

I got out of bed and went to the window. I was just in time to see Timofei turn and shuffle off. It was a terrible sight—the inhuman creature looked even more horrific silhouetted against the rosy rays of the sunrise.

I watched Timofei until he disappeared, and then I stood listening. The house was quiet, and I figured that GM was still asleep. I decided to go right away to look for Innokenti. Maybe I could catch him before he settled in to sleep for the day—or whatever it was that he did. I also wanted to return the lantern I'd taken from the Mstislav crypt—I just wanted to get it out of the house. And finally, I had to retrieve my bicycle from Galina's place—I might need it to get around again.

I dressed quickly and slipped out of the house with the lantern, leaving GM a note telling her that I'd gone for a walk. I would, of course, be gone for more than a little while, and I had a feeling that GM would be angry when time passed and I didn't return. But that couldn't be helped right now.

I had work to do.

The morning was cold, and the light was still low—it would be another half hour or so before the sun itself peeked over the horizon.

I hurried to the Mstislav mansion.

I was loath to enter the crypt again—especially now that I knew that one of its inhabitants had risen once more. It occurred to me that Timofei might be using the crypt as his daytime hiding place, but I quickly discarded the idea. Timofei's body had gone missing, and it could hardly be classified as missing if it returned to the crypt every day. And surely he'd want to stay far away from his tomb—a kost could only be laid to rest again by wrestling him back into his grave. I didn't know if a kost hybrid could be defeated the same way, but I imagined it would still be something he feared.

All the same, I felt my heart hammering as I reached the Mstislav mansion and crept around the massive building to the crypt. The entrance to the crypt yawned open, just as black and forbidding as it had been the night before. I felt a flash of panic, and I considered just dropping the lantern and running off. But I heard footsteps coming toward me over the frost-covered grass, and I knew I had to hide.

I didn't want to get caught trespassing—especially not at the Mstislav mansion. The only place I could possibly conceal myself was in the crypt.

I forced myself to step over the threshold and climb down the steps.

I reached the landing, as I had the night before, and this time, I tripped over some of the tools that the workers had left lying on the floor. I stumbled back against the wall.

I waited, frozen, hoping that whoever was outside hadn't heard all the noise I was making.

The footsteps in the grass approached the crypt, and I held my breath.

I was sure to be found.

But the footsteps kept going, and I set the lantern down and crept back up to the entrance of the crypt.

Very cautiously, I peered out.

I was just in time to see a familiar figure disappearing around the side of the mansion.

It was Maksim Neverov.

His presence at the mansion wasn't that strange—he was, after all, related to the Mstislavs. There was no reason for me to read anything sinister into his being here. He had every right to visit with his family—or to live with them, if that happened to be the case.

But I had to wonder—had Maksim been in Krov back in October? Had he been in the mansion the night I was lured there by Odette?

Had he known what Timofei had been up to in the crypt and in the tunnels that stretched under the Wasteland?

I told myself to forget about it for the moment. I wasn't likely to find out the answers to any of those questions any time soon, and I certainly couldn't ask Maksim about them. In any event, there was no reason for me to suspect Maksim of wrongdoing.

All the same, I was disturbed to see him at the mansion.

I waited for a moment, inside the crypt entrance, watching to see if Maksim was really gone. When he didn't reappear, I ran as fast as I could across the grounds.

Then I hurried away from the Mstislav mansion.

While out the previous day, I'd discovered that Krov had one bus that made a circuit of the town, and one of the stops was the abandoned monastery at the edge of the Pure Woods. I caught the bus and got off at the monastery. Then I walked toward Galina's house.

By the time I reached the house and my abandoned bicycle, the sun was shining brightly in the morning sky.

GM would definitely have begun to wonder what had happened to me.

I went up to Galina's door and knocked, but as I expected, there was no answer. I tried the door, and it was open as before. I peered in, but the house still appeared to be empty.

There had been a faint hope in my heart that Galina might have come home in the middle of the night, but I'd known all along that it was highly unlikely.

I wasn't going to get out of having to find Innokenti that easily.

I pulled the door closed and stood on the step for a long moment. I didn't really want to find Innokenti, and the truth was, I didn't really know where to start.

He'd come to me once when I'd summoned the clear fire in the Pure Woods—attracted by the clear fire itself. Perhaps he could be attracted by it again.

I'd been standing in a sacred place when I'd summoned it, and I figured that that would be the best place to start looking for him. But he would surely be under cover by now. Would he come out of his hiding place during the day to see me? Would I even be able to summon the clear fire?

I didn't know, but I had to give it a try.

I made my way through the white trees of the Pure Woods to the circle of small stones where I'd first called the clear fire out of its otherworldly hiding place. I stepped into the circle and remembered the feeling of peace and contentment that the clear fire had brought me when I had controlled it.

I'd tried last night to summon the clear fire and failed.

I would try again now.

I closed my eyes and reached out with my mind. Softly, I sang to myself the song that would bring the clear fire to me.

But the clear fire didn't appear, and I couldn't recreate the state of mind that had once enabled me to summon it. It was almost as if something were blocking me.

I figured I would have to be more direct.

"Innokenti!" I cried. "Innokenti!"

There was no answer.

I wandered through the trees, calling for Innokenti, but I didn't see him or anyone else. Eventually, I was forced to give up—this clearly wasn't the way to find him. Though I didn't like the idea, I knew I'd have better luck if I tried looking for him at night—after all, that's when the local vampires would most likely be out looking for me.

I began to walk back toward Galina's house.

If I was being honest, I had to admit that I was relieved that I hadn't found Innokenti, and I was even more relieved to be able to put off the search for him until later that night.

Now all I had to do was deal with GM.

I rode my bicycle back to the house, and as I expected, GM was upset.

"Where have you been?" she demanded as I walked in. "You've been gone for hours."

"I was just riding my bike," I said evasively.

"You said you were going for a walk," GM said. "I don't mind, of course, if you go for a walk. But you were gone long enough that I feared something had happened to you. And then all of a sudden you're no longer walking—you're riding."

"I rented a bike yesterday," I said. "I had it with me when I ran into you and Maksim."

GM looked momentarily stunned. I could see that she was reliving the moment of horror when she realized that her granddaughter had found her with the sweetheart of her youth. She'd probably been far too preoccupied with the situation to notice that I'd had a bicycle.

I continued. "I went to see Galina yesterday, and I accidentally left it at her house." This was true—in my haste to get away from Timofei Mstislav, I'd been forced to leave the bicycle behind.

"I went over to Galina's to retrieve the bike this morning, and I rode it back. Making the trip over there took me a little while."

This was also true—I just happened to leave out the fact that I'd gone looking in the Pure Woods for a vampire while I was out there.

GM seemed mollified. "Well, I suppose you can't leave rental property lying around. It was a good idea for you to retrieve the bike as soon as possible. But you should have mentioned that that's where you were going in your note. I would have worried less."

"Sorry, GM."

She was right, of course. Mentioning the bicycle in the note would have given her a good reason for my long absence—I hadn't been thinking clearly.

And that was due in no small part to my anxiety over Innokenti.

My stomach twisted itself into knots at the thought of him.

"What's wrong, solnyshko?" GM asked. "Are you ill?"

"No, I'm not ill," I said. I thought back to Galina's empty house. "It's just—Galina wasn't home, and neither was Aleksandr. And then I heard they were missing."

GM sighed.

"You knew?" I asked.

"Galina and I were in contact when we first returned to the U.S. in October," GM said. "And then Galina broke off contact rather abruptly, which was unusual, as she'd been quite a voluble correspondent. I suspected that something must have changed for her, so I tried to be noncommittal when you asked if we would see her and Aleksandr. I didn't know if she'd see us or not. And then once we arrived here in Krov, I too learned that Galina and Aleksandr had gone missing."

"Do you know what happened to them?"

"No," GM said simply.

"You don't seem very concerned."

"Katie, my relationship with Galina has always been difficult, and Aleksandr I'm sure, is a nice young man, but it may be for the best that they're out of our lives at the moment."

"What if something terrible happened to them?" I asked. "What if they're hurt?"

Or worse, I thought.

"I don't want any harm to come to Galina or Aleksandr," GM replied. "But look how much simpler things are without them. There hasn't been so much as a whisper about the supernatural since they've been gone—except for that little bit of nonsense about the witch-fire. The atmosphere around here is much healthier without them."

I supposed from GM's perspective that that was all true. So far, I'd been able to keep her out of all the supernatural terrors I'd encountered on this trip. In fact, the worst thing that had happened to her was that her granddaughter had met her former fiancé.

I just hoped I could continue to keep her safely out of everything that was going on.

GM's cell phone rang, and she quickly answered it.

"Yes, yes, she's here now, Maksim. Thank you for looking. No, I think I'd better not. I don't know about tomorrow. I'm sorry. But I thank you for your concern."

She ended the call and looked up at me apologetically. "I called Maksim when I thought you'd gone missing. Good man that he is, he went out looking for you."

I could hear GM's fondness for Maksim in her voice, and I felt the stirrings of conscience.

I didn't want to tell her what I'd found out about Maksim's family ties last night, but I felt like I had to. If there was any chance that he could be dangerous, as Odette had suggested, she had to know.

"GM," I began, "I heard yesterday that Maksim was related to the Mstislav family on his mother's side." I paused. "And then, this morning I saw him walking on the grounds of the Mstislav mansion."

GM looked amused. "I know about his mother, solnyshko. I did meet him long before you were born. And I'm not surprised to hear that he was over at the mansion. Since the horrible things Timofei did there, Maksim has been called in by other members of the family to go over both the mansion and Timofei's finances to make sure that there are no more terrible secrets he hid away."

She ran a hand over my hair. "Not all the Mstislavs are bad people, though I can understand why you might think so. And I don't blame you for the way you feel. That's another reason why I didn't want you to meet Maksim. I didn't want his family associations to cause you any distress."

I was greatly relieved—I'd really liked Maksim, and I didn't want to be suspicious of him.

GM began to steer me toward the kitchen that she'd recently stocked.

"Now, I have a feeling that you didn't eat anything before you left," she said. "I insist that you eat something now."

Once in the kitchen, GM pushed me into a chair and began to bustle around.

As she started to pour out cereal, GM's brief phone conversation with Maksim came back to me. "Did Maksim want to meet up with you today?"

"Yes—we'd planned to have lunch together, but now it's out of the question."

"Why?" I asked.

"Don't be silly," GM said.

"Why is it silly?" I asked. "I'm not ill. I'm not hurt. I just went to get my bicycle, and now I'm home again. You shouldn't change your plans because of me."

"You pointed out that Maksim was a Mstislav yourself," GM said. "So how can I see him now?"

"I don't dislike Maksim," I said. "In fact, I like him a lot. It's just that someone told me he was a Mstislav and that you should be careful. I was just worried about you."

"You are sweet to be worried about me."

"GM, I'm glad to find out Maksim isn't dangerous and that all Mstislavs aren't evil."

"That is a good lesson," she said.

"I don't want you to ruin your life because of me. I've seen how happy Maksim makes you."

GM set a bowl and a glass in front of me.

"Eat your cereal. Drink your juice."

"I'll eat if you'll agree to have lunch with Maksim."

GM and I stared at each other for a long moment.

Eventually, she smiled and threw up her hands.

"All right, solnyshko. I'll have lunch with Maksim."

I picked up my spoon and took a bite of the cereal.

GM gave me an appraising glance.

"It's a funny thing," she said. "It turns out you are more stubborn than I suspected."

I had to smile then, too.

That afternoon, GM went out to lunch with Maksim, and I went out on my bicycle again—this time to buy GM a Christmas present.

I had to pass the hours until the time came for me to go out looking for Innokenti, and I figured I might as well do something pleasant.

Back in October, Odette had used a shopping spree as a cover for her need to rest during the day. But she actually had gone shopping—she just hadn't spent as much time doing it as she'd pretended. Odette had purchased a lot of beautiful things, and I'd wondered where she'd found them. I knew about the little row of shops not far from our house, but there was no place there that carried the kind of expensive things that Odette had brought home. I decided to find out where she'd gone shopping.

As I rode up to the Mstislav mansion, I passed a group of girls who were laden with shopping bags—they'd obviously just been doing some holiday shopping of their own. I stopped and asked them where they'd bought everything, and they gave me directions.

As I well knew, there was a road that ran past the Mstislav mansion to the west—that was the road I'd been on a number of memorable times already. It ran past the Wasteland and the monastery. But I learned from the girls that there was another, smaller road that ran past the Mstislav mansion to the east. If I followed that road, which was really more of a dirt path at first, I would eventually come upon a paved road that led to the shops.

I thanked the girls and rode on.

I found the dirt path and followed it past a rather precipitous drop that fell away steeply from the south side of the path—the girls had told me it was known as Mara's Drop. There was no guardrail, and I couldn't help but think that a spill on this path could produce a very unpleasant fall.

Eventually, I left Mara's Drop behind, and the path turned into a wide, paved road. The road led me to a small cluster of high-end shops, and beyond the shops I could make out the roofs of a community of large houses. From what I could see, none of the houses could rival the Mstislav mansion, but they looked impressive nonetheless. I remembered that Odette had once told me that her parents had lived in a big, impressive house. I wondered if I was looking at the community where that house had been.

I turned my attention toward the shops, and I quickly discovered that they were out of my price range. I wandered amongst the high-end boutiques, feeling discouraged, until I discovered a small antiques shop that seemed more down-to-earth. I went inside.

I found a lot of interesting things in the shop—a Russian antiques store was very different from an American one. And one item in particular caught my eye—a necklace.

Lying in a glass case was a slender, silver chain with a graceful pendant—it appeared to be a stylized figure of a woman. I asked to see it.

The figure was indeed that of a woman, and it seemed to be made of iron just like the charm William had given me. The rendering of the woman was more elegant than my cross, but I wondered if it might offer the same protection against the kost. Of course, we were dealing with a kost hybrid now, rather than a regular kost, and I was unsure whether charms of this type had any effect on such a creature.

And it was entirely possible that the necklace had no special properties at all. But I figured any protection this charm might potentially offer would be worth it. GM was very attached to her own cross. But maybe she would wear this necklace, too.

The pendant turned out to be inexpensive, and I bought it. I also stopped and bought a powerful flashlight in a hardware store. Then I rode home.

I had lunch first, and then I searched the house for wrapping paper. I was lucky enough to find some in the attic, and I wrapped up my little box and placed it under our tree.

I stood back then and gazed for a little while at our decorated tree. The moment was so peaceful and so pleasant that it was hard for me to believe that there were horrors waiting for me—horrors that hid during the day and crept forth at night.

It was those very horrors that I'd have to go out to meet tonight.

GM came home not long after I'd wrapped her present, and then time seemed to speed up—the rest of the day flew by.

All too soon the sun set, and I found myself staring out the window in the back door—it was the same door that Timofei Mstislav had stared at so steadily on the previous night. At any moment, I expected him to show up at our house to resume his grim vigil.

I knew he couldn't come in, but I didn't want GM to see him—I didn't want to see him myself for that matter. There was something inherently evil and unnatural in his shuffling yet powerful body that made him horrible to look at, even when he wasn't actively attacking.

And if he did show up, I wasn't sure how I was going to get out of the house to find to Innokenti. I wasn't at all confident that I could get past Timofei Mstislav.

I continued to watch, but he didn't appear.

I wondered how long my luck would last.

"What are you looking for, solnyshko?" GM asked, frowning at me. "You've been standing there for a very long time."

"Nothing. Nothing at all," I said. I wasn't sure I sounded convincing.

"Well, come away from the door. It's time for dinner."

I ate, but I couldn't really taste anything, and I tried not to let myself think that this could be the last time I would ever have dinner with GM.

You have to survive at least till Christmas morning, I told myself. *You have to give GM her present. It's only three more days.*

I smiled a little at my own joke and tried harder to appear normal and unconcerned.

"The Firebird Festival is tomorrow night," GM said. "If it's still what it used to be, it should be a beautiful, joyous celebration. Would you like to go?"

I agreed to go, but I had a feeling that I did so a little too enthusiastically, as my reply caused GM to give me a very strange look. But she didn't make any comment, and she seemed pleased that I wanted to go.

I supposed we talked after that, but at some point I'd stopped listening. It seemed to me that dinner passed by very quickly, and so did the rest of the evening. Before I knew it, I was climbing the stairs to go to bed.

In a way, it was a relief to go to my room—it meant I could watch out my window for the arrival of Timofei Mstislav. There was no doubt in my mind that he'd return tonight. But mercifully, he didn't appear.

All too soon, I heard GM come up the stairs and settle in. I knew that as soon as the house grew quiet, I would have to go out into the night. I would have to find Innokenti while avoiding the vampires that were after me. And if I succeeded in finding Innokenti and further succeeded in securing his help, I would have to go confront Timofei— because I knew he would never stop hunting me.

Don't go to sleep just yet, GM, I prayed. *Stay up a few moments longer.*

But the house lapsed into silence, and I slipped out into the night. The house, the yard, the street were all quiet. There was still no sign of Timofei.

Even so, I was shaking as I climbed on my bicycle and rode in the direction of the Pure Woods.

The night was clear and cold and seemed somehow unnaturally still, as if the night itself were waiting with bated breath to see whether I would live or die.

I told myself not to think like that.

I kept riding and riding until I reached the vast expanse of the Wasteland. I stopped then to turn on my flashlight—I'd be out of range of the village's artificial light very soon. I would go back to the Pure Woods and the stone circle. I'd try to find Innokenti from there.

My flashlight didn't illuminate the road ahead of me quite as far as I would have liked, so I was forced to go more slowly as I rode on. I stopped frequently, too, to send the beam from my flashlight sweeping out in an arc over the Wasteland.

I didn't want anyone sneaking up on me from that quarter.

I'd just finished my latest sweep, when a flutter of movement caught my eye. I felt panic rising in me, but I forced myself to swing the light back in the direction of the movement.

I drew in my breath sharply when I realized what was moving—there was no mistaking what I'd seen.

There was a man, not far away, crossing the Wasteland.

Even though he was moving away from me, I knew exactly who it was.

It was William.

Chapter Twenty

I jumped off the bicycle and let it drop to the side. The terrain of the Wasteland appeared to be rough, and I figured that the bike would only slow me down. In any event, William wasn't far away.

He was moving quickly, but surely I could catch him.

I ran across the blighted plain toward him.

"William!" I cried. "William!"

But he didn't turn around.

He continued to move along swiftly, and I ran after him, keeping him in the beam of my flashlight. I never took my eyes off him—I was sure of that, but without warning, he suddenly vanished.

I stopped and swung my flashlight around in an arc and back again.

William was nowhere to be seen.

I ran toward the spot where I'd just seen him a moment before. A tiny voice in my head warned me that this could be a trap—what if someone was showing me what I wanted to see? But I ignored the voice and kept going.

"William!" I cried. "Where are you?"

Just when I thought that I must have overshot the spot on which William had last stood, I felt a tingle run through my entire body, as if I'd just run through a field of electricity.

The air around me rippled, and I suddenly found myself standing on a cobblestone street. I spun around in disbelief.

The Wasteland had disappeared.

In its place was a narrow, poorly lit street lined by dingy houses. I saw to my shock that a dark castle rose in the distance.

I was positive that none of what was before me had been here a moment ago.

And William was nowhere to be seen.

I took a few tentative steps forward, and my footsteps sounded unnaturally loud in the quiet street.

"William?" I whispered. I had a feeling that this wasn't a place where it would be a good idea to make my presence generally known.

All the same, I didn't want to go back to the Wasteland. I was positive I'd seen William, and if there was any chance that I could be with him again—even for a moment—I had to take it.

And at the moment, everything seemed safe enough. No one had pounced on me when I'd stumbled into this place—whatever it was. In fact, the street before me seemed to be completely deserted.

I moved forward, clutching my flashlight. I walked along the street, until it dead-ended in a building. Then I turned onto the street that ran perpendicular to it. I continued on, on zigzagging streets, into what appeared to be a town of some kind.

I decided to make my way to the castle in the distance.

I soon realized that the place wasn't as deserted as I'd thought. Shadows glided past me and then melted back into the greater darkness. Eyes peered at me from dingy windows and from around corners and then disappeared.

I was just passing a row of shabby houses when a door opened in one of them, and a young woman with golden curls looked out. I turned my flashlight on her, and she drew back into her doorway in alarm. I lowered my flashlight.

She looked out again, and she smiled at me shyly.

"I've not seen you here before." The girl's voice was soft and musical. "Are you lost, child?"

I was wary of the girl before me. I knew only too well that a pretty, innocent face could hide a heart full of treachery. But the girl seemed awkward and a bit frightened herself.

"I'm looking for a friend of mine," I said. "I saw him come in here. Then he seemed to vanish."

The girl blinked, and a look of fear suffused her young features. "He isn't a vampire, is he? There are a lot of them around here."

"Well, yes, he is—kind of," I said.

The girl's eyes widened, and she drew back.

She moved to close the door.

"No—wait. Don't go," I said.

She hesitated for a moment. "Are you a vampire?"

"No," I said.

The girl stepped tentatively out onto her doorstep.

"If you're not a vampire, then why are you looking for one?"

"Like I said, he's my friend."

"If he's a vampire, won't he hurt you—or even kill you?"

"No, he's not like that."

"Would he hurt me, do you think?"

"No, I'm sure he wouldn't."

"You're a strange girl," the young woman said, looking me over. She took a step closer and smiled at me. "But I'll help you."

"What is this place?" I asked.

"Lower your voice," the girl whispered, glancing down the street. "There are a lot of dangerous people in here."

I followed her gaze. A tall, thin man had appeared at the end of the street. He was staring at us steadily. Or rather, he seemed to be staring at me.

"Look here," the girl said. "I don't have any shoes on. You'd better come inside. I'll get dressed properly, and then I'll help you find your friend."

I looked down. Her tiny feet were indeed bare. I glanced toward the man at the end of the street. He seemed to have moved closer.

"Maybe we would be safer inside," I said.

The girl beckoned to me. "Quickly now. I don't like the look of that man over there."

I started forward but stopped, startled, when the girl in front of me suddenly cried out and clapped a hand to her cheek as if she'd just been struck in the face.

A moment later, five razor-thin wounds opened on the girl's ivory skin, and blood began to run down her face.

"You stay away from my cousin!"

I turned. Odette, her eyes bright with fury, was standing by my side. My eyes were drawn to her right hand—her pale fingers were stained red.

"She's mine, Odette!" the girl screamed, still holding her bleeding face. "I found her! You go away! Go hunt for yourself!"

"This one isn't for you," Odette said. "And she isn't for anyone else in here, either. Touch her, and you'll have me to deal with."

The girl stared at Odette with hate-filled eyes, but took a step back. She hurried into her house and slammed the door.

I glanced down the street toward the man who'd been staring at me.

The man had vanished.

I looked back at the closed door through which the golden-haired girl had disappeared.

"She was going to kill me, wasn't she?" I said.

"Yes," Odette replied shortly.

"Was she a vampire?"

"Yes," Odette said. "And you're a fool."

She grabbed me by the wrist. "You've got to get out of the street. I can hold most of them off as individuals, but I can't fight them all if they attack in a pack—which they might do. Food doesn't often wander so innocently into our midst."

Perhaps it was my imagination, but I thought I could feel the chill of Odette's hand all the way through my gloves.

She hauled me down several streets and into a tall, stone tower. I found myself standing in a small, round room with a few sticks of furniture and a wavering, sickly candle. A staircase in the center of the room spiraled up into darkness.

Odette pushed on the metal door behind us, and it slid closed so heavily that the walls around us seemed to shake.

I realized I was shaking myself. I wasn't afraid of Odette—at least not at the moment. But the encounter with the golden-haired girl had left me rattled. She'd seemed so harmless that I'd succumbed to her trap without feeling any suspicion at all.

If not for Odette, I probably would have been murdered tonight—and then I would have disappeared completely.

No one would even have known where to look for my body.

"Thank you, Odette," I said.

She glared at me. "It shouldn't have been necessary for me to rescue you."

"How did you know the girl was going to attack me?" I asked.

"I already told you she was a vampire."

"Yes, I know. But she seemed so scared. She actually seemed to be afraid of me."

Odette's lips curved into a smile, and there was a hint of admiration in her eyes. "Very effective, isn't it? That was Veronika, and that's the trick she plays on all her human victims. She's really only got the one, but it's nearly one hundred percent effective. No one expects a frightened girl to be a predator. She acts like prey, and that sets the prey at ease. I understand it's particularly effective on the males."

Odette tilted her head to one side. "You need to learn not to be so trusting. In any event, I don't need to know Veronika's favorite trick in order to know that she'll attack you. Everyone here will attack you."

She sat down in a rickety chair. "The question is—what are we going to do with you now? I'm suddenly in the very awkward position of being responsible for you. I've never been responsible for anything before. Suppose you start by telling me what you're doing here?"

"Where *are* we?" I asked.

"You are in the village," Odette replied. "Zamochit Village—and we have only one type of citizen here. I'll give you one guess as to what it is."

A fresh wave of panic washed over me. "So, I'm in a village entirely populated by—"

"Vampires. Yes. You're familiar with the term 'zamochit,' aren't you? It's a recent term, as far as we are concerned, and it refers to completely breaking a body—just as our souls are broken."

"How did I get here?" I asked.

"I believe I just asked you that myself," Odette replied.

"I was walking—no—running across the Wasteland," I said. "And then I felt the air around me ripple—or shimmer—or something like that. And suddenly I was standing on a street full of houses rather than in an empty field. I don't have any idea what happened."

"There's a barrier around Zamochit Village—a supernatural one," Odette said. "You aren't supposed to be able to cross it—no non-vampire is. Some of us—like me—have special gifts—certain advanced abilities. Vampires like that created the barrier. And there's another one in the Pure Woods—it surrounds the original vampire community in this area. But the original community was much smaller, and the vampire population eventually overflowed its boundaries. So, the village was built here. Humans don't like the Wasteland anyway, so they tend to avoid it. And the charm of the barrier hides the village from sight and confuses the humans, warding them off if they do wander out here. They just keep walking around the perimeter of the village—never realizing that there's a huge swath of the Wasteland that they can't cross."

"It certainly fooled me," I said.

"Now tell me," Odette said sharply. "What were you doing out in the Wasteland? I thought I told you to go home before you got killed."

I hesitated. Would Odette help me to find William? Or would she force me to leave?

"I'll tell you what you're doing here," she said when I didn't reply. "You came out here looking for Timofei Mstislav, didn't you? I already told you that you can't fight a creature like that. All you can do is run."

She stood suddenly and seized me by the arm. "You're going home right now."

"Odette, wait!" I cried. "I saw William. I was following him. That's how I ended up in here."

She released me. "William Sursur? The one who's up at the castle? The one everyone makes such a fuss over?"

"Yes, William Sursur," I said eagerly.

Odette tapped her chin. "He came for you in the crypt that night, didn't he?" She stared at me for a long moment, and something stirred in her eyes.

"I'll take you to him," Odette said at last.

"You can really do that?" I asked.

"Yes, I can." Odette sat down again. "But I'll have to think of a way to get you safely through the village to the castle. Getting you out would have been comparatively easy—we're close to the border here, though it still wouldn't have been trouble free. But getting you in deeper will be more difficult. Some of the creatures that live here are little more than animals. If we took to the streets to get to the castle, they would eventually be on us in a swarm. They'd tear you to pieces."

I began to feel weak with fear. I sank into a rickety chair next to Odette.

There was a crash and a cry from the floor above us, and I heard heavy footsteps walking overhead. I jumped out of my chair and stared up into the darkness above the spiraling staircase.

"What was that?" I asked. "What's up there?"

"That's the border watch," Odette said absent-mindedly. "He's nothing to worry about. He probably just fell out of his chair."

"The border watch?" I said. "Is he a vampire?"

"Of course."

The footsteps subsided, but I continued to stare upward. I was expecting an angry vampire to come crashing down the stairs at any moment.

"You can relax," Odette said. "That's just Hadrian."

"Hadrian?"

"Yes. He's not a very effective guard—that's why I knew we'd be safe in here."

"What's Hadrian guarding exactly?" I asked.

Odette sighed. "I thought I told you—he's guarding the border—allegedly. There are three other watchtowers similar to this one in the village. They're set close to points at which the supernatural barrier meets the unenchanted Wasteland. Hadrian is supposed to watch the border in case someone like you manages to get past the barrier. He's supposed to detain the intruder and alert the authorities. But intruders are rare, and Hadrian is usually drunk or sleeping—or both—so very little actual watching goes on."

"He's drunk?" I asked. "Does alcohol affect vampires?"

"The kind Hadrian favors does. He drinks fermented human blood."

"Oh," I said. "That's disturbing."

"Yes, it is," Odette replied.

I sat down again, and several quiet minutes passed—there were no further noises from overhead. Soon, however, I began to worry about what could be going on outside.

I glanced over at the heavy, metal door. "Does everyone in the village know that Hadrian isn't a very good guard?"

"Yes," Odette said. "I thought you were finally going to be quiet. I knew it was too good to be true."

"If Hadrian is so ineffective, what's to stop the vampires outside from coming in here to get us?"

"This tower is government property," Odette said. "No one is afraid of Hadrian. But they're all afraid of the group up at the castle. If anything happens to Hadrian, or if this tower is damaged the perpetrators will be punished—severely. And what constitutes 'severe' for a vampire is far more terrible than anything you humans could come up with."

I was silenced, but not entirely reassured.

After another few moments, Odette stood up.

She held out her hand. "All right. It's time to go. I haven't come up with a particularly great plan—in fact—it's pretty simple. But it's the best I can do under the circumstances."

"Where are we going?" I asked.

"Up," Odette replied.

"Up?"

"Yes, up. We have to get over the castle wall, you know."

"Are you suggesting that we fly?" I asked.

"No—not exactly. We're going to glide over the rooftops."

"Maybe you can do that," I said, as panic threatened to overwhelm me. "But I don't think that's something I can do."

"You don't have to be able to do it," Odette said smugly. "As you already know, I have powers that are beyond those of ordinary vampires."

I did indeed know—Odette had used her powers to break the seal on Gleb Mstislav's tomb. She was the one who had set Gleb free—so he could come after me.

Odette continued. "I have some limited ability to levitate objects and people—people have been a little trickier for me, but as long as you hold onto my hand, you should be fine."

I wasn't sure that I liked the sound of this. "We're going to go to the castle I saw in the distance, by way of levitation?"

"Yes."

"But that castle looked very far away," I said. "That's a long way to go off the ground."

"Distances don't mean so much to us," Odette said. "Our speed makes miles seem like nothing at all. Come on. We should leave now. I want to get this over with quickly."

I stood, and the two of us went up the spiral staircase into the darkness. As we ascended, it became harder for me to see, and I wasn't very keen on the idea of stumbling and possibly waking Hadrian from his drunken slumbers. So I went slowly, and I found myself placing my feet on each step as quietly as I could.

"What are you doing?" Odette hissed at me from above. "What's taking so long?"

"What about Hadrian?" I asked.

"He's sleeping," she hissed. "I'm sure of it. Besides, he's harmless."

Odette said he was harmless, but I noticed she was whispering.

I continued to climb the stairs gingerly, and eventually, Odette reached down and hauled me up by my coat.

The room above appeared to be completely dark at first. After a moment, my eyes adjusted to the gloom, and I could see that there was an arched, open window on the far side of the room, through which a little bit of light filtered. I could also just make out a large shape by the window—a man was sitting in a chair with his feet resting on a spindly table that also supported a burned-out stub of candle and an empty bottle. His head was tilted back at an uncomfortable angle.

The man was clearly sleeping, but his bulk was impressive—I didn't want to meet him when he was awake.

"See?" Odette whispered. "That's Hadrian, and he's asleep like I said. In fact, from the looks of things, he's quite deeply asleep—he's completely dormant."

We'd been talking about vampires sleeping as if it was something normal, but I realized that I didn't actually know what that meant.

"Vampires sleep?" I asked.

"After a fashion," Odette replied. "We do have a period of decreased function—which you know about already—you know that creatures of the dark are weak during the day. But we also do need to go through a period of metabolic repair—that's what sleep is. If you have a body, it will always need to fix itself. But Hadrian's current state is more than that. We can go into a state of deep dormancy if we are badly injured but still largely intact. Wounds and injuries can heal over a period of weeks, or months, or even years. I suspect that Hadrian's current state is self-inflicted. Strong drink can induce oblivion in vampires as well as in humans."

Odette pulled me across the room to the window. Then she released her grip on my coat and climbed up onto the spindly table that supported Hadrian's feet.

She climbed onto the windowsill next and perched there, her shape a dark silhouette in the frame of the window.

"Come on," she hissed.

I climbed onto the table and tried not to glance at Hadrian or the bottle. As I reached the window, Odette's dark shape vanished, soaring upward.

I gripped the ledge and looked down into the street below. A single dark shape glided down the street and disappeared. I wondered if the figure below had spotted us.

"Hurry up," Odette hissed.

I looked up, and I could see Odette standing on the tower's pointed roof, a sliver of moon visible just over her shoulder, her red hair fanning out in the wind.

I glanced back down at the street below. It seemed very far away.

"I'm not sure about this," I whispered to Odette. "Are you sure we can't give the ground route a try?"

Odette crouched down and held out her hand. "I can do this. And so can you. Now get out here."

I climbed onto the ledge and grasped Odette's hand. Although I shouldn't have been surprised by her strength any longer, I was startled by just how easily she hauled me up and set me on my feet.

Up on the roof, the air seemed even colder, and the view was dizzying. A strong wind whipped around us, and I found my boots slipping on the roof's shingled surface.

I grabbed frantically for Odette, and she set me on my feet again. I noticed for the first time that she was clad only in a filmy black gown—her gauzy sleeves fluttered to the side, leaving her alabaster arms bare. She grasped my hand again, and this time I was sure—I could indeed feel the chill of her skin through the fabric of my gloves.

"Stay calm," Odette ordered. "And don't let go of my hand. I won't be able to buoy you up otherwise. Remember that."

I wasn't likely to forget.

Odette suddenly leaped forward, and my feet left the solid surface of the roof. I felt my body soar out into the open air, and I twisted and turned in panic, trying to grab onto Odette with my free hand, trying to grab onto anything that would break the fall that was sure to come.

A horrible thought popped into my head.

Had Odette brought me out here to kill me?

All she had to do was let me drop—I imagined she could save herself pretty easily.

Had I been, as Odette had said not so long ago, too trusting?

Of course, Odette could have killed me at any point while we were sitting in Hadrian's tower, or she could have done nothing earlier and simply let Veronika kill me.

These thoughts passed through my mind quickly, and just as quickly, I decided I could trust my cousin. Though panic still coursed through my body as we continued to soar through the air, I tried to quiet my mind, and I clung more tightly to Odette.

We dropped suddenly and landed on the rooftop of a nearby house.

"Stop wriggling so much," Odette said impatiently. "You're going to be fine—for now. Getting to the castle is the easier part. Things will get much harder once we get there."

She took off again, and though I was expecting the feeling of weightlessness that followed this time, it was still terrifying.

Once again, I found myself twisting in the air, flailing wildly for something to grab onto.

Odette brought us to rest on another rooftop.

"Seriously, stop wriggling," she said.

Before I had quite caught my breath, we were off again, and we soared from rooftop to rooftop with dizzying speed.

After several more successful landings, I began to relax just a little bit. I managed to raise my eyes and look around when we came to our next stop, and I realized that we'd halved the distance to the castle. The immense stone structure now loomed much closer, and I could see that its narrow windows were illuminated by a curiously subdued silver light.

"Why is everything so dark around here?" I asked.

"It *is* night," Odette replied. "And as you can perhaps imagine, vampires have an uneasy relationship with the light. Too much of it is hard on our keen senses—that's one of the reasons why we don't like the sun. The sun's harsh light floods our eyes, and its heat can be too much for our skin. There are disadvantages in having super-refined senses. But we do need some light to see by—we can't live in complete and total darkness. So, it might look dark around here to you, but to me it's as bright as day."

Without warning, she grabbed my hand again, and once more we took off into the night.

After several more jumps, Odette brought us to rest on a broad roof with a gentle slope. We were perhaps a quarter mile from the castle, and in the dim light, I could see there was a lot of activity along the castle's parapet wall—there were men in what looked like leather armor positioning themselves into the crenellations of the parapet. The men seemed to have spotted us, and each one trained a weapon on us.

"Are those crossbows?" I asked, squinting.

"Yes. They know we've been headed toward the castle, and vampires are a suspicious group. I told you this would be the hard part."

"Are they going to kill us?" I asked.

"They're certainly going to try," Odette replied.

"But they don't know why we're here," I protested. "Isn't there someone we could talk to? Some sort of gate official or something like that?"

"Vampires don't look for diplomatic solutions," Odette said. "And they're under more strain than usual at the castle these days—they're under imminent threat of invasion. No doubt we look like spies."

"What do you mean by 'imminent threat of invasion'?" I asked, startled.

"I'm sure William will explain it to you," Odette said. "And I'm sure he'll keep the others from killing you once we find him."

She stood up. "I want you to give him a message from me. Tell him that they're planning to attack the human village during the Firebird Festival."

"Who are 'they'?"

"The hybrid army. This information comes from a very good source."

"Why don't you tell him yourself?" I asked.

"Because as soon as we locate your William, I'm going to disappear."

Before I could ask any further questions, Odette had pulled me back into the air. We landed on three more rooftops, and then Odette stopped and turned to me.

"We're going over the castle wall now," she said. "Do *not* panic. Do *not* twist and flail around. This is going to be hard enough without your acting like an idiot. I need to pay attention to what the guards are doing. I can't do that if I have to focus on hanging on to you."

Odette seized my hand. And then, impossibly, we were soaring up into the sky, higher and higher. I felt terror rising in me, but I fought it down. I saw from high up that we were sailing over the castle's parapet. The guards had turned their crossbows on us, and a barrage of flat discs hurtled toward us. The discs split into three razor-sharp arcs and then burst into balls of flame.

Despite Odette's warning, I couldn't help crying out and trying to twist out of the way. I was sure we were going to be killed.

I could feel that we were sinking. And then, somehow we were on the ground.

We were standing in a courtyard, and there were vampires rushing toward us from all sides. Odette, however, seemed to know exactly where to go. Pulling me with her, she ran at blinding speed toward a door at the far end of the courtyard. As we reached the door, a man stepped into her path.

Something flashed in Odette's hand, and one of the discs that had been fired at us shot out and buried itself in the man's chest. Then it burst into a bright ball of flame.

The man fell to the ground, howling.

Odette smashed in the door in front of us, and then she dragged me through the castle's gloomy halls, which were lit only by an odd, silver light.

Vampires came out to stop us, but Odette had another disc in her grasp—this one she held on to. I watched as her slender, white hand lashed out again and again, leaving bloody gashes in faces, necks, torsos, arms.

We reached another door that Odette smashed in.

The door fell heavily to the ground.

Two men stood in the room before us, and they spun around.

I was now looking at Innokenti.

And William.

Odette turned to me, her eyes bright, her face and arms spattered with blood.

"Don't forget that I did this for you," she hissed.

Then, in a streak of black and red, she disappeared.

Chapter Twenty-One

William started toward me immediately.

"What are you doing here?" he demanded.

He was suddenly beside me, pulling me further into the room.

William's eyes flashed fire. "What do you think you're doing?"

I found I couldn't answer him.

I was stunned to see William standing right in front of me. I'd believed he was lost to me forever. I'd believed he'd left me for the Sídh.

And yet here he was with the vampires.

William was clearly very angry. As I looked at him, I felt tears stinging my eyes.

Vampires swarmed into the room, and William turned to face them.

He moved to stand in front of me.

"Get out of here!" he shouted. "Get out of here, all of you!"

The intruders stopped, staring at William uncertainly.

Innokenti looked on in mild amusement.

"Thank you, all," he said evenly. "You have acted quickly and decisively to come to our aid. The flame-haired vampire woman was the truly dangerous one, and she has now departed. I don't believe that she'll return. The one that remains is human—she's as harmless as a kitten. You may all depart. I thank you for your concern and your quick action."

The vampires eyed me as if they longed to tear me to pieces, but one by one, they melted away.

Then I was alone with Innokenti and William. Innokenti continued to look amused.

William continued to look furious.

"Your entrance was somewhat unorthodox, little one," Innokenti said. "But it in no measure lessens our delight in seeing you. Welcome to Rusalka Castle. I must apologize for the overzealousness of our guards. I trust you are unharmed?"

Once again, I found that I couldn't answer—the situation was just too surreal. I found myself looking around the room—looking at anything so that I didn't have to look at William's angry face.

The room we were standing in was well lit, especially in comparison with the rest of the castle. Tables and racks laden with weapons lined the walls. The room itself was vast, and at the far end were several stands supporting bulls-eye targets. A crossbow similar to the ones wielded by the castle guards was lying on the floor a few feet away.

My eyes moved involuntarily to William. He was wearing leather armor like the guards.

"What's going on here?" I asked.

"Target practice," Innokenti said conversationally.

"Target practice?" I said.

"This is our weapons development room," Innokenti replied. "We work in here where the walls are specially reinforced to prevent any accidents from harming the innocent."

His eyes flicked across the room. "Of course the door has unexpectedly turned out to be a weak point."

Innokenti went on, and his tone became reassuring. "But under ordinary circumstances, this room serves its purpose admirably. We test weapons here to make sure that they meet our high safety standards. Then we take them outside to uninhabited areas to do further testing. The locals have seen the flames from our ammunition tests, and in the most amusing fashion, have taken to calling it 'witch-fire.' There's no witchcraft about it, however."

"Why are you telling her all of this?" William asked sharply.

"Why not?" Innokenti's tone was mild. "Do you think she'll use the information against us?"

"Katie, you don't need to know about all this," William said angrily. "What are you doing here? I have half a mind to—"

He stopped and looked away.

I'd known that William didn't want me—he'd disappeared, left me completely alone, and hadn't thought enough of me to even say goodbye. Even so, I was stunned by the coldness of his reaction—I knew he'd loved me once.

How could his love have vanished so completely?

I was suddenly seized by anger.

"What am I doing here?" I said. "What are you doing here?"

The tears that had threatened for so long began to fall. "Why did you leave me alone? Why did you disappear? You left me without saying a word when I needed you the most."

William looked stricken. "What are you talking about? What do you mean I left you? I told you where I was going."

"You didn't," I said. Why would William say something so obviously untrue? "You never told me anything."

"I left you a letter," William said haltingly. "On your dresser, in your room. I thought if I left it there that there was no way you would miss it."

"I never received a letter," I said angrily.

"Even if you never received the letter, Katie," William said, agitated, "all you had to do was use the call. You know that. I gave you the words. I would have come to you from anywhere in the world."

"I *did* call for you," I cried. "When Anton attacked me. I called and you didn't come."

"Anton attacked you?" William asked in horror. He turned on Innokenti. "Was this your doing? Did you send him after her?"

"I can assure you I did no such thing," Innokenti replied. "Anton and I were under strict orders not to harm the human girl."

William didn't seem to have heard Innokenti. He turned back to me. I could see pain and fear in his eyes.

"I'm sorry, Katie," William said. "I never heard your call. I would never ignore it. I'll always come for you—you know that."

"Just out of curiosity," Innokenti interjected, "if Anton did indeed attack you, how did you get away? I hope you'll forgive me for being indelicate, but you're no match for him, or for any other vampire for that matter."

"Someone else came when I called for William," I replied. "He said his name was Cormac. I think he was one of the Sídh."

A look of genuine surprise spread over Innokenti's features. "Interesting. That's very suggestive."

"Do you recognize that name?" William asked.

"I do." Innokenti addressed me. "Little one, may I ask you—this 'dresser' where William claims to have left his letter—is it near a mirror?"

"Yes, it is," I said. "And I remember now—I found a tiny pile of ash on it that I couldn't explain. Is that significant?"

"Perhaps," said Innokenti.

He lapsed into silence.

"I called again after that," I said to William—the words just tumbled out. "But neither you nor Cormac appeared. And then Anton came back. He told me that the Sídh had a way to remove the vampire aspect of your nature. He said that they would cure you and give you back your memories if you agreed to give me up and never see me again. He said that you'd accepted their offer."

William turned on Innokenti furiously. "Did you send Anton to harass her?"

"No, William. I didn't," Innokenti replied calmly. "Don't distress yourself."

"You didn't send Anton to attack her?" William demanded.

"No."

"You didn't send him to tell her a lot of lies?"

"No."

"And I suppose you're going to tell me that you had nothing to do with the fact that I couldn't hear Katie calling to me, aren't you? You're going to tell me that you weren't blocking me from hearing her."

"No, William, I wasn't blocking you."

William's voice suddenly rang out angrily in the vast room.

"Then why couldn't she hear me?"

"I can't tell you."

"Can't or won't?" William demanded.

"I've been instructed to remain silent on this topic. My orders were simply to convince you and the human girl to return to Russia. And in a roundabout way, it appears that I succeeded in getting both of you here. My orders don't allow for explanations of a sensitive nature."

"Your orders," William said bitterly.

"Yes, my orders. You know I exist only to serve others."

William seemed to swell up to twice his normal size. His voice rang out again.

"I want to see them!"

His anger seemed to fill the room, like a living thing, and even though it was all directed at Innokenti, I found myself taking a step back.

"William, please contain yourself." Innokenti's voice was steady, but I could see that he was eyeing William warily. "Be reasonable."

But William was in no mood to be reasonable.

"I want to see them!" he thundered. "Now!"

Innokenti held up his hands pacifically. "Very well—I'll take you to them. But you should know that they'll be none too pleased to be disturbed. They'll just be waking up. And they aren't accustomed to having an interview forced upon them. You risk kindling their ire. Even you are not so special."

William simply stared at Innokenti, and a tense silence ensued.

Eventually, Innokenti bowed his head.

"I will do as you ask," he said. "But remember that I tried to warn you. You may follow me. The girl will be safe enough here."

"Katie will come with me," William said sternly.

Innokenti's eyebrows rose. "You want the girl to see—them?"

"I'm not leaving her alone in this place."

Innokenti gave William a sardonic smile. "There's a phrase in English—'it's your funeral'? If you wish to take Katie along, then who am I to stop you? If you will both follow me, then."

Innokenti crossed the room and stepped over the broken door.

William placed his hand on my back and guided me toward the doorway.

"William, where are we going?" I asked.

"You'll understand very soon. Stay close to me," he said.

Out in the hall, we were plunged back into the strange, silver gloom that seemed to pervade the castle.

Innokenti led us to a tower and then up a staircase that closely hugged the wide, curving wall. He stopped before a large, iron door that was embellished with gold.

"Wait here," Innokenti said. "I will do what I can to smooth your way."

"Wait just a minute," William said. "It occurs to me that you didn't seem very surprised to see Katie show up here at the castle. Did you know she was in Krov?"

"Yes," Innokenti said.

"And you didn't tell me?"

"It was for the best," Innokenti replied. There was a hint of a challenge in his light eyes. "Now, as I said, I will try to smooth your way. One does not interrupt royalty lightly."

Innokenti disappeared through the gold door, which slammed closed behind him.

"What does he mean by 'royalty'?" I whispered.

William said nothing, but he reached out and gripped my hand. I was still wearing my gloves, but even so, his touch was reassuring.

I looked up at him. William's face was set into harsh lines. It was an expression I had seen him wear before—when he'd first met me, and when he'd faced the kost Gleb Mstislav.

It was a face he wore when he met an enemy.

We waited in tense silence.

Eventually, the iron door swung open, and Innokenti reappeared.

"They have agreed to see you," he said.

Innokenti didn't seem entirely pleased about the fact that we'd been granted an audience—nevertheless, he ushered us in.

William and I entered a vast, ornate chamber—it was clearly a throne room. A long strip of thick, blue carpet ran the length of the room, leading up to a set of short steps. The steps led up to a platform, and on the platform sat two intricately carved chairs. An elaborate tapestry with graceful, stylized trees, slender human figures, and a bright, flame-red bird in the center hung behind the thrones.

I wondered if the human figures in the tapestry were actually supposed to be vampires.

The chamber itself was brighter than the halls, but it was still lit solely by the odd, silver light that illuminated most of the castle. In the throne room, however, the light had even more sheen—it was as if someone had captured moonlight and trapped it within the walls.

I took a second look around the chamber. The room was large, but it was clearly empty of living—or nearly living—creatures apart from the three of us. No one else was present.

"Where are they?" William asked impatiently.

"They will emerge in their own time," Innokenti said evenly. "You should be grateful that they've condescended to see you at all. I would advise you to be respectful when they make their appearance."

William made a noise that sounded decidedly derisive.

I heard a door slam shut heavily somewhere close by, and then I heard the sound of footsteps.

William gripped my hand more tightly, and I felt a stab of fear despite his presence.

"Don't speak until you are spoken to," Innokenti said softly.

A corner of the great tapestry behind the thrones lifted—seemingly of its own volition—to reveal a dark doorway. A man and a woman emerged from the darkness and walked to the center of the platform, their hands clasped high in a ceremonial fashion.

They stopped and gazed at us.

The man was tall and lean and dressed in a modern, dark-gray suit. His skin was violently pale, and his hair and trim beard were a sooty black. The woman was also pale-skinned and black-haired. She wore a wine-colored gown of a severe but modern design.

They both wore an aura of power.

As if on a signal, the man and the woman looked at each other and dropped their hands. Then, they seated themselves on the thrones.

The man spoke in a strong, authoritative voice.

"Innokenti, you may approach the throne."

Innokenti started forward and indicated with an elegant gesture that we should follow. He stopped at a respectful distance from the platform.

"You may introduce the petitioners," the man said.

"We are not petitioners," William said sharply.

Innokenti ignored William's outburst and bowed low.

"Your Majesties, may I present to you William Sursur and Katie Wickliff? They have come to petition you for the answer to a question."

Innokenti straightened and stared at us significantly, as if he expected a sign of obeisance from us. But William just stared at the two vampires on the thrones stonily, and I was frozen by fear, completely unable to move.

Both the man and the woman had turned their glittering eyes on me, and I felt like a small animal being calmly surveyed by two great predators.

When neither William nor I reacted, Innokenti continued, addressing us.

"May I present His Majesty, King Hieronymus."

The king continued to stare at me and didn't acknowledge Innokenti's introduction.

"And may I present Her Majesty, Queen Sabine," Innokenti said.

The queen continued to stare at me, also.

I began to feel distinctly uncomfortable.

"So, this is the Little Sun that we have heard so much about," the queen said. Her voice had a breathy, sibilant quality that was oddly charming and inviting.

"Yes, Your Majesty," Innokenti said.

"Do step a little closer, Katie Wickliff," the queen said. She smiled as if she were looking at something she wanted to eat.

"You don't have to do what she says," William said quickly.

William's counsel was unnecessary—I was still frozen with fear. I couldn't have taken a single step closer to the fearsome couple on the platform—even if I had wanted to.

"Are you afraid, Katie?" the queen asked. She smiled even more broadly. "You need not be."

The queen shifted her gaze to Innokenti. "She's pretty, isn't she, Innokenti? She's absolutely perfect."

Innokenti bowed his head in agreement. "Your Majesty is quite right. One shade the more, one ray the less, as the poet said."

Mercifully, the king ceased staring at me also and turned his attention to William. His voice rang out with wintry approval.

"William, we have heard excellent reports of your progress on the new projectile for the crossbows. We have heard also that you are searching for a new item that will aid us in our fight."

"William was actually out looking for that item this very evening, Your Majesty," Innokenti said with an edge of malice in his voice. "He didn't locate it, but we continue to be hopeful."

Innokenti seemed to be hinting at something, but whatever it was was lost on me.

"I didn't come here to talk about the crossbows," William said shortly.

Amusement flickered in the king's eyes. "We are aware of the fact that you have a question, William." The king's tone was tolerant and condescending. "We were going to get to that in due course. But if your question is urgent, you may ask it now."

"Who has blocked my ability to hear Katie call for me?" William said without preamble. "Was it you?"

The queen leaned forward eagerly. "What is it that you say, William? Your question is puzzling. Is it a call for a victim?"

"William began life as a member of the Sídh, my love," the king said, his voice still tolerant. "After his conversion to the noble life of the vampire, I understand that he retained many of the powers that were granted to him by his heritage—one of those is his ability to grant a summoning power known as a 'call' to those he loves. Apparently, he has granted this power to Katie Wickliff, and it is no longer working. Is that the case, William?"

"Yes," William said.

The king glanced at Innokenti. "You could not answer this question of William's?"

Innokenti bowed his head. "I am capable of answering the question, Your Majesty. However, I was forbidden by you from discussing any matter pertaining to this topic. Your Majesty's reasons for imposing a moratorium, were as always, very wise. Most in our community know about the looming threat of the hybrids. Only you, the queen, and I have knowledge of the situation behind that threat. Your Majesty, I believe, wanted to prevent panic."

"I believe in this case that I will make an exception," the king said. "William is a skilled engineer and warrior, and his work is important to us. We may take him into our confidence. Innokenti, answer William's question and any others he may have."

Something like anger flickered in Innokenti's eyes, but it was gone as quickly as it had appeared.

Innokenti bowed his head. "As Your Majesty wishes."

"Who has been blocking me?" William said curtly.

"The Sídh are blocking you," Innokenti replied.

"The Sídh?" William said, his brow furrowing. "And why didn't Katie get my letter?"

"I imagine that the Sídh destroyed it," Innokenti said. "According to you, it was placed near a mirror. And according to Katie, she found a small pile of ash. I would guess that they set the letter alight—they probably couldn't bring it into their world. The ability of the Sídh to act in this world is limited, but they can reach into it through mirrors."

"Who is Cormac?" I asked. "Why did he appear to help me?"

All eyes in the room turned to me.

I hadn't intended to speak, and I was as surprised as anyone that I had—the words had just slipped out.

Innokenti politely ignored the question.

"You may answer the human girl's questions, also," the king said. "We know she is important to William."

A flash of dissatisfaction crossed Innokenti's face, but his voice when he answered was composed.

"Yes, Your Majesty."

Innokenti addressed me. "Cormac is a prince of the Sídh people. He came to your aid because you are the Little Sun. As you no doubt know, it is an infusion of the Sídh bloodline that gives you your unique abilities. The Sídh wish to protect you."

"Are they blocking me, too?" I said.

"In what way, little one?" Innokenti asked.

"I used to have visions," I said. "I didn't have many of them, and I couldn't really control them, but I did have them. And except for one brief vision I had about Anton, they're gone now. And I can no longer summon the clear fire."

Innokenti nodded. "I'm not surprised to hear that. Yes, I would imagine the Sídh are blocking your abilities, too."

"Why would they do that?" William demanded.

"William, I did warn you—both of you. The Sídh believe it is best if you are separated, but their ability to oppose you in this world is limited. So they've brought what pressure they can to bear on you and the young lady. They've taken away powers that derive from them—and it appears that their efforts to keep you apart worked—for a time."

"And their efforts put Katie in danger," William said angrily. "I wasn't able to get to her when she was in trouble."

"And yet here she stands," Innokenti said mildly.

"How do you know all of this?" William demanded. "How much do you know about the Sídh and what they want?"

"I have had no communication with the Sídh directly," Innokenti said. "I'm not working with them against you, if that's what concerns you. But I am the first minister of this community, and as such, it falls to me to watch, to observe—to discern patterns and anticipate developments. And there have been whispers out in the Pure Woods. I hear a little here and there, and I extrapolate. I knew of your relationship with Katie, and I knew the Sídh would work to separate you from the girl. The Sídh won't allow their Little Sun to fall in love with a vampire."

"And what does this have to do with the hybrids?" William asked. "Are the Sídh behind that, too?"

"No, the Sídh aren't behind the hybrids," Innokenti said. "In fact, the hybrids are a threat to them as well as to us. The problem the Sídh have with you is connected to a larger issue."

His tone became discouraging. "It's all very complex. You're out of your depth here, William."

"Explain it to me," William said. "I think I can handle it."

"William—"

"Answer him," the king commanded.

Innokenti bowed his head. "As you wish, Your Majesty."

Innokenti began, and I had an uneasy feeling that I knew where his story was headed.

"Long ago, when the world was young," Innokenti said, "a young man who lived in Russia crossed the Black Sea, looking for great power. He found it, but it changed him fundamentally, and a great darkness was born in his heart—the young man had become a vampire. He sailed back across the Black Sea and returned to Russia.

He converted his entire family, and then he and his family converted others. He became the father of all vampires in Russia. That young man was known as the Werdulac."

I felt a chill spread through my body. Suddenly, I didn't want to know what was going on. I didn't want to know that Odette had been right. I didn't want to be stalked by ancient vampires, or the Sídh, or anyone else.

The desire to run was strong in me. But I stayed where I was.

And I listened.

Innokenti went on. "The Werdulac became the ruler of his own kingdom of the night, and for a time it was sufficient. But then the great lust for power that had led him to cross the sea seized his heart once again. He wanted to conquer the world of the light, also. He looked then to the Sídh, who at the time still walked the earth. The Sídh were—are—ancient spirits of great beauty—some even believed them to be gods. They existed both in this world and the next, and had physical bodies in this world. The Werdulac knew that made them vulnerable."

Innokenti's eyes flicked to me. "After all, anything with a body can die."

He watched me for a moment. If he was disappointed in my reaction, he didn't show it. Instead he simply continued.

"The Sídh were immortal, unless they suffered an injury great enough to cause the death of the body. They couldn't be touched by age or disease, but a sword through the heart or through the throat would end their earthly existence. The Werdulac raised an army of vampires to attack the Sídh—he knew the Sídh were already threatened by the rising tide of upstart humans, and he wanted to strike at them while he believed them to be vulnerable. The Werdulac recruited vampires from all over the earth. The host he mustered was terrible."

William released his grip on my hand and slipped his arm around my shoulders, pulling me into an embrace. I leaned against him gratefully. I knew that the end of Innokenti's story had to lead back to us—to William and to me. And I knew that once we knew, there would be no going back. We'd be a part of this ancient conflict whether we wanted to be or not.

We were going to be trapped.

"The Werdulac and his vampire army marched on the Sídh, but the Werdulac had overestimated his own strength. After much bloodshed on both sides, the vampires were defeated decisively—entirely crushed. The Werdulac himself was beheaded and burned to ash, and the ashes were then entombed in ice—buried so deep, the Sídh said, that he'd never be found again.

"The Sídh did allow some of the vampires to live and forced them swear fealty to the Sídh. That's why vampires dislike mirrors so much—the Sídh defeated us once, and we don't want to glimpse our enemies. That's also why the Little Sun has no particular supernatural power over vampires—because the local ones, at least, have already ceded it to her. Though they don't like to discuss it, the vampires of Krov are honor-bound not to harm the Little Sun."

William made a derisive sound, and Innokenti glanced at him sharply.

"You think vampires have no honor?" Innokenti asked. "You may discover someday that you're wrong."

After a long look at William, Innokenti went on. "Though the Sídh were victorious, they'd suffered losses and were weary. The humans saw their chance and attacked. A tribe known as the Milesians launched an assault on the Sídh. The Sídh were surprised by their strength—and pushed to a degree that frightened even them. Rather than prolong the fighting, the Sídh agreed to a treaty—they would divide the world in half with the Milesians. But the Sídh underestimated the craftiness of the humans, for when the Milesians chose their half of the world—they chose the upper half. The Sídh were bound by the force of their own word to take the lower half. They were forced to retreat underground. The Sídh vanished from the face of the earth.

"In addition, the treaty established the authority of the Little Sun. There are, in fact, a number of Little Suns in the world. Each region has one. As you well know, the Little Sun wields the clear fire to control evil spirits. The Sídh were forced to send one of their number every so many generations to protect the humans in each region of the world from the dark spirits and creatures that threaten them—creatures that humans cannot handle, but the Sídh can."

Innokenti's eyes flicked to me again, and once more he continued without comment.

"And so the Sídh remain in their hills underground to this day, harboring great hatred for the vampires. They were defeated by the human Milesians, yes, but they believe that they would have defeated the humans easily if it hadn't been for the vampires. The Sídh view the humans with some indulgence—sort of like precocious children, but they resent the vampires bitterly."

"So it's over then," William said.

Innokenti spread out his hands resignedly. "That *should* have been an end to it—the Werdulac consigned to his icy tomb, the Sídh trapped under their hills, and the humans masters of the surface. But over the long centuries, the Werdulac, through sheer force of will, began to knit his body back together, to reconstitute himself. The Werdulac cannot yet leave his prison, but he exerts his will over vampires and humans alike."

William hugged me closer. "What does the Werdulac want?"

"He wants revenge. He wants war with the Sídh."

"That's impossible," William said. "He can't get to the Sídh—you said yourself they were banished."

"Unfortunately, it's entirely possible. The Werdulac grows stronger every day, and more people and more creatures fall under his influence. He is, as you know, creating an army of vampire-kost hybrids. They have the strengths of both and few of the weaknesses. And they have one further advantage—the kost can't enter Zamochit Village—they can't pass the supernatural barrier. But the hybrid, with its vampire blood, can pass the barrier. Eventually, they'll grow to sufficient numbers and they'll attack us here."

Innokenti glanced at me then. "Little one, you should tell your grandmother to be wary of her old friends. Some of them may have allegiances she knows nothing about."

Fear seized me as he said the words. "Do you mean Maksim Neverov?"

Innokenti smiled.

"That doesn't answer my question," William interjected sharply. "They can attack us if they want—and we're already working to be ready for them. What I want to know is this—how does the Werdulac propose to get to the Sídh?"

Innokenti nodded his head in my direction. "Through her. The Sídh aren't dead, as you well know. But they are shackled, restrained. Though they're imprisoned, they're still bound to honor their treaty—they must send one of their number to create the Little Sun. And if the Little Sun is killed by their ancient enemy, the vampire—they can be unleashed in full force to combat the vampire. That's why there's a price on young Katie's head. That's why the vampires have been after her. The Werdulac wants her killed—and he wants her killed by a vampire."

Innokenti suddenly moved with blinding speed to stand directly in front of William.

"William, when I came to you and Katie in your charming New World town," he said angrily, "I told you there were two groups that were after her. One group, the Sídh, wants to protect her from all vampires, including you—they will never allow the two of you to be together."

Innokenti leaned close. "And the other group—the Werdulac and his followers—they want to end her life."

Chapter Twenty-Two

Innokenti stopped abruptly, as if he'd said more than he'd intended to say.

A tiny sound that might have been a breathy laugh drew my attention to the king and queen. The queen was sitting forward on her throne, her eyes bright, her full red lips curved into a voluptuous smile. The king, though less open in his reaction, was also riveted. They were both enjoying Innokenti's anger—and William's.

"This is what you didn't think I needed to know," William said furiously, "that the Werdulac intends to kill Katie?"

"No, William, you do not need to know," Innokenti replied angrily. "The Werdulac doesn't intend to kill Katie right away—he only intends to capture her and hold her. He won't kill her until he's fully whole and free again. And Katie isn't the main issue here—she's just one human girl. The main issue is the Werdulac himself. The main issue is the fact that he grows stronger every hour and will eventually break free of his icy prison. The main issue is that he will start a war between the Sídh and the vampires. The main issue is that this community is in danger."

"So that's what you're worried about," William said. "You're worried that the Sídh will attack Zamochit Village."

"No, William. You're not paying attention. I said that one of the advantages of the hybrids is that the hybrids can get past the barrier. The Werdulac intends to attack us—not the Sídh."

"Why would the Werdulac attack vampires?" William asked.

"Because he knows that we protect the people of Krov. He knows that we're honor-bound not to oppose the Sídh—that was the price the vampires paid for their survival. He knows that we'll fight with the Sídh—not against them."

"You will fight against the Werdulac?"

"Yes, William. We will."

"How could the Werdulac know what you will or won't do?"

"His life force is powerful—he has survived the destruction of his body. He is even now breaking the bonds of his imprisonment. And the Werdulac has unprecedented abilities—powers that are awe-inspiring even by the standards of vampires. It's said that his senses alone would make him a wonder—he can see what's invisible even to eyes as keen as ours, and he can hear what's being said over thousands of miles. And, of course, he has spies everywhere. The Werdulac knows what the vampires of Krov have become, and by all reports, he isn't pleased."

"So what do we do against such a powerful enemy?" William said.

"You, William, will go back to your work. You'll build us new and better weapons. The leaders of Krov—His Majesty, the King, Her Majesty, the Queen, and to a lesser extent, their humble servant Innokenti," Innokenti paused to bow, "will take care of the important decisions. We need you to work. We don't need you to meddle in our affairs."

Perhaps Innokenti didn't want interference from William or from me, but I suddenly remembered that I had information I needed to give William—and, I supposed, all of them now.

"I have a message for you," I said. "From a vampire named Odette. She said that the hybrid army will attack the human village at the Firebird Festival."

Once again, everyone in the room seemed to be surprised that I'd spoken.

Innokenti broke into a smile that displayed his gleaming teeth. "Ah, yes, Odette. The most winsome and charming of double agents."

Something in his tone rankled. "What do you mean?" I asked sharply.

Innokenti spread out his hands. "Odette appears to be friendly with all sides lately. She's been here with us in Zamochit Village, and she's also been seen in the company of vampires who are known servants of the Werdulac. It's true that Odette has given us information that's been useful, but I do have to wonder—has she also given information to the Werdulac's camp that's been useful to them? You, of all people, little one, should have cause to be suspicious of Odette's motives. As I recall, she's the one who turned you over to Gleb and Timofei Mstislav. Surely, she must have known that taking you to them couldn't be good for your health. Her presence in Krov was even an argument that William here advanced against your return."

What Innokenti said was true, but I was still oddly offended. "Odette did turn me over to the Mstislavs. But she later changed her mind and helped me escape."

Innokenti raised an eyebrow. "She changed her mind, did she? That was gracious of her."

"Odette is my cousin," I said angrily.

"Tragically, being betrayed by one's own flesh and blood is not so uncommon."

"But Odette helped me again last night when I was in the Pure Woods," I said. "I was in a trance—I thought I'd seen the Werdulac. And then I thought I was falling. I was actually running right into some kind of ritual. I saw Timofei Mstislav—he was being turned into a hybrid. Odette stopped me before I ran into the middle of the whole thing."

William looked at me, stunned. "Did you say Timofei Mstislav?"

"Yes."

"He's been reborn as a hybrid?"

"Yes, I saw him wake up myself. And he saw me."

William turned on Innokenti. "Did you know about this?"

"Yes, William, I did. I knew the Werdulac's people had stolen his body. I knew that they'd been successful in reviving him. From what I understand, after an initial, brief period of obedience, he has proved to be rather rebellious. Apparently he imagines himself as the leader, and he tried to kill several of his fellows. They now have him on a tight leash. As far as Odette saving anyone—"

Innokenti's eyes flicked to me. "Well, her presence was convenient, wasn't it? She simply happened to be lurking near the ritual and intervened just in time to save you, to earn your trust and—"

I interrupted. "Odette said she'd been watching me since I arrived. That's how she happened to be there."

"No doubt she claimed she was worried about you," Innokenti said. "But I would counsel you, little one, to consider your cousin's past behavior when you're evaluating her motives. Isn't it possible that Odette is watching you so that she can report back to someone else?"

I wanted to protest, but I had to admit to myself that I couldn't be sure Innokenti was wrong.

William, however, was not concerned with Odette at the moment.

"So Timofei Mstislav is something else you didn't think I needed to know about?" he asked Innokenti angrily.

Innokenti gave an elegant shrug. "There was no point in telling you. We aren't entirely sure we can kill the hybrids yet. Letting you know about him would only make you anxious and distract you from your work."

"Why has Timofei Mstislav been revived?" I asked, though I had a terrible feeling that I already knew the answer. "Has he been brought back because of me?"

"I believe the reasons he was chosen are twofold," Innokenti replied. "The first is practical. It's easier to raise a kost when you have a body that's in good condition. Since Timofei's death was relatively recent, he was a good candidate for resurrection. Bodies that are in an advanced state of decomposition are harder to raise. However, I know that the Werdulac's camp is working on raising older and older bodies. If they can marry a kost spirit to a desiccated corpse, then the infusion of vampire blood on top of that will repair the body and give it new strength. Vampires, as you may know, have marvelous abilities to heal their own bodies. The Werdulac's force is a small one right now. Once the Werdulac's people can raise old bodies, they will have an army ready to go."

"What do you mean?" I asked.

"Did you never wonder about the Wasteland?" Innokenti asked. There was an odd gleam in his eye.

"I heard it was the site of a human village centuries ago," I said. "And now this castle and the rest of Zamochit stand on its surface."

"Yes, but what happened to the people of that original village?" Innokenti asked. "More specifically, what happened to their bodies? I know you've seen the tunnels that run under the Wasteland. Do you know what's in them?"

I suddenly felt cold. "Are you saying that the bodies of those villagers are in the tunnels?"

Innokenti smiled. "Exactly so. The tunnels were built for other reasons, but after the village was destroyed, they became vast catacombs. There are thousands of mummified bodies below us, just waiting to become the Werdulac's army."

"Stop it." William started forward. "Stop trying to scare her. You're trying to distract us from the real question—was Timofei Mstislav raised from the dead so he can hunt Katie?"

"William, I can assure you that the development of the hybrid army isn't something I bring up to 'distract' you. The danger is very real. And I believe that I said there were *two* reasons why Timofei Mstislav was revived—I was getting to the second one. In addition to Timofei's relative 'freshness,' he was also revived because he'll seek Katie out. He'll be an excellent tracker."

A sense of dread settled over me. I had confirmation of what I'd feared—Timofei had indeed been brought back to hunt me down. The nightmare I'd lived through back in October was about to begin again.

Through the haze of horror that enveloped me, there came another fear.

"What about the people of Krov?" I asked. "Is Odette right that the Firebird Festival will be attacked?"

"Yes," Innokenti said. "However, we already knew about that, so her information isn't actually very helpful."

"Why?" I asked, feeling panic rising in me. "Why are they doing it? If the Werdulac's force is still small, as you say, why is the army going to attack the Firebird Festival?"

"To draw us out—to test our strength. They know that we protect this village, and that we'll be drawn out by a supernatural threat. They want to see what we have in our arsenal. They also hope to draw you out, little one. The fact that you can no longer command the clear fire is hardly common knowledge. Since the hybrids are part kost, you certainly might be expected to try your power against them—if so, you might then be captured—and you have proved elusive so far. The stronger the Werdulac grows, the more frantic he'll be to have you kidnapped."

The air was suddenly torn by a horrible, high-pitched wail. The wail rose and fell in a steady pattern, and I realized after a moment that what I was hearing was a siren.

"If I'm not very much mistaken," Innokenti said calmly in the interval between wails, "that sound means someone is here for the little one now." He gave me a wintry smile. "That's the alarm we set for the hybrids."

The king rose from his throne.

"Come, my love," he said to the queen. "We must get you to safety right away."

The queen had been staring around her wildly, her eyes bright. At the king's words she rose and rushed to him.

The king placed a protective arm around the queen, and the two of them disappeared behind the tapestry.

"Does this mean that Timofei Mstislav has tracked me here?" I asked Innokenti.

"That is possible," Innokenti replied. He appeared to be completely unperturbed by the siren. "Of course, it's also possible that Timofei's powers weren't needed. Odette may simply have told the Werdulac's people that she brought you here. There are definitely hybrids attacking us at the moment, but Timofei may not be amongst them."

"Watch Katie," William said to Innokenti sternly. "Don't let her out of your sight—even for a moment. I'm going to take care of the intruders. Katie had better be here when I get back."

William vanished from the throne room.

I didn't even have time to attempt to stop him.

"William is a man of decision," Innokenti said with a distant hint of amusement in his tone. "I like that about him."

Innokenti wasn't someone who inspired confidence in me, but I couldn't help turning to him.

"William will be all right, won't he?"

I thought back to the look in Timofei Mstislav's eyes when he'd spotted me in the Pure Woods. I thought, too, of the great physical power that his father had possessed. Timofei would surely have that power and more. Innokenti had said that Timofei wasn't necessarily here, but I had a strong feeling that he was. And who knew how many others were with him?

Could William handle the hybrids?

"I have every confidence in William," Innokenti said calmly. "I believe in him in a way that I have never believed in anyone or anything in my life."

He gestured with one elegant hand. "Would you like to have a seat, little one?"

I was startled. "On the thrones?"

"Yes, of course, on the thrones."

I glanced nervously at the tapestry behind which the king and the queen had disappeared.

"Won't they—the king and queen—won't they mind?"

"I imagine that they'll never find out," Innokenti replied. "They're on their way to a secret, safe location as we speak. Please, do be seated. The thrones are very comfortable, I can assure you."

"You've sat on the thrones before?" I asked.

Mischief gleamed in Innokenti's eyes for just a moment. "Every chance I get."

With one last glance toward the tapestry, I climbed the steps to the platform and sat on the queen's throne. Innokenti sat on the king's.

Innokenti and I sat side by side in the strange, silver light of the throne room while the wail of the siren rose and fell with unsettling regularity.

My nerves were frayed, and I cast about for something to do that would distract me from worrying about William. I didn't know exactly what he was facing outside this room, and it was terrible knowing that there was nothing I could do to help him.

I thought then of the charm William had given me. I had a sudden longing to see it—I knew it would make me feel calmer. I peeled off my gloves and unbuttoned my coat.

It was only as I did so that I realized that the throne room was actually comfortably warm. I wondered—did vampires have need of warmth? I glanced at Innokenti and very nearly asked him if vampires felt the cold. But Innokenti looked back at me, and his cool gaze was, as usual, disturbing.

The question died on my lips.

As Innokenti continued to stare at me, I was strongly tempted to run from the room—I felt like a rabbit sitting next to a hungry wolf.

But William seemed to trust him, and I could trust William again—couldn't I?

I looked away from Innokenti and pulled out my necklace. I gazed steadily at the charm as I turned it over in my fingers. Despite my surroundings, I began to feel calmer.

"What do you have there, little one?" Innokenti asked.

"It's a charm," I replied. "A gift from William. He said it would protect me from the kost."

Innokenti gave me his unnerving smile. "It will indeed. And someday you may find that it has properties that even William doesn't know about."

He didn't elaborate, and I hesitated to engage him in further conversation on the topic.

As I looked back down at the charm, my mind drifted. I thought of all the people who were going to go to the Firebird Festival tomorrow night—even GM wanted to go. And I thought, too, of how little they suspected the danger they were in.

They had no idea they were going to be attacked.

I realized that William and the vampires probably had some sort of plan to deal with the hybrids, since they'd apparently known about the attack all along.

But in all likelihood there would still be an attack—the vampires would fight the hybrids, but they wouldn't be able to stop the attack from happening entirely.

People would die.

An idea began to form in my mind.

"Whatever William is facing right now is because of me, isn't it?" I said after some time had passed.

"Don't sound so mournful," Innokenti admonished gently. "You're hardly at fault."

I persisted. "But it *is* true."

"Yes, whatever contingent of the hybrids that is out there is most likely present because of you."

"Innokenti," I began slowly, "if I need to talk to you tomorrow, during the day, is there some way I can find you?"

Innokenti stared at me for a long moment. I had the disturbing impression that he could read my thoughts. His next words, however, dispelled that notion.

"What is in your mind, little one?"

"I can't tell you yet. Can I see you tomorrow if I need to?"

"Yes, of course."

Mercifully, the wail of the siren suddenly stopped, and silence settled on the throne room.

I looked up expectantly. "Does that mean the hybrids are gone?"

"I believe it does," Innokenti replied. "Or at least I hope it does. If our side was successful, your William should be back with us soon."

I realized that I needed to act quickly then.

"How can I find you tomorrow?" I asked. "If I do need to talk to you."

I remembered how fruitless my earlier search for Innokenti had been.

Innokenti grinned. "You can always attract a vampire with the red elixir of life. Come to the edge of the Wasteland tomorrow and spill three drops of blood. I will come to you then."

"Does it have to be my blood?" I asked.

"No," Innokenti said, his eyes faintly mocking, "the blood of an animal will do just as well."

William suddenly ran into the room, and he was beside me in an instant.

Both Innokenti and I rose from the thrones.

"What happened, William?" I asked. "You weren't hurt, were you?"

"No, I wasn't hurt."

"Is Zamochit Village safe?" Innokenti asked. "Were the invaders repelled?"

"Yes, the village is safe. We've warded off the threat. The hybrids won't be back tonight."

"How many of them were there?" Innokenti asked.

"There were three," William said shortly.

"Was Timofei Mstislav one of them?" I asked.

William ignored my question and put an arm around my shoulders. "Come on. We have to get you home."

"You haven't answered the young lady's question," Innokenti said. "Was Timofei Mstislav present?"

"I'll give you a full report when I return. Right now I have to get Katie out of here."

William steered me out of the throne room.

Innokenti's voice floated after us.

"They won't allow you to be together, William. Remember that."

William took me by the hand and led me through the dim halls of the castle.

The anxious eyes of vampires followed us as we passed.

It was strange and wonderful to be walking beside William and to feel the warmth of his hand. I'd believed I'd never see him again, and yet here he was—he hadn't left me, he hadn't abandoned me. I had him back.

"William—"

We shouldn't talk in here," he said. "Let's get out of the castle—out of the village—out of earshot."

We continued to move through the halls, and once more I found myself crossing the courtyard of the castle. Soon we were on the other side, moving toward the front entrance.

William stopped before the massive front doors, and I pulled on my gloves and buttoned up my coat.

William gave me a serious look.

"The streets will still be dangerous for you," he said. "But I think the attack by the hybrids will have convinced many of the villagers to stay inside. All the same, we should still move quickly."

William pushed the massive front doors open.

"Ready?" he asked.

"For what?"

"To run."

He picked me up suddenly then, and I wrapped my arms around his neck.

Before I knew it, we were off into the streets of Zamochit Village, moving at blinding speed. Houses, buildings, figures blurred into one as we flew past them. We navigated twisting, winding streets, and I had to close my eyes several times as we negotiated tight corners.

At long last, we approached one of the watchtowers, and beyond that, there appeared to be nothing but darkness. William sped forward into the darkness, and I felt the air around me ripple.

William stopped running and set me down.

It was hard for me to see, but I looked around. We were standing in the vast emptiness of the Wasteland. I looked back in the direction from which we'd come. Zamochit Village had disappeared.

"We got out of there more easily than I'd expected," William said. "They must all be genuinely frightened."

"Are vampires as strong as the hybrids?" I asked.

"No, not even remotely," William replied. "Vampires are to hybrids as humans are to vampires."

"It's no wonder that they're scared, then," I said. "How did you fight the hybrids off?"

"I have more power than an ordinary vampire," William said. "And I didn't fight them off exactly. It's more like I scared them with our new weapon."

He glanced back in the direction of the village. "We'd better get you home."

"I have a bicycle around here somewhere," I said. "But it's a little too dark for me to see properly."

"I'll find it," William said. He held out his arm to me, and I took it. Then he led me back toward the road. Soon I could feel its solid surface under my feet, and we began to walk along it.

"Wait here," William said after a moment.

He trotted down the road and returned with my bicycle.

"Thanks," I said, smiling. It was good to be with him.

We began to walk down the road again. William was pushing the bicycle, and I held onto his arm as a guide through the gloom.

The night was cloudy and cold, and the stars and the moon were out, but their light was dim. All around us was quiet.

"Are we far enough away yet to make talking safe?" I asked.

"Yes," William replied. "They won't be able to hear us out here. In any event, it's more of a precaution than anything else. Everyone back in Zamochit Village should be too preoccupied at the moment to spy on us."

We walked on, and though there were questions I wanted to ask William, I waited.

I could tell he was turning something over in his mind.

"Katie, I'd never do that," he said suddenly. I looked up at him. He was staring down at the road, and lines of strain were visible in his face. "Anton told you that I gave you up in exchange for getting my memories back and being freed of my vampire nature."

He looked at me then. "I'd never do that. I'd never give you up for anything. You have to believe that."

"William, when you disappeared, it was hard for me," I said slowly. "I thought I'd never see you again. I thought you had abandoned me—and abandoned me when I had a price on my head—when I was being hunted."

William closed his eyes, as if he felt a sudden pain. "I'm sorry, Katie. I left the letter—I told you to call me any time you needed me. I knew I could get to you in an instant. It never occurred to me that the Sídh would interfere."

"Why did you leave?" I asked.

"I thought I was helping you," William said. "Innokenti came to me again. He told me that in addition to the vampires that were after you, someone was building an army of vampire-kost hybrids to come after you, too. But he also implied that he didn't know who was behind it—though I realize now that he never said that explicitly. I thought I could work on defeating the hybrids and try to find out who was responsible for all your troubles at the same time. I had no idea that Innokenti knew all along."

"Why did you write me a letter?" I asked. "Why didn't you just tell me in person?"

William's jaw worked, but he didn't say anything.

"I suppose I was afraid," he said at last.

"Afraid of what?"

"It's hard to explain exactly. I was afraid you'd be angry. I was afraid you wouldn't want me to go—and I had to go. I had to do what I could for you. I had to protect you.

"At the same time I was worried about what would happen when I came back. I was afraid you would forget about me—I was afraid I would come back to find that you didn't want me anymore."

William gave me a serious look. "I wrote you a letter because I love you. And I was afraid that I would lose you."

"You'll never lose me," I said.

William looked at me for a long moment. Then he went on.

"I have some questions for you now. Why did you come here to Krov? Why did you come into Zamochit Village?"

The hurt, the despair I'd felt when I'd thought William had left me came flooding back, and suddenly I felt like I couldn't breathe.

"Originally I decided to come here to look for you," I said haltingly. "But eventually I lost hope."

I stopped and drew in a deep breath. "It still hurts to talk about it."

I stopped again and went on when I could. "Like I said, I lost hope, but I still decided to come for GM's sake. And then tonight, I spotted you accidentally. And I had to speak to you just one last time. I followed you—I didn't know where you were going—and I wound up in Zamochit Village. I had no idea such a place even existed."

"So followed me into a town full of vampires, even though you believed I had abandoned you?"

"Yes."

"Why did you do that?"

"Because I love you."

William bowed his head. "I told you before—you're too young to know what love truly is."

"I'm not too young," I said. "I love you. I'm not wrong about that."

"I'm not used to anyone loving me," William said quietly.

We walked on in silence after that, and I could feel his love, bright and shining, encircling me once again.

We walked on to the Mstislav mansion and then through the rest of town. Eventually, we reached my street with its two working streetlamps.

We stopped in front of my house, and I suddenly realized just how tired I was. But even though there had been moments of pure terror for me on this night, I knew I wouldn't have traded it for anything—I had William back again.

William looked up at the house. "I suppose your grandmother has no idea you've been out wandering around tonight."

"I have to admit that that's true," I said.

William shook his head. "Sometimes I don't know what's wrong with you. Go inside. You'll be safe there. There are special protective charms on this house—and they're strong."

I was startled. "That's true. But how did you know about that? I only found out because Odette told me."

William frowned. "I don't know—I just knew it the first time I saw the house."

"Odette also told me that the charm keeps out vampires," I said thoughtfully, "as well as other creatures like kosts. But the house allowed you to come in. I wonder why?"

"I don't know," William said once again. "But I do know that you should stay away from Odette from now on. Now go on inside and get some sleep—you need it. And stay in the house tomorrow—all day and all night. Whatever you do, do *not* come out for the Firebird Festival. The vampires and I will take care of the hybrids. I'll come to the house when it's safe for you to come out again."

William walked the bicycle over to the side of the house and propped it up.

"So, now that I've seen you safely home, it's time for me to say good night." He gave me his crooked half smile.

On impulse, I ran over to him, grabbed him by the collar, and kissed him. We stood together for a long moment, and I thought that I'd be perfectly happy just to kiss him forever.

William stepped back for a moment and then leaned in to kiss me again. He finally stepped back with decision.

"You're going to make me forget why I'm here," he said. "Now get in the house. And stay there."

I slipped into the house quietly, and even though I knew William would be long gone, I hurried to look out the front window, hoping to catch a glimpse of him as he left.

He was no longer there, as I'd suspected, but I closed my eyes and pressed my fingers lightly to my lips.

The memory of his kiss still lingered.

Chapter Twenty-Three

I awoke the next morning feeling alert and full of energy. I'd actually slept very little—most of the night had worn away by the time I'd made it back to the house.

All the same, I didn't feel the lack of sleep—every nerve in my body was alive and tingling.

I had decisions to make, and I made them quickly.

The germ of an idea had begun to grow in my mind last night, and now I knew for sure what I'd have to do.

William had warned me to stay away from the Firebird Festival.

But that was exactly what I couldn't do.

I got ready for the day quickly, and then I went downstairs. I had breakfast with GM, and afterward she went out to see Maksim.

I was uneasy as I watched her leave the house. I had to wonder about what Innokenti had said during the night—he'd implied very heavily that Maksim was in the service of the Werdulac.

I'd felt twinges of suspicion myself, and Odette had also warned me about him.

But I wasn't sure I could trust Innokenti on this—in fact, I wasn't sure I could trust him at all.

And yet, I was planning to seek him out this very morning—to summon him with blood as he'd said I might. Even if I didn't trust him, I still believed he could help me with what I needed to do.

So, I'd trust that GM would be safe with Maksim—at least for the present—and I'd trust that I'd be safe with Innokenti.

Once GM was gone, I hurried outside. I had to move quickly and get started before I gave myself too much time to think about what I was going to do. I retrieved my bicycle from the side of the house where William had left it, and I felt a pang as I touched the handlebars. I couldn't help thinking of the way William had looked last night. It was hard for me to believe in the clear light of morning that I had him back—it was almost as if I'd dreamed the entire thing.

It was also hard for me to face the terrible truth that I might lose him again very soon.

I would lose him because I might lose my own life.

I rode through town to the Mstislav mansion and then out into the Wasteland. A light snow had fallen in the short time that I'd slept, and the tires of my bicycle crunched in the snow as I rode along. Once I'd reached a spot that I judged to be sufficiently remote, I pulled off the road and surveyed the blank expanse that stretched before me.

I'd always believed that snow brought with it a great stillness, and this snowfall, light as it was, was no exception. The morning air was quiet—nothing stirred as far as I could see.

I suddenly felt very alone, and I stood very still.

I felt for just a moment as if I were the last living creature on earth.

I quickly shook off my abstraction. I had a vampire to summon.

I took off my gloves and took out the knife I'd brought with me—it was the Swiss Army knife that Branden had given me back in Elspeth's Grove. I figured using this knife was safer than using any of our larger kitchen knives—but this was hardly the use Branden had intended the knife for when he'd given it to me.

Innokenti had said that three drops of blood would summon him.

I wasn't very enthusiastic about cutting myself, but it was preferable to the alternative. Innokenti had said that I might use animal blood, but I couldn't really bring myself to do that.

It would have to be my own.

I pushed up the sleeve of my coat and quickly slashed a thin red line down my arm, bracing myself for the bite of the knife. The cut itself wasn't actually that painful, and I let the wound bleed onto the knife.

I then let several bright drops of blood fall onto the clean white blanket of snow. The red droplets spread out and then sank in, melting the snow where they fell with their warmth.

More than three drops had fallen, but I figured that that didn't matter—I had a feeling that Innokenti had just been waxing poetic when he'd given me his instructions. All that was truly necessary was that blood was spilled.

I looked around then, expectantly, but the white plain before me remained empty. Innokenti didn't appear.

I let a few more drops of blood fall onto the snow.

I looked around again. But no one appeared out in the Wasteland. Everything was silent and still.

I continued to stare out over the vast, white plain. The morning wasn't especially bright, but even so, the snow reflected back all available light, and my eyes soon began to burn. I continued to look out over the Wasteland until I was forced to shut my eyes.

Once my eyes were closed, tears began to sting the back of my eyelids. Part of that was simply the effect of the snow glare, but part of it was frustration—Innokenti hadn't come like he'd said he would. I began to realize that he had deceived me.

After a moment, I wiped my eyes with the back of my free hand and looked around again. As I feared, Innokenti still hadn't appeared.

And I knew now that he wasn't going to.

Feeling foolish, I wrapped the knife in a handkerchief I'd brought, and I unrolled a length of gauze. The cut wasn't deep, but I'd come prepared with bandages, just in case something had gone wrong. I wrapped the gauze around the thin wound and tucked in the end of it.

My eyes continued to tear, and I closed them and rubbed them once again. When I opened them, I was startled to find myself staring at a broad expanse of black cloth. Involuntarily, I jumped back. I could see then that the black cloth was actually clothing covering a human form.

I looked up. I found myself staring into the cool gray eyes of the vampire Innokenti.

"Tears, little one?"

I took another step back.

"I—I thought you weren't coming," I stammered.

Amusement glimmered distantly in his eyes. "The tears are for me, then? It's been a long time since anyone has shed tears for me. Of course, over the years, many have shed them because of me."

I had an uneasy feeling that Innokenti had chosen the manner of his appearance purposefully.

"You're trying to scare me," I said angrily.

Innokenti smiled and spread out his hands as if in confirmation.

"Why?" I asked.

"It's what I do," he said simply. "Perhaps it would be better for you to be scared."

His eyes drifted to my wounded arm.

I took another step back.

"Innokenti, I summoned you for a reason," I said, trying to sound confident. "I need to talk to you."

The vampire looked up at me with eyes that burned with a dark intensity. Innokenti's usual courtly manner had disappeared—he seemed now like the dangerous, blood-drinking creature he was.

He took a step toward me. He kept going.

The urge to run welled up within me, and I stumbled backward. But I'd come to the Wasteland with a purpose, so I forced myself to stop and stand still.

"I need to talk to you," I said again. I could hear a tremor in my voice.

Innokenti stopped then, too, and the intensity in his eyes faded. It was replaced by another faint glimmer of amusement. He seemed pleased by the effect he'd produced, and his manner became business-like.

"After you requested a meeting last night," he said, "I have eagerly awaited your summons. How may I be of service to you, little one?"

I took a deep breath and tried to calm my racing heart. Innokenti had a bizarre sense of humor.

"We have to stop the hybrids from attacking the Firebird Festival tonight," I said.

"Nothing would make me happier. But, alas, what can we do? I fear we will have to wait for them to make their move. We don't know where they are at present. The Werdulac's people are good at hiding the hybrids. We believe they may even be hidden in a different location every night."

"But you do know a few things about them," I said. "You knew Timofei Mstislav had been resurrected. And you said he'd been put on a leash—or something like that. You said they had him under control."

"That is true," Innokenti replied.

"Was he there last night?" I asked. "Was Timofei Mstislav one of the hybrids who attacked the castle yesterday?"

"Yes," Innokenti said. "William, I imagine, would prefer that you not know, but yes, he was there."

"So, he came to find me."

"I believe that he'd been released to track you—as a test for the Firebird Festival."

"Then we can use me as a target," I said.

"I beg your pardon?" Innokenti said.

"If the hybrids are attacking the Firebird Festival because they hope, at least in part, to draw me out, then I'll show myself, somewhere, in a very obvious way. I'll draw the hybrids to me, get them to attack me, rather than waiting for them to attack the festival."

Innokenti's eyebrows rose a fraction. "You intend to offer yourself up as bait?"

"Yes."

"An intriguing idea."

"Do you think it will work?" I asked.

Innokenti stared at me steadily for a long moment. It was impossible for me to read his expression.

"I do believe it *will* work," he said after a time. He tilted his head to one side. "I wonder, do you truly understand what you're suggesting, little one?"

"Yes, I do," I said.

"Are you sure?"

"Yes," I said. "I'm sure."

Innokenti shook his head. "It's dangerous, little one—very dangerous. What exists of the Werdulac's army will be assembled in its entirety tonight. If you show yourself, Timofei will lead them all to you. We will attempt to stop them—to destroy them, actually. But there is no guarantee that we will succeed. The hybrids are ferocious. And they want you. If they capture you, your life will effectively be over. You will live, of course, until the Werdulac is completely free of his icy confinement, but you will be his prisoner, and he will sacrifice you when it suits him."

"I understand," I said.

"Do you really? Reflect for a moment on what it might be like to be the prisoner of the Werdulac *and* Timofei Mstislav, little one. Think on it very seriously."

I thought, as I had before, of the way Timofei had looked that night in the Pure Woods when he was revived—I remembered the burning hatred in his eyes, and I felt a wave of horror wash over me.

"If you are captured," Innokenti said softly, "your life will be forfeit. There will be no hope of rescue."

I had no doubt that Innokenti was right, and a strong desire to turn and run for home rose up within me. I quelled it.

"You're trying to scare me," I said.

"As I said, that's what I do. There are times when you should be afraid."

I was suddenly aware, once again, of how eerily quiet our surroundings were.

"The hybrids are going to the Firebird Festival to kill people, aren't they?" I said.

"As many as they can. They want to make a strong impression."

I looked over the desolate white plain that stretched behind Innokenti. I knew that that clean, white surface concealed tunnels full of dead villagers. If we didn't draw the hybrids away from the festival, more villagers would go to join their neighbors under the ground.

"But you do believe my plan could work?" I said. "If I show myself, the hybrids will come?"

"I believe Timofei will be drawn to you, and the others will follow him—especially since there is a charm on your house, and the hybrids cannot get to you there. You will succeed in provoking an attack. They will lose their focus on the festival, at least while they hunt you."

"I want to do it, then," I said. "I want to draw them away from the festival."

"Even if it may cost you your own life?" Innokenti asked.

"Yes," I said.

Innokenti made no reply, and I was left to listen to the silence.

As I waited for his response, it seemed to me that I could feel the cold more keenly than I could before.

"I'll need you to help me," I said after some time had passed. "I don't know how to go about setting myself up to be found."

"If I agree to this," Innokenti said, breaking his silence, "it occurs to me that William won't approve. How does he figure into your calculations?"

"I actually hadn't done much in the way of calculations," I said. "Does he have to know?"

"Not at first. But when the alarm is raised and all of our men go out, William, of course, will be amongst those called. And he will naturally see you once he arrives on the scene."

Innokenti tilted his head to one side. "However, it occurs to me that it could actually be a good thing for William to see you there—it could provide him with a little extra incentive. There's nothing like having to protect someone you love to give you strength you never knew you had. And, of course, by the time he sees you, it will be far too late for him to stop you from carrying out your plan—you'll already be in the middle of things."

Innokenti paused. "Seeing you in danger will be very hard on him. Doesn't that matter to you?"

I couldn't help wincing at his words. "Of course it matters to me. But I can't let innocent people be killed. I have to do this."

"I just want you to be sure that you count the cost of what you are doing," Innokenti said. "The total cost."

"I know what I'm doing," I replied. "I know it's dangerous."

"I will give you one last chance," Innokenti said. "You could lose your life. You could end your days as the prisoner of a reanimated corpse with a thirst for revenge. Is that a risk you accept?"

"Yes. I accept it."

Innokenti stared at me for a long moment. Something in my tone seemed to get through to him.

"Very well. I agree to your plan and accept your sacrifice. We will need to work out what to do."

"How many hybrids are there?" I asked.

"We believe that there are about a hundred of them," Innokenti replied.

"And how many are on our side?" I asked.

"Alas, we number only fifty," Innokenti said. "Oddly enough, vampires aren't natural fighters, and they're difficult to train and discipline—vampires in their natural state are lone hunters like tigers."

"So recruitment isn't easy?" I said.

"Indeed it is not," Innokenti replied. "That's another one of the advantages that accrue to the hybrids—I imagine the kost part of the hybrids helps make them more amenable to commands and organization. But our troubles don't end there. In addition to our smaller numbers, we have a limited number of the weapons we need. Very few things are effective against the hybrids."

"What kind of weapons do you use?" I asked.

"I believe you saw something of them the other night when you paid us a visit at the castle," Innokenti replied. "William has been instrumental in developing them."

"I did see guards with crossbows," I said. "Is that what you mean?"

"Exactly so. There are some challenges involved in killing a hybrid—he has the strengths of both the vampire and the kost. Though a wooden stake can often be damaging, to kill a vampire properly, you must cut the head off and then burn the body. To kill a kost, you must wrestle it back into its grave. To kill the hybrid, you must do both.

"So, that's where the crossbow comes in. It shoots an iron disc that opens out into three curved blades when it's fired—and the iron, when it makes contact with the skin, has some efficacy in blunting the greater strength that comes to the hybrid through its kost side. The disc is also coated with a substance that ignites. When this bursts into flame, it damages the vampire half of the hybrid, thus weakening the creature further. Then it may be possible to behead the creature. The head and body—which will continue to fight with terrifying strength—must then be placed back into the proper grave and burned to ashes."

"That doesn't sound easy," I said.

"It isn't," Innokenti replied.

"How do you know which grave to take the hybrid back to?" I asked.

"We have paid close attention to all of the grave robberies in the area—in fact, we have detailed lists with photos of the grave sites and of the deceased when they were still living. We like to call it our scouting report."

"So you'll use your scouting report to match the right bodies with the right graves," I said.

"Yes."

"That doesn't sound easy, either," I said.

"I must confess that the odds of our overall success aren't good in this battle. We are outnumbered and, in many ways, outmatched. The whole thing is quite a challenge."

Innokenti paused. "Are you certain you still wish to do this? There is no dishonor in backing out. You didn't truly know what you were up against until my explanation just now. And I hope you will forgive me for pointing this out, but you are ill-equipped to defend yourself against such a threat."

"I was chosen once to protect this town," I said. "Even though I no longer have the ability I was originally granted, I still have to do what I can to help."

"I cannot dissuade you?" Innokenti asked.

"No," I said.

"It is my lot to defend this village, also," Innokenti said. "You may not think so, but I do understand."

Something flickered in Innokenti's eyes that might have been sympathy, but it was gone as quickly as it had appeared.

"What I suggest is this," Innokenti said. "We should set up a situation that will attract attention, but that doesn't seem staged. The Werdulac has placed a price on your head that is very attractive to vampires. Most of the vampires who live in communities know better than to go after you—they know the offer is a trap. I doubt very much that the Werdulac will make good on his promises.

"But there are plenty of rogue vampires—lone hunters, as I said— who are still out to collect you. I propose that we set up a chase. We'll have a vampire we can trust pursue you. Once we have attracted the attention of the hybrids, you and your pursuer will lead them to a prearranged ambush spot in which we'll hide some of our vampire warriors. And then once our ambush is sprung, we'll alert the rest of the warriors, including William. Unfortunately, we *will* have to wait until nightfall to put our plan into action—the hybrids are unlikely to be sufficiently active to take the bait until darkness is upon us."

I couldn't help shivering.

"You want to have a vampire chase me?" I asked.

"Yes. I think you should be chased into the Pure Woods. There's a large clearing with a castle keep that we know about, and I think we can create a bottleneck there and pick the hybrids off one by one. We know the woods well, and I actually think the trees will be a help rather than a hindrance. If we were to choose an entirely clear area, the way would be clearer for our crossbows, but I also think that out in the open we'd be more likely to be overwhelmed. What do you think?"

I tried to consider the tactics, but I was too alarmed by Innokenti's first suggestion to be able to think about anything else clearly.

"Which vampire are you going to have chase me?" I asked. "Odette?"

"No, not Odette," Innokenti replied. "I don't think we can trust her. But I have the perfect man in mind. I think you should work with Anton."

"Anton?" I said in disbelief. "But he attacked me. He tried to turn me over to the Werdulac."

"Yes, I know that now," Innokenti replied. "I discussed the issue with him after your accusation, and he confirmed it. That's what makes him so well suited to the task. The Werdulac's camp will believe that he's genuinely after you. And he was terribly repentant when I confronted him about you. I'm sure he would like a chance to redeem himself in your eyes and in the eyes of our community."

I found it hard to believe that Anton was repentant about anything. "You trust him?"

"Yes," Innokenti replied simply. "If this life has taught me one thing, it's forgiveness." He paused and gave me a mirthless smile. "That's a joke, by the way. But very genuinely I do trust him. Anyone may be tempted."

I took a deep breath. "Anton."

"You may still back out if you wish."

"No," I said. "I see the logic of choosing him."

Innokenti grinned broadly, showing his teeth. "You're a brave girl."

I didn't feel very brave at the moment. In fact, I began to feel the stirrings of panic. "Is there anything I can do—in the event that things don't—go well with—"

I paused. I was having trouble forming my words.

"In case things don't go well with Anton?" Innokenti asked.

"No—"

I was determined to think as little as I possibly could about Anton's involvement.

"No," I said. "I mean if we succeed in luring the hybrids out, and one of them gets to me—is there anything I can do to protect myself?"

Innokenti considered the question. "Nothing comes to mind. We will do our best to protect you, of course. And William will certainly do the same."

"What about my cross?" I asked. "The one you saw the other night at the castle. You said it had special properties I might not know about. Will it help me with the hybrids?"

"Actually, I believe you should divest yourself of that particular object. I'm not certain how effective it is against a hybrid, but if there's any chance it will throw the hybrids off your trail, then you'll want to get rid of it. We don't want them to be confused."

"Oh," I said faintly. "I'll leave it at home, then."

"Very wise."

I cast my mind about desperately.

"What about William's search?" I asked.

"I beg your pardon?" Innokenti said. "I don't know what search you are referring to."

"Last night you said he'd been out searching for something that would help in the fight against the hybrids. An 'item' I think you called it."

Innokenti laughed—a sound that startled me.

"Ah, yes," he said. "William's quest. Are you familiar with the work of the great vampire philosopher and visionary Orpheo?"

"I'm afraid not," I replied.

Innokenti waved a hand. "Don't feel bad—few humans know of him. Orpheo has long since been turned to ash, but when he was alive, he was something like your Nostradamus. He's the author of a famous quotation—*Sacer ignis exitus mundi*. It translates as "'The world will end in—'"

"Holy fire," I said.

Innokenti seemed pleased. "Yes, 'holy fire,' very good. Orpheo predicted that there would be another war between the vampire and the Sídh. His devotees even believe that he foresaw the resurrection of the Werdulac. Some further believe that this particular quotation should be interpreted literally—as in the world *will* end."

"What do you believe?" I asked.

Innokenti gave an elegant shrug. "I believe in fighting for my life." He gave me a sardonic look. "One romantic interpretation of this quotation is that the Werdulac may be defeated by a famous vampire sword known as 'Ignis Sacer'—as you said, 'holy fire.' William subscribes to this interpretation."

"What do you mean by 'vampire sword'?" I asked.

"It's a sword that drinks the blood of its victims and becomes stronger," Innokenti said. "It's supposed to be the most powerful sword the world has ever known. William, bless his innocent heart, has begun to search for it."

Innokenti's mocking tone was beginning to make me angry. "What's wrong with William looking for this sword?"

"Orpheo, like Nostradamus, was largely a fanciful man. The sword is not real. The sword is a dream. There is no magic talisman that will save us from the Werdulac on this night or on any other night. Nothing will help us here. What we have on our hands is a good, old-fashioned fight. We cannot place our faith in legends, no matter how attractive."

Innokenti suddenly glanced around. "I hope you'll forgive me, little one—I shouldn't spend too much time out here in the daylight. It's possible someone will see us talking and report us to the Werdulac. We don't want to endanger our plans.

"This is what we'll do tonight. We don't know exactly when the hybrids will attack the festival, but I imagine they're planning to inflict as much damage as they possibly can. So they'll want to wait until the festivities will be in full swing—when the most people will be out and about and a little, shall we say, incapacitated from merrymaking? I can't imagine that the hybrids would attack before midnight. You should go to the festival around ten o'clock, and then wander away from the crowd at around eleven to begin the staged chase. The hybrids should be stirring by then, and we should still be ahead of their attack."

"I can do that," I said. "I'll get away by eleven. How do I find Anton?"

Innokenti gave me a disturbing smile. "Anton will find you."

Innokenti moved then with startling swiftness, and in the next moment he was gone.

I spun around, looking for him.

The Wasteland was empty.

I figured Innokenti was gone, so I turned to go myself.

Then I heard a voice in my ear.

"Let us pray, little one, that you haven't sealed your own fate."

Chapter Twenty-Four

Time seemed to speed up after I returned home. All too soon, the day passed me by, and the sky began to darken. Night fell with alarming swiftness.

After dinner, I sat up in my dark bedroom, looking out the window, watching the stars come out. I no longer feared the appearance of Timofei Mstislav—I knew he was under control.

Or he would be until he spotted me tonight.

My heart sank when I heard GM start bustling around in her room—I knew she was getting ready for the Firebird Festival.

She was excited about the festival.

I was dreading it.

The plan I was to follow tonight was what I wanted—what I'd chosen for myself. But now that the time to leave was nearly upon me, my stomach had begun to twist itself into violent knots. I knew that there was every chance that our side would lose tonight—that the hybrids would overwhelm us, and I would be lost to the Werdulac.

And then the hybrids would still attack the festival.

And even before all of that, I would have to deal with Anton.

I didn't trust him—at all—and it occurred to me that he might just kidnap me himself and turn me over to the hybrids. That way he could try to collect that precious reward of memories that he'd told me about.

Fear flooded through me at the thought—the possibility of being betrayed by Anton tonight was a very real danger.

But I had to try. I had to do what I could—even if it meant the end for me.

Reluctantly, I turned on the light and began to get ready for the festival myself. Mindful of Innokenti's advice, I took off the charm that William had given me.

I felt strangely alone without it.

As I walked down the stairs, GM looked up at me expectantly.

"Katie, you'll see something truly marvelous tonight. No one can celebrate the way we Russians can. There will be music and dancing and—"

She stopped and looked at me searchingly.

"What is it, solnyshko? What's wrong?"

I smiled and tried to appear as if I were really excited about the night ahead of us.

"Nothing's wrong. I can't wait to go to the festival tonight."

"Yes, yes, something is wrong," GM said. "I can tell."

As I reached the bottom of the stairs, she put a hand to my forehead.

"Are you ill?" she asked anxiously. "You were terribly ill the last time we were here. I hope this isn't a reoccurrence of that sickness."

I thought back to the fever I'd had after Odette had poisoned me, and an involuntary shudder ran through me.

GM was watching me closely. "I knew it," she said. "You *are* ill. We'll stay home."

"No, I'm not ill," I said quickly. I fought down the panic that was rising in me. I couldn't let GM keep me home. I *had* to go tonight. "I'm fine, really. I want to go to the Firebird Festival."

I pasted a smile on my face.

"You're sure about this?" GM asked, looking me over critically.

"Yes, I am. GM, please. I really want to go."

"All right," she said after a moment. "We'll go. But if you begin to look really bad, I will insist that we go home."

I tried to make my tone reassuring. "Okay, GM. That sounds reasonable enough."

I couldn't help smiling a little for real then. "You always think I'm ill. Or that I'm about to be."

GM touched a strand of my hair. "I worry about you, solnyshko."

"Everything will be fine," I said.

I really hoped that was true.

As we went out to the car, I glanced at my watch. It was just about ten o'clock.

I had one more hour to go.

The drive didn't take long, and GM and I soon reached the main square in front of the Mstislav mansion. She slotted the car into a space in amongst a big jumble of cars.

GM slipped her arm through mine, and she smiled at me. I could see how excited she was. I suddenly wished that the evening could be exactly what she believed it to be—a clear winter's night with a simple, safe, small-town celebration. Little did she—or any of Krov's residents—know what waited in the dark to attack them and shatter their peaceful world.

The square was full of people eating, drinking, laughing, talking. There were live musicians, and somebody seemed to have brought a radio—two styles, one traditional, the other modern, clashed in the winter air, fighting pleasantly for the attention of the crowd.

The air was full of the aroma of food, and both electric lights and open flames illuminated the square, which was hung with hundreds of paper lanterns representing the Firebird.

"Later tonight there will be performances illustrating the folktales that are told of the Firebird," GM said. "Dances, plays, things like that."

A fair-haired man, his pale cheeks tinged red by the cold, handed both GM and me plastic cups filled with a dark liquid. He winked at us and disappeared into the crowd.

From the scent of the liquid, I guessed it was spiced wine. I looked around for a place to set it down. As I did so, I realized that I also had to find a way to get away from GM. At the moment, I wouldn't be able to slip away without being noticed.

"I know what is in your mind," GM said.

I felt a flash of panic. "You do?"

"Yes, of course. You're worried about the wine. A sip or two will probably not hurt you. But make sure it is only a little."

I was relieved. I'd thought for a moment that she knew I was planning to disappear from the festival.

"No, thanks," I said. "I don't want it." I really didn't. I needed my head to be clear.

GM smiled approvingly. "It's true what I always say—you're a good girl. Let's find a place to set these down. I'm sure that on a night like this, no one will mind a few extra drinks sitting around. I think I see a spot on that table over there."

GM steered me through the crowd, and just as we were setting our plastic cups down, I spotted a tall, silver-haired man moving toward us.

It was Maksim Neverov. I was both elated and dismayed to see him. I was happy because I had a feeling he'd provide the distraction I needed to get away from GM. But at the same time I was worried—Innokenti's hints about Maksim and my own half-formed suspicions suddenly hit me again. GM's seeing him during the day was one thing. Would it be safe for me to leave her with him on a night like this?

An even more disturbing question popped into my mind.

What if Maksim was in on the attack tonight?

He saw the two of us and lifted a hand in greeting. GM saw him, too, and her face was instantly suffused with the same light that always seemed to appear whenever he was around.

GM looked happy to see him—truly happy. She was usually very sharp—except where matters of the supernatural were involved. I wondered—could it be that she was deceived in him?

Perhaps she couldn't see what she didn't want to see.

"Good evening, Anna. Good evening, Katie," Maksim said warmly. He bowed over each of our gloved hands in turn. Then his eyes lingered on GM. "I'm truly lucky to find myself out and about on such a fine evening and in the company of two such beautiful ladies."

"Oh, Maksim," GM said, delighted, "you knew we'd be here. There was no luck involved at all."

"Forgive me for reminding you, Anna, but you've disappeared on me before. I repeat that I am lucky."

"Oh, Maksim," GM said again.

Maksim and GM continued to talk, and it was clear to me that they only had eyes for each other. While their conversation went on, I glanced at my watch several times. All too soon, my hour was up, and Maksim and GM were still engrossed in one another. It was about time for me to slip away.

I had to hope that Maksim had nothing to do with what was planned for tonight—or if he was, that what I was about to do would be enough to distract him from his part in it.

Someone on the far edge of the crowd set off a few firecrackers, and Maksim and GM turned, laughing, toward the sound. They were so absorbed in each other that I figured it would be a little while before they noticed I was missing. And once they did notice, they wouldn't be too alarmed—at first.

I decided now was the time to disappear.

I ducked into the crowd and made my way toward the Mstislav mansion, which sat at the far end of the square. Once I was free of the crowd, I could see the mansion itself, looming pale and ghostly at the end of its dark, tree-lined drive.

I glanced back toward the crowd and saw four young men carrying a large, flame-colored figure of a Firebird on a litter. Behind them trailed a line of girls in traditional Russian dress, carrying baskets and scattering handfuls of rose petals. The petals looked like feathers that had fallen from the great bird.

A cheer went up from the crowd as the Firebird came into view.

I hurried on.

Soon I had passed beyond the Mstislav mansion, and the warmth and safety of the festival were growing more and more distant every moment.

There had been no further snow since the early morning, but the day had been cold, and none of the snow had melted. A thin layer of white still blanketed the ground as I walked on toward the Wasteland.

I realized suddenly that I no longer had a flashlight—I'd lost it somewhere in Zamochit Village. Even with the snow and the starlight, the Wasteland would be hard to cross in the dark. Not only that, but I didn't even know where the castle keep was that I was supposed to go to. I wondered with a sinking feeling how I was going to lead Anton on a chase if I couldn't see where I was going and didn't know where to go.

I glanced at my watch. It was five minutes past eleven.

Innokenti had said that Anton would find me, but I waited, and Anton didn't appear. I looked around—I was at the edge of the Wasteland, and as far as I could see, I was completely alone. I found myself in the uncomfortable position of both hoping to see Anton and hoping he wouldn't find me.

Minutes passed, and I began to feel the cold more keenly. Suddenly, I felt something brush against my hair, and I turned around quickly.

No one was there.

I turned back and was startled to see Anton standing before me, grinning.

"Hello, Sunshine," he said.

I stumbled backward away from him in a panic.

"Relax," Anton said. "I'm on the side of the angels this time—however dark those angels might be."

I took another step back. I hadn't seen Anton since he'd shown up at my house back in Elspeth's Grove. He'd seemed threatening then, and here in the dark, in the cold, his eyes glittering, he was even more so. My heart was beating wildly, and I couldn't seem to find my voice.

Agreeing to put on a sham chase with Anton no longer seemed to be a good plan—or even a plan I could go through with.

"Tongue-tied?" he said with an unpleasant smile. "Like I always say, I have that effect on a lot of women."

I suddenly felt a strong desire to run, and I stifled a hysterical laugh—running was exactly what I was here to do.

Anton continued. "Since you're not in a very talkative mood this evening, I suppose it will up to me to sustain the conversation. I must confess, however, that I'm disappointed that you've come back here. I'd hoped you would take my advice and stay home. Since you *have* come here, I've been forced to keep an eye on you again, and it's been exhausting. There have been even more attempts on you in Krov than there were in Elspeth's Grove."

"You've been—been—"

"I've been looking out for you, yes," Anton said. "You know, this village is a dangerous place at this particular time. And you seem to have a knack for getting yourself right into the thick of all the trouble. Our meeting here is a good example of that."

I drew in a ragged breath and tried to force myself to be calm.

"You're here for real, aren't you?" I said when I was at last able to speak a complete sentence.

A look of genuine confusion flickered across Anton's face.

"I'm sorry?" he said. "I'm not imaginary if that's what you mean. I'm definitely very solid."

"I mean this isn't a trap, is it?" I asked. "A circumstance that sprang up that you'll take advantage of?"

"I still don't know what you're talking about," Anton said.

"You're not going to kidnap me and turn me over to the Werdulac, are you?"

"Oh, so that's what you're getting at." Anton seemed amused. "No, of course not. And if I *were* going to do such a thing I'd hardly stand around talking with you. I would have carried you off already. You'd never even have seen me coming."

"That's reassuring," I said.

"I told you," Anton said. "I'm with the good guys—such as they are." He gave me a sardonic smile. "Sorry—I'm afraid I'm always going to have to add a qualifier whenever I try to cast our little community of vampires as the heroes."

We stood for a moment in silence, and Anton glanced around.

"You may not know this," he said, "but the hybrids are on the move now. Their lead bloodhound, Timofei Mstislav, is already on the scent. We had better get this show started."

He paused. "Are you waiting for me to lunge at you, or what?"

The thought of Anton lunging for me sent a flash of panic through me that I had to fight off.

"Innokenti said we should go to the old keep in the Pure Woods," I said with as much calm as I could summon. "I don't know where the keep is."

"I should have thought that was obvious," Anton said. "You said yourself it was in the Pure Woods."

"I don't know where in the woods it is," I replied, irritated.

It was strange to be afraid of Anton and angry with him at the same time.

"I knew what you meant," he said. "I'm exasperating, aren't I?"

I stifled an angry reply—this wasn't the time to get distracted by an argument.

"I also can't see very well in the dark," I said, "and I forgot to bring a flashlight."

"This is your lucky night," Anton said, grinning. "I happened to anticipate your very human difficulties, and I brought something that will help."

He reached into his coat pocket and pulled out something small and glowing.

"Take off your gloves and hold out your hands," he said.

Quickly, I did as he asked.

"Now cover this as soon as it touches your skin," Anton said. "You don't want to let this get away just yet."

He placed the glowing object into my outstretched hands, and I swiftly cupped one hand over the other. Golden light streamed out from between my fingers, and something fluttered softly against my hands—it felt like I was holding a butterfly.

"What is it?" I asked.

"I believe you would call it a 'will-o'-the wisp,'" Anton said, pronouncing the last word in English. "Also known as *ignis fatuus*, or 'foolish fire.' The greatest pleasure of this delightful little creature is to lead people astray. This one is a friend of mine. He's agreed to help us out."

"Ignis," I murmured. "There's that word again. *Sacer ignis exitus mundi.* The world will end in holy fire."

Anton looked at me in surprise. "Where did you hear that?"

"From Innokenti," I replied.

"There are many interpretations of that saying," Anton said, his tone unexpectedly serious as he echoed Innokenti's sentiments on the topic. "Some people think it means either a famous sword, or simple fire itself, can defeat even the most dangerous of enemies. Others take a more metaphorical approach and think that 'holy fire' refers to the fire of a courageous heart. I think something different—I think the saying can be interpreted literally. The world *will* end—for us anyway, for vampires—not for humans. Ultimately we will all burn and die. There is no magic, no fire of any kind that will defeat our enemies. There will come a day when all of us cease to exist."

"That's horrible," I said.

Amusement glimmered in Anton's eyes. "You think so? I imagine that most humans, if they knew about us, would be glad to be rid of us."

He glanced around and then went on with some urgency. "You know, we'd really better get moving. As I said, this particular will-o'-the-wisp is a friend of mine. He'll lead you to the old keep."

"You're sure about that?" I asked. "He won't lead me astray?"

"No, he won't," Anton said with a smirk. "This one owes me a favor—a big favor. He'll lead you to the keep safely, and he's also agreed to use his powers to give you a little more speed. That's why it was necessary for you to hold him in your bare hands—that allows the transfer of power. The effect will only be temporary, however."

"So what do I do?" I asked.

"Just let him go," Anton said, "and then follow him." He gave me a wolfish grin. "I promise I'll make the chase look good."

I wasn't sure I liked the sound of that.

I opened my hands, and a golden, luminous sphere leapt up into the air. I thought I saw a tiny figure hovering in the center of the glow, but before I could get a good look at it, the sphere bounced off, and hung in the air a few yards away.

Anton held out a hand. "After you."

The will-o'-the-wisp wasn't terribly far away, so I simply walked toward it. I was just close enough to reach out and touch it when it suddenly darted away.

I ran after it.

The will-o'-the-wisp moved with dizzying speed, and somehow, startlingly, I found myself able to stay just behind it. I could feel energy running through me that surely must have been transmitted by the will-o'-the-wisp.

All around me was dark, despite the snow, and the golden glow ahead of me was the only real source of light I had. The will-o'-the-wisp bounced and danced and gamboled in the night, and I was overcome with a strong desire to possess it. I had the feeling that the light was the key to a great treasure—if I could catch the will-o'-the-wisp, it would lead me to a horde of gold and riches that glowed as brightly as the little creature did. I forced myself to shake the feeling off.

I knew I couldn't afford to get lost in the fantasy the will-o'-the-wisp was spinning.

I chased the dancing light across the Wasteland, and it seemed as if there was nothing and no one left in the world but me and the little glowing imp. I glanced behind me, looking for Anton, but all I could see was darkness. I panicked—what if the will-o'-the-wisp had led me the wrong way? What if we had shaken off Anton and were no longer headed toward the keep?

What if the will-o'-the-wisp couldn't be trusted?

Suddenly, there was a snarl in my ear, and I glimpsed a flash of glittering eyes and sharp teeth.

I cried out, and mocking laughter echoed around me.

I realized that I hadn't lost Anton, and even though that was technically a good thing, I couldn't help running even faster.

The will-o'-the-wisp danced on, always tantalizingly just out of reach, and Anton continued to make his presence known from time to time in the most disconcerting manner possible.

Eventually, I spied the ghostly pallor of the Pure Woods looming in the distance up ahead of the bouncing will-o'-the-wisp.

Soon we plunged into the trees.

The will-o'-the-wisp led me on a dangerous chase, darting close to the petrified tree trunks that loomed suddenly out of the dark and veering away at the last possible moment. Incredibly, I found myself able to follow the wisp's treacherous, tortuous path, and I slipped through the trees without so much as a scratch from an outstretched branch.

We ran at breakneck speed deeper and deeper into the woods. Before long, we had crossed into territory that I didn't recognize—the woods were far larger than I'd realized.

I followed the golden sphere of light into an expansive clearing, and by the light of the luminous trees, I could see a dark shape on the top of a hill. A round, stone cylinder of a building reached up to the sky—it was a solitary tower.

I realized we'd reached our destination—the tower before me must be the keep.

I then realized with a jolt that I'd seen the keep before. Back in Elspeth's Grove I'd had a dream about this keep—and about being chased by Anton.

I'd also dreamed that I'd fallen from the keep to what had surely been my death. Of course, in dreams no one ever really died. But parts of my dream had suddenly turned out to be real. What if it would all turn out to be real?

Fear began to gnaw at me.

The will-o'-the-wisp darted around to the other side of the keep and vanished from my sight. I hurried after it and was just in time to see the golden sphere disappear into an open doorway.

A quick glance to the side showed me that there was a sheer drop behind the keep—one much steeper than Mara's Drop in the town. It was certainly a good spot for a fortification. No one would be able to approach the keep from the back—it was far too dangerous.

I plunged into the keep after the will-o'-the-wisp and was startled to hear the heavy door through which I'd just passed slam closed behind me. I felt another surge of panic then, and I scrambled after the will-o'-the-wisp.

The golden sphere bounced ahead of me down a hall, and then it began to surge upward. I realized that it was mounting a staircase. I ran after the will-o'-the-wisp, stumbling and slipping on stone steps that spiraled up into the darkness. The glowing sphere that led me on was the only source of light I had now. I was terrified to lose sight of the will-o'-the-wisp, and in my haste to keep up, I fell, badly skinning the palms of both my hands.

I got up and kept going.

The will-o'-the-wisp led me all the way up to the top of the stairs, and then out through a trapdoor in the roof, where I broke out into open air once again. We were at the very top of the keep, and I could see the ghostly trees of the Pure Woods in a pale ring far below us. The will-o'-the-wisp darted up to the crenellated wall of the keep and leaped over it, disappearing from view.

I rushed after it and prepared to leap off the parapet wall.

Something like an iron band wrapped around my arm and pulled me backward with terrific force. I stumbled into a solid body and looked up into the glittering, dark eyes of Anton.

"I wouldn't recommend going that way, Sunshine," he said. "You're likely to find that first step a little steep."

I looked back toward the parapet and realized with horror that I'd been about to leap to my death.

"I—I don't know what I was thinking," I said to Anton. "Thanks. I'm glad you were here. Really glad."

He shrugged. "It wasn't your fault. Will-o'-the-wisps can be like that, even when they help you. You had to be entranced or else the speed enhancement spell wouldn't have worked. And our little friend had fulfilled his part of the task and couldn't help throwing in a little mischief at the end. He knew I was following right behind you and would stop you. At least I think he knew that."

I tried to step away from Anton, but I found that he held me solidly against him.

"It's okay," I said. "I won't jump now. You can let go."

He smiled. "Are you sure?"

"Yes," I said.

Anton's smile deepened, but I felt his grip relax.

I walked toward the parapet wall and looked over it. There were flashes of fire in amongst the trees.

I could also hear screaming.

"What's going on?" I asked.

"Our people have been hiding in the woods around the keep, waiting for our arrival. Now that we're here, and we've successfully induced the hybrids to follow us, our people have launched their attack with the new weapons. Soon they'll fall back to the keep. And then, with any luck, we'll pick off the hybrids one by one. They should keep coming, even if they're being destroyed. Past experience says they're a pretty tenacious group."

There were more bursts of flame and more screams.

"Is William out there?" I asked.

"No," Anton said. "He's back at the castle with a small group of our newer recruits. He's getting them ready to defend the villagers at the festival. Innokenti thought it would be better if William didn't know about what was going on here till he saw it for himself—he was afraid William would put a stop to it. He'll be here, though, as soon as the alarm goes up, which should be happening right about now. As much as I hate to say it, William's one of our best fighters. We need him for this."

Anton continued to watch the flashes of fire in the trees, and I was surprised to see he wasn't moving.

"You're staying?" I asked.

"Yes, of course." He tilted his head to one side. "Did you think I'd leave you?"

"So you're one of them?" I asked. "You're one of these vampire warriors?"

"Yes—did you ever doubt it? I said William was *one* of the best. Well, I am *the* best. I'm the best protection there is."

"Where's your armor?" I asked.

"Under my coat," Anton replied. "I thought I'd surprise you."

There was a flurry of motion below us, and I turned back to look over the parapet wall.

The vampires with their leather armor and their crossbows were backing into the clearing on all sides. They turned swiftly toward the keep and sprang onto its walls.

They began to climb.

As I watched, dozens of vampires surged toward me, and I backed away from the edge to give them room.

The last thing I saw before the ground below was lost to my sight was a hybrid, staggering out of the trees, with a disc lodged in its chest. In the darkness, I could see the white, angular smoke of the hybrid swirling in awkward, violent shapes around its body.

I knew there would be others behind him.

"Stay in the center," Anton shouted to me. "We'll cover the circumference of the roof. They won't be able to get up here."

I shuffled back a few feet, looking around to see what I could do. I was soon surrounded by vampires—all of whom were armed. They were leaning over the parapet, aiming their crossbows and firing.

From the ground below, I could hear horrible, inhuman screeching mingled with wild cries. I knew those cries only too well—it was the sound a kost made when it attacked.

I moved back a few more feet, looking around for a spare weapon of any kind, but there was nothing I could use. A vampire rushed past me, and I found myself backed up so that I was standing on the trapdoor in the floor.

The trapdoor flew open with sudden force and threw me to the ground—and I thought for one horrifying moment that the hybrids had broken through.

Then a familiar, well-loved face showed itself above the space in the floor.

"William!" I cried.

He turned and looked at me, and shock spread over his face.

"Katie!"

William quickly climbed onto the roof. He dropped his crossbow and rushed over to me.

"What are you doing here?" he demanded, pulling me to my feet. His face darkened. "I wondered why the hybrids were gathering here. Did Innokenti trick you into doing this?"

"No," I said. "It was my idea."

William's expression grew even darker. "I'm sure that's what he led you to believe."

Five other vampires had come out of the trapdoor after William, and he began to pull me back toward them.

"I'm getting you out of here," William said grimly.

"I'm not going," I said, twisting in his grasp. "I can't leave."

"You can't stay here," he said. "It's too dangerous."

A hand landed on William's chest.

"What's dangerous is leaving the keep. The woods are crawling with hybrids."

I looked up. Anton had suddenly appeared beside us.

William released me and seized Anton.

"I should have known you were part of this," William said furiously. "Katie's been tricked. She doesn't understand what she's gotten herself into. I'm getting her out of here now. And if you try to stop me, I'll tear you apart."

"Anton is right," said a new voice.

I turned to see a pale, fair-haired vampire standing just behind us—he was one of the small group who had followed William through the trapdoor. He appeared to be young—probably about the same age I was. Of course with vampires age was hard to tell—it was entirely possible he was hundreds of years old.

"Anton is right," the fair-haired vampire said again. "If you try to take the human girl through the woods, the hybrids will capture her and kill you. If you truly value her life, you will allow her to remain."

William turned a face full of fury on the pale vampire, but he loosened his grip on Anton and pushed him away.

"She'll stay for now," William said. Then he stepped toward Anton. "But if anything happens to Katie, I'll hold you accountable."

"Just do what you're supposed to do," Anton said contemptuously, "and everything will be fine."

Anton walked back toward the parapet, and the fair-haired vampire went to his own post.

William seemed reluctant to leave me. "Stay here and keep your head down. Nothing will harm you while I stand."

"This is where I want to be," I said.

William gave me one last despairing look and then retrieved his crossbow and rushed off to the parapet wall.

I stood next to the trapdoor and listened to the sounds of the fight all around me. The crossbows sang with deadly regularity, and I could hear the shrieks of the hybrids as they were struck by the razor-sharp projectiles. I couldn't see what was going on, but I could imagine the scene below, with hybrids swarming out of the trees and being hit with projectiles that then burst into flame—hacking off limbs, lodging in chests, cutting into necks.

But beheading the hybrids, I knew, was only part of destroying them. They still had to be wrestled back into their graves and burned to ash. And as far as I could tell, the entire vampire force was in the keep—there was no one left on the ground to do the wrestling or the burning.

I began to think about the odds against us, and a sense of uneasiness settled over me. The hybrids would keep coming, and we were outnumbered.

What if I had doomed us all?

The shrieks from below continued, and I began to move toward the parapet, taking care not to jostle any of the vampire defenders. I wanted to see what the situation was like on the ground—if I could get down to the ground myself, perhaps I could draw some of the hybrids away from the keep, and give the vampires a better chance.

But as I reached the parapet edge, I was startled to hear a shriek close by.

I turned to see a hybrid, its green-flame eyes burning with hatred, appear over the top of the parapet, angular smoke swirling around it. The creature's large, death-pale hand was wrapped around the handle of an axe.

As I watched, the hybrid buried the axe deeply in the shoulder of a vampire defender right next to me. The vampire dropped his crossbow and wrenched the axe out. Then he swung it in an arc, aiming for the hybrid's neck.

I turned away quickly.

Unfortunately, as I looked to the other side, I saw another pair of flame-green eyes rise up over the parapet. A new hybrid bared its teeth in a feral cry.

I looked away again and spotted yet another hybrid. This one also had an axe, and he began hacking away at the two vampires defenders on either side of him. The hybrid was shot in the chest by a third vampire, and I heard him scream as he fell away from the parapet.

But there were more cries from our circle of defenders, and more and more hybrids appeared over the parapet wall.

There were too many of them. We were soon going to be overwhelmed.

The sounds of the fight continued to swirl around me as I spotted a dropped crossbow and began to run toward it.

But I'd only made it halfway when I heard an ear-splitting shriek close by, and I twisted around.

One of the hybrids had successfully made it over the parapet and was now standing on the roof. Angular smoke was swirling around him in a thick haze, and I realized that I was the only one who could actually see it—it was invisible to the others. The smoke was a defense mechanism of the kost—a field that could jam an enemy's senses. I saw several vampires stumble and fall, and I realized with horror that the smoky haze generated by the hybrids was doing its work—it was attacking the vampires' keen senses and clogging their eyes and ears.

For his part, the hybrid that had attained the roof of the keep was standing over a hapless vampire, trying to hack at him with an axe. The hybrid shrieked in triumph.

I ran toward them—I had a half-formed idea that I was going to push the hybrid over the parapet.

A moment later, I cried out when someone grabbed me by the arm and hauled me back.

It was William.

"Katie, you can't," he said. "You can't join the fight. You'd never survive. I'm getting you out of here. Now. No arguments this time."

William dragged me through the trapdoor, and we ran down the spiral staircase in the darkness.

He then pulled me out of the keep, and we ran at dizzying speed down the hill toward the ring of pale trees at the edge of the clearing.

As William pulled me along, I saw the blurred forms of several wounded hybrids flying past us.

William stopped suddenly, and I looked around, disoriented. We'd just reached the trees, and someone had stepped into our path.

It was Timofei Mstislav.

It struck me once again that he was much as he had been in life—he was still sleek and superficially handsome. There were changes in him, of course, which I'd glimpsed elsewhere in these same woods—his eyes now burned with an unholy flame, his skin now had the intense pallor of death—and there was something else—an added sheen to him, an unhealthy glamour that all of the hybrids had. They were both beautiful and terrible.

With angular smoke swirling off him, black where it touched the white trees, Timofei stared at me now, his eyes burning with hatred. William interposed his body between Timofei and me.

Timofei was lost to my sight.

William had slung his crossbow over his back earlier, and he now brought it forward and raised it.

He fired several times in rapid succession—it seemed that the crossbow had the capacity to hold more than one disc at a time. And then when he was out of ammunition, he reached into the armor that he wore. It turned out that the leather garment wasn't armor after all—it was really a place to store the lethal discs.

William reloaded the crossbow with lightning speed and prepared to fire again.

A large, dark figure suddenly hit William from the side, knocking him to the ground. The figure then wrenched the crossbow away from him. By the light of the trees, I could see that the attacker was one of the still-intact hybrids.

With William's body out of the way, I could see Timofei Mstislav once again. He smiled malevolently and started toward me.

William jumped to his feet and grabbed me by the hand.

"Run!" he cried.

We flew through the woods at blinding speed, and we moved so fast that the trees became a white blur. We ran on and on, and I realized that we must be close to the edge of the Pure Woods. We would soon be out in the Wasteland.

I began to believe that we could make it.

Then something snaked around my ankle and held it fast, and my hand was pulled out of William's grasp.

I fell to the ground heavily, and suddenly I found myself being dragged backward along the forest floor with terrifying speed.

I tried to grab onto something—anything—that would stop the dragging, but I couldn't find any purchase on the frozen ground.

There was a sound of splintering wood, as William rushed after me, and I felt a jolt as my backward progress came to an abrupt halt. I was jerked suddenly to my feet and held in an iron grip.

I knew without looking around that Timofei Mstislav was the one who held me.

"Stop!" cried a harsh voice right next to my ear. "Stop or she will die."

Icy fingers wrapped around my neck, and William skidded to a halt just in front of me. He stared at me for a moment and then took a step forward.

"Stop!" Timofei cried again, and he gave me a shake.

William froze.

"Move back," Timofei ordered.

William took a step back.

"Let her go," he said. His voice was full of cold fury. "Let her go, or I will tear you apart."

"You threaten me?" Timofei asked. His voice in death had a strange, metallic quality to it. "I'm no dumb brute. I'm not to be ordered around like an ordinary kost. And you killed me once before, remember? You can see how effective that was."

"Let her go," William said furiously.

"I've captured the girl they all want," Timofei said triumphantly. He gave me another shake. "The girl who helped you to kill my father. The two of you are responsible for his death and mine. And for that I'll have my revenge on you both. You, I will kill tonight. The girl will be killed later. But you will both die. And you, William Sursur, will come with me now. You'll walk just ahead of us. You'll stay where I can see you."

Timofei gave my neck a painful wrench, and I was forced to walk forward. William, his eyes bright with anger, turned and walked in front of us.

The cold from Timofei's fingers spread down my neck and ran through my body. I couldn't fight off an involuntary trembling as he forced us to walk on.

Timofei pushed the pace so hard that I stumbled and fell. He pulled me to my feet with such force that I cried out, and William started back toward us.

"Stop!" Timofei cried, squeezing my throat. "Stop! Or I'll kill her right now."

William stopped.

"Turn around and walk," Timofei commanded.

William obeyed.

"Fall again and this ends right now," Timofei said to me in a harsh whisper.

The three of us marched grimly onward.

I soon realized that we were headed back toward the keep, and I felt the fear that filled me escalating. Timofei wanted us to be surrounded by hybrids. He wanted to ensure that there would be no escape.

William and I were trapped.

After an eternity of walking, my body slowly freezing from contact with Timofei's icy skin, we reached the keep, where the fight between the hybrids and the vampires raged on. But instead of leading us toward the hybrids, Timofei forced us to walk along the edge of the sheer drop that fell away from the back of the keep. I glanced over the edge of the drop. All I could see was darkness.

"Keep moving," Timofei commanded.

I tried to control my trembling, but between the cold from Timofei's grasp, and our proximity to the edge of a dangerous drop, I shook even harder.

I feared I would stumble.

And if I stumbled, either Timofei or the fall would kill me.

Then the unthinkable happened. William stumbled, falling over the lip of the drop.

"William!" I screamed.

"Get back here, William Sursur!" Timofei shouted furiously.

Timofei dragged me over the lip of the drop, and I saw with a faint measure of relief that there was actually a broad ledge on the other side. William was lying face up on the ledge. Beyond the ledge, the ground fell away sharply into the deep, dark valley.

"Get up!" Timofei shouted.

But William didn't move.

Timofei pulled me toward William's motionless body.

"Get up!" Timofei shouted furiously. "Get up now!"

With blinding speed, William launched himself at Timofei, somehow missing me completely and knocking Timofei to the ground.

"Run!" William screamed at me. "Run!"

I stumbled backward a few paces, but I was unable to leave William.

I couldn't just run and leave him to die.

William held Timofei pinned to the platform of the ledge for a few moments, then Timofei, his eyes burning with hatred, threw William against the wall of the drop. Timofei lurched to his feet, grabbed William, and sent him flying back over the top of the drop. William was propelled into a tree, hitting it with such force that the tree cracked and began to rock on its roots.

Timofei started toward me then, and I scrambled back quickly, stumbling hard against the wall of the drop.

William jumped back onto the ledge and lunged for Timofei, the two of them falling heavily onto the solid surface of the ledge. They struggled briefly, and Timofei came out the winner. He lifted William up off the ground and wrapped him in a grotesque embrace. He seemed to be trying to break William's ribs.

William let out a terrible cry of pain.

I looked around desperately and spotted a big, heavy broken tree branch. I caught it up and began to pound on Timofei's broad back.

Timofei dropped William and turned toward me, wrenching the tree branch out of my hands. He caught me by the neck once again and then lifted me up.

He threw me, and I felt myself soaring first, and then falling through the air into the deep valley below.

I knew I would never survive the fall.

There was a terrible crash.

Then everything went black.

Chapter Twenty-Five

I was aware of light on my face first. Then I could feel warmth. I moved my arms and legs experimentally, and they seemed to be working.

I wondered—why wouldn't they be working? Why had I thought of that?

My mind was cloudy.

I opened my eyes.

I was lying in a bed in an all-white room. Sunlight streamed in through a window nearby.

GM was sitting by my bedside. When she saw that my eyes were open she started forward.

"I'm here, solnyshko. I'm here. You're safe now. I'm taking care of everything."

"Where am I?" I asked.

"You're in the hospital," GM said, taking my hand. Her grasp was reassuringly warm.

"Are we still in Krov?" I asked.

"We're still in Krov."

I frowned. I felt the stirrings of memory. I remembered moving through the air in the dark—

"How did I—"

I stopped when Maksim Neverov walked into the room. I felt a flash of panic, and I sat up in bed. I remembered that I had reason to be suspicious of him—but then I'd decided to trust him—hadn't I?

Maksim smiled when he saw me. "How's our girl? It's good to see you awake at last."

"I'm not entirely sure what happened," I said. "But I think I'm okay."

Maksim came to stand beside GM, and I found that I was pleased to see him, despite my misgivings.

"Your doctor told us you'd be fine," Maksim said. "But it's a relief to see it's true."

GM smiled first up at him and then at me. Seeing the two of them together, looking at me with concern and relief in their eyes, I felt for a moment like I actually had a mother and a father. It was a good feeling.

"We should call the doctor back now," GM said. "He'll want to see her. I'm sure there are some tests he'd like to run."

"Maybe we should wait a little while, Anna," Maksim replied. "Let's give Katie some time to enjoy being fully conscious again."

"Fully conscious?" I said. "How long have I been out?"

"Don't be distressed," GM said quickly. "You were brought unconscious to the hospital about twelve hours ago. But the doctor says you just received a small bump on the head—he was quite sure that you'd be all right."

She frowned. "All the same, you do appear to have quite a few bad scrapes and bruises. What a terrible time you must have had."

I put a hand up to my forehead and shifted into a more comfortable position in the bed. I really did feel fine, though a fog still sat over my memories. I realized that I hadn't expected to be okay—why hadn't I expected that?

"You said I was out for twelve hours," I said. "So it's Christmas Eve?"

"Yes, it's late afternoon on your American Christmas Eve," Maksim said in a gently teasing tone. "Though, as I told you, the real Russian celebration isn't until New Year's."

GM touched a pendant around her neck, and I realized she was wearing the necklace I'd bought her along with her usual cross.

"I hope you don't mind, solnyshko. I opened your present to me early. I was worried—even though they told us everything would be all right—I had feared—"

She broke off and wrapped her fingers around both the cross and the primitive female figure.

"I just wanted to open your gift as soon as possible," GM said. "I thought that opening it might somehow bring luck for both of us."

"Luck?" I said with a little smile. "That doesn't sound like you."

"When there's nothing you can do, but you wish you could influence events—" GM shrugged. "Sometimes you can't help but look to luck."

I was really happy to see GM wearing the charm—I hoped it would do more than give her luck. I hoped it would protect her.

"Do you like it?" I asked.

"I love it, solnyshko." GM clutched her necklaces tighter and shook her head. "I'm sorry—I'm so sorry that I lost track of you last night at the Firebird Festival. Otherwise, I'm sure you wouldn't have fallen."

Fallen. I *had* fallen—because I'd been thrown. I'd been in the forest—Timofei and the hybrids had attacked—

The fog over my memories suddenly shifted, and I saw in part. A few images from the night came back to me hazily.

"What happened at the keep?" I asked. "What happened with the hybrids?"

GM blinked at me in surprise. "I don't know what you mean by 'hybrids'—but how did you know about the keep?"

"Do you mean the keep in the Pure Woods?" Maksim asked me.

"Yes," I said. "That's exactly the one I mean."

"Perhaps Katie overhead some of the doctors and nurses talking," Maksim said, turning to GM. "Maybe she processed the news subconsciously."

"In that case," GM replied firmly, "Katie doesn't need to know anything about it. It will only upset her."

"Keeping Katie in the dark could upset her, too," Maksim said gently. "Her imagination could run riot. Sometimes it's best to face upsetting facts."

GM sighed. "Very well. I suppose the news is all over town anyway."

She turned to me. "Some of the bodies that were stolen from their graves were found this morning. They were found at the old castle keep in the Pure Woods. Many of the bodies had been damaged or decapitated. One of the bodies that was found was that of Timofei Mstislav."

Panic ran through me—the hybrids had been found—as had Timofei Mstislav. And their bodies hadn't been burned to ash. Did that mean that they were still alive? The whole terrible night in the woods suddenly came flooding back to me.

And what about—

"William," I said frantically. "Where is William? Is he okay?"

GM sighed again. "Always back to the boy. Just when I think we've seen the last of him."

"Oh, Anna," Maksim said. "How can you be so hard-hearted? William did bring Katie to the hospital. I think we can be grateful to him for that."

"William brought me here?" I said. "So he's okay?"

Maksim smiled. "Yes, of course. William is okay. You're the one who fell—not William."

"Where is he?" I asked, sitting up straighter. "Is he here?"

"I imagine he's in the lobby," Maksim replied.

"In the lobby?" GM said sharply. "I told him to leave."

"I doubt he listened, Anna."

"I have to see him," I said. I threw off my covers and swung my legs over the side of the bed.

Maksim held up a restraining hand. "There's no need for you to get up. I'll go and fetch him."

He turned and bowed to GM. "With your permission, of course."

GM waved a hand. "Yes, yes. Go ahead. If he's indeed still here, you may bring the boy in. I can see that Katie won't be at peace until she sees him."

Maksim bowed again and left the room.

I sank back gratefully against my pillows—my sudden exertion had left me feeling dizzy.

Part of that dizziness was physical weakness, but part of it was born of sheer relief. I now knew that William was all right—somehow he'd survived our encounter with Timofei Mstislav. I wiped at my eyes—I suddenly realized that they were brimming with tears.

I glanced over at GM then. I was glad to have a moment alone with her—I wanted to find out exactly what had happened last night. It seemed as if what I'd done had actually helped to spare everyone at the Firebird Festival.

And somehow I'd survived the whole thing, too.

"So, what happened last night?" I asked. "Did anything unusual happen at the festival?"

"Apart from your nearly scaring the life out of me?" GM said. "Why is it that every time we come to Russia you end up in the hospital? I hope this is a habit we can break."

"Tell me everything you remember," I said. "I want to know exactly what happened."

GM stood and looked out the window for a moment. Then she turned back to me.

"I suppose your memory might be a little fuzzy," she said. "That would certainly be understandable. There isn't actually a lot to tell you. Last night Maksim and I were talking and laughing, and I suppose the two of us got separated from you in the crowd. We heard the firecrackers, and then the main procession with the Firebird statue came through. And then—"

GM stopped and closed her eyes as if the memory were painful. "And then we looked around and realized we didn't know where you were." She shook her head. "I can't believe that I lost sight of you. We went in search of you. We found a police officer, and he helped us look. Soon, others joined us and helped to look, too.

"None of us could find you. Eventually the festival began to wind down, and there was still no sign of you. I began to fear—"

She broke off and took a calming breath.

"And then that boy of yours showed up. He told us he'd taken you to the hospital—he said you'd fallen. So we hurried here, and he came with us. You were unconscious when we arrived. That's basically the whole story."

I was relieved. GM didn't seem to have seen anything out of the ordinary.

The hybrids hadn't attacked. The plan had worked.

GM frowned and went on.

"There's a fairly deep depression not far from the Mstislav mansion. It's by the side of that little road that leads to the newer shops and houses—it's called Mara's Drop. I assumed that you'd fallen over there, but now I realize that I don't know where you were or what you were doing. What was going on last night?"

I chose my words carefully. "I went to a place where I knew William was likely to be eventually."

"You didn't arrange to meet him?" GM asked.

"Definitely not. William was surprised to see me—I think it's fair to say he was actually shocked."

GM seemed a bit mollified. "Well, I suppose that's something. So what happened once you saw him?"

"I did fall," I said. "And I blacked out. As I was falling, I remember I didn't think things would be okay—I didn't think I'd survive—"

My voice faltered.

"Yes, yes, don't think of that," GM said quickly. "You're going to be all right now. The doctor will examine you, and he'll pronounce you well. I'm sure of it."

She took a deep breath. "Now about this boy—"

"GM, please. His name is William. He had dinner at our house not too long ago."

"About this William," GM said. "Did he follow you here to Krov?"

"No. William was here before we were. As he told you at that same dinner, he used to live in Krov. He was here—visiting."

I finished my last sentence rather weakly.

But GM didn't seem to notice.

"And this William—he *did* follow you to Elspeth's Grove?"

"Yes, but you knew that. He did move there to be near me. He told you that at dinner, too."

"I just want to be sure of my facts," GM said.

"And after we all had dinner together you said you were okay with him—or at least that you would tolerate him."

"That was before he made you unhappy, solnyshko. You were heart broken—I could see that. Why should I forgive him for breaking your heart?"

"There was a misunderstanding," I said. I would have to try to explain without giving too much away. "William came here to Krov, and I didn't know that. I thought he'd left me. And I didn't have any way to contact him, but he didn't know that. He thought I knew how to reach him. We just got all mixed up."

GM sighed. "My dear girl, you will be the death of me."

Maksim came back into the room then.

William was right behind him.

I wanted to run to him, to throw my arms around him, to kiss him.

But I forced myself to sit still. I could feel GM's eyes on me.

There was also every possibility that I'd fall if I tried to stand up.

William rushed to my side, and I thought for one tantalizing moment that I was going to get that kiss. But he suddenly pulled back and stood rather awkwardly by the bed.

"Katie," he said. "Katie—"

He stopped and started again. "You look perfect. You look beautiful. You look—perfectly beautiful."

I was pretty sure I looked terrible. I'd only been awake for a little while, and I was aware now that my face was scratched and sore.

But the look on William's face made me want to kiss him even more.

The doctor came in next.

"I hear my patient is up now," he said with an air of pleasant authority. "I'm going to have to ask everyone to leave."

Don't leave, William, I pleaded silently. *Don't leave the building.*

Maksim and GM left, and William went with them. I felt a sharp pang of loss.

I had a terrible feeling that he might disappear again.

I passed the doctor's neurological tests, and after all my cuts and scrapes were dressed, I was discharged from the hospital. GM and Maksim took me home.

William hadn't waited with them.

GM and I spent Christmas Eve together quietly, sitting by the tree that we'd decorated with my father's ornaments. The night certainly *seemed* peaceful, and I would have enjoyed it more if I hadn't been so worried.

From what I'd learned about the hybrids, it was clear to me that some of them had to have survived—their bodies hadn't been burned. So there was every possibility that they would rise again and attack me or the village. And one of the bodies that hadn't been burned was Timofei Mstislav's. I wondered—could the vampires still get to the bodies and finish them off? At the very least, it was something I could hope for.

And then there was William. What if he'd gone away in order to protect me again?

What if he was gone for good this time?

"You don't look well, Katie," GM said at last. "You don't have a headache, do you?"

"No—no headache."

"Be sure to say something if you do have a headache. The doctor said that was important."

"I'll be sure to say something, GM."

We continued on in this manner for some time—I would worry silently, and periodically she would ask me how I felt. Eventually, I rose to go to bed.

"Good night, solnyshko," GM said as I left the room.

"Good night," I replied.

I was tired and aching, but sleep was elusive. I continued to worry about the hybrids and the village—I had no idea what was going to happen during the night. Of course, my house was supposed to be supernaturally fortified against invaders, but it was hard to imagine that it could stand against an army of determined hybrids.

I drifted off eventually, and when I woke up, rosy dawn was lighting up my window. I hurried downstairs and was delighted to find that GM was in the kitchen, looking happy and unruffled. I was deeply relieved. Our house had clearly not been attacked in the night.

I only hoped the village had been so lucky.

"Merry Christmas, Katie."

"Merry Christmas, GM."

She gave me a present—a little wooden bird with fanciful scarlet plumage that was suspended from a loop of gold string.

"It's a Firebird," GM said. "I found it in the hospital gift shop while you were still out. The Firebird is said to be able to heal any illness—I thought it might bring you luck. It's supposed to be a tree ornament, but you can use it for any purpose you wish."

I gave GM a hug.

We went into town a little while later to have lunch with Maksim.

I was relieved to see that Krov, like our house, had escaped attack.

I knew, of course, that the fact that Krov hadn't been attacked last night was no guarantee of future safety. There was no reason that the village couldn't be attacked tonight or the next night or the next.

And there was no sign of William.

GM and I stayed in Krov for two more days—she wanted to make sure I was truly fit for travel—and then we left for Moscow.

The hybrids didn't attack, and William didn't appear.

And I felt his absence more keenly every day.

Once we arrived in Moscow, we lingered. GM was still nervous about my health, and she contacted my school to see if I could come back a few days late. She wanted to stay in Moscow through New Year's Day, and I was due back in school the very next morning.

GM was able to get me an excused absence, and New Year's Eve found us once again in Red Square. The night was very cold, but the square was beautiful—it was all lit up, and I felt as if I'd walked into a celebration in an enchanted land.

The square was full of people, and I watched a couple walking arm in arm, their heads bent together. I thought of William.

I felt a pain so profound that I thought it would tear me apart.

And then suddenly, impossibly, I saw William walking toward me through the crowd. I blinked. I was sure I was seeing things.

But William didn't vanish, and he kept moving toward me.

Soon, he was standing right in front of me, and he gave me the crooked smile that I loved so much.

"Hello, Katie. Hello, Mrs. Rost."

GM eyed him warily.

"Hello," she replied.

"Mrs. Rost, may I take Katie for a walk? I promise you I'll bring her back safely."

GM seemed resigned. "Very well."

"Forgive me for noticing," William said. "But you don't seem at all shocked to see me. It's almost as if you expected me."

"I did expect you," GM replied. "I knew you'd be back."

I looked at her in surprise. I had known no such thing.

"We'll be back soon, I promise," William said.

We walked off into the crowd, and I clung to William's arm.

I was half afraid he'd disappear again.

"How did you know where to find me?" I asked. Despite what his presence implied, I was suddenly struck by doubt. "You did come here to see me, didn't you?"

"Of course I came here to see you. I know where you are all the time now."

"Where have you been these last few days?" I asked. "I was worried—"

"About the hybrids?" William asked.

"Yes, I was worried about them, but I was worried about you, too."

"Well, the hybrids are a real worry," William replied. "And I'm glad you're getting out of the country."

I felt a chill steal over me. "The hybrids weren't all killed off?"

"No, they weren't," William said. "We managed to destroy about forty of them. But the rest of them survived. And they've disappeared. We have to find where they're hiding before they're strong enough to attack again."

"I heard that headless bodies were found by the keep," I said slowly. "And that one of those bodies was Timofei Mstislav's. Is he—did he—"

"He survived," William said grimly. "Along with the other hybrids that the villagers found. They took the bodies to the morgue, and they all disappeared before we could get back to them to destroy them."

I couldn't help shivering, and William put his arm around me as we continued to walk.

"I'll look after you," he murmured into my hair. "You'll be safe while you're with me."

"And what happened the night of the festival?" I asked. I couldn't help shivering again. "I was sure I would die. And that you would, too."

William's expression grew harsh and a muscle worked in his jaw.

"I thought you were lost to me," he said. "I saw Timofei throw you into the valley. I saw you crash against an outcropping of rock as you fell. I leaped forward and caught you. I set you down, and then a rage came over me. I took out one of the discs. I hacked him to pieces. I—"

William broke off. "Once I was sure Timofei wouldn't come after us, I took you to the hospital. I've stayed by you ever since then. Even if you didn't see me."

"Why did you hide from me, then?" I asked. "I was terrified that I'd never see you again. William, I need you. You have to know that by now."

He looked away. "Katie, I didn't come to see you because of what I've put you through. It's been hard for me to work up the courage to tell you this."

William stopped and I waited. Something was clearly tearing him apart.

"Katie, I'm sorry," he said. "I'm sorry I left you alone in Elspeth's Grove. I thought you could call me—I had no idea you were cut off from me. I had no idea that I couldn't get to you if you were in danger. I can't believe what nearly happened to you because of me. Katie, I hope you can forgive me."

"I forgive you," I said.

William looked at me warily, as if he suspected a trick. "Just like that? After all you've been through?"

"Just like that—I forgive you."

William hung his head. A muscle worked in his jaw again.

We walked on in silence for a time.

"I'm not used to being forgiven," William said in a low voice.

He stopped walking and pulled me close.

"So, how does that work exactly?" I asked. "When I call you and you appear—or, how did it used to work?"

"It's a little complex," William said. "Katie, I'll never leave you again. You'll never have to rely on that call. I'll always be with you. When I thought I'd lost you—"

He stopped.

"I'll always be with you," he said again.

"I'll always be with you, too," I said. "I love you."

"I love you," William said.

He looked around. "I think we're far enough away now." His crooked smile had returned.

"Far enough away for what?" I asked.

William bent his face close to mine.

At last I had my kiss.

Thank you for reading!

Thanks for reading *Firebird*! If you enjoyed it, please leave a review at your retailer of choice:

Amazon
Apple
Barnes & Noble
Google Play
or
Kobo

Thank you very much!

Other Books by Catherine Mesick

Pure, Book 1 of the *Pure* series

Dangerous Creatures, Book 3 of the *Pure* series

Ghost Girl, Book 4 of the *Pure* series

Coming soon!

Little Sun, Book 5 of the *Pure* series

About the Author

Catherine Mesick is the author of *Pure*, *Firebird*, *Dangerous Creatures*, and *Ghost Girl*. She is a graduate of Pace University and Susquehanna University. She lives in Maryland.

Visit the author's website at catherinemesick.com and her Facebook page at facebook.com/PureBookSeries. You can also connect with her on Twitter at twitter.com/CatherineMesick.

Sign up for Catherine's newsletter at http://eepurl.com/cXS5_z.

www.ingramcontent.com/pod-product-compliance
Lightning Source LLC
Chambersburg PA
CBHW030546180626
46816CB00005B/1429